HAVEN FOUND

Book 6
The Guard Trilogy Extended Series
The Guards of Haven

N. L. Westaway

Original Cover Photo by Engin Akyurt
Cover designed by Beach House Press

This book is a work of fiction. Names, characters, places, and incidents either are products of the author's imagination or are used fictitiously. Any resemblance to actual persons, living or dead, events, or locales is entirely coincidental.

N. L. Westaway
Visit my website at www.NLWestaway.com
ISBN: 979-8-9907502-1-0
Printed in the United States of America

First Publication: September 2024 Beach House Press

Haven Found

To the reader,

This novel, like the other books in succession, is not a standalone story. Book 6, *Haven Found*, is the next in series and carries the reader forward from the original story in The Guard Trilogy, into The Guard Trilogy Extended Series, *The Guards of Haven*.

The Guard Trilogy
The Guard – Book 1
The Unseen – Book 2
The Believer – Book 3

The Guard Trilogy Extended Series/The Guards of Haven
The Haven – Book 4
Haven Lost — Book 5
Haven Found — Book 6
TBD — Book 7
More to come….

This book is dedicated to Monica & Fred.

*"Remember your name. Do not lose hope—what you seek
will be found."*
— Neil Gaiman, Instructions

*"I looked at him like a stranger, someone I'd never seen
before, and he looked at me like I'd been lost to him for a
thousand years and finally found."*
— Emme Rollins, Dear Rockstar

*""I believe that imagination is stronger than knowledge. That
myth is more potent than history. That dreams are more
powerful than facts. That hope always triumphs over
experience. That laughter is the only cure for grief.
And I believe that love is stronger than death."*
*— Robert Fulghum, All I Really Need to Know I Learned in
Kindergarten: Uncommon Thoughts On Common Things*

Acknowledgements

To my beta readers, I thank you once again for your patience and
for your support of my storytelling.

To the readers, thank you for your devotion to the stories and the
characters within them.

Prologue

Rental Home of Natalie Harwood, July 7th, 2022, Ottawa, Canada

Teeny set the cardboard tray of Tim Horton's coffee on the dated dining table. "Brought you a coffee. Thought you could use it since there's never any in this house," she stated, coming to stand behind Natalie at the head of the table in one of the mismatched dining chairs. "Whatcha doing?"

"Thanks," Natalie said, taking her coffee marked with the code B2S for 'black two sugars' from the tray. "I'm waiting to see my status update." She tapped her laptop screen. "This is my student account for Ottawa U. I'm watching for it to change to accepted or rejected for the program I applied for." Natalie pointed to the lower corner to show her friend the countdown next to the status that currently showed as 'submitted'.

"Looks like only one more minute left." Teeny noted, leaning in over Natalie's shoulder.

The minutes on the counter hit zero and Natalie refreshed the page. "There," she said, tapping the screen again, "status updated, *waitlisted*."

"Waitlisted?" Teeny questioned, her face scrunching like something stunk.

"Ya, expected as much. I got an email already updating me that I'm on the waitlist for January. Won't know officially about my acceptance until early December, but I wanted to see the status change, anyway."

"Well, that's good enough for me—pour me a glass of wine girl! Let's celebrate! Been a long time coming." She dropped her purse on the table next to the coffee tray.

Natalie blew out a breath, her expression filled with discontent.

"What's with the face?" Teeny asked. "You're not having second thoughts after waiting so long to apply—are you?" Teeny put her hands on her hips. Tina Barone, a.k.a. 'Teeny', was a feisty and curvy Italian 5 years senior to Natalie. She stood all of 5 foot nothing in high heels to Natalie's towering 5 foot 9, yet she could still pull off an intimidating posture.

"Yes, no—I don't know," Natalie said, freeing her shoulder-length pale blonde hair from the hair tie only to twist it back into a knot and secure it with the hair tie again. "I'm kind of old to be starting university, don't you think?"

"What old—you're not even 21 yet!" Teeny bellowed, clapping her hands several times. "Not until January 1st anyway—Baby New Year."

"But I'll be attending class with 18-year-olds, who bring their lunches to class and sip through straws jabbed into drink'n-boxes," Natalie whined, assessing Teeny's outfit. She was dressed for her part-time job at her parent's bakery in her usual uniform of tan coloured cotton pants and a white golf shirt with the bakery logo on the breast pocket. Natalie glanced down at her oversized vintage Led Zeppelin t-shirt, the one she'd gotten for a dollar at the local thrift shop, then blew out an exasperated breath, repeating the loosening and retying of her hair again.

"So what?" Teeny said, waving a dismissive hand. "You're a mature student. People older than you go back to school all the time. It's no big deal. Besides, you've already done part-time online courses already, so it's not as though you're new to post-secondary education." Teeny gave Natalie an encouraging smile.

Natalie shrugged and picked at the frayed edges of her cutoff shorts. "I bet none of the other students have to sling beer to pay their rent."

"Hell—none of them are old enough to even drink beer," Teeny countered, smirking.

"Nice, very nice," Natalie said. The two of them worked together at the same bar downtown. She waited tables while Teeny worked her second job behind the bar as head bartender. It was Teeny who had gotten Natalie the gig when she'd first moved to Ottawa.

"Did you tell the roomies?" Teeny asked. "They'll be stoked to have you on campus with them, and you know they'll help you out if needed." Teeny grabbed up her purse from the kitchen table and adjusted it on her shoulder. Then she snatched up the remaining coffee, a double espresso, from the cardboard tray.

"It's still not a done deal, but I'll tell them over pizza when they get in from class—you wanna stay?" Natalie asked. She was the only female in the four-bedroom, two-and-a-half-bath rental house she shared with three full-time students who attended the same university she'd be going to. Two of her roommates were brothers, twins actually. Her third roommate the twins met on campus when they'd first put up the post in the student lounge about looking for roommates. The post had also been placed online and was how Natalie had found the rental listing. When she viewed the house, it had been clean and so had the bedroom she'd been shown. The room came furnished with a simple double bed, nightstand, and a low three-drawer dresser, and a decent closet. The only thing she hadn't been thrilled about was the fact the bedroom was in the basement. Although, she would have her own bathroom and wouldn't have to share it with anyone since the others had a larger full bathroom on the second floor near their bedrooms. It would be private, she had considered, *and* the rent *was* cheap. That was mainly due to the fact that the twins' mother owned the property. And honestly, it had been exactly what she'd needed at the time, considering how slim her options had been.

"Love to—can't. Parents are expecting me at the bakery today, but thanks. Rain-check on the wine too—I gotta jet." Her parent's bakery was down around the corner on Preston Street right in the heart of

Little Italy. She only works there two days a week, mainly because her parents don't like to leave her younger brother there on his own. He's only a year younger, but tends to slack off when no one is there to keep an eye on him. It had been two years ago on the same day Natalie had seen the rental, that she and Teeny had met. After she had signed the rental agreement, she had walked over to Preston Street to catch the bus and had noticed the bakery. She had gone in to check out the place, mainly to see if they were hiring. They weren't, but funny enough, Teeny's brother Matteo—Matty, had shamelessly hit on her. Natalie kindly brushed him off, and because of the snub to her brother, Teeny had taken an instant liking to her and had mentioned that they were looking for waitstaff at the bar she worked at.

"Okay, no worries, next time. By the way, I took an extra shift tonight," Natalie added with a shrug.

"Did you tell the bosses yet?"

"About school—no," she said, shutting down her laptop.

"What's the hold up? They're your biggest supporters—next to me, of course."

"Yes I know. They'll be happy for me, proud for sure, but it'll mean I'll have to give up my day shifts with becoming a full-time student. Might have to find another job, and something part-time, more than likely."

"Maybe they'll let you work part-time in the new year," Teeny suggested, adjusting her purse again, this time sweeping her long, waist-length curly dark hair over her shoulder to hang down her back.

Natalie turned in her seat to face Teeny. "Well, I've been working full-time days there for almost 2 years, and I've saved enough for my tuition and books etc., plus about 6 months of rent, but I only have until January before school starts to save more. I'm going to need more funds sooner rather than later." Natalie pulled a loose thread from the frayed edge of her jean shorts. "And those prime evening shifts will already be spoken for by then, you know that. Only reason I'm working tonight is because one of the evening waitresses asked if I could help her out this one time."

"Look, once you get your official acceptance and your school schedule, you'll be able to see what shift options are available," Teeny said, reaching out to pat Natalie's arm, giving her an encouraging yet sympathetic grin. "And don't forget to update your mailing address — still shows your old place on your profile," she added as she turned and headed for the front door. "Later," she called over her shoulder.

"Gater," Natalie countered. "I'll do it when I register officially. I still have lots of time," she called out just as Teeny shut the door.

Back at home after her evening shift, Natalie readied herself for bed, changing out of her work clothes and into another oversized concert t-shirt to sleep in. She piled her hair up into a messy bun, washed her face and brushed her teeth, and then went and climbed into bed. Before plugging in her cellphone to charge on the nightstand, she wrote a quick text to Teeny, even though she knew she was probably asleep and wouldn't see the message until tomorrow.

She wrote,

> *Hope things went well at the bakery. I need to drop over and see your parents again soon. Roomies were excited about my news, bosses were very proud too as expected, and I had a good shift. But alas, I was told the likelihood of changing my weekday shifts to nights is a no-go, but they suggested I circle back once I got my schedule, like you had said. Guess we'll see. Chat later xo*

Chapter 1 

The old-fashioned bell over the door jingled.

"Hello," Kris heard Leo say. "You were the one reading the sign in the window earlier."

Kris glanced up then and his mouth gaped. "Jana?" he said in disbelief.

"Hi." Jana gave a little wave, her beautiful smile beaming back at him. "I'd like to apply for the general manager's job."

"What… are you doing here?" Kris asked, straightening from leaning over to read Leo's laptop screen.

Jana pointed a thumb over her shoulder in the direction of the large front window. "I saw the job posting and considering I'm currently in need of a job, I thought I'd apply." She shrugged, her expression sheepish. "Looks like you are getting closer to opening day." Her nervous smile appeared forced. "Great bell, by the way."

Kris continued to stare at Jana as she glanced around the bar's interior and the renovations in progress. She wore a white sundress with some kind of periwinkle blue flower dappled throughout the cotton fabric. Her blonde hair was pulled up into a high ponytail. Seeing her standing there as the sunlight beamed through the front windows felt like a dream. When he said nothing in response, Jana shifted, as if to go back the way she came in. "Where are you going?" he asked.

"I'm sorry—clearly I've made a terrible mistake," she said, embarrassment evident in her expression as she attempted to make her escape.

In a blink, Kris was at her side, folding a hand around her forearm, halting her in her tracks. Jana's eyes shot up to his face, then back to the bar where he'd just been standing. "Don't go," he pleaded. "I'm the one who should be sorry—you just caught me off guard." She looked down at his hand then. "Please stay. Come meet my…." He let go of her arm then, realizing the confusion that crossed her face was probably from rationalizing how he had gotten to her side so fast.

"I'm Lane—Kris's niece," Lane interrupted, rushing over to where they stood, holding out her hand in greeting. "*Jana*, is it?" she confirmed, taking a final step closer, hand still out.

As though in a trance, Jana glanced down at Lane's hand then back slowly up to her face. "Yes… I'm Jana… pleased to meet you, Lane." She clasped Lane's hand and shook it, then glanced back to Kris, further bewilderment clear in her expression. "Neice?"

"Uncle Kris…," Lane said, giving him a chin-nod before turning back to point to the bar. "…and Uncle Leo, aren't actually related— they're longtime close friends of my fathers and are like family to us. I've called them *uncle* as long as I can remember."

"Welcome," Leo said, traversing the distance to where they all stood now. "Kris, why don't you have Jana sit down?" He extended an arm toward the couches in the lounge area near the front of the restaurant.

"Yes, Jana, please—come sit," Kris said, swiftly moving to guide her to the nearest couch. Leo gave Kris a stern expression, eyes bulging, and eyebrows lifted for emphasis at words not yet spoken, as Jana began her gradual relocation towards the lounge area.

Jana glanced up at Kris, still stunned. Then she glanced back at Lane and Leo before turning back as Kris gently settled her down on the couch. "Thank you," she said, placing her purse to one side, evidently still bewildered as she scanned the rest of the open space of the bar.

"Can I get you something to drink?" Kris asked, taking his own glance around the ski lodge styled interior he and Leo had chosen to go with. "We aren't open for service yet—obviously, but we do have some waters and sodas in the bar fridge." He glanced over to the bar to see Leo had returned to his spot at the computer and Lane was once again sitting across from him.

"Water?" Jana said, pulling Kris's attention back. "I'm feeling a bit...."

"Right away," Kris said before she finished her sentence, dashing to the bar, mindful this time of his speed.

"What do you think she's doing here?" Kris asked Leo in a whisper.

"Applying for the manager's job, apparently," Leo said, giving him a facetious grin.

"Don't get me wrong—I'm thrilled to see her," Kris countered, cracking open the water bottle, pouring some of the contents into one of the glasses he'd washed from an earlier box.

"Thought you said she owned a bakery in Iceland," Leo questioned.

"She does—she did," Kris scrambled out. "Apparently, something has changed."

"Well, go find out what the deal is," Lane cut in. "She's very pretty, by the way."

"She's more beautiful than I remember," Kris said, taking a sip of the water he'd just poured.

Lane tapped the side of the glass. "Go—that's for her, remember?" She shook her head, then pointed over to Jana.

"Right—shit," Kris said, rushing around the bar, glass in one hand, open water bottle in the other.

The bell over the door jingled then as the door was opened once more. The lone Earthbound Seraph entered, giving Kris a quick glance and nod before he headed in the direction to where Leo and Lane were at the bar.

"Hey, Shayne," Kris said in acknowledgement before turning to hand Jana the glass of water.

"Another Uncle?" Jana asked, staring up at Kris as she took the glass from him.

"No-no—just an old friend," Kris said, cutting a quick glance at the bar. "Shayne is coming to work for me—us, as the bar manager." Kris lowered himself down on the adjacent couch across from Jana, setting the water bottle next to a stack of coasters on the low table between them. He grinned when he saw she was staring at him. Nervous, he said, "The bell is from the previous business—I kept it because it reminded me of the bakery." He glanced at the door, then back at her. Then he frowned. "What do you mean you're in need of a job—what happened to the bakery?"

She took a sip from the glass of water. "Right—that." As though gathering herself, she took in a long breath, and then said, "I sold the bakery—to the restaurant owners next door." She stared down at the water glass in her hand. "Sold my father's old place too," she continued hurriedly. "Met these ladies at the bakery looking for a property—one big enough to host women's retreats. Since it's just 30 min from Seydisfjordur to Egilsstadir—they thought it was the perfect location, secluded yet not too far from town. And well, I haven't done much traveling—so here I am," she rushed out as though losing the conviction in her words.

"I can't believe you sold the bakery," he said, leaning in, hoping for further explanation. "What do you plan to do now?"

"Truly, I hadn't thought that far ahead. And I realize now I shouldn't have shown up unannounced—but I came straight here after my endeavor to find you in New York. I would have chickened out had I waited, though." She wrapped both hands around the water glass.

"You went to New York... looking for me?" he questioned, impressed by her boldness. He recalled her telling him she'd never travelled outside of Iceland.

"Yes—I went to your restaurant." Jana took another sip of water. "Frank is... quite...," she started, then swallowed hard. "... she said you mentioned me ... that you had come back *a changed man*." Continuing not to look him in the face, she stared down at the glass in her hands.

"Why didn't you tell me you were coming?" Kris leaned his elbows on his knees.

"I figured you would have told me not to," she said, glancing up briefly before focusing back on her hands. "But after the way you had looked the last time I saw you—at the hospital, I just needed to know—see for myself you were truly okay," she fumbled out, her attention still on the water glass.

Kris leaned back against the couch and blew out an audible breath, grasping the reality now that she was really here. "Jana…," he started to say, then felt a flush of embarrassment recognizing he was in his grubby work shirt and cargo shorts he'd worn for unpacking the bar supplies. He leaned forward to hide the packing dust smudges on his white t-shirt.

"Frank gave me one of the new coasters—for this place," she said, taking one hand off the glass to snatch a coaster from the stack on the low table. "Told me she'd probably get an earful for doing so." As if unsure what else to say, she took a long sip from the glass before setting it down, placing the coaster under it. Then she looked at him.

"That explains it," Kris said, nodding, pouring the remaining water from the bottle into Jana's glass.

"Explains what?" She took the refilled glass and raised it to her lips as she continued to look at him.

He ran a hand through his hair, considering it was probably as disheveled as his clothing. "How you found me—not that I was hiding. Frank is the only one from the restaurant who knew where I was."

"How come you didn't tell me you were… starting a new project?" She set the glass back down without taking a sip. "Wait—you don't have to answer that—I'm sorry—I shouldn't have come here—I'm intruding," she scrambled out, grabbing up her purse.

"No," he said, putting his hand out for fear she would try to leave again. He had wanted to contact her several times after his goodbye email, to tell her about his new plans, but had felt it best he step away, let her get on with her life. "Fact is, I never dreamed I'd see you again, Jana." He wondered often what it would be like to be with her again now that his memories were intact. "You need to understand. I've never been close to anyone—except maybe Frank."

"What about…?" Jana began, glancing over to the bar.

"Lane and Leo?" Kris stole a look back over his shoulder to the bar, then turned back to Jana.

"Your niece said you were close with her father," she added, focusing back on him.

"Fathers—plural, her parents, yes. We've known each other for years, but…,"

"You wrote you were doing some *changing*—working on becoming a better person," Jana said, lifting one shoulder in a shrug, reciting the words he'd written in that last email he'd sent her.

Kris was relieved she hadn't gotten up to leave. "And that I had a lot to make up for," he added, doing his own recalling of the words he'd written. "My past actions." He leant back again, resting the palms of his hands on his knees. "It wasn't until I lost my memories—got them back, I mean, that I understood what a bastard I'd been… and realized the lack of closeness in my life—was my own fault. I'd done it to myself. But I'm working to change that now. It's the reason I came back here. It's the reason Leo and I are working together on this new venture. I needed—wanted, to be closer to my brothers."

"Came back… *here*?" Jana questioned. "*Brothers*, right. I remember you wrote about that, too." She shook her head as though puzzled by the word.

Kris sighed. "It's complicated."

"And now I've made things even more complicated."

"Honestly, yes…," he started to say. Then he closed his eyes and dropped his head, running his hands through his hair. He heard Jana stand then, and he opened his eyes and reached out for her. "… but that doesn't mean I don't want you here," he finished, taking her hand in his. Guiding her around the low coffee table and swiftly making room on the couch, he gently pulled her to sit next to him. She rested down at his side, staring at his hand holding hers. The feelings he had for her, the ones that had grown so intense during his stay in Iceland, the strong attraction he'd felt then, he had never experienced anything like it before. And now, having her next to him again, he could barely catch his breath as he stared at her lovely face. "Jana… I knew I could never return to Iceland again, but I never stopped thinking about your kindness and friendship…," he began, then trailed off to stare down at the top edge of his tattered socks poking free of his work boots.

"But that's all it was," she said, causing him to lift his head.

Gathering up his truth, he gazed into those light blue sparkling eyes of hers. "No… it was so much more than that… however, I never anticipated you'd ever come looking for me." He placed his other hand over hers.

"But it's complicated," she said, reciting his words back at him. Tears formed in the corners of her beautiful eyes, and she gave him a weak smile before placing her free hand over the top of his.

"Jana, you deserve… well, you deserve better than me, that's for sure."

"I have time… if you want to explain… the complexities." She drew in a breath. "I'd love to learn more about you—your life, about the others, your *brothers*." She exhaled a breath as though trying to settle her nerves.

"My family," he simplified, knowing his brothers, his existence— all of it, was going to be tough to explain considering he wasn't sure how much he should or would be permitted to share.

"Where are you staying?" came Leo's inquisitive voice from behind them.

The bell over the front door jingled again, grabbing all their attentions.

"I'll see you later, Uncles," Lane called out as she held open the front door.

"It was nice to meet you, Lane," Jana tossed over to her.

"Nice to meet you too, Jana," Lane responded, giving her a quick wave before exiting.

"You should stay with us if you haven't secured lodgings yet," Leo said then, his tone adamant.

Kris felt his mouth gape at Leo's words, watching as he came over to stand next to where they sat on the couch.

Jana too focused up at Leo. "I checked into a little hotel up the way—left my suitcase there in the room," Jana informed him.

Surprise had sounded in Jana's voice over the invite, but no one was more surprised than Kris was, and he continued to gape at Leo.

"Kris," Leo redirected, "help Jana get her things and meet me back at North Haven. I need to circle back with Lynn first, then we can discuss Jana's visit." Leo smiled at Jana, sincerity clear in his words about her staying with them.

Kris stared up at him, dumbfounded. "Okay—will do," he said in replace of the gaping, standing then to fulfill the request.

"Lynn—she's your estate executor," Jana said to Kris, drawing his attention from Leo.

"Right—yes," Kris responded, shocked, yet still excited at the prospect of Jana being a part of his world.

"Kris, we need to review that *name* still, the one I found in my research," Leo stated, eyebrows raising, his expression intense, reminding Kris there were *other* matters besides Jana being here that needed discussing.

Chapter 2 

The Beach House, August 1ˢᵗ, South Florida, USA

Yesterday, I'd been so preoccupied with swirling thoughts over my brother losing his dog Skye, Purah's latest visit and information about Thaddeus, that I hadn't had the mental capacity to circle back with Lane. I had asked her to contact me with updates each time she and Lyndon spent time together, and she had, so I assumed her text from yesterday asking me to call her was of a similar nature. Today, however, I was better equipped mentally to deal with whatever news she had to share.

I leaned a hip against the kitchen counter as I hit dial on the contact number I had for her.

"Hi, Lynn," came Lane's youthful voice through the cell's speaker as I switched it to hands-free.

I set the cellphone on the kitchen island and pulled open the fridge door. "Hey, sorry I didn't call yesterday…," I began to say.

"It's all good," she cut in. "But I have other stuff to tell you, though."

My brain buzzed. "What's up?" I asked, pausing before pulling out the ingredients Redmond would need to make our lunch. It was an exceptionally hot August day in South Florida, and I lingered in the open fridge door for an added chill boost despite the A/C pumping cool air through the house vents.

"First, on the Lyndon front. I was supposed to meet him today at the group home, then we were to head out to this bar-restaurant Rachel told me about."

"This would have been your first time hanging with him outside of the group home, yes?" I shut the fridge door, then removed the hair tie from my wrist and swiftly threw my long hair up in a loose bun.

"Correct—was supposed to be, but he had to cancel—said his boss needed to see him."

I rolled my eyes. "And?" We were both well aware of who his *boss* was.

"Well…," she said, then paused, "…I was just at Uncle Kris's new place. I told him and Uncle Leo I was considering asking Lyndon to come there with me—once it's open. That way, they could see for themselves how he is."

"What did they say?" I asked, staring over at the sliding glass doors to the patio. At this time of day, the humidity outside clung to the glass of the doors in a similar manner you would see on windows of an indoor pool, giving the impression it was foggy outside when it wasn't.

"Uncle Kris said it would make an interesting date, and I had to remind him it wouldn't be a *date*. Uncle Leo didn't say anything."

"I know you trust Lyndon, and the others seeing him might help them to trust him too—if he's all you say he is."

"My thoughts exactly," she agreed.

I turned back to the fridge and opened it again. "I can't wait to come up and see the new place. I used to go there—when it was Stoney Monday's—back when I was your age," I affirmed, my mind reminiscing of days long past.

"I read about that bar, actually. Found an old article linked to the history on the building," Lane stated, her use of the word *history* making me feel old. Then she said, "Speaking of Uncle Kris's new place. You… are not… going to believe… who showed up just before I left."

The hairs on my arms bristled, but it wasn't from the cold coming from the fridge. "Dare I ask?" I huffed out a breath, shutting the fridge.

"Jana!"

"Wow!" I shouted, surprise and relief mingling. "That's a better answer than I had expected."

"I know—right!" she said, still excited. "Before I left, she and Uncle Kris were deep in conversation. Then Uncle Leo interrupted them, saying she should stay with *us*. But that's all I know. I was already heading out at that point, so."

"Speaking of your Uncle Leo, I need to reach out to him on a few things anyway, so I'm sure he'll catch me up."

"When are you coming up again?" Lane asked, shifting the subject.

"Not sure," I said, leaning my lower back against the kitchen island. "Why?"

"Was nice having another female in the house," she confessed. "Talking to you… about everything is much easier than talking to my dads, or my uncles. There are no *wives*. I don't have any aunts, you know?" Her words ended with an audible sigh.

"I hadn't considered it before, but I can understand being the only female in a house with all that testosterone would be more than challenging." I'd had it bad growing up with brothers and mostly guy cousins, but Lane's circumstances were a whole new level. "I'm always here if you need to talk—about *anything*. Consider me your *Aunt* Lynn. We can even video chat if you want," I suggested, fully open to being her surrogate aunt.

"I'd love that," she said, and I could almost hear her smile. "We can exchange schedules—that way I won't be interrupting your family time."

"You are family, Lane," I said. "You, your dads, your uncles, we are all family now."

"Thank you, Lynn—*Aunt* Lynn. You don't know how much that means to me."

I did know. "I'll send you my schedule later today." It was important to have people in your life that you considered family. "And you send me yours—when you have time, and we'll book a video chat. Cool?"

"Cool. Thanks again," she said before hanging up.

Redmond came through the door from the lower level into the kitchen then, beads of sweat blistering across his handsome face. He was followed by the girls, who were both carrying plastic bags from the local office supply store.

"Hiiii Mum," Ryley called out as she maneuvered to the dining area, plopping her bags down on the table. She cleared away a sweaty wisp of hair from her face that had come loose from her ponytail.

Hayley grinned at me, the bangs of her fair hair sweat-soaked and stuck to her forehead, but she said nothing as she passed by and then slid her bags onto the table next to her sister's. I'd given them both high ponytails before they had left with Redmond to go shopping, but clearly, they hadn't helped in abating the heat.

"Hot out there, eh?" Even shorts and tank tops felt like too much clothing in summer here.

"South Florida in August—good times!" Redmond gave me a sarcastic grin.

"Nice haul," I said in greeting, walking over to stand at the table in front of the bags. I leant down to get a dewy kiss from each of the girls. "How did it go?" I asked Redmond, stretching up to give him a kiss next when he came to stand beside me.

"Success," he said, wiping his brow and pulling open the bags by their handles to reveal the contents.

"When I was a kid, we didn't start school until after the Labor Day long weekend."

He nodded. "Same here."

"September 5th is still a holiday here," Hayley said, reminding us.

"The studio is closed that day," Redmond shared with a winsome grin.

"And I'm off on that day, too," I informed them.

Rylie clapped her hands together. "We can make it a family long weekend," she said, adding to her sister's comment, grinning playfully up at her dad and me.

"How about the two of you go through the supplies with your Mum—run through the list the school provided to make sure we didn't miss anything," Redmond suggested, handing me a pen, and the printed list he'd used at the store. His grin was mischievous now as he turned in the direction of the kitchen.

The girls nodded, then took off, dashing up the hall towards their bedrooms. Thirty seconds later, they returned with their school bags in hand, setting them down on the bench seat across from the shopping bags. They were using the same light green and pale blue knapsacks from last year, since they were still in good shape. Neither had any theme to them so they wouldn't be considered 'last years' trend, and besides, the girls liked them just fine.

"Okay, I'll read from the list, and you hold up your matching item before putting it in your knapsacks, and I'll check it off the list. Okay?"

They both nodded again, then simultaneously dumped out their shopping bags onto the table. "Ready," they said in unison.

"First item…

6 composition notebooks

Ryley held up a package showing a short stack of light blue notebooks, while Hayley held a similar pack, though each of her notebook displayed different colours.

"Check," I said, drawing a line through the first item on the list.

The girls placed the notebooks into the open mouths of their knapsacks.

"Next…

6 pocket folders

They each help up their supplies. Ryley had similar coloured pocket folders to that of her notebooks, and Hayley, like with her notebooks, each of her pocket folders matched in colour to their corresponding notebook. This was another indicator of how very different they each were from one another and how differently they liked to organize their school work.

"Great!" The remaining items finished off the list…

24 Pencils with erasers
1 red ball-point pen
1 box of 12 colored pencils
2 Low-odor dry erase markers (black only)

1 24 count of crayons
3 highlighters, blue, green, yellow
1 pair of scissors
5 glue sticks
5 packs of square sticky notes, yellow
1 plastic pencil box

… although the pencil box and scissors for Ryley were blue and Hayley's were green such that they didn't get mixed up.

"I've already bought you each new running shoes for PE," I said then. Ryley was in a standard size 5 for her age and Hayley was in a size 4, yet I still managed to find the same style in both sizes. Hayley had grown some over the summer, however Ryley was still 4 inches taller and had about 10lbs on her sister.

"Can we go play outside in the backyard?" Ryley asked, zipping up her knapsack.

I glanced at the glass doors to the deck. The humidity had lessened some. "We're going to have lunch soon," I said, pointing at the clock on the wall.

"What are we having, Da?" Hayley inquired, zipping her bag closed.

"My special grilled cheese," he answered, pulling a loaf of bakery bread and his special mustard seed mixture from the fridge drawer.

"GOAT!" Ryley shouted, attempting to tighten her ponytail.

"Goat?" I questioned, giving her a repulsed face.

"Greatest. Of. All. Time, Mum," Hayley clarified with an exaggerated eye-roll and swipe of her damp bangs.

I turned the corners of my mouth down, giving her an *excuse-me* face in response, then shot a glance Redmond's way. "Have *you* heard that expression before?"

"Sure—I'm hip," he said, grinning proudly as he strode to the patio door.

"Ya—no, if yer still using the word *hip*, you aren't hip," I tossed back with an amused chuckle.

He laughed, nodding agreeably. "I do make a mean grilled cheese sandwich, though."

"That you do, my love. That. You. Do."

Redmond slid open the patio door for the girls to exit. "I'll call you when it's ready."

"Take Summer and Snow with you. Try to stay in the shady areas—it's still stifling out there. And no going up the path to the beach without us—you hear me?"

Grumbling, Hayley said, "We only ever did it that one time." She stepped through the open door.

"It was after our last day of camp," Ryley added, following her sister out the door.

"Scared your mum half to death," I called out before Redmond slid the door shut. "And *their pleas fell on deaf ears*," I said, feeling the relevance of the phrase.

Redmond chuckled and shook his head. "So, did I miss anything exciting while we were out?" He returned to the kitchen area.

"Just got off the phone with Lane before you got home," I said, meeting him at the kitchen island.

"Anything new on the Lyndon front?" Redmond asked as he took a large cast-iron pan, two grill weights, and a small pot out from the pot drawer. He set the pot on one of the stove burners, setting the heat to low. Then he added half a stick of the butter I'd set out into the pot.

"Nope. Only that she wants to bring him to Kris's new restaurant—once it's open, so they can meet him—see what he's like." I slid the wooden cutting board and cheese grater over Redmond's way next to the cheese and other items I'd pulled out of the fridge for his lunch prep.

He took the cutting board from me and proceeded to grate the cheese and diced the onions and leeks. "That would be an interesting... *introduction*," Redmond said with a hint of apprehension in his voice, more than likely fatherly concern. Then, from the cupboard next to the stove, he pulled out two large metal mixing bowls. Into one of them he tossed the grated cheese, onion, leeks, some salt, regular whole-grain mustard, and the pickled mustard seed mixture he had prepared first thing this morning.

"She trusts Lyndon—wants them to trust him, too." I shifted from the island to lean my hip against the counter where Redmond had all the ingredients arranged.

Redmond's eyebrows raised in response, though he continued to stir and combined the contents in the bowl.

"I know-I know. I'll believe it when I—they see it. And yes, interesting for sure," I admitted. "And you are not going to believe who Lane said showed up at the restaurant."

Redmond stopped mixing and stared at me.

"Don't worry, it's not anyone bad." My own imagination had fired up similarly when Lane had said the same to me, mainly because we had spoken with Leo the night before about how Thaddeus was believed to be heading to Brazil. Leo had restated that before relocating to Ottawa, Nic had originally been located there, but nothing concerning had occurred for years at that location, nor had any other Earthbound been living in that region, including any of Thaddeus's followers. Although based on this revelation of Purah's, Leo said that Nic would be going back soon to check out the lab for any signs of Thaddeus or his devotees.

"Who?" Redmond asked, tapping the mixing spatula on the inside edge of the bowl.

"Jana," I said wide-eyed, raising my eyebrows.

"Wow," Redmond said, pausing to move the pot with the now melted butter off the heat to a cool burner. He then placed the cast-iron pan over the hot burner and set it to medium heat.

"That's what I said when Lane told me." Assisting with lunch prep, I removed several slices of the bakery bread from the paper bag and set the stack on the cutting board.

"What else did she say?" Using a pastry brush, Redmond began spreading the melted butter over one side of each slice, placing each back in the stack on the cutting board buttered sides facing each other.

"Not much, really. Just that Leo had asked that Jana stay with them." Helping again, I removed the gruyère and cheddar cheese slices from their respective packages, setting them next to the bread. "How'd you like to be a fly on the wall for those next conversations?"

Redmond whooped out a laugh, then furthered his masterpiece by placing the gruyère cheese on one slice and the cheddar on the other, with about 1 inch of the cheese hanging over the edges of the bread. "Oh, I'm sure we'll hear all about it, eventually," he added, grabbing up the water squeeze bottle next to the stove, checking the heat of the pan by releasing a dribble of water over its surface. The water splattered, indicating the pan was hot enough. "It's ready."

"Okee dokee," I said, handing Redmond the full mixing bowl in exchange for the squeeze bottle. Then I watched in amazement as my talented husband expertly divided the grated cheese mixture evenly, piling one scoop of the mixture atop the first slice of bread and another atop the adjacent slice. Then he skillfully placed both halves into the heated cast-iron pan.

With the remaining empty metal mixing bowl, he covered the masterpiece. "Water," he requested like a surgeon asking for a scalpel.

"Water," I repeated, handing him back the squeeze bottle.

Using his handy-dandy kitchen tongs, Redmond tipped one side of the bowl up and squeezed a small amount of water around both slices of bread, then immediately covered the sandwich again with the metal bowl to trap the steam. He repeated this process several times over the next few minutes. "Melted and shiny," he said then, lifting the hot bowl with the tongs and placing it to the far side of the stove.

"Spatula," I said, handing him a metal flipper.

"Thank you, nurse," he countered in his professional doctor tone. Using the spatula, he flipped closed the first sandwich and then placed the grill weights atop it. "Need to let it crisp up before I flip it," he added before moving on through the steps for the next sandwiches.

"Right," I said, my stomach groaning with impatience as he toasted the other side of the first sandwich.

As each sandwich was fully toasted, Redmond transferred the grilled cheese goodness to individual plates, slicing them diagonally. "Eh, Voila!" he announced, placing the last of the grilled cheese sandwiches onto the plate closest to where I stood watching.

"My hero!" I said, faking a swoon before crossing the kitchen to the patio door. I slid open the door and called out, "Giiiirls, come get cleaned up—lunch is ready!"

A dual call of, "Okaaaay!" came from under the deck.

I left the patio door open despite the waft of hot air coming through it and walked back towards Redmond just as my cellphone rang where I'd left it on the kitchen island. "I guess we'll find out sooner rather than later. It's Leo calling," I shared, hitting answer and then speaker. "Hi, Leo."

"Hey, Leo," Redmond call out.

"I have you on speaker," I said, tearing paper towel sheets from the roll to use as napkins.

"Hey, you two. I just wanted to let you know—confirm really, that I'm sending Nic to Brazil. He leaves tonight. He'll be posing as a conservationist interested in a tour of the lab."

"Clever, but are you sure he should go alone?"

"Don't you get any ideas," Redmond scrutinized, grabbing the makeshift napkins from my hand.

"I'm not saying for me to go…." Although I would have had Leo asked me to. "… it's just that backup is always good."

"It's all good," Leo said. "Jules reached out to a few of her connections there so he will have contacts and a secure place to stay while he's there *and* help should he need it."

I nodded, even though Leo couldn't see me.

"Good to hear," Redmond said when I didn't respond.

"Yes—good news," I said. "I hope to meet her next time we're in Ottawa." I knew Jules had been in Brazil for her job, though she had not been involved in any monitoring of things like Nic had previously done. Both she and her son Mason were in Ottawa now, and I was more than anxious to meet them both.

"She is eager to meet you too," Leo stated, before switching topics. "I have some follow up news on our search for Anael's daughter."

"Did you check the Ontario adoption records like I mentioned?" Originally, the records for adoptions in Ontario had been sealed, but I'd informed Leo about the Access to Adoption Records act, the one that had come into being and allowed me to request my own adoption records.

"Yes! I'd been exploring other databases with no hits, but your suggestion was a winner. Sadly, the records did show the adoptive parents are deceased, but that does make their names public record now."

"Did you find anything else helpful?" I began filling plastic cups with water from the fridge dispenser.

"Not really, although I did another type of search on one of those family lineage websites. I was able to locate the parents' names and the mother's maiden name. The public tree was actually under her name, but it was quite limited. The time stamp showed no updates had been done for years. Fortunately, it did show the mother had a sister, however, there doesn't seem to be any other living relatives on either side."

"How old would the daughter have been when the parents died?" Redmond asked, picking up two of the water cups I'd set on the island to take over to the dining table..

"They died in January of 2012 and based on her DOB, she would have just turned 10 years old at the time.

"Is there any chance she went to live with the aunt?" I asked, transferring the remaining two water glasses over to the table.

"That's what Lane had proposed when I found the tree."

"I spoke to Lane earlier by the way—she told me about your surprise visitor," I said hurriedly, hearing clambering noises from outside traveling up the back stairs to the deck.

"Yes, it was quite an unexpected *reunion*," Leo acknowledged, just as panting dogs and giggling girls came scampering through the open patio door.

Chapter 3 

When Lyndon had spoken with Lane about their upcoming outing, he had to lie as to why he couldn't meet up with her. Since mid-May, they had been spending a lot of time together with Taylor, and today would have been their first time to venture out just the two of them. He knew he would have had to call on a different form of bravery to meet with her in public, but he hadn't wanted to give up any chance of spending time with her. He'd even purchased new clothes for the occasion, since she seemed to like the way he had changed up his wardrobe. Regrettably, he had to miss the opportunity due to having to tend to the needs of his ever-demanding boss. Lyndon loathed the feeling of being beholden to Thaddeus and being treated like his personal errand boy. He hadn't been privy to Thaddeus's plans before they'd all ended up on Earth, but he was determined more than ever to come up with his own plan, one that would involve Taylor's safety and their freedom.

Lyndon had informed Thaddeus of the newest lead on this Ms. Westlake, how the woman had married a man with the last name *Lockridge*, and whom Lyndon had been told by the man's father, currently lived in Florida, Miami to be more precise. Thaddeus hadn't questioned where he had gotten this information, and Lyndon had opted not to share. Lyndon had, however, insisted he needed to stay local, keep an eye out at the brother's house as well as the group home, should the target or perhaps one of the other women was to show up at the locations. He still had lookouts stationed at these locations but stated to Thaddeus he would prefer to watch these places himself.

Fortunately, the lie had worked, mainly due to the fact it had been Thaddeus's idea to keep watch on the homes and workplaces of the other women with the hope of catching this Westlake person at one of these locations. Although, Thaddeus *had* questioned why she would have used her maiden name on the sign-in sheet at the group home. Lyndon hadn't understood why it even mattered, but in response, he had suggested it may have been to hide her identity, but there was no way to know for sure.

The latest step of many in Lyndon's plan towards freedom had involved convincing Thaddeus he needed to send Zuriel to Florida in his place, and he'd breathed a sigh of relief when he had gotten Thaddeus's buy-in. The only reason Thaddeus had agreed was because he didn't care *who* pursued the lead, just that someone was on it. This suited Lyndon just fine because he was currently waiting for Zuriel to check in, having already instructed his fellow tracker where he had needed to go in Miami.

Lyndon checked the time on his cellphone just as it vibrated in his hand. "Z," he said, answering on the second vibration.

"I'm here," came Zuriel's jovial voice in response.

"You at the condo?" Lyndon had texted him the address of the residence he'd found in his preliminary internet search, the one having been owned by *William Lockridge*, but he had provided Zuriel with *both* surnames just in case, and details about the woman's association to the medical arena.

"Not yet. I'm in Coconut Grove, in a social area they call *The Grove*, but I'm close by. I have the location you sent me and will be heading there soonest." There was a pause, and then Zuriel let out a whistle. "It's beautiful here by the way—with all the tropical greenery, palm trees—reminds me of the rainforests in Brazil, and oh the ocean views are magnificent, much like the Atlantic ocean where it touches the rainforest. Quite the change from New York City. I was glad to get the assignment, grateful to get out of the city, frankly," he added joyfully. "But wow, is it hot here."

Lyndon couldn't help but grin. "Okay, great, Z—let me know what you find out," he replied, adding a little levity to his own words.

"You got it!" Zuriel said before ending the call.

It wasn't often Lyndon heard such delight from one of his own, but he had always enjoyed Zuriel's company and respected the positive attitude he embraced in spite of what had happened to them. Thaddeus, on the other hand, thought Zuriel was a fool for his optimistic view of the circumstances. Thaddeus did, however, recognize Zuriel was a *follower*, and he liked those who obeyed. Zuriel did what he was told, although he hadn't come with any skills Thaddeus had felt were useful, other than his skill at being compliant.

Zuriel's devotion while serving among the stars had been focused on Earth's mammals, specifically those who lived in the oceans. His abilities involved communication with them even over long distances, though Lyndon was not privy to how he did it. All he knew was it had been Zuriel's aim to make sure there was a balance kept in the ocean between the largest of the oceanic mammals, the blue whale who are also the largest animal to have ever existed on Earth, and a variety of species throughout their entire food chain to the tiny swarms of zooplankton like krill that the blue whales ate. Both Zuriel and Marcus had come from the star *Taygeta* and had originally been assigned to work out of the Brazil facility, but they'd been reassigned to New York City when there was no longer a need for them at that location.

Other than Julianna, who was now in Ottawa, that information Lyndon had yet to share with Thaddeus, there had been no other Earthbound in that region of the world for quite some time. Interestingly of late, Thaddeus had informed Lyndon he was heading to Brazil of all places, for what, Lyndon didn't know, nor did he care.

Although, any day Thaddeus was away, was a good day in his books.

* * *

Coconut Grove, Miami, USA

Zuriel slid his cellphone into his vintage leather messenger bag as he strolled down the shady palm tree covered sidewalks from the park towards Coconut Grove's center town known as Coco Walk. He'd chosen this bag over a rolling style suitcase as it was easier to carry while flying and was large enough to carry extra clothing and anything else he needed for a short stay. Before take-off from New York, Zuriel had read that Coconut Grove was Miami's premier lifestyle destination and just south of downtown Miami and The Beaches. He had chosen the neighborhood for his arrival not just because of its proximity to the address he'd been given, but also because he'd read about the quaint scenery and atmosphere and its nearness to the ocean. He'd landed before dawn at the far end of the large grassy area that looked out to the ocean, and it wasn't until he'd found the main entrance into the area that he'd discovered it was a historical state park called The Barnicle. Luckily for him, no one had yet been on duty to catch him exiting, as apparently you had to pay to enter, and he would have had to explain how he'd gotten in without doing so. He intended to return later when it was dark, and the place was closed for the day such that he could sit peacefully at the ocean end of the property to enjoy the moonlight reflect off the water. For now, he allowed himself the beautiful 30-minute walk along the path that ran next to the road and under the arching banyan trees leading to the address Lyndon had instructed him to check out.

Zuriel approached a condo building surrounded by palm trees and meticulously manicured grounds, which, based on the property sign stating 'Waterway Towers', was the location he was looking for. As he advanced towards the main entrance, a man who appeared to be in his late 40s, wearing a doorman's uniform, exited the building to hold open the door for him. "Good morning, sir," the man said, motioning for him to enter. "How can I be of service?"

"This is an incredible location, the views and that tropical breeze — just amazing," Zuriel said in response, though he appreciated the air-conditioned space of the front lobby on such a hot day.

"Yes. They are quite amazing, sir. Are you here to see one of the residents? Shall I call up to them for you?"

"Actually, I'm here to talk with the manager," Zuriel said, adjusting the shoulder strap of his messenger bag.

"The supervisor for the building is not here at the moment. Is there something I may assist you with?" he asked, remaining near the main entrance.

Zuriel glanced around the lobby, hanging one hand leisurely around the strap of the bag. "Do you know when he will be back?"

"Sorry, not until the end of the day, sir. Is there anything else I may help you with?"

"Do you know William Lockridge? I believe he lives here. He's actually the one I need to speak with." Zuriel gave the man a friendly smile.

"Yes, I know Mr. Lockridge. But I'm sorry again, sir, he hasn't lived here for quite some time—several years, in fact." He smiled back.

"Oh, I see. That's unfortunate, for me I mean. You wouldn't know where he moved to—his change of address, possibly?" Zuriel asked hopeful.

"We don't keep that kind of information at the front desk," he informed him, pointing a hand towards the small security office.

"You don't suppose the building supervisor would have that kind of information, do you?" Eager, he wrapped both hands around the messenger bag's strap.

"Anything regarding past residents would have been forwarded to the main office offsite," the doorman stated before looking back over his shoulder.

Just then, an older man wearing the same uniform as the younger man, one whose appearance displayed a stature of a man years past standard retirement, came through the entrance. "Hello. Everything okay?" he asked the younger man.

"Yes-yes. Misterrr…?" the younger doorman started to say.

"Zuriel," he finished for the doorman, tightening his grip on the strap.

"Mr. Zuriel was just inquiring about a past resident." The younger doorman clasped his hands behind his back.

"Who would that be, may I ask?" he questioned, his query directed at the other doorman.

"Do you remember Mr. Lockridge?" the younger doorman asked the elder, releasing his hands from behind his back to relax at his sides.

"Oh yes, William, of course—and his lovely wife, Lynn," he said, turning from the younger man to focus on Zuriel.

"Would you, by any chance, remember where they moved to?" Zuriel was doing his best to be polite while trying to be patient with these two humans.

"It was Palmetto Bay, if I recall correctly. Though, where exactly, I couldn't say." The old man put a finger to his lips as though probing his memory banks. "But I do remember they were moving into their first house. A young couple like that needs more room for children and family." He held his finger in the air like he was adding an exclamation point to his comment.

Smiling innocently, clearly having no valuable information of his own, the younger man opened the door, then stood back to make way for Zuriel to leave.

Zuriel nodded his understanding. "Well, thank you—this has been helpful," he said, conceding at the man's not-so-subtle hint for him to go. "Say, would you know of any restaurants nearby where I could get something delicious to eat?"

"Closest would be The Grove," the younger doorman said, pointing an open hand in the direction Zuriel had come from.

"Of course," he acknowledged, nodding before exiting the building. Whistling a joyful tune, Zuriel headed back out to the path he'd just traveled and continued up the road. He *was* hungry, although instead of taking the long hot walk back to the grove, he stopped under the shade of a large banyan tree to pull out his cellphone and do his own web search for this William fellow.

After several tries alternating between the two surnames, he found an address that appeared to be right in the heart of Palmetto Bay, though the map showed it would take him over 3 hours to walk the distance. Conversely, it was only a short drive to get there, so without hesitation, he hit the icon on his cellphone for the ride service, then plugged in the address for the destination. Within 4 minutes, a white eco-friendly Prius pulled up alongside him where he stood under the banyan tree.

A scenic 20-minute drive later, the Prius pulled onto a halfmoon shaped driveway in front of a large single storey home, and then he exited the car to walk the short distance to the front door. Before knocking on the door, he checked himself in the reflection of the window nearest to the large double-door entrance to the home. He always made the effort to maintain a well-groomed appearance, having his dark hair cut short and stylish and parted to one side, and for this journey, he'd opted to travel wearing new dark jeans, white tennis shoes and a teal golf shirt. Fortunately for him, despite the scorching heat of the day, he did not appear to be a sweaty mess yet. Even so, with the local temperature as hot as it was, the first chance he got, he would be swapping out his jeans for walking shorts. He nodded at himself in the reflection, then knocked once on the door and waited.

When no one came to the door, he knocked a second time.

He knocked a third time before leaning to peek through the window. There were no cars in the drive, but then he noticed the far end of the driveway extended up around the boundary of the house. Intent on checking the side of the home, he turned and descended the short rise of stairs from the front door. Just then, a car drove up and pulled into the driveway of the home across the street. A young woman in deep purple hospital scrubs exited the vehicle. "Hello," Zuriel called over to the woman, briskly crossing the street to her side.

The woman stopped to look his way. "Hello," she said in kind before glancing briefly back and forth up the street.

"I'm here to see Mr. Lockridge, but no one seems to be at home."

"Uhm, sorry, I haven't met the neighbors yet. This is only my second day working here."

"My apologies. I assumed you lived here."

"No-no, but I can check with my clients. Please, have a seat," she said, waving a hand in the direction of the patio couch and chairs under the covered porch.

"Thank you," he said, taking the last step up onto the front porch as the woman went inside the home.

Several minutes later, she returned, assisting an elderly man through the front door, trailed by an equally aged woman. The woman appeared to be much spryer than the man but was still quite frail despite her ability to walk unassisted. "This is…," the young woman began in introduction.

"Zuriel," he affirmed, realizing then she was, in fact, the nursemaid to the elderly couple she'd referred to as *clients*.

"… Mr. Zuriel is the gentleman I mentioned that's looking for the neighbors across the way," the nurse said, louder than needed. She eased the old man into the cushioned chair while his wife rested down onto the couch at the end nearest her husband's chair. The nurse took the other chair next to the old man.

"Come sit. I don't bite," the old woman said in an equally loud voice, giving him an encouraging smile.

Zuriel remained standing now in the shade of the porch.

"That's because she hasn't got her teeth in," the old man said just as loudly, giving a hearty laugh followed by an abrupt cough.

Zuriel understood then that the loudness had been for the benefit of the old couple.

The old woman laughed and patted her husband's knee. She grinned at Zuriel, showing him she did in fact have her *teeth in*. "We don't see the neighbors very often anymore," she said, addressing no one in particular.

"The husband is a musician," the old guy stated, moving his arms and hands as though he were playing an invisible guitar.

"And they have the cutest little girls," the wife added, pulling free a hardcover novel out from under a decorative pillow near the arm of the couch.

"Wait, no, he works for the cruise ship," the husband said then, confusion blanketing his wrinkled face.

"No, silly, that was the other one," his wife corrected him, patting his knee again.

He nodded, then swiftly proceeded to literally nod off, soft snores escaping his open mouth almost immediately.

The old woman patted her husband's knee a third time before slipping on a pair of thick reading glasses, focusing her attention on the now open book.

"Sorry, they get confused easily," the nurse said in a softer voice. "Not much help, I'm afraid. Oh—look." She pointed to a jeep pulling into the driveway of the house across the way.

"Please excuse me," Zuriel said, moving away from the seating area to descend back down the stairs.

"You may be in luck after all," the nurse called out to him.

"Who was that?" Zuriel heard the old woman ask in confusion as he stepped onto the grassy lawn.

"Thank you," he called back over his shoulder as he reached the edge of the property.

A short heavyset dark-haired young man exited the jeep as Zuriel strode once again up the driveway. "Good morning," Zuriel said, addressing him, hand already out in greeting.

The young man swiftly latched a karabiner of keys to a belt loop on his shorts before gripping Zuriel's outstretched hand. "Morning," he said kindly, though his expression was one of puzzlement.

"Mr. Lockridge," Zuriel said with delight, shaking the man's hand with exuberance. "I was hoping to catch you at home."

The man shook his head and said, "Sorry, friend, the name's Cortez, not Lockridge." He gave Zuriel a crooked smile, then pulled a bandana free from the pocket of his shorts.

"Oh… I'm terribly sorry—my mistake," Zuriel apologized, his enthusiasm deflating.

"Are you looking for the previous owner?" Mr. Cortez queried, wiping the bandana across his sweaty forehead.

"Yes, the Lockridge family," Zuriel said, his enthusiasm rising again.

The man rubbed his jaw with his other hand. "I don't recall that name, but the owner before me was Westlake."

"Westlake?" Zuriel said with surprise. But perhaps the house had been sold under the wife's name, he considered. "How long ago was that?"

"Back in 2016," he said, patting the back of his neck with the bandana.

"You wouldn't happen to know where they moved to, would you?" Zuriel asked with a reluctant smile.

"Nah, never met them, actually. Only know the name because it was on the paperwork when I contracted to buy the place."

Zuriel gave him an understanding nod. "I'm terribly sorry to have bothered you," he said, defeated, turning and heading back down the drive.

"Oh hey, I used Coconut Grove Realty, if that helps. They're in The Grove. Slim chance—but they might have more information for you."

"Thank you, I'll give them a try." Zuriel waved and then strode on up the street. He blew out a whistled breath, recognizing this was going to be harder than he had anticipated. He already intended to return to The Grove for lunch once he'd secured his target, but now, along with his hunger, he was feeling woeful about the assignment having already hit a dead end. The chance of getting any information from the real estate office would be slim at best, as the man had said. Nonetheless, he was determined to make the most of this beautiful day. Turning his frown upside-down, he pulled his cellphone from his bag, stopping once again under the shade of a large tree. He hit the icon on his phone for the ride service, then punched in the return address to The Grove.

On the ride, Zuriel had asked the driver for a lunch recommendation in the area to where they had been headed and the driver had kindly obliged, dropping him off out front of a restaurant on Greenstreet, aptly named the Greenstreet Café. And now happily seated on the patio in the shade, he perused the menu and was further joyed to find plant based meals available. He'd never been comfortable with the idea of eating meat, especially fish, even those deemed as bred for consumption. In fact, he was opposed to any harm towards animals of all kinds and had been sickened over the cruelty he had witnessed after he and the others had been stranded here. He didn't enjoy hunting down these halflings either, but he'd rather track one of them before he'd ever harm an animal.

Over a vegan plate of truffle fries coupled with a Smashed Avocado Impossible Burger, Zuriel performed several more internet searches using the surnames but found no new records or house purchases other than the sale of the Palmetto Bay home. *"I'm not ready to go back to New York,"* he murmured under his breath, searching now for the business name Coconut Grove Realty. The GPS on his phone showed that the place should be right in front of him, and he glanced up from his phone. Panning the area, he spotted the partial name of the realty office on a sign peeking out from the corner of the building where two streets intersected.

Done with lunch, Zuriel dropped his napkin on the empty plate, then grabbed up his satchel and stood, tossing more than enough cash for the check and a tip on the table before dashing out of the restaurant's patio area to head across the street. At the real estate office entrance, he paused briefly to look around before entering the establishment and then pulled open the door.

He was immediately greeted by an average height casually dressed middle-aged man. "Lovely day. Are you enjoying the weather?" the man asked. He had a name tag pinned over the embroidered agency's name on his coral coloured golf shirt that read 'Alejandro' next to the word 'agent'.

"Beautiful, yes," Zuriel responded, "although I wasn't prepared for the temperature of the day. I'll be changing once I get to a hotel." Zuriel chuckled, looking down at his denim pants.

"Yes—it takes some getting used to," the agent said with a nod.

"I am grateful for the brilliant A/C and airflow." Zuriel pointed to the ceiling fan.

"I take it you are new to the area. Visiting, or are you looking for your next home?" The agent extended a hand. "I am Alejandro."

"I'm Zuriel—pleased to meet you. I uhm—I'm just visiting… for now," he said, shaking the man's hand. "I am hoping you can help me—I'm looking to get some information."

The agent turned, sweeping an arm towards a wall of photos that displayed numerous homes for sale and what Zuriel guessed were spots of interest, noting the parks and green spaces as well as waterfront docks, store fronts and restaurants. "Our lovely little neighborhood was established back in the late 1800s. Miami's oldest neighborhood," the agent stated. "It has been home to an A-list roster of tycoons, adventurers, artists, writers, and musicians alike." He turned to look back at Zuriel, then went on with his sales pitch. "It's a little Bahamian and a little bohemian, drawing influence from its original Bahamian settlers and an influx of artsy inhabitants from decades past. We've had residents such as David Crosby, Jimmy Buffett, Tennessee Williams, Alexander Graham Bell, and Madonna—just to name a few."

"Wonderful," Zuriel cut in, impatient. "I read all about the area before my arrival—it was described as a warm and welcoming escape from the stresses of city life."

"Correct you are," Alejandro agreed. "We have a combination of chef-driven restaurants, charming sidewalk cafes, chic boutiques, lush parks, and a glittering shoreline decorated by sailboats, making it a destination brimming with scenic serenity and natural splendor." He pointed at several of the photos as he gave his shpiel. "Where did you say you arrived from?" The agent tilted his head like an inquisitive dog.

"New York City," Zuriel disclosed, having no need to lie.

"My, that is quite the contrast and reasonable as to why you are seeking an escape from the stresses of the *big city*." He gave Zuriel an understanding smirk. "Where will you be staying on your visit? We have some lovely hotels just walking distance from here." He extended his other hand as if indicating the direction to them.

"Right, yes—no, I haven't figured that out yet," he said, adjusting the strap of his messenger bag, the fabric warm on his shoulder, contemplating how to bridge the conversation towards the details he actually needed.

"I can provide you with some recommendations if you'd like, while we discuss your options to purchase a home in our lovely neighborhood." The agent's smile widened.

"Actually, what I'm looking for is… information on a home—a sale of a home, the transaction in which your agency brokered."

The agent's smile dropped, though he swiftly managed to regain a more pleasant expression. "Is this a property you are interested in acquiring?" He asked cheerfully.

"Possibly," Zuriel lied, attempting to secure the man's further assistance. "It's a home in Palmetto Bay. The last sale was in 2016. Seller was Westlake, and the buyer was Cortez."

"Hmmm, 2016 you say?" the agent questioned. "I don't believe we would have any records from that far back in our files here. I'd have to check with my wife," he added, turning and pointing to a plump middle-aged woman at the far desk. "She's the record keeper. Stores the older paperwork in the home office…."

Zuriel's interest in what Alejandro was saying faded out as his attention fixated on the female client the agent's wife was currently speaking with. Heart pounding in his chest, Zuriel's stare dropped to the woman's feet. Her pink painted toes were adorned by white strappy sandals and whose elevation barely took her past the 5 foot height mark. He pulled in a breath, his gaze travelling up her bare ankles to meet the edge of the sage green cropped slacks she wore, traveling further still to the white sleeveless blouse that crisscrossed gracefully over her breasts. She was petite yet had subtle curves. Her glossy red hair was affixed into a smooth bun at the nape of her creamy neck. Her heart-shaped face shone with a pale flush across cheeks that bunched as her full lips spread into a wide smile. Sunlight streaming through the large agency windows lit up her exquisite face, illuminating the greenish hue of her stunning eyes. Zuriel's breath caught as she laughed at something the other woman had said, his heart pounding faster at hearing her joyful giggle. She reminded him of that actress who had played Lois Lane from the Superman movie, the newer one. He loved movies but preferred the lighter, less edgy stories like that of *Leap Year*, the same actress having appeared in both.

"*Mr. Zuriel*… Mr. Zuriel," came Alejandro's voice, yanking him away from his… *ogling*.

Zuriel turned his attention back to the agent, uncomfortably aware he had been ignoring the man *and* that he had been staring at the young woman for far too long. "Yes, sorry… something caught my eye out the window. I apologize. You were saying?" He cut a glance over the agent's shoulder to see the woman was still chatting with the agent's wife.

"If you are looking for a new home with more ease, we have some lovely condos in the area. I can make some arrangements to view them during your visit, and while I have my wife look into the sale of that house you mentioned."

Before answering, Zuriel took another covert glance, spotting the redheaded woman just as she exited the establishment. Anxious over her sudden departure, Zuriel said, "Let me get back to you on that." He gave the man a quick smile, then darted for the door.

Outside, he spied the woman as she sauntered up the sidewalk. She was quick in her stride despite the high sandals she wore, and he quickened his pace to catch up to her. He felt a sudden pang of guilt for leaving the real estate office so abruptly and leaving poor Alejandro hanging, but this woman had seized his fascination. When she stopped to cross the street, he slowed his pace, then continued to follow as she ventured across the road to head up Main street.

"Z, what are you doing?" he mumbled to himself, followed by a response of, *"No idea."* There was something captivating about this human female. He'd never had any interest in the females in New York, as he found most of them too intense. They were fashionable, and walked a lot, but he didn't understand anyone who didn't value their sleep. That had become one of his favorite things next to eating food since being trapped on Earth. He was open to all sorts of different types of people and experiences, however, he found the women of New York City overly success driven and money oriented, and not much into nature, not in the way he was.

He continued after her as she took a left just past what looked like an ice cream shop at the end of the main thoroughfare at the crossing of Grand and Virginia Avenues. Stepping stealthily back out of view and around the side of the storefront, he noted she'd stopped to cross another street. He spied around the edge of the building, watching as she made her way forward to the far side of the street. He continued his measured pursuit several strides behind her as she took the walkway up to a spectacular five story building lushly covered in tropical foliage. He paused for a brief moment, taking in all the splendor and greenery adoring the upper levels of the structure before following her inside.

Zuriel stepped into the building, welcomed by the rich details of the arches engraved into the wood doors, and the exquisite scent of blooming flowers in what he now realized was the lobby of a hotel. Zuriel's gaze traversed the luxurious haven of tranquility, its serene, calming ambience that instantly instilled in him a sense of being one with nature. The profusion of greenery inside seamlessly blended modern convenience with an organic aesthetic. "Astounding," he said aloud, gazing up through the open-air roof to the sky and the tropical flora adorning the interior balconies.

"Good afternoon, sir," came a man's voice, drawing Zuriel's focus back down to earth. The man was youngish, 30s maybe, wearing a stylish light grey suit, and he stood behind a prominent check-in desk. "Are you currently staying with us here at the Mayfair House Hotel & Garden?" the man asked when Zuriel focused his awareness on him.

"Currently, no," Zuriel said, shooting a glance in the direction of the elevators. "But I will be," he added, just as the female he had been pursuing vanished from view behind the elevator's sliding door.

Chapter 4 

On the drive to pick up her luggage from the hotel, Jana found she couldn't help but sneak glances across at Kris. In the restaurant, she had noticed right away his appearance was different. He seemed *bigger* somehow. His skin, the tone of it was healthier, his hair was thicker, and his eyes were a brighter navy blue. Even his voice, the cadence of it, sounded richer, clearer, and he was even more handsome than she remembered. She had wondered, worried more so, that with his restored sharper mind, he might see her differently too. Her appearance may be less appealing to him than he had recalled, considering he—his mind, had not been functioning at its best during their previous time together.

Kris had not looked her way, and they'd spoken little on the ride to his home, North Haven he had called it, giving her reason to believe there must be a South Haven, though she had not made any inquiry to such. When they'd arrived at the odd-looking home, they'd been warmly greeted by family friends Max and Julian, the lovely couple who she was told took care of the home and its residence. Julian had been the one to show her to a beautifully designed modern bedroom. The room had a king-sized bed with grey bedding and a tufted grey headboard that took up most of the wall it was up against. On the far side of the bed was a nightstand with a small armchair next to it. There was floor-to-ceiling sliding doors on the opposite wall to the bed she discovered was a closet. Over the bed there were high windows covered by white blinds that matched the white of the window frame perfectly. Julian had revealed the attached bathroom behind the door at the far end and pointed out the small fridge next to an armchair designed in the same fabric as the headboard. Max and he had been given the heads up they were on their way, so the fridge had been stocked with glass bottles of fresh filtered water provided for her arrival along with a variety of fruit which would all be replenished at her request. Lastly, she'd been shown the temperature control unit adjacent to the light switch, should she find the room too hot or cold. Her tiny hotel room had been quaint, and she would have given the service there a rating of 7 out of 10, but this room and the treatment she'd received here had surpassed that, scoring beyond 10 out of 10 on the way to a 20 out of 10 if the first 15 minutes post her arrival were any indication. Although, to her dismay, before she'd even been shown to her room, Kris had excused himself with the reason being he needed to speak with Leo, stating it would give her time alone to unpack and freshen up. She hadn't packed much for her trip, and she hadn't needed any freshening up having come straight from the hotel to the restaurant, but she had appreciated the alone time, mainly to get her bearings for whatever was to come.

Jana crossed the room and put her purse on the small table next to the chair and then placed her suitcase on the chair and opened it up wide. She wasn't sure how long she'd be here, so she left everything in the suitcase, taking out only her toiletry bag to set on the counter in the bathroom. Like the bedroom, the bathroom was painted in a soft grey with white trim. Along with the elegant sink and sleek modern toilet, there was both a beautiful shower and a free standing tub for her to use. The lighting in the bathroom was adjustable and gentle like in the main bedroom space. There was no artwork on the bathroom walls, though the sea-foam coloured tiles in the shower were arranged in subtle curves simulating ocean waves. Everything about this guestroom was so peaceful, she mused as she stepped back into the bedroom space.

Grabbing her purse off the table, she felt her cellphone vibrate within it. She pulled her cellphone from the side pouch to see that Geir had texted, again,

Are you okay?

She wasn't sure how to answer that. The time on her cellphone displayed it was 3:45 pm, making it 7:45 pm in Iceland and more than likely, Geir was finishing up his workday. She hadn't answered any of his earlier texts since speaking with him about heading over to the restaurant. Jana knew she needed to send something back soon or Geir would be calling, and she wasn't ready to talk about how confusing her day had been so far. He would know by her voice something was up, and she wouldn't be able to hide her anxiety from him over the phone. Instead of going into a long explanation on what had transpired since their morning chat, she chose to respond with a simple answer,

All good! Met some of Kris's family. I'll be staying at his home instead of the hotel. Will share more later. Have a great evening.

Geir must have been okay with her answer because he responded with,

Finally. I was starting to wonder if I should be contacting Interpol for your whereabouts. Looking forward to hearing all about it.

She sent him back a smiley-face emoji, relieved she wouldn't have to explain more yet. Her words weren't lies, they just weren't details.

With showing up the way she had, she hadn't known what to expect, really. When she'd walked into the restaurant, she hadn't known for sure if Kris would even be there, and she certainly hadn't anticipated to be staying in this house—his home, a home she was coming to realize was shared with both his friends and family, not that it mattered. So far, those she'd met had been lovely and kind, though it was all just a lot to take in, considering Kris was the only person she had thought she'd be speaking with.

A soft knock sounded on the bedroom's door, and she stood quickly from where she'd been sitting on the king-sized bed. "Come in," Jana called out.

The door opened without a sound and in the opening stood Julian. "Greetings," he said in his gentle tone. "I thought you might be in need of some nourishment and perhaps bored with staring at the four walls of this room." He chuckled. "I have prepared a variety of tasty items for the household should you wish to join the others for an early dinner."

Jana smiled, warmed by the gentle gracious nature of this *friend of the family*. She checked her cellphone again to see it showed the time was now 4:00 pm. She hadn't eaten before venturing to Kris's restaurant, and it hadn't been open for service, plus she had been so nervous she doubted she could have stomached anything then. While she'd waited in the bedroom, she'd eaten all the raspberries and blackberries from the container in the small fridge, but now she welcomed the offer of a real meal. "You are a mind reader," she said, her smile widening. She had been left alone for several hours and though the time to gather her thoughts had been welcome, she had begun to wonder if she'd been abandoned, even speculated if she had been locked in this room. She hadn't tried the doorknob, instead she'd pushed the ridiculous thought of capture out of her mind. But she *was* hungry, and the room was beginning to feel a tad confining. It had nothing to do with the room itself and everything to do with the anxiety rising over her decision to travel all this way to find a man she realized now she barely knew.

"Well, I do have my talents," Julian tossed back at her. "And I'm told one of them is cooking." He winked at her. "Shall we?" He released the doorknob and extended his other arm to the hall, indicating the way to go.

"Yes, yes—lets," Jana said, standing, hunger and excitement shoving away her nervousness as she left the bedroom to follow him.

At the end of the hall they emerged into the open concept living space she had walked through when she'd first arrived. Julian continued on in behind the kitchen island where his husband was currently setting out large white dinner plates. Max gave Jana a joyful wave, and she raised her hand in response.

At the extra-long kitchen island sat two large men with their backs to her, taking up space on two of the eight stools that lined the island. She glanced at Julian, and he winked at her again.

"Jana, wonderful to see you again—join us," Leo said as he turned in his seat. He stood then, crossing the short distance to where she had stopped. "If you're hungry—you're in luck. Julian is a master in the kitchen."

Leo, she obviously recognized. His striking features and massive size had not escaped her attention at the restaurant when they'd first met. He still wore the same seasonal clothing, shorts and a t-shirt he'd had on earlier in the day when they'd met at the restaurant. But the other man, he was new to her.

He stood then as well and turned her way, though he stayed where he was leaning an elbow on the back of the stool. "Hi, I'm Nic," he said with a kind smile. He, too, gave her a quick wave. Jana noticed, unlike the other men in the room, he wasn't wearing summer clothing, instead he wore sage green hospital scrubs. She grinned at Nic, then stole a glance at Leo before focusing back on him. He was equally tall and of similar muscular build to both Leo and Kris, but unlike Kris and Leo who wore their hair short and modern, Nic had a shimmer of long jet black hair that hung loose down his back to his waistline. The skin of his arms and face displayed a blend of rich bronze and warm russet tones. His face was a mesh of cultures, a straight nose and square jaw suggestive of First Nations heritage, melding with the exotic appeal reminiscent of Polynesian features, both heritages she had only observed in TV shows or movies, although she had never… ever… seen a man quite like Nic.

When his full lips parted in a smile, revealing perfect white teeth, she felt a tiny blush heat her cheeks. "Hi," she all but choked out. *This was all so… bizarre*, she thought. They were all so bizarre, but at the same time being here felt safe, comforting, and she found she was beginning to adore the friendly welcoming faces of everyone under this roof.

"Have a seat," Leo said, encouraging her to move forward. Like Julian had, with directing her up the hall, Leo extended an arm directing her toward where to sit.

She felt suddenly foolish for standing there and gawking at the two impressive men and moved swiftly to the island, choosing a stool to the right and at the end of the island nearest the walkthrough into the main kitchen area. Two stools to her left separated her from where Nic now sat again. Leo too, had returned to his seat at Nic's left.

Jana surveyed the open kitchen space before turning her attention back down the island. "So, Kris has… *two* brothers? Wait—no, three brothers—I almost forgotten about Hayden—Den," Jana rushed out. He'd been the one her friend Geir had reached out to when Kris had been in the hospital. She knew Kris only partially she had come to realize, but she had been told *of* Den via Geir. He'd stated Hayden was even bigger and taller than Kris, and now with meeting both Leo and Nic, Jana found herself wondering if it wasn't North Haven she was staying at but was in fact *Heaven* itself.

"Six," Max said before the others could reply, setting a wine glass in front of her on the island next to the white dinner plate. "Red or white?" he asked then, holding up a bottle of each. "Or sparkling water, if you prefer."

"Red," she said, staring intently at Max, unable to look back down the island to the others. *Six*? *Geir is not going to believe this*, she mused further, speculating if the other brothers she had yet to meet were as extraordinarily gorgeous as the man she had originally come all this way to find. "Where's Kris," Jana asked, continuing to watch Max as he filled her glass.

The sound of a door opening behind her at the far end of the living space pulled Jana from her thoughts, answering her own inquiry. Freshly showered and changed into a dark pair of walking shorts and a crisp white t-shirt, the man of her dreams and recent musing, shut the door and then strode across the expanse of the living room to stop directly in front of where she sat.

"Jana, sorry to keep you waiting so long," Kris said, reaching out to caress her shoulder before taking the stool next to her.

"That's my fault, actually," Leo said, his tone apologetic. "We had to brief Kris on a few things—update him on one of our… *ventures*." Leo smiled at her then shot a glance Kris's way.

Kris nodded at Leo before turning back and giving Jana an innocent grin.

At the lack of further details, Jana turned her attention back to Max. "How did you and Julian meet?" She loved hearing how other couples found each other.

"My dear sweet husband and I met while working for Leo at his architectural firm," Julian answered for him, then pulled an extra-large dish of bubbling lasagna from the oven. He then cut into it with something similar to what you would use to cut and dish out pie. "We're both retired now, but we help to take care of the place, as you already know."

"How long have the two of you lived here?" she asked, drawing in the intoxicating aroma of melted cheese and sauce.

"Awhile," Max answered then, using oven mitts to lift and carry the hot dish over to the island to place it on one of those mats made for serving from hot dishware. "We raised our daughter here."

"You have a child? I adore children. Where is she?" Jana shot a glance down the line of men, noting they resembled a line of hungry lions waiting to be fed. She watched as Max dished out the cut serving onto their waiting plates. Like well-disciplined children, they waited to dig in until everyone had been served.

"She's at the school library, though I wouldn't let her hear you call her a child," Julian chuckled out, handing Jana a basket filled with warm bread rolls.

Jana took one and passed it down the line to Kris. "Ah, she likes to think she's all grown up." Jana broke the roll open and placed it on her dinner plate.

A laugh of amusement escaped from Julian. "She is, all grown up, that is. She's doing her master's at the university here in town."

"You met her at the restaurant earlier," Kris said. "*Lane.*"

"Oh my gosh—Lane, yes." Jana had liked her sassy nature.

"I know—I look too young to have an adult daughter," Max joked, placing a generous serving of lasagna on her plate next to the roll. "Too much?" he asked when she glanced up at him.

"It's perfect—I'm starving," Jana said, still staring at him. "I can see the resemblance now—to both of you, interestingly enough."

Max slid a butter dish in front of her plate. "She gets her looks and wavy locks from Julian and her dark features from me," Max stated, reaching over to give Julian's thick wavy salt and pepper ponytail a gentle tug.

Jana grinned at the playfulness, then picked up the butter knife and sliced off a small wedge of butter from the dish. "And she grew up here?" Jana questioned. It was clear by Max and Julian's appearance they were much older than Kris and the others and could easily have a grown child, but Julian had said they had raised her *here*. She shot the others a puzzled look, then turned her focus back to Max. He too was looking at the others, though the expression that rented his face was one of anguish, as though he'd shared too much.

"Okay folks, I need to get moving," Nic said, interrupting the uncomfortable silence. He stood from his place at the island, revealing he had already finished his meal, his once overflowing plate now cleared. Then he stepped to the side of his stool, sweeping his long shiny hair back with both hands to secure it in a black elastic hair tie. "Cancer and evil waits for no one," he said like a superhero, giving his ponytail a toss over his shoulder.

"Night shift?" Jana queried, ignoring the weird awkwardness that lingered. At her question, Nic turned to look at Leo. "Oh wait—that's right, it was you who helped Kris get healthy again, wasn't it?" He was a valuable friend to have, and his demeanor was calming and that would be helpful in his work, she mused.

"Night shift—yes, you could say that, and yes," Nic said, his smile sympathetic as though there was a third *yes* in agreement with how things had suddenly gotten weird. He gave Kris's shoulder a pat. "Hope to see you later, Jana," he added before turning and dashing off to the main door.

"Same!" she called after him, noting then that Kris and Leo too had similarly clean plates, having devoured their meals as well.

"Let me show you my space in this big, strange house," Kris offered, sliding his stool away from the island.

She looked down at her still full plate, then glanced swiftly to Max and Julian who were now tidying the dishes, then she returned her focus down to her hand. She still held the butter knife, having not yet married the butter slice with her roll, let alone taken a first bite of her meal. "You and your brothers are fast eaters," she answered Kris, bringing the butter to meet her dinner roll before looking back at him.

"Right, sorry," Kris apologized. "When you're finished, of course."

In the meantime, Kris and Leo discussed plans for the upcoming Grand Opening of the restaurant, while Jana slowly ate her meal, not wanting to add an upset stomach to her now rising uncertainty about this place and its occupants. Before she had finished her meal, Leo had excused himself, and like Nic, he had stated his hopes of seeing her later.

"Ready?" Kris asked when she'd set her cutlery down on the plate.

She swallowed her last sip of wine and gave a satisfied grin. "Yes," she answered, dabbing her mouth with the cloth napkin she'd been provided. "Thank you for a lovely meal," she said, addressing Max and Julian, who were seated at the far end of the island enjoying their own generous servings.

"You are most welcome," Julian said, again giving her a wink. "And don't let those heathens rush your future meals." He gave Kris a stern look while pointing his fork at him. "Come by the kitchen before bed. I'll have a sweet treat for you." He pointed his fork at Kris again. "Not you."

Max snorted a laugh then. "You're not going to want to miss it, Jana."

Jana rubbed her already full tummy. "Should have warned me to leave some room." She blew out a heavy breath and smiled appreciatively at the good-natured duo.

"I'll eat her portion," Kris proposed, licking his lips.

"I'll save some of the special surprise for you, Jana." Julian narrowed his eyes at Kris, then smirked. "But not you."

Kris gave a fake *cry* much like a disgruntled 4-year-old. "You are soooo mean," he said as he took Jana's hand, leading her away from the kitchen towards the row of inner doors to the private suites.

Via the second door in the lineup, they passed through an empty lower area to take a set of stairs up to the second floor and into what appeared to be Kris's bedroom. Jana noticed it was much like the one she was staying in. "Are all the rooms in the house like this—the bedrooms, I mean?"

"They all start like this, but my brothers have since put their own personal touches on their suites. Each has an upper bedroom and lower living space like this one. Though I haven't done much with mine yet, as you saw by the sparseness of the lower level."

"You've been here a few months now, so why is that?" she asked, scanning the books that barely filled one shelf on the bookcase nearest the bedroom's entrance.

"My condo in New York was spectacular, designer décor, expensive art, high-end kitchen appliances, etc. but none of the things felt personal. The stuff was more like expensive trophies that had no meaning." He shrugged. "When I moved here, I only brought my clothes and left everything else behind."

"I can understand that—fresh start and all." She picked up the lone framed photo at the end of the line of books.

"What about you—where did you put all your personal items and keepsakes from your father's place?" He frowned then. "Where are you living now, for that matter?"

"At Geir's," she said, her words the answer to both questions, feeling no further explanation was warranted. "Gay Pride Parade?" she questioned, holding up the framed photo of Frank and Kris under a banner that read the same.

Kris said nothing, only took the framed memory from her to linger serenely on the image.

"I have a question," Jana stated then. "I think I know the answer, but I feel the need to ask—just for clarity."

"Ask away." Kris returned the frame to its spot on the shelf.

Jana pressed her lips together, then asked, "Are you... *gay*?" It would explain the reason all the men staying here were so attractive, she speculated. Geir would have thought it paradise being with a group of men who resembled extremely buff fitness models.

"Ha—no," Kris laughed out. "But I do support the community 150 percent, and it's not just because Frank and Ina are a couple. My New York City restaurant has been a staunch supporter of the LGBTQ2+ community for years through events and donations to Pride celebrations and The Center."

"The center?"

"It's the name of the community place. For almost 40 years, it has been a welcoming space with resources for residents and visitors to the city. That photo is from one of the events we hosted."

"I recall you were very interested in learning about the *community* in Iceland from Geir," she reminded.

"Yes, I figured my past connection to the community in New York must have fed my interest despite my lack of memory of it. And it's no wonder you felt the need to ask about my sexual orientation." He paused to glance back at the photo. "Regardless of my obnoxious past, I have always believed everyone has the right to be themselves, be with who they want, and love who they love."

"I agree with you. What do mean, '*obnoxious past*'?"

Kris blew a breath through his nose. "When my memories came back, one of the things I was forced to face about myself was that I had been… an indulgent womanizer. One of many *disgusting* things from my past I'm not proud of."

"So you've been with… a lot… of women—had a lot of partners?"

"Yes." Again he blew out a breath. "Although, it's not the number I consider disgusting, it was my treatment of these females—women I engaged with."

Jana frowned, her anxiety returning.

Kris held up his hands. "I'm not an abuser—nothing like that. Nonetheless, I have caused unwarranted harm to the hearts and self-esteems of these women. I was often cruel in the way I used them to satiate my needs, brushing them off, never spending more than one night with any of them regardless of their efforts to gain my favor or more time with me."

"Great, and here I am, traveling all this way just to see you. You must think I'm a fool." Jana brought her hands up to cover her face.

"Quite the opposite, honestly," Kris said, gently removing her hands from her face to hold them. "I think it was brave of you to go to New York City, to come here, not knowing what or who you might find. And if it makes any difference, I'm not *that* guy anymore."

"You are *healthier*." She glanced briefly down at his hands holding hers. "And I recognize other changes in you. But I find myself searching…." She looked back up into his face. "…I came here to find that person, the one I found on my father's property… the man I believed I made a connection with."

"No," he said abruptly, letting go of her hands and stepping away.

She felt a tiny sting in her heart at the sudden absence of his touch. "No—we didn't have a connection?"

"No—I mean yes, we had a connection, but I'm not speaking of the *me* you met in Iceland. I'm talking about the *me* before that, the crappy friend and shitty brother, the philanderer. The *me* you met—the man I was when I was with you… well, I'm endeavoring to be *that* guy, to cleanse myself of the horrible bastard I was." Kris took a step closer to her again. "I never stopped thinking about you, Jana. Our time together… are some of my favorite memories."

"You said *had* a connection. It's gone for you now that your memories are back. And like with the other women—you just feel what, regret now?" Jana crossed her arms over her chest, the ache in her heart intensifying.

Kris took another step closer, their feet almost touching. "Jana, I only have one regret from our time together," he said, raising a hand to tuck a strand of her hair behind her ear. His fingers settled against the side of her neck.

"Only one?" She tilted her head back and gazed up into his beautiful, deep blue eyes.

"That I hadn't been brave enough to do this." He leant down to her and pressed his lips to hers.

Jana closed her eyes as his hand slid around to the back of her neck, deepening the kiss. A muffled *chime* sounded, and Kris softened the kiss, only to intensify it again before pulling away.

He stepped back, his concentration fixated on her as he drew his cellphone from his shorts pocket. He let out a slow sensual breath before glancing down at the cellphone. "Figures," he said, focusing back on her with a mischievous smile.

Jana tilted her head in question. "Is it the restaurant?"

"Nope—Julian," he said, sliding his cell back into his pocket. "He's just pulled out that *special surprise* from the oven." He gave her a couple eyebrow raises before taking her by the hand and leading her out of the bedroom and back down the stairs to the main level.

Out into the common area, he let go of her hand to do a relaxed jog over to the kitchen. "Are those Pastelitos de Guayaba I smell?" Kris asked before glancing back at her as she approached the kitchen island. "Jana, you're going to love these. Julian makes the best Cuban pastries."

"He learned from the best," Max stated, tilting his chin at Kris as he took one of the barstools.

"I used your recipe, Kris," Julian confessed, wiping the palm of his hand on a tea towel that rested over his shoulder.

Jana took the barstool next to Kris. "They smell incredible."

"I do hope you like them. I was a tad nervous making them considering your culinary baking expertise," Julian said, before sliding a small plate with a delicate pastry her way. "They may be a bit hot— so be careful."

"I'm pretty sure I've burnt my fingerprints off already with working on my own baking," Jana said with a smirk. She picked up one of the warm desserts from the plate, examining the expertly constructed puff pastry. She glanced at Julian and then Max before taking a bite. As she savored the treat, she noticed Kris watching her intently. Fully delighting in the dessert, she closed her eyes, falling deeper into the buttery ecstasy. Heaven, Jana thought, although not as heavenly as that first kiss she'd just shared with Kris.

"What do you think?" Kris asked eagerly.

"Absolutely delicious," she said, opening her eyes as she finished savoring. "The filling is amazing, and the cream has a beautiful texture," she added, licking the corner of her mouth. "But I can't make out the fruit ingredient you used."

"Guava," Julian shared.

"Guava? I have never tasted that before. It's fabulous—you'll have to show me how you made these." She licked at the guava filling that oozed out from the bite she'd taken.

"I could show you—but Kris is the real expert with *this* recipe. I'm sure he can show you." He smiled at her, then winked at Kris.

Jana took another more generous bite, then turned in her seat, scanning the long open space of the living room, then the pool tables and bar, and the *two* sitting areas. "What is this place exactly? I mean, I understand it's your *home*," she said, addressing no one in particular. "And there are individual suites—like the one Kris occupies now."

"It was a project of mine—renovating it," came Leo's now familiar voice from behind Jana. She turned his way as he grabbed up one of the pastries from the tray. He took a big bite before claiming the open seat beside her. Swallowing, he said, "… and changing it from an old, abandoned motel into this. We have this common area…." He turned his stool to face away from the island, extending an arm in a wide arc in the direction of the lavish yet inviting living room. "…and each of my brothers has their own private space—like Kris's, outfitted to their particular needs."

"The guestroom—your room, and Lane's room, as well as our bedroom and private lounge are on this side of the house," Max added, pointing a thumb over his shoulder. "It was Julian, and I who designed the kitchen." He wrapped an arm around his husband's shoulders and gave him a peck on the cheek.

Jana turned her seat to match Leo's, then focused her attention on Kris. "Max and Julian said they met Leo on the job—is that how you met him and the others?" She glanced at Leo and then back at Kris. "Obviously you are not *actual* brothers, genetically related, I mean."

"Foster system," Leo answered for him. "Then when we graduated high school, we all went our separate ways."

"So you all met while in the same foster home—here in Ottawa?" Jana popped the last of the warm pastry into her mouth. "Mmmm," she added with a tight smile.

Kris gave her a pleased grin. "No," he said, turning in his seat so he faced them, shooting Leo a grimaced look. "Our foster parents live up north in Nunavut, aiding the communities in need there. That's where we *met*, First Haven. That's the name of the group home."

Redirecting, Leo said, "I have my business here, and a few years ago I renovated this place and then I reached out to all of them to have a reunion of sorts. Several years back, I offered to share this place as a home-base, so to speak."

"Homebase?" she questioned, shifting slightly in her seat to reach back for the remaining pastry on her plate.

"We all travel so much with our different careers, it made sense," Kris clarified, stretching to grab a pastry from the serving platter that held the rest of the desserts.

"But hadn't you been living in New York City before I met you?" Jana asked before taking a bite of the warm goodness.

"Yes, but now we all agree it just doesn't seem practical to have seven separate homes anymore, where more often than not they are left basically empty except for a change of clothing, maybe some personal items, and expired food in the fridge," Kris explained with a shrug.

She grasped the concept, she did, but the explanations she was getting felt a little too… *rehearsed*. "Are the others—the other brothers, traveling at the moment?" She took a quick glance down at the lengthy lower legs of both Leo and Kris. *No leg hair*. She took a closer look at their arms and each of their faces, noting their arms were also hairless. Their cheeks and chins too appeared as though freshly shaven. Kris's made sense as he'd just showered, but she also recalled how he'd never used the shaving items she'd gotten him in Iceland. It had been Geir who had witnessed and then shared that Kris's body had been completely hairless.

"Well, Den is down south, Florida," Leo said, pulling her from her thoughts. "He travels between there, here, and Amsterdam. Ben teaches at the university here and is travelling from Japan at the moment, so he'll be here for a longer stay with the new semester starting soon. Marq is in Italy managing his gallery, though he plans to open another here in the very near future, and he travels to Florida on occasion now as well. And Zach is in Norway.

"He's a firefighter, but he's the only one who doesn't travel much," Kris added, devouring the remains of his second pastry.

Or was it the third pastry, Jana pondered, watching his luscious lips as he chewed. She pulled her gaze away and chose to ask a different question. "But, he still has a suite here?"

"Correct. Mainly for when he comes for visits," Kris stated. "By the way, Zach has a ton of books in his suite—a full wall of bookcases. I'm sure he wouldn't mind if you borrow some. I know how much you love reading."

Jana turned her head towards the island and caught Max placing a second warm treat on her empty plate. "Thank you," she said to him, snatching it up from the plate.

"There are plenty more," he said in a not so quiet whisper. "I'll hide some for you, so these barbarians don't get them all."

Jana laughed. "Must be hard having to feed such big…."

"Mouths?" Julian cut in.

"Heeey?" Kris whined.

Jana laughed again. Turning to Leo she asked, "And what is in Florida that has some of you traveling there?"

"South Haven," he said, leaning back and stealing two pastries from the serving platter. "It's another home-base, a newer one."

There was her confirmation that there was in fact a *South* Haven. "Right. So that's it, you share this space as a home and simply get a hotel room when travelling places other than Florida?" She swiveled her stool to look at Kris.

Not answering her, Kris looked at Leo, giving him an intense stare as though he needed assistance with the answer to her question.

"What?" Jana volleyed her attention back and forth between the two silent men. "What am I missing? Or what aren't you telling me?"

"We all have our own lives, jobs etc….," Leo began. "… and we also work together… as a team."

"Like… a sports team?" Jana shook her head. Though a sports team would explain why they all had such fit muscular builds, assuming the other *brothers* were of a similar physique.

"No-no. Maybe it would be better if we just show you," Leo said. "Let's finish enjoying these delicious treats first. Then we'll tour the rest of the place, and I'll explain what it is we do when we are not attending to regular jobs."

Chapter 5 

Leo gave Jana the tour to end all tours, explaining as they went what they were involved in, showing her the underground spaces they utilized for the team's top-secret ventures, but it was upon entering this last room, the *weapons* room, that Jana recalled something Geir had told to her. "My friend Geir—the one who had reached out to Hayden," she said as she stared at the array of weaponry. "He told me they met in Belgium while attending college, that at the end of the semester Hayden had stated he'd been recruited by some special ops team—I'm guessing this is that team, yes?" Eyes wide in astonishment, Jana still couldn't fully comprehend what she'd just been told despite the evidence she'd witnessed on the tour, like all the weapons lined up at the far end of the room.

"Yes, you are correct," Leo agreed, turning away from the armory's entrance.

"Den is an expert in hand-to-hand and he has taught all of us this specialty," Kris explained further.

"He obtained a degree in criminology—at the University in Belgium, *and* he speaks fluent French. As his day job he has worked as a bodyguard, protecting various high-profile people over the years," Leo added. "I myself work as an architect, and my contribution to the cause is my photographic memory for anything relating to structures and buildings," he shared, directing her back towards the stairwell they had come down.

"After you," Kris said, pausing, smiling sweetly at her before pushing open the door to the stairwell for her to go first.

As she ascended the stairs, Leo continued with his running down of the team lineup. "Nic, who you met, is actually following up on a lead this evening, but he normally works as an Oncology Nurse at the Queensway Carleton Hospital by day—or night shift, as it were. He loves science, his specialties are genetics and diseases, his current focus being on children at the hospital."

Jana stopped when she hit the top step. "That would be a difficult vocation working with sick kids," she said, pondering Nic's choice.

"Some of the stories he's shared are beyond heart wrenching," Kris said as he came to stand next to her on the landing. "I'm not sure how he does it. That's a completely different kind of strength."

"You'll have time to talk to Nic about his work, I'm sure," Leo said, his tone sympathetic as he placed his thumb on a scan pad next to the door. "Marq has his gallery, but he specializes in surveillance and security, internet and structure security, including biometrics." He removed his thumb and punched in a security code to open what she'd been informed was a solid reinforced fireproof door. Its purpose was mainly to keep the wrong people out of the lower level. The heavy door made a loud click and then swooshed into a space in the wall like a pocket door.

Jana stepped through the now open doorway into the same hall to where her room was located off of. The walls outside of the stairwell appeared the same as the rest of the walls in the home, but were reinforced and fireproof, she was also told, though she hoped to never be in a situation where such extensive measures were needed for her protection.

"And we can't forget Zach," Kris said then, drawing Jana from her musing. "He's our resident expert in pyrotechnics and explosives. He and I speak the most languages of the seven of us, the 30 most spoken," he finished as they all returned to the common area.

Jana spotted Julian in the kitchen, wiping down the big island. He waved at her and smiled. She waved back, pleased to see his kind face. Not that Leo wasn't kind, it was just that Julian and Max seemed more like her, average and not all superhuman like the others she'd been introduced to.

"Let's have a seat," Leo suggested, directing them to the closest seating area in the large open space. "I'm sure you have a ton of questions after all we've shown you."

"I'm still trying to absorb it all," Jana said, her head reeling from all the details and what she'd observed in the lower level of this otherwise lovely *home*.

The men remained standing as Jana sat down in the middle of the huge couch. Leo sat then in one of the two chairs across from the couch, while Kris took up space next to her. Jana turned to face him. "What is your expertise—dare I ask?" She tried her best to keep her expression neutral even though her brain was imploding.

"I'm a chef and restaurant owner," Kris joked, giving her one of his charming smiles. "Even Superman had a day job."

"And he's an expert in weaponry, especially knives, of all kinds," Leo elaborated, kicking Kris's outstretched foot with his.

It was clear Kris remembered who Superman was now, but Jana didn't smile back at him. Instead, she shook her head as if it would help ease the load of information she'd been given. "I'm sorry, I came here hoping to find you, Kris. Talk to you, make sure you were truly okay— I even hoped that maybe…," Jana rushed out, then paused. "I see that you are okay—more than okay… now I'm presented with all this… and I'm expected to accept that you're part of some kind of elite special forces group?" Kris opened his mouth to speak, but Jana held up her hand. "What about Frank—is she part of this?" She had the muscular physique for it, Jana considered before dropping her hand.

"No, but she knows about what I do—we do," Kris confessed.

"It's not illegal, is it? Please tell me you're fighting human trafficking or something equally horrific, please." Jana wrung her hands in her lap.

"Sort of…," Kris began, as another interior door into the main living space opened at the far end.

It was the last door along the line of doors next to where she and Kris had exited from earlier. Jana shouldn't have been shocked by who came through the door, witnessing yet another massive man who appeared to be in his mid-thirties like the others. He wore a grey tank top and long black gym shorts, and he strolled leisurely towards where they all sat. He was built like the others, but unlike them, his complexion was noticeably fairer, as was his hair, his pale eyes gleaming a light blue.

"Ben, good of you to join us," Leo said when the large man stopped in front of them. "Jana, this is Bennet Frost."

"Please to meet you, finally," Ben said, nodding at her, his smile gracious.

"Hello," she responded, "Leo said you were travelling from Japan."

Frown lines appeared between Ben's eyebrows as he glanced to Leo. Turning back to her, he said, "Yup—snuck in through the front entrance to my suite. Needed to clean up after… the flight."

"Did you eat yet?" Julian called from the kitchen. "I'm just putting away the leftovers, but I can heat some up for you, if you wish."

"That'd be great—thank you," Ben said, turning briefly in the direction of the kitchen. That's when Jana noticed his strawberry blond hair was secured back in a braid down the middle of his back. She stole a glance down at his legs and then his bare arms. *No hair.*

"We just finished showing Jana the tactical areas and equipment," Leo said.

Ben turned back and nodded, his expression casual, like all of this was a typical day for him.

"You're the professor," Jana said then, recalling that tidbit from all the other details Leo had shared on their tour of all things secret-agent-like.

"I am. I teach Human Kinetics at the university," he said like it too was no big deal, though she liked the casual way he spoke and the relaxed way he carried himself. She would have enjoyed having a teacher like him, and it wasn't because of his handsome looks, it was his calm manner she found appealing.

"Science is his thing—more specifically the study of all living things—big and small," Kris interjected, smiling at her again as if hoping to appease her discontent.

Ignoring Kris, she glanced back up at Ben and said, "You're the one who trained the others to fight." Leo had said Ben was a 'master of movement and martial arts'.

"Only touch and pressure point combat, *and* reverse weight influence—martial arts that require no strenuous force. Den does the more physical hand-to-hand." Ben lowered himself into the chair next to Leo. "In my program at the university I also teach athletic enhancement and stamina, along with Thai chi, meditation, and nutrition," he said, all nonchalant and without a hint of arrogance.

"And he makes a mean turkey chili," Julian said, handing off a tray to Ben with a plate of lasagna, two dinner rolls slathered with butter, and a large glass of water. "I'll be retiring for the evening, so you're all on your own for the rest of the night." He pointed his forefinger at each of them as though he were telling a group of children not to stay up too late.

Jana checked her watch to see it was only 8 p.m. When she glanced back up at Julian, he gave her a sympathetic smile. *"I've got a juicy romance novel waiting for me,"* he directed at her in a mock whisper. He gave her several eyebrow raises before turning his focus back to the others. "If you get hungry, please help yourself to anything you want in the fridge." He smiled at her again, then turned and proceeded off to his private quarters.

"Jana," Kris said, drawing her attention. "You asked what we were fighting."

"We fight a common enemy," Ben stated.

"An extremist group," Leo clarified. "One whose members are scattered around the world and under the guise they are helping kids— sick kids, but in reality, what they're doing is experimenting *on* these children."

"Experimenting on kids—what the… for what purpose?" she questioned. Not that any reason would validate the abuse of children.

Leo crossed his thick arms over his massive chest. "They're looking for specific people—children mainly, the offspring of those who carry a unique set of genes, ones of interest to this faction."

"We are also trying to locate these kids, but for the purpose of keeping them safe and out of the hands of this group," Kris added. "We also keep watch on the labs."

"Labs? There are labs—plural?" Jana asked. "Wait—why aren't the police involved, the FBI, CIA, whatever, or some other secret branch of the government?" She may not be worldly, but she wasn't naïve either.

"It's not known to the government," Ben said before taking a huge bite of his remaining roll.

"If the authorities were to get involved, we fear the group would take their experiments underground and out of reach," Leo explained, uncrossing his arms to rest his hands on his thighs. "Right now they function publicly, and we can keep watch. The key thing is they don't know they are being watched."

"What do you mean, they function *publicly*?" Jana felt her unease rise.

"The group functions disguised as a well-known medical foundation, one that promotes falsehoods about its research and treatments," Ben said, laying his fork down on his now empty plate.

Thoughts racing, Jana continued to stare at his plate. "How many of these people are out there, the ones with these unique genes?" She shifted her stare up to Ben's flawless complexion. "What is so special about their genes, anyway?" She forced herself to blink as her mind halted on the impending truth.

"Let's just say it's a superior gene mutation," Ben said, holding her gaze. "The number of them is unknown."

"Our work is on a case-by-case basis," Kris stated, drawing both Ben's and her interest his way.

Jana paused briefly to appreciate Kris's handsome face before turning to Leo and asking, "Are you searching for a child right now—do you have a case right now, I mean?"

"Yes," Leo said, his expression serious.

"It's painfully obvious I've come at an inopportune time," Jana said, realizing her poor timing. "Had I known...."

"I'd say it was perfect timing," Leo interrupted. "Because there is one more thing we need to tell you... and it involves you—your father, actually."

"My father?" Jana shifted her gaze to each of them, one by one. "You're not going to tell me he was involved in this secret group of yours, are you?" She swallowed hard, wishing she had her own glass of water.

"No—that's not what I'm saying…," Leo began.

Jana raised a hand, palm facing out. "Although I wouldn't have put it past him had he been involved." Jana nodded her head. "He was *that* kind of man—putting others' needs before his own, especially children."

"Jana…," Leo began again.

"Hold up!" Jana said, putting both of her hands up as if she could stop the onslaught of information. "Don't tell me you think *he* helped the bad guys—because my father would never get himself involved in anything so vile." Jana bent her arms, wrapping her hands around the back of her neck.

"No…," Leo attempted to say.

But Jana cut him off. "I'm not saying he wouldn't have wanted to aid your cause—but I would have known if he was involved in something like this—it was just the two of us, and we were very close. Besides, he never—and I mean never, did any traveling once I was born. Well, other than that one time he went to New York—I told you about that," Jana rushed out, directing her words at Kris, "but that was over 20 years ago."

"He isn't—wasn't involved," Leo finally got out.

"What then?" Jana dropped her hands back in her lap.

"That trip, the one he took to New York City…," Kris started to say.

"What about it?" she questioned, interrupting once again. This was all too much, she thought.

Continuing, Kris said, "…you said he met someone, a woman, when he was there." Kris turned his upper body to face her.

"So?" She shrugged, raising her palms up in question.

"That woman, the one he met, she…," Kris tried to continue.

"She what—she's involved?" Jana asked, cutting him off again. "Did she get him involved—is that it?" Jana placed her palms on the sides of her neck.

"Jana, no—nothing like that… not exactly," Kris said, yanking her hands away from her neck, holding them in his.

"Then what, *exactly*?" Jana huffed out. "Wait—is this why you were in Iceland? Were you trying to track down this woman through my father?" She pulled her hands free from his grasp. Kris tried to take her hands again, but she crossed her arms, tucking her hands in her armpits.

Kris let out an audible sigh. "No… I was in Norway for my restaurant. I was to travel after to meet up with my brothers at First Haven, to see… our foster parents." He ran a hand through his hair. "How I ended up in Iceland—came to be on your father's property, was a complete accident, a coincidence, I assure you."

"And what about the amnesia? Was that genuine or pretend?"

"My condition is real, what happened, the memory loss and illness from the sulfur—it's all real. Although I hadn't known how severe my sensitivity to sulfur was until then."

"Riiiiight. And I'm supposed to take your word for it—that this is just all one big coincidence, that this organization you work for just happens to be looking for the same woman my father met—so many years ago? Seriously?" She glanced at Ben, then Leo, and then focused back on Kris. "What kind of game are you all playing at?"

"Jana, please, you have to believe…," Kris began his plea.

"Do I though?" Jana relaxed her arms. "How do you even know who this woman is—that she's even the same person my father met?" Jana slid her hands under her thighs.

Kris drew in a breath. "Well, because…."

"She's a client of ours—I guess you could say," Leo cut in. "Though she is not the one we are looking for."

"Who then?" Jana asked, withdrawing her hands from under her legs, palms open in question again.

"It's her daughter we're trying to find," Ben shared then.

Jana gasped. "Her daughter is missing?"

"No—but she *was* given up for adoption," Leo said. "We believe the daughter is one of these children who carries the unique genetics."

"And we need to find the daughter before the others do," Kris said, his expression weary. "I'm sure you can understand why." He moved to take her hand, but she slid it under her thigh again.

"What does this have to do with my father?" She glared at Kris.

"Well…," Kris started to say.

"Spit it out," Jana said, her patience running thin.

"Your father's name was on the original birth certificate," Kris finished, his face impassive.

"What?" Jana slid free her hand, meeting it up with the other in her lap.

"His name was used on the records with the adoption agency," Leo said, rewording the information for her like it would make it any more plausible.

"Backup," Jana said, raising her hands again to stop any more details. "My father… conceived a child with this woman? How can that be?" She dropped her hands once again on to her lap, staring at them as though they held the answer. "He would have told me."

"Your father never knew about the pregnancy, much less the baby," Leo clarified.

Jana lifted her head to look at Leo. "Are you sure… I mean, are you 100 percent sure he's the father?" Jana's head ached and her throat felt dry.

Leo nodded. "Not unless there is another *Reider Stephansson* out there—who just happened to have been visiting New York City from Iceland at the time of conception. I'd say it's a pretty sure match."

"The birthmother—your client, does she know where her daughter is?" Jana believed Kris had lost his memory, that he hadn't kept this from her, but had she not come here would they have told her, reached out to her, she wondered.

"She doesn't, but we know who adopted her, *and* we've found the daughter's name," Kris said, slowly reaching for her hand.

She let him wrap his hand around hers. "Where are they?" Jana asked, relishing the warmth of Kris's hand now as it clasped hers.

"They were living in Buffalo, but the parents are deceased—car accident," Leo said, mournful.

"Oh my gosh," Jana cried, "and the girl?" Jana put her free hand to her mouth, focusing on Leo.

"The daughter wasn't in the car," Ben assured her. "But she was only 10 years old when they died. Records show she went to live with a family member—an aunt."

"It was spring," Jana recalled, "April 2001 when my father went to New York. I turned 11 years old that fall." Jana did the calculations in her head. "That would make the daughter 20 years old now," Jana said, realizing the missing girl was no longer a child.

"Correct. We are leaving tomorrow to go see the aunt," Ben said then. "The woman lives here—in Canada, Toronto, to be precise."

Kris squeezed her hand. "I understand this is a lot to take in," he said, his words gentle.

She wasn't mad at Kris, but she couldn't look at him. "Is that all of it? Tell me that's all of it," she directed at the two men across from her.

"It's enough for now," Leo said, his tone sympathetic.

"Try to focus on…," Kris began to say, his voice hinting with levity as though there was a bright side to all of this.

Jana turned to stare at him. "Focus on what? The fact I have a sister out there I've never met?" she interjected before turning back to Leo. "One who—from what you've said is potentially in grave danger. You're right, it is enough… for now."

Chapter 6 

"You're still in your uniform. Did you come straight from the hospital?" Den asked when I entered the training area from the garage. He was in the middle of arranging the floor mats for what looked like some hand-to-hand training.

"I had a feeling I might be late, so I brought my gear with me just in case." I held up my gym bag to show him. "Let me change." I fluttered the collar opening of my short-sleeved work shirt. "It's scorching outside, and I just about died from the heat inside my SUV. Had to have the air-conditioning cranked the whole way. I'll be right back."

Den said nothing, only shrugged and continued with his arranging.

In less than 10 minutes, I returned with my bag in one hand and my running shoes in the other, padding across the floor and onto the mats in my sock feet. I'd changed into black leggings and a snug black tank top, with my hair secured back in a long tight braid. I dropped my gym bag near the bench at the edge of the mats. "What are we working on today? I'm guessing close contact?" I sat on the bench to put my shoes on.

Instead of answering my query, Den asked, "Do you wear the same uniform all the time?"

"I don't always wear the same thing. Sometimes I wear a white golf shirt instead of the long-sleeved button-down, but the khaki pants are a must." I smirked up at him.

"What is your role there again?" He squinted as if examining me.

"I'm part of the support staff that does the patient transport. But my role is only to retrieve the wheelchairs. I don't typically interact with patients." I double knotted my laces.

"That's right—now I remember." He pushed the last of the big mats into place. "Why doesn't the support staff wear scrubs?"

"I wish we wore scrubs. But it has something to do with us blending in with the public while at the same time making it clear we work for the hospital—should someone need our assistance. They don't want us to be mistaken for medical staff, is my understanding."

"How was your shift?" Den kicked the edge of the last mat into place.

"Uneventful," I said, pushing up from the bench.

Den traversed the mats to come stand at my end. "Which I'm sure is welcome, considering you work at a hospital."

"True. My last pass was by the Behavioral Health Center, and it was quiet as well since they have no new patients, which is a blessing for them, I'm sure." I gave him a tight grin.

"Have you witnessed any of the psych patients?" he asked, doing a few quick stretches, twisting back and forth at the waist, his spine cracking.

I copied his movements, although my back did not crack. "Not yet, but I'm not allowed inside the ward. You have to have special security clearance to enter, so staff just leave any unused chairs at the entrance hall on my side of the doorway for pickup." I paused my stretching and put my hands on my hips. "Why all the questions about my volunteer gig?"

He shrugged again. "Just curious."

I surveyed the padded mats arranged out in front of me. "More hand-to-hand exercises today?"

He tilted his head from side to side, his neck making a popping sound. "Yes—but no. I actually want to work on some attack maneuvers."

I dropped my hands from my hips. "When am I ever going to need to attack anyone?"

"No bonehead. I'm going to teach you some more about how to get out of an unexpected attack. Similar to the other self-defense techniques, but these are more about escaping a hold verses fending off someone coming at you." He bent his large torso forward and down touching the palms of his hands to the mat.

It was impressive how limber Den was for such a big guy. "Phew—because I'm a lover not a fighter," I laughed out.

Den's laughter joined mine. "You could show the girls a few of these in case they have any run-ins with bullies. Or I could come to your place and teach them. How are they doing? Ready for school? When do they start?" he asked, shifting his stance to a wide-leg straddle stretch.

"Probably best you teach them—they'd like it better, anyway. You sure are full of questions today." I double checked my laces were tied securely. "They're ready for school. Redmond took them to get the rest of their school supplies, but they don't start until August 10th." I checked the elastic around the end of my braid. "When I was a kid— up in Canada, school never started until after the Labor Day long weekend. Here it varies from state to state, but I still find it too early for them going back in mid-August considering their school year isn't over until the end of May."

"They'll be starting fourth grade," he said, as though recalling they were in third when he'd met them. "I never went to primary school, but it does feel long for kids that age." He nodded.

"Right, I forgot. Straight to college and university for your lot. At least you didn't have to repeat high school on a loop like the vampire characters from those Twilight books." I lifted a foot, pulling it up behind my butt for a quad stretch.

Den's eyebrows pinched in confusion. "What?"

"Vampires, they never age." I dropped my foot and then pulled up the other to complete the stretch. "The ones from the books had to keep doing high school over and over—in different places. The younger they could start out looking—the longer they could stay in one place, at least the teen vampires."

His brows went from pinched to raised.

"Oh, never mind," I said, clasping my hands behind my back to stretch my shoulders and chest.

He laughed. "Hey, Leo told me about Purah visiting again. Said she overheard Marcus talking to Thaddeus about some new project—cellular regeneration," he said, coming to stand right in front of me.

"Yup," I confirmed as he gripped my shoulders and spun me, my back facing him. "You know, I think there was a little sparkle between Leo and Purah."

"Reeeally?" Den asked, his tone curious. "Been forever since he's had any interest in a female."

"How are things with you and Gavin?"

Den spun me back around to face him. "Look who's the curious one now," he said before spinning me to face away again. "He keeps asking if I want to come help out at the school, volunteer with activities and such."

"You should do it. The girls would love having you there." Redmond and I were both very fond of Den, and the girls adored him. Gavin was a great teacher and a wonderful friend, so of course we were hopeful there was something between the two of them.

"Ya, maybe."

"Whatever." Switching topics, I asked, "What would happen if Purah got in trouble for coming to Earth—without assignment, I mean?" I stole a peek at Den over my shoulder. "Do you think she'd end up like the other Earthbound? Or if she chose to come down—to stay, would she be considered *Forsaken* like other angels who choose to give up their divine existence?" I turned to face him.

"Hard to say. There's no real precedence for something like that."

Shifting gears, I asked, "Do you think Purah is right about Thaddeus heading to Brazil? Leo said he's sending Nic to check things out."

"Nic used to watch that location when Marcus was overseeing the lab there," he said, turning me back to face away.

I was full of questions, but Den didn't seem to have the answers, or maybe he didn't want to answer. "Well, as long as Thaddeus's focus is elsewhere and not on finding me—the further away the better, I say."

"None of Thaddeus's followers are there anymore. Marcus and Zuriel the tracker from Taygeta, relocated to New York, don't forget."

"Marq told me Nic relocated to Ottawa when it seemed no other Earthbound were in the region—including Thaddeus's guys." My recall of the name *Zuriel* came with the memory of Marq showing me the map with the most recent whereabouts of the Earthbound and their migrations. I went to turn around again, but he stopped me mid-twist.

"Correct," Den confirmed. "Now focus."

We spent the next two hours going through a variety of moves to defend against an attacker, starting with basic counter moves should one find themselves in an armbar chokehold. We ran through elbow thrusts to the torso, over-the-shoulder fist to the face, and backwards fist to the groin. Den explained the fist to the groin was also good if the attacker has both their arms wrapped around your torso, same with a reverse headbutt. We then moved onto more complex maneuvers for when a knife is used by the attacker, which I recognized would take much more practice on my part.

"Okay, since you have your hair tied back—great for training but also great for an attacker, let's try a few techniques to escape this type of restraint. Turn facing away from me again," Den requested.

I turned away, taking a casual stance and then felt tension on my neck as Den gripped my braid.

"Lift both your hands up and over your shoulders to grab my wrist—the one holding your hair. Set your feet so that you're balanced, using your hands to resist my movements."

I followed the instructions, attempting to resist as he yanked me around like a rag doll.

"Even if the attacker is stronger than you and can pull you around, this move is meant to force them off balance." He stopped tugging but still held my braid tight.

"What do I do next?" Den released my hair then, and I turned to look at him.

"I'm getting there—turn around." He did a circle movement with his index finger.

I turned around, and he grabbed my braid again.

"You are going to twist and turn towards the assailant," he said, this time not yanking me to-and-fro.

I followed his instruction again, raising my hands up and over my shoulders to grip his wrist and then twisted.

"Now go for a hit to the face or go under my arm to throw me off balance," he instructed. "Then kick the knee or groin—if you can't get in a good punch to the face."

I attempted a knee kick, but obviously he was ready for it and dodged my foot.

"The idea is to turn your whole body right away and strike them as quick as possible," he said, releasing me and giving some distance between us. "Remember, movement and striking are two different things."

I nodded, out of breath. "Does it matter which way I turn?" I rested my hands on my hips, gathering my breath. Den hadn't even broken a sweat. It was always like that.

"It's best to turn towards them—away from the hand holding your hair," he said. "That will give you more opportunity for strikes." He fisted his hands and bounced on his toes.

"If they are behind me, how will I know which way?" I gave him my best confused face.

"When you try to turn, you'll know which way is best when you feel the resistance."

"Okay, what about if my hair is loose and they approach from the front and grab it?"

"If someone approaches you—even just to chat, the minute you feel unsafe or they start to close the distance, the main thing is to get your hands up in defense."

I put my hands up in a defensive stance when Den stepped closer.

"Move with them, never let them get to the side or behind you," he said, taking a step to the right and then the left.

I mirrored him, moving as he moved, keeping him at my front. "And what do I do if they get a hold of my hair from the front?"

Den stopped his sidesteps and swiftly grabbed hold of the front of my hair. "It doesn't have to be loose for them to get a grip of your hair."

"Clearly—ouch!" I grabbed his wrist with both hands.

"You're instinct will be to do what you just did, but don't. You're going to need to put one hand—the one opposite, up to my hand holding your hair," he said as I struggled. "I know it goes against your every instinct, but it will help with the pain of them gripping your hair or them ripping it out."

I switched up my grip to one hand as instructed.

"Now brace your stance, wrap your other hand around my wrist and turn it inward, forcing me to go with you as you turn your head towards the ground. If you do it right, this will break their hold."

Doing it again as instructed, I turned and… almost broke his grip, but he started pulling me side to side and back and forth.

"They may try yanking you around, so do your best to regain your stance, move with me," he said as he continued to yank me back and forth.

"Obviously, I'm not strong enough to break your hold," I said, hanging on for dear life.

"If that happens, then you're going to release their wrist—but still keep hold of my hand holding your hair. Bring your free arm up and over my extended elbow and try to bring my elbow down. This will make it harder for the assailant to move you around."

I followed his commands and turned… but it didn't work.

Then Den said, "But unlike the first attempt at turning the wrist forward—like you just did, you are now going to turn away from me and throw me off balance."

I followed through in the current direction, and Den released his grip.

"Hopefully they let go."

"Hopefully?" I questioned, rubbing my head.

"There is no perfect technique, best thing is to not get in that situation in the first place. Let's go again. Ready?"

"Ready," I said reluctantly.

With lightning speed, Den grabbed hold of my hair again and I attempted the maneuvers once more. "Faaack, I think I just cracked my halo." I yelped as my head made contact with the knuckles of his other hand.

Den released my hair and stepped back. "You're not going to master this technique right away. This is why we train. Again?"

I put up a hand. "I need a breather," I said, rubbing my aching scalp with my other hand. I rotated my neck, turning my head side to side. Biding my time, I said, "I'm guessing you heard about Jana showing up at the new restaurant—and that Leo asked her to stay at North Haven, eh?"

"Oh yes," Den said, extending his arm in the direction of the bench. "We all got a lengthy briefing on her arrival, plus the odd correlation about her father's name being on the birth certificate for Anael's daughter."

"Lengthy briefing?" I questioned as I moved past him to sit on the bench.

"Think about it," he said, taking a seat next to me. "If Jana is staying at North Haven, Kris and the others there would need some kind of backstory."

"Something that made sense for why a crew of men like you guys live together," I laughed out.

"*Straight* men," he added, chuckling at his own comment.

I smiled and shook my head. "And what did they come up with?"

"Superheroes," he said, "just kidding." He laughed again.

"Har-har." I punched him in the arm and regretted it instantly. "Ouch!" It was like punching a concrete wall. "I'm done."

"Serves you right," he said, sticking out his tongue. "Don't you have to pick up the girls, anyway?"

"Yes—and oh-my-gawd you've been hanging out with them waaaay too much."

At the end of our driveway, I opened our mailbox and grabbed up the usual weekly flyers from inside. Then I took hold of the handle of our recycling bin and rolled it back to the shade of the carport. Mixed in among the fliers was a postcard from Queensland, Australia. The card had a phrase on the front that read, *Wish you were here* with a photo of a koala bear. On the back was a brief handwritten message,

> *Australia is amazing! Put it on your bucket list.*
> *We are off to Brisbane tomorrow but will probably be in Sydney by the time you get this. Hope all is well.*
> *Love to Redmond and the girls.*
> *~ Vicki*

"Short and sweet," I said aloud as I tossed the flyers into our recycling bin before positioning it next to the yard waste and garbage bins in the carport. Then I heard the distinct rumble of a motorcycle.

Redmond drove in on his Harley just then, pulling into the carport next to where I stood in front of the bins.

"We need to take a ride together soon," I said when he shut the engine off.

"We've got plenty of options now for people to watch the girls. Maybe we make a weekend of it?" He swung a leg over the bike to dismount from his ride. His white t-shirt was dotted with sweat marks. "Where are the girls?"

"Doing tomorrow's chores."

"Already?" he asked, removing his helmet and sunglasses.

"They asked if we could all go for a nighttime walk on the beach after dinner *tomorrow*—and I said if they finish their chores for today and *tomorrow* before dinner tonight, we would."

"Why not do a walk tonight?" Redmond removed his wallet and cellphone from the side bag of the bike.

"They want to do a special walk to wish Gramma Sally a happy birthday tomorrow." My heart swelled at sharing their request.

"Oh, that's sweet of them." He leaned down and kissed my forehead.

"I thought so too." I tippy-toed up and kissed him on the lips, then we strode together through the carport. "Speaking of walks on the beach, I forgot to tell you who I saw on my walk the other day."

Redmond stopped in his tracks, worry blanketing his expression. "Tell me it wasn't Purah visiting again."

"Noooo. Do you remember me telling you about that new on-call doctor at the hospital, the one working with the Behavioral Health Center?" I stopped at the door as Redmond stepped forward, wrapping his hand over the knob.

"Refresh my memory." He turned the knob then pushed open the door leading into the lower level.

"I need to shower first. I'll refresh your memory later once the girls are in bed. Plus, I have more on the topic of Jana staying at North Haven."

Redmond paused again, turning to shoot me another worried look.

"It's nothing to be concerned about," I said, turning him around and pushing him through the open door. It wasn't. Den had given me the story they were using before I had headed out, and it was a good one.

Once the girls had been tucked in, instead of staying up to watch TV, I insisted that Redmond and I make our way to bed early so I could circle back on the earlier topics I wanted to share with him.

After shutting the bedroom door, I went and set my cellphone on the nightstand, changed into a pair of pajama boxers and a tank top, and then I padded down the short hall connected to our ensuite bathroom.

"So tell me about this doctor you met on the beach," Redmond said as I entered the bathroom area.

I paused to admire my husband as he stood shirtless in front of his vanity wearing nothing but his boxers, then said, "Dr. Stone—Grier. We met back in February at the hospital—she seemed really nice." I moved to stand in front of the sink on my side of the bathroom.

"And you saw her on your beach walk?" he questioned, turning to look at me in the mirror, toothbrush paused in his mouth.

"Yup. We got to talking, and she told me she bought that cute little beach cottage up the way from us—the one we loved so much." I took *my* toothbrush from the ceramic holder.

"That place has been vacant for a while." He continued brushing.

I opened my toothpaste and squeezed a short line of it onto my toothbrush. "I know—I was thrilled to hear she owns it now—someone nice. She'll be working from home—doing her practice from there." I turned on the tap and ran the toothbrush under the running water.

"We should invite her over," he suggested before swooshing his mouth out with water.

"She said she was heading back to Miami—and wouldn't be back until September when she was officially on call at the hospital. But we did exchange numbers." I began brushing my teeth.

"We can drop off a house warming gift once she's settled in."

I paused my brushing. "You're sweet," I garbled through a mouth full of toothpaste, then finished brushing and rinsed my mouth out. "That's a wonderful idea." I set my toothbrush back in the holder. "Hey, I know we usually have our date night during the week, but how about instead of doing our usual Friday *lunch*, we do our date night this Friday instead?" I suggested, examining my reflection in the large vanity mirror over the sink.

"Sounds like a plan—but we're still doing family roller-skate night though, right?" he asked, coming to stand behind me. His arms snaked around my body, his hands coming to rest over my now flat stomach. He gazed at me in the reflection over my right shoulder and gave me a squeeze, causing me to wince. "Did I hurt you?" he asked, alarmed, releasing his arms from around me.

"Mat-rash," I said, lifting the back of my tank top to show him the marks on the backside of my ribs. "And yes, skate night is still on as usual."

"Let me put some ointment on those scrapes," he said then, reaching and pulling open the top drawer of my bathroom cabinet. "I've had plenty of those scrapes myself, as you know." Redmond retrieved a tube from the drawer, then he knelt to gently rub in the first aid cream. It was the good kind with the anesthetic, and he applied it over all my boo-boos.

Done, he tossed the tube back in the drawer, then returned to standing behind me. Looking at me in the mirror again, he ran his fingertips up my arms and over my shoulders, stopping to give me a soft massage over the muscles near my neck, all while gazing at my reflection. "Your shoulders have rounded out. Your arms are leaner and more muscular, and even your legs have gotten leaner." He ran his hands down over my hips and butt.

"My speed and endurance have all improved too." I was stronger over all. Even my ankles, knees, and hips were stronger, having done endless repetitions with exercises for balance and agility. "I'm a lean mean fighting machine." I held up my fists.

Redmond shifted his attention to his own reflection in the mirror, stretching his neck by tipping it slowly side to side. Then he rolled his shoulders, causing a cracking noise to come from both. "I'm just getting older," he said with a sigh.

"Nah!" I said, turning to face him. "And you're still as handsome as the day I met you." I pulled his face down for a kiss.

"Any weapons training yet?" he asked, resting his hands on my hips and looking past me into the mirror again.

I dropped my hands from his face. "Nope." I tried to step away, but he held me in place.

"So you haven't tried firing your gun yet?" He kissed my forehead.

His hold on my hips was gentle, and I shifted, turning to face back to the mirror. Ignoring his comment I said, "Den mentioned he could come teach the girls some defense techniques for dealing with bullies—should the need arrive." I reached for the jar of my nighttime eye cream.

"Might be good for them, being able to defend themselves." He turned his face to one side then the other, examining his jaw in the mirror.

I shrugged, hating the idea of them ever needing such a thing. "Speaking of…," I began, before dabbing some of the cream under my eyes. Then I continued, explaining what Den had told me about Jana's arrival.

"And Leo asked that she stay with *them*?" he questioned, leaning around me into my mirror, examining the tiny lines under his own eyes.

"Ya," I agreed, moving away from the sink area, heading back up the hall to the bedroom.

Redmond followed behind me.

"I think he wants to feel things out, see if they can trust her with the real deal. In the interim, they provided her a different narrative, something a little more plausible—about how they work as a covert team involved in tracking down these special kids, before the bad guys do."

Redmond flipped the switches to turn on the ceiling fans.

Together, we flipped back the bed covers and climbed in.

I went on to tell him the full details on the backstory they'd concocted, then shared the last bit about how it was Jana's father's name on the records for Anael's daughter.

"Wow, that's got to be a real head-shaker for her," Redmond said, dragging the covers up to his chest. "Hearing about what Kris does besides the restaurants…." Redmond did finger quotes for the word *does*. "…and the fact that her now deceased father is linked to their latest target."

"Biologically linked, making her and Jana half-sisters," I affirmed, turning on my side to face him. "Leo told Den that Jana had been pretty shaken by it all, but she'd calmed soon after and even welcomed the idea that she had a sister."

"Did Den say anything about how Kris was navigating Jana's arrival?" Redmond turned his head to look at me.

"Leo told him that he's never seen Kris behave like this over a female. Meaning he'd never shown any concern for a woman or her feelings before. And whatever transpired between them while he was in Iceland had evoked the *old* Kris, the one that gave a shit about humans and his own kind—the Seraphim, I mean." I folded my side of the covers partially back to rest my arm atop the cool fabric while sliding my other arm under my pillow.

"If they can establish trust with her, have her be part of *the knowing*, she could continue to be a great influence on Kris." Redmond adjusted his pillow then stared up at the ceiling.

"It's still a lot to grasp—you know that. You had to absorb a lot when we started dating."

"Been there—done that—bought the t-shirt," Redmond tossed back.

"Although, for them, there's the whole aging thing to contend with. Would be like dating a vampire, growing old while they stayed young and handsome."

"They still age—don't forget, just not as fast as humans, and they function just like humans, albeit they have wings, so there's that." Redmond continued to stare at the ceiling.

"Look at Den and the girls' teacher. If they got serious, wouldn't Den have to explain why he isn't getting older as fast?"

"I suppose." Redmond turned his face my way again. "You could always ask him."

"What?"

"If he has ever had to explain things to a human before?"

"I asked him about how things were with Gavin earlier."

"What did he say?"

"He ignored the question. I've never asked any of them about involving humans before—other than Max and Julian—and Lane, of course. Wasn't sure it was my business." I turned away to the other side remembering I needed to plug my cellphone in the charger. "But then I guess we are all in this together, secrets and all."

"Ask—find out how Leo bridged that topic with them."

I turned back and rested my head down on my pillows, staring up at the ceiling as he had, pulling the covers up higher as the cooler bedtime A/C settings kicked in. "Maybe that's the reason why he offered for Jana to stay with them, so she could meet Max and Julian. Then if the time comes, they could ease her into the true details."

"Would be good to have other humans there to cushion the blow, I suppose," Redmond suggested before reaching over to his nightstand and shutting off the light.

I turned my face to look out through the bedroom windows at the starry night. "Only time will tell, I guess."

Chapter 7 

Residence of Sherran Anderson, August 6th, Toronto, Canada

Jules held the door open, standing half in and half outside the cramped vestibule that led into the six story brick apartment building while Ben hit the call button next to the label with the name S. Anderson written on it for apartment 204. When no one answered, he hit the button again. The scratchy buzzer sound resonated in the small, mostly glass walled entry way again.

Jules wrinkled her nose. "Guh!" The small space had the faintest stink of urine.

"What is it?" questioned a gravelly voice through the tiny intercom speaker.

"Hello, we're looking for Natalie Harwood," Ben said.

"Natalie? What do you want with her?"

Ben glanced at Jules. "We are from the law firm who handled her adoption, and we have some important information for her."

In leu of a response, the door made a similar annoying buzz indicating the door was now unlocked for them to enter.

Ben pulled the door open and followed Jules as she proceeded into the main floor lobby.

"Doesn't seem to be an elevator, but the apartment is only on the second floor," Jules stated with a half grin. "No air-conditioning either. Interesting domicile," she added as she advanced up the filthy stairs in front of her. The stairwell stank of cat pee.

At the top of the stairs there was a smudged plaque with an arrow indicating that apartment 204 was to the left, each floor having only three apartments on either side of the stairs. Together they moved left, stopping at the second apartment in.

The door was ajar, but Ben knocked anyway.

"Come in," came the same gravelly voice they'd heard in the entryway. Apparently the gravel in the voice hadn't been because of the intercom.

Ben pushed the door open, and they were immediately assaulted by the stench of smoke, stale cigarettes, and body odor.

"Don't just stand there with my door wide," the gruff female voice said.

Jules led the way, stepping inside the tiny apartment.

The main living area contained both the kitchen and living room in one. Like the halls and stairwell, the apartment had no A/C, either. Against the far wall on an old brown couch sat a woman with long stringy, sweat-soaked tawny blonde hair. Her skeletally thin legs extended out from under the below-the-knee cotton housedress she wore. Her feet were bare, her toenails yellow and overgrown, and based on her wrinkles and age spots, she appeared as if in her late 60s or even early 70s, though the records they had stated the aunt was merely in her 50s.

"Sherran Anderson?" Jules asked. The small space was stifling, so she unbuttoned her suit jacket and flapped one side. She'd done her long hair up in a tight bun to appear more professional, but now she was grateful it was up and off the back of her neck.

"Yes, but you can call me Sherry," the woman said, stalked by a phlegmy cough. Smokers cough by the looks of the cigarette butts piled in the ashtray on the side table next to her, and the fact she was lighting a cigarette with a still burning butt of another. She snubbed out the latter in the already overflowing ashtray. Her hands and arms were thin and vein-ridden like her legs.

"Mrs. Anderson," Ben began, choosing to unbutton his suit jacket as well.

"That's Miss. I'm not married."

"Miss Anderson, I'm Mr. Frost and this is my associate, Ms. Forest." Ben loosened his tie and then released the top button of his dress shirt.

"Frost and Forest," Sherry repeated, trailed by a coarse laugh that quickly morphed into a choking cough. "Are your other colleagues Wind and Winter?" She chortled, then coughed again.

"Winter and North, actually," Jules stated, schooling her features, holding back her disgust for the woman.

Sherry waved a dismissive hand. "Whatever." She took a drag of the cigarette. "What do you want with my niece?"

"We have some paperwork for her," Ben said, patting the cross body satchel that hung at his hip. "Is she home at the moment?"

"She's not here."

"Do you know when she will be back?" Ben patted his forehead with the back of his hand.

Sherry took another draw off her cigarette. "My guess is never."

"What do you mean?" Jules asked.

"She up and left me two and a half years ago," she said, coughing into her fist, "and after everything I did for her, too."

"Does she live nearby? It's extremely important we speak with her—deliver these papers," Jules pushed, eager to get out of the stink and heat of the apartment.

"If it's a cheque, I can make sure she gets it. Besides, she owes me." She blew smoke out her nostrils like a haggard old dragon.

"Since she's an adult now, legally we have to work with her directly," Ben clarified.

"Were you not provided funds to take care of Natalie?" Jules questioned. They both knew Anael had provided ample funds to the future adoptive parents, the remainder of which was transferred to the aunt after the parents' deaths.

The woman snorted, coughed, and then said, "That was the deal. The bank account had to be opened in her name and the money was direct deposited there. I managed the money, had full access until she went to the bank on her 18th birthday and locked me out. Ungrateful little…."

"Miss Anderson—Sherry, we need to find Natalie," Jules interrupted, losing patience with this horrible woman. "Do you know where she lives now?"

She took another long draw off her cigarette before answering. "She moved to Ottawa. Sent me the change of address to forward her mail—not that she had any." She shifted then, maneuvering to push up off the couch, but when her efforts failed her, she pointed a brown and yellow tobacco stained finger to a pile of magazines at the far end of the couch.

Ben promptly began shuffling through the stack of magazines, the dates on them he noticed were from over two years ago. "Got it," he announced, holding up the address form, now faded with age and ruined further by several coffee rings.

"Do you know why she moved to Ottawa?" Jules asked.

"Not sure. But she did mention wanting to go to school for some kind of sports science program or something." She shook her head, as if unsure.

"She could be attending one of the Universities," Ben suggested to Jules. "Both the universities in Ottawa have sports medicine departments." He raised a knowing eyebrow.

"The city college has programs and courses that align with that course of study, too." Jules was well aware he worked for one of those university departments, after all.

"I wouldn't be surprised—she was a smart kid, too smart for her own good if you ask me," Sherry interjected before letting out another rattled cough. Then she lit another cigarette with the end of her almost finished one.

"Do you have a recent photo of her?" Jules asked, hopeful yet disgusted at having to witness how this woman lived.

"Recent—no, but there's a framed graduation photo of her on the kitchen counter." She pointed the two fingers that held her cigarette in the direction of the kitchen area.

Jules went to the counter but found no framed photo. "I'm sorry I don't see it."

"It's there," Sherry said, glancing out the living room window as if she were unconcerned about their need to find Natalie.

Jules looked again, lifting a plastic bag up off the counter that contained a half loaf of molded over bread. Under it lay the framed photo, tiny ants scrambling across the glass front. "Found it," Jules announced, shaking the ants off into the small sink, banging the side of the frame for good measure. "Do you mind if we borrow this?" she asked, shaking a persistent ant loose.

"Keep it—I don't need it," Sherry said with a sneer and a cough, followed by an *I couldn't care less* shrug.

Chapter 8 

Lyndon hadn't heard a word from Zuriel other than a short text saying he was checking another lead. Which was fine with Lyndon because he'd been saddled with ridiculous errands given to him by Thaddeus via Amahle that had taken up most of his time this past week. Right now, his focus was on getting back to the group home as soon as possible because he knew Lane was scheduled to be volunteering today.

When he entered the large playroom, he spotted her sitting at their usual table in a chair next to Taylor. Her back was to him as he approached, though he could see she was holding up one of Taylor's hands, palm facing outward as she arranged his fingers in a fist with his thumb tucked in between his index and middle fingers. "T… for Taylor," she said, annunciating the letter T as she mimicked the hand gesture.

"What are you two up to?" he asked in his softest voice, hoping not to startle her. She was wearing navy shorts and a sleeveless top that had purple and navy stripes. She had her shoulder-length wavy black hair pulled up into one of those hair claw-clips, the high position of it exposing the smooth length of her neck.

"Oh—hi," she said, looking up at him with a sunny smile as if happy to see him. "Thought I might try teaching Taylor some ASL. Help him communicate more." Her smile widened. "That forest green t-shirt looks amazing on you, by the way."

"Th-th-thank you," he said, feeling a flush warmth ring his neck. He'd purchased several new casual shirts and lightweight jeans to wear now that he was making an effort with his appearance. "How do you know how to do sign language?" he asked, selecting the seat next to her.

"I took it as an elective course when I was doing my original degree. Are you familiar with ASL?" She turned in her seat to face him.

"Familiar, yes—I've seen it being used. But I don't know how to sign." He lifted his hands and wiggled his fingers.

"I'm lucky, I have a friend who is fluent, someone I can practice with—further my own knowledge. I can teach you some basics… if you like. You can practice with Taylor when I'm not here." She wiggled her fingers like he had.

He gave a quick smile and nodded. "I'd like that."

"Can Taylor read?" she asked him, though she looked at Taylor when she did.

He appreciated that she always made a point of giving Taylor her focus when she talked about him. She told him once that she felt it was rude to talk about him like he wasn't here. It was one of the many things he admired about her, how she always considered Taylor when they were all together. "He knows his numbers—up to one hundred, plus his letters, days of the week and months." Lyndon reached over and gently touched Taylor's cheek with the back of his fingers. "He doesn't care much for reading, but he does love being read to, as you know." He smiled again, recalling when he'd read the story about the mermaid to both of them.

"Yes," she said, nodding. She turned to look at Taylor again and his bright green eyes beamed back at her.

"Time for your exercises," came the voice of Taylor's mobility therapist as she entered the room.

She was one of the few treatment specialists Lyndon trusted to work with him, as most of the therapists were male. She was quite muscular for a human female, but strength was needed while working with those with physical challenges, he had been told.

"Hi, Lane," she added when she reached the table, "Nice to see you here again."

"Wonderful to see you too," Lane said, before turning her attention back to Taylor. "Are you ready?" She raised her hand, making a fist with her folded fingers facing forward, then motioned like she was knocking on a door. "Yes?" she asked then.

The gesture Lyndon realized was ASL for *yes*.

Taylor made the sign for the letter T she'd just taught him, then he mirrored her gesture for yes.

"Wow, you are a fast learner. T is for Taylor. Well done. Would you like to learn more next time?"

This time he nodded and repeated the yes sign before clapping his hands.

"Thank you for spending time with me," Lane said to Taylor, making the sign for what Lyndon could only guess was for *love*, crossing both hands over the middle of her chest.

In response, Taylor placed the palms of his hands overlapped against his chest.

"See you soon," Lane called out as he was wheeled away out of the playroom.

"Do you have to leave now?" Lyndon asked, knowing her volunteering time here was almost over.

"Nooo," she said playfully, tilting her head to one side. "Do you?"

"No," he said, enjoying the continued lighthearted way she interacted with him.

"Then how about you show me your living space?" She gave him a crooked grin.

Still nervous, he threw caution to the wind. "Okay," he said, rising from his chair. When she asked to see his living space that first time, he hadn't said no, instead he had said perhaps *another time*. And now he supposed this was *another time*.

A surprised yet pleased expression spread over Lane's lovely face, and she swiftly got up from her chair to stand next to him. "Let's go," she said, placing her purse crosswise over her chest. "Lead the way."

Lyndon led the way to the elevator, then used his security fob that allowed for the elevator to descend to the lower level. The elevator opened to the white hallway he always made sure to keep clean. He extended his hand for her exit first, then passed by her to go left up the hall.

"What's down that way?" Lane asked, pointing to the right.

"Water heater, furnace, stuff like that." He shrugged his shoulders, then used his security fob once again to open the way to his private living area.

"Would you like a refreshment?" He asked, striding to the kitchen area and opening the fridge. "I have lemonade, aaaand water." He looked back at her as she stood near the entrance.

"I'm good actually—but thank you," she said, remaining where she was as though taking in all that his simple space had to offer.

He grabbed the water pitcher and then picked up the single overturned glass from the dish rack. His throat was parched, and he was suddenly a tad too warm with Lane now in his home.

"What a marvelous kitchen for such a small space," she said, sauntering forward finally into the kitchen area.

"I like to cook." This was his favorite space, and he'd put in a high-quality chef's style kitchen with all the bells and whistles when he'd designed the lower level space. Lyndon poured the cool liquid into the glass, then lingered in front of the open fridge before replacing the pitcher back inside. He took a gulp of the water as he shut the fridge door, then leaned back against the kitchen counter. He'd designed the counter in a C shape. Running along the same wall as the entrance, was the fridge next to a short stretch of counter with a sink, where he was, that then took a right angle and stretched out in a lengthier counter with a gas stove in the middle, more counter and then another right angle that continued with an equal length of counter as the fridge and shorter counter combined, all of which had cabinets or drawers. There were shelves above the sink area and on either side of the stove top, allowing for a vent in the upper space and a full oven below. To the left of the oven was a small dishwasher, to the right was a two-stack set of deep drawers that contained all his pots and pans.

"I see that," she said, sliding free one of the many cookbooks he had lined up on the counter next to the stove. "Would you cook for me sometime?"

He folded his arms awkwardly over his chest, still holding the glass of water. "I… I would be honored to prepare a meal for you," he said, stunned at the fact she would want him to. They hadn't even shared a meal together out at a restaurant yet.

"Do you have a specialty?" Lane flipped through the cookbook, stopping at the pages tabbed with sticky notes.

"I can make whatever you like—you choose," he said, then realized how arrogant that must have sounded. But he *was* an excellent cook. It had been a passion of his to learn how to prepare foods from different cultures.

"Anything?" she asked, her tone skeptical.

He nodded in response to avoid sounding smug.

"Let me think on that," she said, withdrawing another cookbook to flip through its pages. "Wouldn't want to make it too easy on you." She slid the cookbook back into its place.

"I welcome the challenge," he said with a grin, loosening his arms to take another sip of water.

She gave him a devilish grin, then left the kitchen to stroll to the other side of the open room.

Lyndon admired how calmly and casually she moved around his personal space. He, on the other hand, was a nervous wreck, and he gulped down the remaining water from the glass. He was proud of what he'd done to the once cold, sparse basement, converting it to a cozy living space that was his haven away from Thaddeus and all his depraved activities. Lyndon had made an environment that contained everything he needed along with some things he actually enjoyed. The open space was divided into four distinct areas. To the right of the entrance was a solid wall. On the other side of it was the bathroom. The workmen had install efficient yet stylish elements consisting of a white pedestal sink, a sleek, modern white toilet and a sizable glass front shower that took up most of the space with the back and side walls finished top to bottom with light blue glass tile. Like the door into the apartment, the bathroom entrance faced the same direction and opened to the hybrid area for both working at his desk and for sleeping. To the left of this space, in the opposite corner from the bathroom, was his second favorite area that contained his bookshelves and the armchair he used when reading.

Lane stopped in front of his wall of books and pulled one free of the shelf. "Michael Jordan's biography?" She turned the cover his way. "Did you play sports when you were younger?"

"No. I just enjoy biographies. Did you?" he asked, still holding the empty glass, uncertain what to do with his hands.

"Basketball. Funny, though, I wasn't any good at it. The gym teacher thought I'd be a natural since I was tall. Turns out I'm a geek—not an athlete."

"A geek?" He crossed his arms over his chest again, switching the empty glass to his other hand.

"That's me. I actually liked school as a kid. Still do." She lifted her shoulders in a shrug, raising both her hands palms up.

"How is your program going?" he asked, uncrossing his arms, turning slightly to set the glass in the sink. "You're doing your master's, you said, yes?"

"Yes. And it's really great. I should be done by January. Then I'm hoping to find an internship. And I'd eventually like to do my PHD." She gave a subtle one-shoulder shrug, then focused back on the wall of books. "You have quite the collection. Excellent variety of topics *and* genres." She glanced over at him.

"I like to read," he admitted, matching her one-shoulder shrug, glancing briefly over to the well-worn leather armchair and accompanying ottoman set up next to the bookshelves.

"Several classic children's books, too. Looks like you have a full Dr. Seuss collection." She turned and smiled sweetly at him. "Those were my favorites."

He grinned, leaning his hands back on the counter behind him. "They were some of Taylor's favorites." He enjoyed them as well.

"How is work going?" she asked, as though to keep the attention on him.

"Fine, I guess. The boss is away." His fingers gripped the edge of the counter, causing it to make a creaking noise.

"Where did he go?" she asked, her head tilted back to read the spines of the books on the upper shelves.

"Brazil." *The farther away, the better*, Lyndon considered.

"Interesting. So does that mean you will have to go there too?"

"Hell—no. Sorry, I mean *no*, not if I can help it." He felt his face heat with embarrassment for his aggressive tone.

"Does he travel a lot?" she asked, seemingly unfazed by his forceful words.

"Some. Are you sure you don't want something to drink?" he asked, needing something to do besides just standing in the kitchen.

"I'm good—thanks," she said with a brief glance his way. "How long will he be away?" she asked then, returning her attention to the shelf with the children's books. "Green Eggs and Ham." She held up the thin book. "Another cookbook?" She smirked.

He went to say no, but then realized she was teasing. "One of my favorites," he teased back, chuckling at her playfulness. "As for my boss, not sure exactly, but it's looking more and more like it will be an extended trip—permanent, maybe." He wished Thadeus would stay away permanently.

Lane nodded, then returned the children's book back to the shelf.

Then he added, "Any day he's away…."

"…is a good day, I bet," she finished for him.

He watched as she straightened and slowly scanned the rest of the room.

"It doesn't feel like you're in a basement," she said. "And I like the creamy white walls and ceiling colour."

"I didn't want it to feel like the dungeon space it had once looked like, considering there are no windows."

"I hadn't even noticed there were no windows," she said, continuing to scan the space.

He was so pleased she liked his home. "The drop-ceiling was removed as well."

Her scanning of his space stopped on him. "Where do you sleep—I don't see a bed?" she turned his way again. "You do sleep, right?" she asked, teasing him once again.

He laughed. "Yes—I sleep, at least I try to." He pointed over to his desk setup. "Murphy bed, behind the desk."

She crossed the room over to the desk where he had his computer and monitors set up. "Do you *ever* have to travel with your boss?"

"No—never." Lyndon remained where he was, comfortable with letting her check out what little there was on the desk. He always made a point to lock away any weapons or important documents in the desk drawer, should someone find their way into his private space. It was unlikely, but he still felt he needed to be cautious.

"Where else does he travel to?" she asked as she went towards the bathroom.

She was full of questions, but he found he didn't mind if it meant she would stay longer. He was coming to enjoy having her down here. "Norway... New York City... Rome. Amsterdam. Japan...," he called out, listing off some of the locations Thaddeus frequented as she disappeared into the bathroom.

"Those are some spectacular places—not that I've been," she cut in, her voice echoing from within the bathroom.

"…and Brazil," he said, ending the list when she came back into view, "but I was surprised he was headed there."

"Why is that?" Lane returned to his desk, turning and resting her backside against the edge of it, placing the palms of her hands down on the surface.

Lyndon copied her stance by leaning back against the kitchen counter. "Because there aren't any…," he began, halting before he said *test subjects*. He'd almost said too much, and swiftly switched to, "…we haven't done any work there in years."

"What does your boss do for a living—or do I even want to know?" she asked, stretching her lengthy legs out in front of her, crossing them casually at the ankles.

Lyndon barely processed what Lane had just said, his concentration lost as his focus fell transfixed on her lean tanned legs.

She spoke again, though he scarcely registered it. "*Lyndon*," she said, her voice firmer now, yanking him from the rudeness of gawking at her.

"I'm sorry," he said ashamed, promptly straightening from his casual leaning to turn his gaze away and onto the nothingness of the adjacent wall.

"Sorry for what?" she asked him, her question genuine, as if she'd not just caught him staring at her legs.

"Let's just say he's in research and leave it at that," he said, eager to change the subject. *Was the air-conditioner not working*, he wondered, because his body felt much too warm.

"Okay—I'm sorry, didn't mean to upset you," she said hurriedly, pushing up from the desk as if suggesting she was going to depart.

"No-no, you didn't." He gave her a sincere, reassuring smile to show her he wasn't upset with her. "He's just someone I don't like to think about, let alone talk about." His upset wasn't with her, and though he loathed Thaddeus, he was disappointed with himself for lingering so long on her bare legs. "How about we pick a different topic?"

"Alright," she agreed, returning to lean against his desk and showing no indication she was about to leave. "Is there anyone you work with that you *do* like?"

"Zuriel," he said without thinking, "but I don't really work with him much."

"Hmmm… have you always lived in Ottawa?" she asked, continuing with her inquiries.

He didn't care she had more questions and was relieved she hadn't bolted for the door. "Mostly," he said, relaxing some, drawing in a calming breath.

"Where did you work before this job? Or maybe a better question would be, *what* did you do before this job?"

"What I did before was considerably different from what I do now." He had been proud of his vocation before. The only thing he was proud of now was his time with Taylor.

"Tell me." Lane tilted her head to one side.

"You might not believe me if I told you." He relaxed further, leaning back against the counter again.

"Try me." She removed her hands from the desk to cross her arms below her chest. Then she raised her eyebrows as though to emphasize his task.

"Well," he said, then paused, pondering how much he should share. "My work involved the morphogenic processes relating to the changes in an organism's behavior, morphology, and physiology in response to unique environments." He'd said it like that to tease her, wanting very much to return to their playful banter.

Lane's eyebrows creased. "Come again?" she said jokingly, her lips tightening and clearly holding back a smile.

Success, he thought, before adding, "I did research on the biology of regeneration, asexual cellular processes."

Lane raised one skeptical eyebrow then and gave him a half smile.

Lyndon laughed. "See, I told you that you wouldn't believe me." This felt so wonderful, he mused, grateful for the ease of their continuing conversation.

"It's not that I don't believe you, I'm just… not sure I grasp what exactly you did for work." Her eyebrows pinched again.

"I basically studied different species and their capability for regeneration. Like when a starfish grows back an arm. Every species— human to bacteria, has the capacity of regeneration," he simplified.

"Impressive," Lane said, nodding, giving him a head to toe once over as though seeing him with a new perspective.

"What sort of work do you want to do when you complete your degree?" he asked, redirecting the attention back on her. That was enough about him.

Lane uncrossed her arms to rest her palms back on the desk. "After my master's in environmental engineering is done, I'd like to get the type of job where I can help to improve the ocean systems and optimize human-marine life interactions."

"Inspiring goal," he said with a grin. She may not understand his previous work, but there was no uncertainty in his mind that she was brilliant. "That was Zuriel's area of expertise before we—before he came to work with us."

"Really? I'd like to meet him—get his feedback on some of my ideas," she said, her tone filled with enthusiasm.

Lyndon smiled but said nothing, realizing he should probably be a bit more careful with what details he was sharing.

"It's a shame you don't work in that field anymore, because it sounds fascinating. Better than working for that asshole boss of yours."

"It most certainly was," he agreed. How he wished he could show her the wondrous things he'd seen, share with her the true work he had performed over the millennia.

"Then why don't you go back to it?" She pushed off the desk again and briskly crossed the short distance back to the kitchen area.

"It's complicated," he said, stiffening when she stopped directly in front of him. Lane was so close to him he could smell the fresh scent of her shampoo. And as she stared up at him and into his eyes, he found himself falling into the lapis blue depth of hers. He swallowed, his throat suddenly dry again.

"You have the most beautiful eyes," she said softly, shocking him with her words. No one had ever considered anything about him as *beautiful*. "The colour is so complex… like the lush dark green of a forest." Lane's gaze shifted to the scarred side of his face, and she raised her hand to brush away the curtain of shoulder-length hair he used to shield that side from view. Before he could muster any words, her attention moved to his lips. "How did you get that scar?" she asked, her eyes lifting to gaze up into his again.

Lyndon pulled in a slow breath through his nose, taking in the fresh scent of her. "That… is a story… for another day," he answered, *his* focus dropping now to her mouth. He liked that she didn't wear lipstick, as the colour of her lips was reminiscent of pale pink rose petals. When he refocused on her eyes, she took a hesitant step back.

"I'm going to get you to tell me more, one of these days," she countered with a playful smirk.

Lyndon let the air out of his lungs gradually as the haze in his brain cleared. Oh, how he wished he could come clean, maybe even tell her… *everything*. But he was a fool to think in maybes.

"I should probably get going," Lane said, observing him still as she stepped away and over towards the door. "By the way," she said, pausing and turning back. "I get that it's a big deal having someone down here, and I'm grateful you trusted me enough to show me your home."

He took two strides in her direction, then reached around her to grip the doorknob. "You are always welcome here, Lane," he said, leaning into her briefly before pulling the door open.

When he held the door wide, she went to step through then paused. "Do I need you to activate the elevator?" She shot a glance up the hall.

"No—only for the way down," he shared, giving her a small grin.

She nodded and then continued through and up the hall.

He watched from the doorway as she pressed the button to call down the elevator. When the door slid open seconds later, she looked back his way. "You know—you should really come meet my uncles. Perhaps I could take you to their new restaurant—once it opens."

Chapter 9 

Jana set her latest book she was reading next to the mug on the counter and then plugged in the kettle Julian had left out for her evening tea. It had been quite a week full of information to absorb, and her first couple of nights here had been filled with restlessness and very little sleep. Julian had suggested a valerian root tea, sharing he had found it helpful for sleepless nights whenever he was feeling anxious, and when she had tried some on her second night here, it had worked for her too. The tea had become a nightly ritual that had also helped her feel more at home as well.

Everyone she had met here and at the restaurant so far had been kind and courteous, nevertheless she still couldn't shake the apprehension she felt staying in the home of people she barely knew. The unease wasn't regarding these men specifically, it was more as though the reality of things were escaping her, the vagueness of information, the certainty of her new circumstances were somehow lost in shadows. Since the big discussion about what he and his brothers were doing, her father's indirect involvement with it, and the fact she had a half-sister they were trying to find, her days had been spent with

Kris at the restaurant. She'd been assisting where she could while learning more about the plans for the grand opening.

The distraction with keeping busy at the restaurant had kept her mind off thoughts of a sister she had yet to meet while Kris did his best to assure her they would find Natalie. He had also taken the time to explain further how he had abandoned his role here, abandoned his brothers when his restaurant had taken off and the attention of notoriety had inflated his ego. As a part of it, he'd lost focus and had fallen into excessive drinking, lavish spending, and questionable morality with disregarding others, women in particular, with his philandering ways. He wasn't proud of it and had said if it weren't for his chance meeting with her; he feared he would have never found his way back, found his integrity. His brothers had granted him forgiveness, as had those closest to him, including Frank, so he was adamant about working towards redemption. He'd even promised he would continue to work towards proving his worth to her if she'd let him.

Jana had assured him she'd witnessed his worth already. Kris may not have had his memories then, but she believed what she had observed during the months he was with her in Iceland was his true nature. She and Kris had grown closer over this first week, and she'd felt the connection they'd made in Iceland returning. Early evenings were spent sharing dinner with Julian, Max, occasionally Leo, and sometimes Lane, who had explained she was well aware of the goings on here. After dinners with the others, they spent quiet time alone relaxing in his private quarters on the main level, stretched out on the L-shaped sectional couch that took up most of the space. They'd talked for hours, discussing their day at the restaurant, asking each other basic get-to-know-you questions, like what's your favorite colour, favorite food etc., and exchanging memories now that Kris had some he could share with her. The best part of their alone time had been the fact that they held hands almost the whole time, though Kris had not made another attempt to kiss her. She understood, or at least tried to comprehend, how difficult it would be to venture into a committed relationship, when parts of your life had to remain secret. She recognized that Kris was going slowly as a part of his regaining trust and respect, and it was obvious by the way he interacted with and spoke to her that he wanted her here. It was the same welcoming feeling she got from the others at the house.

Tonight, Kris was staying late at the restaurant with Leo to go over the timeline for the rest of the renovations still to be done. When she'd arrived at the house earlier, Max and Julian had just been leaving for the restaurant, heading over to discuss the kitchen part of the renovations. After they had left, she'd gone and changed into jeans and an oversized heather grey t-shirt of Kris's, then set herself up at the kitchen island alone to eat the delicious meal Julian had prepared and left warming in the oven for her. He'd also set out a book for her, the romance novel he'd been reading, topping it with a sticky note on the cover that read,

If you enjoy paranormal romance, try this. It's a good one!

She'd only brought one book with her for the journey but had finished it the night she'd arrived in Ottawa. She'd not slept well that night due to the unfamiliar surroundings and all the bizarre information she'd learned about the man she'd come all this way to see. As for the rest of her books, they were all packed away, stored in Geir's home in one of the spare closets, along with most of her clothing and other items she'd chosen to keep. She'd sold her father's home with its contents and had left most of the household items in her old apartment above the bakery when she'd handed off ownership. For this trip Jana hadn't brought much with her, just the basics, and other than a few pieces of clothing and toiletries she'd purchased this week, she hadn't thought to get another book. So it had pleased her greatly when Kris had shown her the stacks of books in Zach's suite. She had yet to meet Zach, but Kris had assured her that he didn't mind one bit if she borrowed his books, and had even recommended a few, one of which she was currently reading. When she'd flown from NYC to Ottawa, the title on a hardcover version of the same book had caught her eye as she'd passed the airport bookstore. *Daisy Jones and the Six*. The ratings she'd found on the book had been excellent, and she'd like the idea of reading a story about an American band in the 1970s and was thrilled to have found it amongst the piles in Zach's room. She was enjoying the writing style and how the author had used interviews from the band members to further the story.

The teakettle whistled and the auto shut-off kicked in. Jana poured the steaming water from the kettle into her mug to steep the tea, its woodsy aroma permeating the air. Julian had warned her it had a strong smell and was slightly bitter. She found it tasted similar to black licorice, which she actually liked and was grateful for the simple comfort. At the sound of the main door opening, Jana turned around to see Ben, the university professor by day covert operative by night, come through it. "You're back. Did you have a successful venture?" she asked, dipping the tea bag up and down. She hadn't seen him since that first day they met.

"Hey, Jana. I'm guessing Leo hasn't updated you yet." Ben took several long strides over to the kitchen. He'd been in shorts and a t-shirt last time, and today he wore tan cargo pants and a pale blue short-sleeved collared shirt that matched the colour of his eyes.

Jana tossed the tea bag in the trash bin. "No—and I didn't want to bother him about it." She had been dying to hear about what, if anything, they had discovered, considering it was her half-sister they were searching for.

"The address we got for her was a temp week-to-week place, but it has been over 2 years since she lived there, and no forwarding address, I'm afraid," Ben shared, entering into the main kitchen space. "But we'll find her." He pulled open one side of the industrial sized fridge and pulled out a large bottle of orange juice. "The aunt said Natalie was interested in attending school here in Ottawa, so Jules said she'd check with the local college and two universities tomorrow to see if she is registered at any of them."

Jana nodded. "Smart." They were both university professors, she knew that, and it made sense they would know how to search student files. "Before coming here, I hadn't known much about Kris other than he owned a restaurant, and I hadn't anticipated it was just his *day* job. The sister stuff was just the topper. It's strange to think I have a sister out there. Although I guess she's kind of like me, her parents are also gone."

He set the bottle down on the counter, then opened the cupboard next to the fridge to retrieve a tall plastic cup. "But unlike you, she had the misfortune of being raised by a terrible substitute for her parents."

"Do I want to know?" she asked, tucking the paperback book under her arm.

"When we find her—and you two finally get to meet, I'm sure Natalie will share all the crappy details about her parental replacement."

Jana nodded her head slowly in understanding. "I had a chance to chat with Lane, and we talked about how both of us grew up being an only child, and about my now having a half-sister out there somewhere. She said she had always wanted siblings, especially a sister, since she had two fathers for parents and was surrounded by mainly uncles."

Ben poured juice into the cup, then returned the bottle to the fridge. "I never thought about that before—the lack of female company she would have been missing growing up. She was always such a happy kid." He took a sip of the juice.

"Oh, she's not *unhappy*. She was just pleased I was here—not that she feels lacking. It's more about having another female in the house." Jana gave him a reassuring smile. "Speaking of parents. I was told *Jules* went with you to speak to the aunt." She hadn't met Julianna yet, though she'd met her son Mason at the restaurant as he'd been helping Kris with the menu. He was a lovely young man with a talent for cooking. She had learned more about Jules's background, how she had been in Brazil working on an environmental project, that like Ben, she was now a professor at the university, *and* that Lane was one of her grad students. Jana had also been told Jules was aware of the covert initiative due to the fact her son carried the unique genes these nasty individuals were hot after.

"Yes, she was helpful in getting the woman—the aunt, to talk," Ben confirmed. He tossed back the last of his beverage and then rinsed the cup before placing it in the large industrial dishwasher near the sink.

"Kris showed me the photo you rescued from the aunt, the one Leo texted to the others." Jana had studied the smoke-stained and obviously neglected photo of Natalie, comparing their similarities and differences. She had an exceptional beauty even in the school photo. "I wasn't much older than Natalie when I found out that my mother had died. That was the reason my father went to New York City. He only told me about meeting someone when I was much older, but not the details. And he would have told me if the woman—your client, had ever reached out to him, *and* he wouldn't have kept the pregnancy a secret from me had he known." Jana knew her father would have liked to have more children, but *'it hadn't been in the cards'* he'd told her. "I would have liked to have siblings growing up, though I adored my time with my father, and I *never* felt like I was missing out with not having a mother. Geir has been much like a brother to me, and he was like a son to my father, especially with him taking over his veterinarian practice." Jana shifted the book, hugging it to her chest with one arm.

Ben opened the fridge again. "Geir, he's the one who contacted Den?"

"Yes." Jana leaned into the fridge and pointed at the containers that held the leftovers from this evening's meal.

"Thanks," he said, sliding the glass storage dishes free.

Jana stepped back, making room for him to prepare his meal. "Do you have a photo of Natalie's birthmother?"

"No, but I can tell you she greatly resembles Anael. Though you and Natalie have the same shaped faces, hair colour, and your eyes are alike. You look much like sisters. Do you look like *your* mother?" Ben took a large dinner plate from the long open shelf with the angled plate rack.

Jana thought of the remaining photos she still had tucked away in that memory box. "Yes, very much, but I have my father's eyes. Natalie's eyes look like his but are a much darker blue, so she must have *her* mother's eye colour."

He nodded as he dished out food onto the dinner plate. "The similarities of *your* mother to Natalie's birthmother may have been the reason your father had been drawn to Anael all those years ago."

She'd wondered as much, and now that she'd seen the photo of Natalie, she knew how similar in appearance their mothers must have been. "I don't think my father ever stopped loving my mother."

Ben paused his meal prep to look at her. "They say some love never dies."

Chapter 10 

The Beach House, Sunday August 14th, South Florida

In preparation for the group video chat, I adjusted my bed pillows behind me against the headboard and positioned my laptop out in front of my crossed legs for better comfort. Then I hit the video icon to dial. "I got a postcard from Vicki," I said when the faces of both Mac and Alison appeared on the video screen.

"Me too," Alison said. "Seems she and Eric are having a great time traveling. Australia is a big place to see, so they'll be gone for some time, I'm sure."

"Gotta do it while you still can," Mac stated, adjusting the neck of the chocolate brown off-shoulder shirt she was wearing. "We always think we have time. Watching my parents' health decline reminds me how every moment is precious." Mac sighed. "You two have been through this already. The aging of parents, their memory issues. My mother's memory is getting worse. It's so scary to watch her struggle, and I don't know how to help her. She gets frustrated and then ends up crying when she can't remember something."

"Oh Mac, I'm so sorry you are going through this—it's heartbreaking watching your parents decline. You feel so helpless," I said, my heart aching for her.

"If you need assistance finding resources or services to help her or them, I'm well connected," Alison offered. "I know you feel alone in this, but we're here to help you through it."

"I'm really sorry I can't be right there by your side," I said, feeling the pain in the distance between us. "Please don't be too proud to take Alison up on her offer."

Mac nodded slowly, then hung her head. "You've both experienced so much loss, I don't want to burden either of you."

My heart squeezed. "We love your parents. We love you. Nothing is ever a bother."

"I'm just a phone call away, Mac," Alison reassured her. "I can even help you navigate options for senior living, so you are prepared if that decision needs to be made." Alison scribbled something in her notebook.

Mac lifted her head. "I promise I'll reach out Alison, take you up on sifting through all the options and aid available." Mac gave a weak smile. "Derek said he'd be on the call but would be late," she said then, redirecting the focus.

"And Redmond said he'd catch Luc and Darius up later," I said, helping to lift the heaviness. "So it will be just the three of us until Derek hops on." Mac had texted me earlier that Olivia wouldn't be on the call because she was busy tending to the new program she recently started with training new doulas.

"Rachel said she was interested in learning more about magic," Mac shared. "I already showed her a few things she could use with her patients at the hospital."

"She's been working on the geriatric floor and loves working with the senior patients," Alison added.

"Wasn't she working with Nic in the pediatric oncology ward?" I asked, feeling a little out of the loop.

"She was," Mac said, "and she said she had learned a lot while working with him, but the weight of trying to remain stoic had been difficult with witnessing so many sick kids."

"You know what that's like, Lynn." Alison frowned.

I nodded. "But I'd only ever worked with babies, not with older kids, and it had been emotionally challenging, although it had been exceptionally rewarding to care for those tiny patients." Needing to shift topics again, I asked, "What type of spells did you show her, Mac?"

"Like Olivia, she can't do *real* magic, so I gave her the ingredients and casting words for an herbal sachet remedy to the promote health of her patients." She held up her open grimoire, tapping the recipe on the page.

"Can't hurt, especially if it gives her peace of mind when she feels powerless with using standard medicines," Alison said.

"I don't blame her," Mac said. "I'm finding it harder than I thought working with these mothers and their babies. It's great when things work out but when they don't...."

"Did something happen?" Alison asked.

Mac blew out an audible breath. "No. I'm just not sure I want to keep doing what I'm doing...." She paused again, taking in a long breath of air.

"Keep doing what?" I questioned, unsure what exactly it was she wanted to stop. "Magic?"

"Not magic, no. My work at the hospital with Olivia," she breathed out. "She loves it, even the difficult days, but she has a real knack for helping in a way I can't. I'm fine with providing the clinic with the products I make, the natural topical creams and such that help with relaxation and healing. I'm just not so cool anymore with dealing with the heart wrenching stuff, you know." Mac played with the black hair tie around her wrist.

Mac was such a tender-heart, she has always felt things so strongly. "Do you need to be there? For the hard stuff, I mean?"

"Olivia pretty much has everything covered. I just think she likes having me there to chat with." Mac forced a grin.

"Well, of course she does. And she appreciates your support in the work she does," I said, knowing I'd love having her with me to chat with at work, too.

"Working with kids, especially those with compromised health or in difficult circumstances can be daunting," Alison said. "I deal with it in my line of work with children's services and it can get overwhelming at times, but I do find it rewarding to help. Mac, if you don't find it fulfilling, don't force yourself to be in that arena. You have to respect your own needs. It's not a vocation most people choose to be in."

"Olivia would totally understand if you needed to step back from some or all of the patient stuff. Focus on just the administrative tasks," I suggested.

"She has people to do that—the admin part, so other than bringing in the creams and ointments, I don't actually fill any specific role. Plus, she's got several trainees that help out in the clinic." Mac yanked the hair tie from her wrist and twisted her long hair up in a loose, messy bun using it. "I'll talk with her tomorrow when I see her at the clinic."

"You'll work it out," I said, reaching forward to lift my laptop, stretching out my legs to set it then on my thighs.

"Agreed." Mac gave me a small grin. "How is your volunteering going?" she asked, doing her own redirect of the conversation.

"Uneventful, thank the goddess," I chuckled out.

Mac's grin widened.

Alison glanced down at herself. "Excuse my messy appearance, I've been baking," she confessed with a cheeky grin, attempting to brush away the flour on her shirt. Her black shirt had a hand shaped swipe of something white near one of her shoulders. "How are the girls?" She asked, glancing back up.

"Good-good," I responded with a chuckle at her failed try at dusting herself off. "They started back at school this past Wednesday."

"I still can't get over how early Florida kids go back to school," Alison said. "We still have until after Labour Day weekend for Kevin's start."

"Ya, I still find it weird," I agreed.

"Are you guys still doing family skate night on Thursdays?" Mac asked.

She and I used to go roller-skating every weekend when we were in junior high. "We missed the last two Thursdays, but I'm sure the girls will be asking to go soon. I'm thinking with them back in school we should probably switch it to a weekend thing."

"Still meeting with Redmond for your lunch dates on Fridays?" Alison asked. "I keep suggesting to Ken we should do something like that."

"Well…," I started to say.

"What—well, what?" she demanded.

I laughed at her enthusiasm and interest. "We changed that up." I paused to laugh again. "We did an actual date *night* on Friday two weeks ago instead of the lunch date."

"Niiiiiice," Mac said, "I think I could use a *date night*. One that didn't involve watching hockey on a big screen at the local pub, that is."

"Why the change?" Alison questioned. "Not that I don't approve."

"Priorities," I said. "We've been so focused on *family* time and everything else, we forgot about *our* relationship." I smiled, remembering how nice it was to have adult conversations over a nice meal, to hold hands, and to have genuine time alone. "Don't get me wrong, I love time with the girls—family time, but I missed my husband."

"Yup," Alison said. "Maybe I should talk to Ken about a date night, too."

"Adulting is hard," Mac said with a laugh that ended in a snort.

Alison giggled too, then said, "Based on the text you sent, I take it you have some otherworldly news for us." Alison tapped her notebook with her pen.

"Affirmative," I said, before going on and maneuvering through all the details about Jana's arrival and the ploy Leo and the others were using in opposition to telling her the complete truth.

"How are they going to explain the rest? Do you think they even will?" Alison asked, jotting down the update in her notebook for her records.

"I'm not sure. Redmond thinks I should just ask one of them about relationships between the Earthbound and humans, but I kind of did already. I got Marq and Den's take on it, but not in any great detail. I feel funny asking them about their love lives." I made an *eeeww* face.

"Have they told you any more about the Nephelium born from such couplings?" Mac inquired. She made an *eeek* face, then chuckled.

I shook my head. "Nothing other than this search for Anael's daughter, but that's part of what I wanted to tell you about." Leo had kept me up to date on everything, but this was the first time Mac and Alison had had time to chat with me.

"Spill," Mac demanded, loosening her bun only to redo it tighter.

"Okay, where do I start…," I said, then paused. "Hmmm, you know about Jana now but there's one more thing, well, two but…," I said, pausing again, trying to decide which order to give the other details. "Aaand you already know the scoop about how Anael left First Haven to venture out on her own all those years ago, and that her daughter is of a concerning age—wings and such, but get this, Jana's father… well, he's the guy Anael slept with. Her daughter is Jana's half-sister." I paused to let the details sink in.

Mac blinked, slowing as though digesting my words. "Uhm, what?" She turned her head as if giving me the evil eye.

"I know-I know, it's the most bizarre coincidence, wild timing for sure, but he just happened to be in NYC at the same time Anael was there. Apparently, Anael holds a striking resemblance to Jana's mother, Kris told me. Obviously, he didn't know it when he met Jana—brain fog and all, but he saw photos of her mother when he was with Jana in Iceland. He'd noted how much Jana and her mother looked alike, and when he regained his memory, he found he couldn't ignore the likeness between her mother to Anael."

"Okay and?" Mac pulled her hair loose again.

"Not that the correlation between the mother's isn't freaky enough, but they now have a photo of Anael's daughter too—and she also resembles Anael, and of course, the daughter and Jana look *just* like sisters."

"How did they get a photo of her—the daughter?" Mac asked, running her fingers through the now free hair.

"Leo found information on the adoptive parents. Unfortunately, they were killed in a car crash. He found only one living relative—an aunt."

"Yeesh, sounds like the start of a YA coming of age novel," Alison stated, before adding more to her notebook.

"Harsh right? But Leo located the woman—the aunt, and it seems the daughter went to live with her after the parents died."

"Did they reach out to the aunt?" Mac asked, hopeful.

"Even better, Ben and Jules went to talk to the woman. She lives in Toronto—if you can believe it." I adjusted the pillow behind my head.

"At this stage—after my time in—playing with magic, I realize now almost anything is possible," Mac said, smoothing her hair over one shoulder, securing it near her jaw with the hair tie.

"Was the daughter living with the aunt?" Alison questioned, eager for more details.

"No, but they did get the photo from her and a forwarding address."

"Please don't say *you're not going to believe this*," Mac said with a smirk.

I laughed. It was a lot of crazy information and chance happenings, but this wasn't the last of it. "It's. An. Ottawa. Address," I said, drawing out the *you're not going to believe this* last tidbit before delivering the not so great part of the details.

"Shut up!" Alison shouted. "Where?" She leaned into her screen, waiting.

"Ya about that," I started, then frowned, morphing my face to express my own disappointment. "The address was 2 years old. She's no longer there and left no forwarding address."

"Ooooh, man!" Mac roared in frustration.

I knew it was crappy news. "Neighbors said she was only there a few months."

"What is her name?" Mac asked then.

"*Natalie…* Natalie Harwood. Why?"

"Mac, if you say that you know this girl, I'm gonna need to go buy a lotto ticket," Alison joked.

Mac cackled. "Nope—don't know her. But, Lynn, do you know if Leo checked public records for her?"

I shrugged a shoulder, uncertain. "I'm guessing he did along with his other searches, but he would have told me if he found anything."

"Public records—the Library and Archives Canada, that is, are great if you are interested in things like censuses, military records, passenger lists, immigration, or naturalization records," Alison said, "Leo already has her adoption records, so unless she enrolled in the military, committed a crime, or—God forbid, is in a cemetery, chances are he won't find her address."

"That's true," I agreed. "The aunt mentioned Natalie was interested in going to school in Ottawa, so Jules checked the college and universities there." I adjusted my pillows again.

"That's a good option. Any luck?" Alison asked.

"Some. She *was* registered at Algonquin College for some part-time online courses but seems those were dated back when she'd first move to Ottawa. The account only had that original address they'd gotten. The universities were a bust so far too. Nothing showed she was registered at either."

"So far?" Mac questioned, chewing the skin at the edge of her thumbnail.

"Ya, Leo said Ben told him that professors can't see the names of students if their profile has a status of *submitted*, *waitlist*, or *accepted*."

The line between Mac's eyebrows deepened. "Not even the *accepted* status?"

"Nope, not until they make a *commitment* deposit, and the status changes to *future start*. Once a student starts classes, their status then changes to *active*. And that's only helpful if Natalie has enrolled in one of the universities."

"How soon can they check for a status change?" Alison asked, glancing up from her note-taking.

"The Fall semester starts soon, so in a few weeks, I'm guessing," Mac supposed. Since her oldest son attended university, she would know better than any of us. "Although the winter semester doesn't get started until January. Statuses then won't change until the first week of December."

"Hope they find her before—you know," Alison said with a swift tilt of her head.

I rolled my shoulders. "Before wings burst out from her back, you mean?"

Alison gave a noticeable shudder, then asked, "Has Mason got his wings yet?"

I rolled my shoulders again, uncomfortable at the idea of wings bursting out of anyone's back. "Yes, it was shortly after he and Jules arrived in Ottawa, Leo told me."

"How did that go?" Alison asked, her face contorting in worry.

"Good… I guess you could say, considering he was aware it could happen. Nic said he had been there to help him through it, but I didn't ask for the traumatic details." I grimaced.

"Ya—no need for that," Alison assured us, her face still a contour of concern.

"Is he the only other *adult* halfling besides Natalie?" Mac asked.

"Not sure, but I'll follow up with them on that." I'd wondered that myself. "I'm looking forward to meeting Mason and Jules."

"You're not the only one. Derek is itching to meet her too," Alison said, knowing as we all did that it had been ages since he'd had a woman in his life.

"Derek is itching to meet who?" Derek's questioning face appeared on the screen.

"Juuules," I confirmed, giving him a smug smile.

"I resemble that comment," he said, giving me an equally smug grin.

"Like I said before, get yourself up to Ottawa and go visit with aaaall the ladies."

"Leo did say I could borrow one of the suites at their place, if I ventured north. Might have to take him up on that offer." Derek rubbed his hand over his jaw as though considering the trip.

"Lynn, did you get a chance to look at the links I sent about the Magic Mirror?" Mac asked, redirecting the two of us. "I sent it to Derek too—told him what happened."

"A bit, but found the information confusing," I confessed. "I recognized the name John Dee from the second link, though."

"I found another reference about a magic mirror as well," Derek stated. "The Tang dynasty 618–907 has a book entitled Record of Ancient Mirrors. Emperor Cao Rui and the Wei Kingdom of China gave several bronze mirrors to Queen Himiko of Wa and were considered rare and mysterious objects. It was described as a *source of honesty* reflecting all good and evil without fault and why Japan considers a sacred mirror called Yata-no-Kagami to be one of the three great imperial treasures."

"Tang dynasty… Yata-no-Kagamiii," Alison said, jotting down notes on what Derek had just spewed out. "Check!"

Derek grinned and then went on. "The first magic mirror to appear in Western Europe was owned by the director of the Paris Observatory, who brought several mirrors back from China, one of which was magical. Later, two engineering professors presented several models to the Royal Society of London they had brought from Japan, calling the artifacts 'open mirrors'. This was the first time expert observations were made regarding their construction. More recently, the Cincinnati Art Museum discovered they had a Chinese magic mirror in their collection, dating back to the 15th or 16th century. It was a small bronze one which had seemed quite unremarkable but was found to have a more complex style of Chinese script and it reflected an image of Amitabha Buddha. But as far as I could find, that's all it did, really."

"Amitabhaaaa Buddhaaa," Alison said aloud once again, adding to her notes from Derek's description. "Go on."

I rubbed my hand over the back of my neck, feeling a headache coming on. "Not sure that applies."

"That was my deduction as well," Derek conceded. Then he went on. "Besides, it's the John Dee one that is more interesting. He, as you know, is the guy who alleged he summoned angels. Dee claimed that for ten years, he and his scryer Edward Kelley received messages through a mirror, one with a wooden case covered in tooled leather. He believed the messengers were angels. Kelley thought they were demons and begged to end the rituals. Dee, with the assistance of Kelley, created a *Holy Table* anchored by *Enochian* sigils, upon which this mirror acted as a portal to commune with the heavens in search of ancient wisdom. The mirror was called the *Obsidian Mirror* and considered an esoteric artifact. But John Dee was not the first person to use this mirror. The mirror itself was made by the Aztecs of South America to communicate with a god called Tezcatlipoca — the harbinger of discord. I couldn't find why, but it was sometime in the 17th-century when art historian Horace Walpole inscribed a handwritten quote on the case, something to do with Samuel Butler's poem Hudibras. He spelled Kelley's name wrong, but let me read it to you,

> *Kelly did all his feats upon*
> *The Devil's Looking Glass, a stone;*
> *Where playing with him at Bo-peep,*
> *He solv'd all problems ne'er so deep*
> *The Black Stone into which Dr Dee used to call his Spirits*

Derek ended the poem, then said, "If what happened with the girls is similar to what John Dee did with that obsidian-holy-table-thing to talk to angels, you may need to speak to Gabriel about the mirror. Since he's the one who made it," Derek suggested. "It's possible he did something to it, maybe to keep an eye on them when he's not around?"

"I can ask, but the mirror incident happened before Gabriel gave the twins their mirror. It was in *my* mirror that Hayley saw Ryley in her bedroom."

Alison raced to finish her notes, then asked me, "Have you talked with Redmond about it?"

"No—was going to, but nothing has happened with the twins since then. Although I could have sworn I saw something in my mirror."

"What?" Mac asked, eyes wide with interest.

I blew out a breath. My head was definitely aching now. "It was after I caught Ryley looking at herself in my mirror. I reminded her they had their own mirror now. It was just a flash—not even sure I saw what I think I saw. Could just have been my imagination—projecting, you know, in correlation with what Hayley had seen in my mirror that first time."

"I highly doubt that," Alison said, knowing my *flashes* usually meant something.

"Mac, are there any spells that can—I don't know, make a mirror a conduit or something," I queried, running the charms of my necklace back and forth along its chain.

"I've read that a lot of magic practitioners use mirrors with their spell casting," Derek interjected.

Mac chewed again at the corner of her thumb nail. "Okay… I'll… look into it."

Chapter 11 

The Group Home, Friday September 2nd, Ottawa

Lyndon pushed through the main door of the group home just as Lane rounded the corner to the entry hall. "Lane, I was hoping to find you here."

"Hey, I was just heading out," Lane said. "I haven't seen you in a while. Where have you been?"

Lyndon checked the time on his cellphone. "Aren't you scheduled to be here another hour?"

"Normally yes, but the family of the young girl I was supposed to be assisting called saying they were taking her out for the afternoon." She shifted her tiny crossbody purse around to rest at her lower back. "Everything okay?"

He shrugged.

"Is it your boss?"

"When isn't it my boss?"

Lyndon stepped forward in Lane's direction as one of the other volunteers came through the door.

Lane gave them a quick wave. *"Did something happen?"* she whispered, leaning in closer to him.

She was close enough he could smell the soft fragrance of her shampoo, and he took in a long, deep breath. "I uhm, just got word he's back in town and he's looking for an update on… a project I'm tending to."

"It's obvious you detest the guy. Why do you work for someone you dislike so much?"

He blew out a frustrated breath. "It's complicated."

"I know, you said that before. How about we go downstairs and talk?"

"Sure," Lyndon said. He had spent several nights daydreaming about their first shared time in his home. Lane had seemed very interested in getting to know more about him and had been fascinated by the array of books he had on his bookshelves. After she'd perused his cookbooks, she had even requested he cook for her. He had thoroughly enjoyed their exchanges and the teasing moments. And it wasn't the first time she'd touched his hair, brushed it away from his face, and though she never recoiled when seeing his scars, this time her touch had felt different, more… *intimate*, as she'd studied his face. Once he'd relaxed, he'd welcomed the closeness, the tender way she had gazed into his eyes. She had even described his eyes as *beautiful*, in fact.

When Lyndon opened the way into his apartment, Lane immediately walked to the far side of the room. "Besides your boss, tell me what else is frustrating you," she said, resting herself down in his armchair.

He liked how tall she was and took in the long length of her as she stretched her legs out on the adjacent ottoman. She was wearing a long-sleeved, raspberry coloured pullover that flattered her dark wavy hair, with an ankle-length denim skirt that split at the knee to show the tops of her brown leather boots. He crossed the short distance to her, then asked, "Do you mind?" He pointed to the ottoman.

"Limited seating, right," she said with an amused laugh. Lane shifted her legs to set her feet on the floor.

"I'll work on that," he said, bending over and moving the ottoman away just enough that he could sit down in front of her.

"Are things not going well with the *project*?" she inquired, setting her small matching leather purse on the floor next to the armchair.

Instead of answering her questions, Lyndon asked, "Has anyone ever told you how Taylor came to live here?"

"All I know is what the residential counsellors told me, that he'd been given back to Children's Services—how the foster parent couldn't handle the extra care, with him being autistic."

Lyndon nodded and relaxed his posture, placing his hands on the tops of his knees. The ottoman was a tad uncomfortable for him, considering his size, but he'd make do until he could set up a better seating arrangement.

Lane tilted her head as though assessing him. "It's obvious you and Taylor have a special bond, and he is safe and happy here with you and the others."

"I like to think so," he said with a grin. "Tell me something good—something happy, about your life."

"Hmmm." Lane brought a finger to her lips as if searching her mind. "My uncles are having their Grand Opening next month, for the new restaurant," she stated, raising that same finger up in triumph. "Would you like to go with me?"

"You mentioned that the last time you were here," he recalled. If his chaotic world allowed it, he would go anywhere with her. "When is it exactly?"

Lane sat forward in the chair. "October 1st, it's a Saturday night," she announced, hands in the air, her expression hopeful.

"I'll have to see…," he began.

"About work. I know," Lane finished for him, slumping back in her seat.

"I'm sorry about that, about how it always gets in the way."

Lane rested her hands in her lap as if in defeat. "It's okay."

"What is your favorite food?" he asked, hoping to shift her mood.

"Oh, that's a tough one." Lane put her finger to her lips again.

Lyndon waited. "How about favorite *type* of food?" he asked then.

She sat forward again, smiling, resting her elbows on her knees. "It's a toss-up between Mexican and Indian, *aaand* Italian." Her smile was full of mischief. "Oh, and I love Japanese food too," she laughed out. "But if we are talking street fair—I'll take Poutine from a food truck every time."

He laughed with her, thrilled he'd been able to improve her disposition. "I'll make note of those and surprise you."

"Okay, I'm game." She laughed again, resting back in the chair once more. Lane adjusted herself in her seat, extending her long legs out to one side of the ottoman.

Noting her discomfort, Lyndon lifted himself up from the ottoman and pushed it further back from the armchair, so she had room to stretch out her legs. "Tell me more about your life," he said, positioning himself back down.

"Like what?" Lane readjusted herself, crossing her legs at the ankles out front this time.

Focusing on the lovely features of her face, he asked, "What is your family like?"

"Well, I have two dads," she said, leaning to one side and resting her left forearm on the arm of the chair. "It's not a secret, but it's not typical either."

"And your… mother?"

"No mom. They used a surrogate."

"I see." He nodded, trying to remain impassive while still fully understanding the use and need for surrogates. He'd been witness to Thaddeus's use of human females for his testing purposes.

"I grew up surrounded by uncles," Lane added, using air quotes to emphasize the word *uncles*.

"What do you mean?" he asked, his question sincere.

"My uncles are essentially… well, they're basically close friends of my fathers'. They have been wonderful to me my whole life, so it felt more natural to just call them *uncle*."

"Sounds quite nice," he said, bending one of his knees, struggling with the comfort of the low seat. "No… *aunts*?"

"Yes… well, sort of. But similar to my uncles—they're close friends of the family."

"Do you have… siblings?" He watched her intently.

"Only child," she said with a one-shoulder shrug. "Now you tell me something about your life."

Lyndon extended his leg again, then bent up the opposite. "I don't have uncles or aunts, or siblings, or parents for that matter," he said, harshly, recognizing too late his tone was in reflection of his painful posture.

She nodded but didn't prod him for more on the family topic. "Do you like to travel?" she asked, as if to keep the focus on him.

"Depends," he said in a softer voice, bringing his extended leg back to meet his bent one, adjusting his position on the seat.

Lane bent her elbow and rested the side of her head against her open hand. "Do you have to travel much with your job?"

"Some." Lyndon placed a hand over the outer edge of the ottoman, leaning to the side in the same direction Lane was.

"Do you make a good living doing what you do?" Her eyes dropped to his feet. "Nice shoes."

"They're new." Interestingly enough, his loafers were the same colour as the leather boots she was wearing. "I didn't always have money—like I do now. I relied on Thaddeus for everything when I first came here. He'd made plans for the future, and I had not."

"Thaddeus is your shitty boss?" she asked, glancing up, her eyes explored his face like she was assessing each of his features.

"Yes," he said, realizing he'd spoken his name aloud to her. "We were more like partners once, and well, he's also Taylor's benefactor. He funds this place."

"What kind of work do you do for this, *Thaddeus*?" She swept a thick wavy length of hair behind one ear, then leaned her cheek against her hand.

Lyndon brought his feet together, letting his knees fall open as he inclined forward. "Mainly research and running errands." He really needed better seating, he scrutinized, leaning his forearms on his open thighs.

Lane mirrored him, resting her forearms on her closed thighs, then tilted forward in her seat to gaze at his face. "Were you hurt on the job?" she asked, her gaze going to the scarred side of his face.

"No," he said, when her gaze remained on his burns. "I haven't always been grotesque."

"Grotesque?" Lane pushed up from leaning on her forearms. "I think you're handsome—thought so the first time I saw you out back in the snow." She leant back again in the chair, crossing her arms. "How do you know Professor Forest?" she asked then.

Lyndon hadn't been expecting that reaction, nor that she would ask about Julianna. He had hoped they were past that screw up of his from the time he'd followed her and confronted her at the university. "I guess you could say we all once worked together." It wasn't a lie.

"Was that when you worked in bio regeneration?" she questioned further.

"Yes," he answered honestly.

Lane tightened her crossed arms. "Did the two of you date?"

"Date?" he said confused, followed by a firm, "No!" when he understood what she was getting at.

"Have you ever been married?" she asked before he could get his bearings.

He frowned, feeling as though he were being interrogated.

"Or maybe I should have asked if you *are* married?" When all he could manage for a response was to stare at her, she asked, "A girlfriend, perhaps?"

He sat up. "No, neither. Are you?" he shot back. He hadn't been comfortable asking that type of question before, but there it was.

"Married, no—not yet."

He swallowed. "Does that mean you are spoken for… *engaged*?"

"No-no." Lane shook her head.

"Boyfriend?" he pushed, question gates open now.

She shook her head again. "What about the caregivers here—are you sweet on anyone?"

"Yes—no, I mean yes," Lyndon said, giving his own head a good shake.

Lane's eyebrows squeezed together.

"I'm interested in someone, but not one of the caregivers," he clarified. "And you, are you *sweet* on anyone here?"

"Maybe?" she said, her eyes still pinched as though he'd said something to piss her off.

His cellphone vibrated in his back pocket, and he pulled it free as it progressed to ringing. "It's…," he tried to say.

"Your boss," Lane said, cutting him off, her lips tightening and emphasizing her scowl.

"Yes," he said sheepishly, before hitting answer and bringing the cell to his ear.

"What is the update from Zuriel?" Thaddeus's demanding voice shouted in his ear.

Lyndon tore his gaze from Lane. "I'm waiting on one," he responded, rubbing his fingers over his forehead. "But I think this lead may have gone dry." He didn't dare look over at Lane. He took the call in her presence, worried she'd leave if he asked to take it in private.

"Well then, get him back here—even if you have to drag him back yourself. The debrief will be at my lab." Thaddeus hung up.

"Lane, I'm so sorry," he said, refocusing back on her and giving the back of his neck a rub.

"Another errand?" she asked, dropping her crossed arms, her annoyed expression morphing to one of disappointment.

She wasn't alone in her disappointment. "Yes," he said, frustrated, "and I have to make another call." This one he needed to make in private.

"I understand," Lane said, leaning over to grab her purse before standing. "I'll see myself out."

Chapter 12 

Cleveland Hospital, September 3rd, St. Lucie County, South Florida

Yesterday, Zuriel had gotten another call from Lyndon, but once again he did not pick up. Lyndon's message this time had sounded urgent, even demanding, that he report in with an update. Zuriel reluctantly hit dial for Lyndon's number.

"Why haven't you reported back in?" came Lyndon's enraged voice.

"I was waiting for something solid to report back," he said in defense. "Had to wait to speak to the condo manager—actually had to make an appointment," he lied. "Pretended to be a P.I. and found out that this William guy sold the condo and moved. I called the manager the next day asking if he knew where the guy had moved—or a forwarding address, maybe. The manager recalled it was the Palmetto Bay area," another lie. The front door guy, the older one, had told him that. "I finally found the new address and went to check things out. No one was home, so I went around and spoke to the neighbors. Most of the neighbors are new to the street and don't seem to know anything about anything. Though one of them stated the older couple across from the house might know something—apparently they've lived there a while. Sadly, when I spoke with the older couple, their recollections were scattered. They had a nurse's aide tending to them, and she told me the neighbors I was looking for were away and were supposed to be back later that day. Unfortunately, the nurse had it wrong. I waited, but no one showed. I had been waiting to speak to them." More lies.

"And?"

"Well, I just got back from speaking to them. Turns out, the owners of the house are not who I expected to find. The guy I spoke with bought the place in 2016 and other than the details on the purchase paperwork, he didn't know anything about the previous owners," Zuriel explained. This part was true. Although, as far as he was concerned, the lead to finding this Lockridge guy was a dead end. In the meantime, he hadn't been wasting his time. Instead he'd been spending time watching and hoping to see that alluring female again. She was all he could think about. He had eventually spotted her again, heading in the direction of the real estate place, and he'd followed her once again, only this time he'd waited outside. When she'd left the agency, she'd been on the phone, and he'd overheard her speaking about moving to a place called St. Lucie where her new job was at Cleveland Hospital. She'd stated to the caller that she had signed her physician's contract back in February, *and* that she had already secured a house there. He didn't know *where* she was moving to—the exact address, but he was determined to find out, so he chose to toss Lyndon another lie. "The new owner did, however, say the seller's real estate agent mention they might have been moving further north, some place called St. Lucie county." Zuriel's plan was to use this ploy of the target moving north as a way for him to stay in Florida. "I'm going to go check it out."

"I don't know, Z," Lyndon expressed. "It might be better to come to Ottawa, research the lead from here."

"Didn't you say the woman worked in the medical field or something? There's a major hospital up there—so let me go check out this lead and get back to you." Zuriel held his breath, even crossed his fingers knowing this was a long shot.

"Fine—but make it quick."

"10-4," Zuriel said, letting his held breath go. He felt guilty for lying to Lyndon, but he wasn't interested in actually tracking down this target or her husband.

In truth, he missed his life among the stars of Pleiades, his role of watching over the ocean's gentle giants and the tiny sea creatures. He hadn't wanted to do this new role, none of them had, but there hadn't been any other options, considering Thadeus had been the only one with a plan. He had considered taking off like Ariadne had, but he believed now he was too ingrained in this life to find another way out. As Lyndon had expressed to him several times, he, too, felt stuck. But he respected Lyndon for the difficult choices he'd made regarding Taylor, his devotion to watch over him now, plus he was the best at what he did, the best tracker of those who had been designated as such. Marcus, on the other hand, was an asshole, always had been, in his mind. He wasn't nearly as monstrous as Thaddeus, but he did enjoy indulging in all that this planet had to offer. However, he suspected Marcus too hated being beholden to Thaddeus and had chosen to make the best of the situation as he saw fit.

Unlike Marcus, Zuriel chose his indulgence wisely, and he had enjoyed his stay in Coconut Grove at Mayfair House Hotel & Garden. The room he had acquired radiated a sense of calm, with its deep soothing tones and subtle interplay of light and shadow. The visual motifs of the furniture echoed the organic lines he'd seen in nature and further reinforced the hotel's connection to the lush surroundings. Even the colours used, the bold teal and orange hues, had reminded him of tropical landscapes. But now he stood waiting on the light grey paved walkway of a plain white hospital, its name displayed overhead in a basic blue and green lettering, the location to where the heart of his attention had taken him. To *her*.

It had been another excruciatingly hot day, and though dusk had begun creeping in, Zuriel still had not seen his Dr. Stone. Then, just as he checked the time on his phone for the hundredth time, the main doors into the hospital spread open, and there she was. Dr. Stone exited alongside another much older woman with short white hair who wore scrubs under a white medical coat. The two continued to the right of the entrance to stand under the covered awning. When he'd gone in earlier through the main entrance, he had noticed a display of photos depicting the new-to-the-hospital physicians. To his luck, one of the photos had been of her. The only reason Zuriel knew her name now was because it had been engraved into a silver placard fixed to the bottom of the photo frame.

Zuriel's cellphone vibrated in his hand, drawing his attention away long enough that he saw it was another call coming in from Lyndon. "Hey, what's up?" he asked, focusing his attention back on the lovely female.

"Where are you?" Lyndon questioned back.

"I'm checking out that lead I told you about." It was a half-truth, he mused.

"Interesting. Looks to me like you're just standing outside the entrance to a hospital."

Zuriel turned to find Lyndon briskly striding his way. "I'm staking out the hospital," he replied into the phone despite the fact Lyndon was now within earshot.

"Looks like you're spying on those two women." Lyndon tilted his chin in their direction. "Neither of which is the woman you were sent here to find."

Zuriel glanced back and forth between his doctor and Lyndon, his brain scrambling for an explanation that would secure need to stay here.

"I'm not sure what it is that you're up to, Z," Lyndon said, "But Thaddeus demanded I bring you back—if there was no update. Is there an update? Because it looks to me like your focus is on other *things*."

Anxious, he said, "Lyndon, you don't understand."

"Then explain it to me."

"You see that woman there," Zuriel began, pointing in the direction of his Dr. Stone.

"I see two women," Lyndon interrupted. "And neither is our target."

"The doctor—the younger one." Zuriel sensed sweat gathering around his collar, a trickle of it escaping to run the length of his back.

"Yes—what about her?" Lyndon said, his tone impatient.

"Dr. Stone—*Grier*. I adore that name. It is resplendent, like her," he rambled out, glancing over at her. "Look at that flawless skin, her gorgeous red hair, those dreamy blue eyes—they convey so much, and that supple, kissable mouth." He turned to look at Lyndon. "She has a dazzling smile. She is simply the most beautiful female on this planet."

"Have you have been watching her this whole time?" Lyndon questioned him.

"Not the whole time. Just after I hit a dead end with the lead you gave me." Zuriel turned to look at her again. "And her voice is so sweet… yet sexy."

"So you've spoken with her?"

"Not exactly, but I have heard her speaking."

"You're infatuated, yet you haven't even had a conversation with this female?"

Ignoring him, Zuriel said, "She's intelligent, funny—very personable. She's warm and kind. Genuine—she really cares about others, and classy—selfless, really. I was amazed by her complete lack of arrogance. Exquisite as she may appear, I find her to be absolutely breathtaking, but nothing compares to how lovely a person she is on the inside. She's the most perfect female I have ever met." It was brutally hot, and Zuriel noticed then that Lyndon had not changed to accommodate the weather in South Florida.

"I won't lie to you, my friend. I grasp the whole enamored thing, but I'm serious when I say you need to come back with me." Lyndon wiped the sweat from his brow.

"Let me just check out this one other lead," Zuriel pleaded.

"Seriously, are you going with that BS again?"

"No, this is a *real* lead on the husband. I found out the guy works for one of the cruise lines here in Florida." What he said wasn't a lie. He'd done another online search and found records of a William Lockridge working for a popular cruise line. He had taken the leap based on something the neighbors, that old couple, had mentioned, but what he wasn't telling Lyndon was the fact he had already checked the cruise line lead. He'd contacted the company and had been told Mr. Lockridge had been transferred to the Japan office and had been there for several years now. He didn't want to tell Lyndon this because he knew he'd either get yanked back to New York or sent to Japan.

"You can come back later—do whatever you want, *after* you speak with Thaddeus," Lyndon said.

"He's back from Brazil?" Zuriel asked. "I got the impression he was in *do-not-disturb* mode."

"He was—but he's back—for how long I don't know. Look, just report to him that the trail ran dry."

Chapter 13 

The Beach House, Sunday September 4th, South Florida

The massive body of a man hung lifelessly in front of me. Thick straps ran around his waist and shoulders, his feet suspended several inches off the ground. Long lengths of chain attached the straps to a hoist mechanism on the ceiling. His upper body is bare, his legs covered by filthy hospital scrubs, the edge of the waistband stained with fresh and dried blood. His bare back is a tragedy of open gashes and boreholes. Blood and pus seep from the hollows. The stench from the wounds coupled with the reek of sweat emanating from his skin is so rancid I cross my forearm over my mouth and nose, pressing into the crook of my elbow. There is a small table next to him. On it are pieces of long thick bone, much like a femur, though the man has both his legs. I step around him and stare up into his magnificent yet bloody and bruised sweat-covered face. A groan and hiss of pain escape his swollen mouth, eyes fluttering open to reveal he still lives. Soft, tiny voices call out from behind me. I turn to see a floor-length mirror on the opposite wall. I approach the mirror only to find it is actually a window and I press my hands to the glass, leaning in. Through the window I see two small figures huddled together in a tiny bed, their mouths open, screaming, their faces panicked. It's then I recognize the tiny figures are my daughters and I call out their names, but no words release from my mouth, only muffled sounds as though I were screaming underwater.

I try again, but nothing comes out. I pound my fists on the glass, but they can't hear me, and then… I hear it… voices… screaming.

Screams yanked me from the horrific visions of my nightmare, and I bolted up in bed, my awareness targeting to the floor-length mirror on the far wall. An image of my daughters huddled together in Hayley's bed reflected back at me. Tiny cries called out then from the other side of the house, stealing my attention away. I flipped back the bedcovers, briefly catching my leg in them as I scrambled from the bed. Down the hall I ran, heading towards the shrieks.

I found the girls together in Hayley's room in the same position I'd seen them reflected in the mirror. "I'm here-I'm here," I reassured them. "What happened?" I sat on the bed and wrapped my arms around both of them.

"We had a bad dream," Ryley whined. She loosened her tight grip from around her sister to curl an arm around my ribcage.

"I just had a bad dream too," I said in a soft voice, hoping to calm them. "What was yours about?"

"The hanging angel," Hayley said, her voice lowering to a whisper. She snaked a tiny arm around the other side of my ribs.

"Same one you did, Mum," Ryley added, giving my side a little squeeze.

"What's going on?" Gabriel asked, appearing next to the bed. "Where's Redmond?"

Redmond rounded through the doorway into Hayley's bedroom. "Did I hear my name?" he asked, oblivious to the goings on.

"Where have you been?" I asked him, doing my best to remain calm for the girls.

"I went to get bagels," he said, stun-faced, holding up the bags from the bagel shop. "What happened?" he asked, finally recognizing something was clearly wrong.

"Bad dreams," I said, letting go of my grip on the girls and altering my position to hold their hands. "Com'on girls, let's get some food into us—it'll help chase away the icky dreams."

Filled to their tiny brims with bagels and cream cheese now, we released the girls out to the backyard with Gabriel and the dogs to play. Any remaining imagery of menacing dreams now vanquished, I redirected my attention to Redmond. "I had another one of those dreams. And the girls had the *same* one, Ryley told me."

"You all had the same dream? That's never happened before—has it?" Redmond questioned, clearing the mess from the bagel bonanza.

"Not that I recall." I picked at the barely eaten bagel on my plate.

"Was it a replay of that first dream or something else?" Redmond pointed at my plate. "You gonna eat that?"

"No—my stomach doesn't want it, sorry." I handed him the plate. "The dream was similar and different. But there was something else," I said, leading him through the experiences I'd had with the girls and the mirror in our room, explaining how I saw the same thing again in my nightmare. "I told Mac and the others about the first incident," I confessed.

"Why didn't you tell *me* about the mirror thing?" he demanded, shutting the dishwasher door harder than needed.

"Didn't want to worry you—plus I thought maybe Mac could find something to help explain it."

He shoved the bagel bags into the recycling bin under the counter and then slammed the bin drawer shut. "Like what?"

"Something magic related—I don't know," I said, getting up from my seat at the table to go over to him. "I'm sorry—I shouldn't have kept it from you." I wrapped my arms around him, pressing my cheek against his sternum.

He returned the embrace, his arms enveloping me. "Could this have something to do with the mirror Gabriel made for them?"

I loosened my grasp and stared up at him. "Maybe, but it happened before that, though there is only one way to find out." I stepped back and called out, "Gabriel!"

He appeared in the kitchen a second later. "Everyone seems to be fine now," he informed us, smiling happily, and pointing a thumb over his shoulder at the backyard. "What? Did something else happen?" His joyful expression turned grim.

"That mirror you made the girls," Redmond said. "Did you do anything to it?"

His grim expression switched to one of confusions. "What are you talking about?"

"He means did you do any kind of angel protection whammy on it?" I clarified.

"No—of course not. Why would I?" he asked, hurt showing across his face as though he'd been assaulted.

"Lynn saw them—the twins, through the mirror in our room," Redmond said, before explaining the first occurrence and then the latest. "When she woke from her nightmare, she saw the twins in Hayley's bed reflected in the mirror—the same position she found them in Hayley's room."

Gabriel raised his hands in surrender. "It's just a normal mirror, I swear it," he insisted, turning his hands palm up in submission.

"How do you explain what's happening, then?" I asked.

Gabriel dropped his hands to his sides. "I can't—but I also wouldn't lie to you, Lynn."

"I know, I'm sorry," I said, coving my face briefly with my hands. "I just don't understand what is happening."

"What about your friends? Did you tell them about the mirror—what happened, I mean?" Gabriel glanced back and forth between Redmond and me.

"They know about the first time," I shared. "Mac sent me a few links about magic mirrors, but nothing I read fit. Derek tried to explain some stuff about John Dee using one to conjure angels, but...." I shook my head. "I asked Mac to explore spells that use mirrors."

Redmond drew a hand over his jaw. "Perhaps it has something to do with the twins' growing abilities."

"It is certainly possible. The challenge with their capabilities is that we don't have any reference to humans like them, or *you,* for that matter," Gabriel explained. "But I'll look into it—ask the others if they have any thoughts on what could be happening."

I nodded, and Gabriel was gone without another word. Redmond just stared at me, and I shrugged. A text chime emanated from my cellphone on the kitchen island. I grabbed it up to see the text was from my new doctor friend. "It's a text from Grier. Says she just wanted to let me know she's officially moved in and on call now at the hospital." Her text had brightened my mood, but then the phone rang in my hand. "Leo," I announced to Redmond before answering it. "Hi, please tell me you have something wonderful to share." I put my cellphone on speaker.

"Not exactly… unless knowing the whereabouts of Thaddeus is considered wonderful," he said.

I let out a weighted sigh. "This is too much."

"Did something happen, Leo?" Redmond questioned.

"My contact at the Celaeno building just informed me that Thaddeus is back in Ottawa."

Redmond glanced at me, then asked, "You have someone on the inside?"

"A civilian. She's part of the gardening crew who takes care of the plants in the greenhouse."

"Wasn't Nic watching for him in Brazil?" Redmond further questioned.

"He checked out the facility, but there was no sign of Thaddeus having been there, and no one has seen him or any of his minions in months. If he *was* in Brazil, he wasn't at his facility."

"Something told me he might be back in Ottawa," I said then.

"Something?" Leo questioned.

Redmond leaned his knuckles on the island, bending his arms and hovering over the cellphone. "Lynn had another one of those dreams," he said. "And the twins had the same dream she did."

"When was this?" he inquired.

When Redmond glanced at me again, I nodded for him to go on. "Last night—early this morning rather," he said.

"Do you think… I mean… is it possible… could that angel be in there now?" I asked, speaking up then. "I know he wasn't previously, but… I considered what happened before was possibly a premonition, but now with the twins dreaming about him… maybe Thaddeus has him in his lab now."

"I can't fathom who it could be," Leo said. "My brothers are all accounted for."

"Has to be one of the Earthbound, with those gouges in his back," I expressed, my upper back suddenly aching.

"Have you seen Purah?"

I raised my eyebrows. "No, why?"

"No reason." There was a pause. "Other than she might have some insight for us if she's been traveling to the other facilities likes she sometimes does." There was another pause. "I'm not sure what to tell you, Lynn, Redmond, but rest assured, we'll keep watch."

"Keep us in the loop," Redmond said.

"Will do. And let me know if you hear from Purah," Leo said, ending the call.

Leo seemed a tad preoccupied with wanting to know where Purah was, I mused. But right now, I didn't have time to entertain the idea. "I need to let the ladies know Thaddeus is back," I said, typing out a group text to Mac, Olivia, and Alison,

> *Just heard from Leo that the big-bad is back in town.*

Olivia was the first to respond, though all she wrote was,

> *OMG!*

I sent another text, this one directed at Mac,

> *Mac, did you find anything about spells and mirrors yet?*

Mac sent a brief response stating she'd not found anything like what I'd experienced, then sent a summary of what she had found,

> *Nearly every culture in the world attributes some superstition or myth to mirrors. In modern wicca, practitioners use mirrors for introspection, glamour spells, repelling negativity, scrying, and sometimes as a gateway to alternate dimensions.*

Alison texted next,

> *I recorded this in more detail for the records. But I'm guessing something mirror related happened. Am I right?*

I paused briefly to gather my thoughts, then wrote,

> *Yes, but this time it was in a nightmare. I had another one of those dreams this morning, but the alarming thing was that the twins both had the same dream I did.*

Olivia responded immediately with,

Please don't ask me to go back to that facility. I'm not comfortable with any of this and I don't want anything to do with someone who could do such a thing as you described.

I had anticipated something like that from Olivia, and I responded with,

I understand. And we won't.

I created a new separate text, sending it just to Mac and Alison, saying,

I'll circle back with the two of you if I find out more information.

Mac sent a peace sign emoji back, and I got a thumbs up one from Alison. I set my phone back on the island and looked over at Redmond, who had been waiting quietly as I'd texted my friends.

"How did they respond to the news?" Redmond asked, arms folded.

"Olivia was freaked out, of course." I rolled my eyes. "Mac sent a summary of what she found on mirror spells, and Alison said she made a record of it, but unfortunately nothing relates to what occurred," I shared with him before turning and heading off across the living room to our bedroom.

Stepping into our walk-in closet, I promptly realized I was going to need something to step up on if I was going to get what I wanted. Returning to the bedroom, I spied the step ladder I'd used the other day to adjust the spring mechanism on the window blinds. "Bingo," I said, snatching it up and hustling back into the closet.

Once on the ladder, I reached in behind the stack of photo albums and pulled free the gun safe that was hidden there. When Redmond entered the closet, I already had the safe unlocked and my gun out of its confines.

"Now you're going to learn how to shoot?" he questioned.

Not answering, I drew the gun from the soft pocket pistol holster, checked the safety was on, then turned it over in my hands. It was definitely smaller than Redmond's gun. I flicked on the laser and pointed it at my shoe rack. The memory of Kris's words echoed in my head, *"Wherever the red dot is, a bullet will follow."* Despite feeling more comfortable with the gun's weight, shooting the gun still wasn't something I was ready for. I shut off the laser and ran my fingers over the gun's textured grip. "No, although I *am* going to ask Den to come over to work with the girls—teach them some self-defense," I told him, before sliding the gun back into the holster.

Chapter 14 

It was one thing for me to have these disturbing dreams, but it was unacceptable for the twins to suffer the same fate, nonetheless the girls tried to assure me they were fine. I knew they were resilient for their ages, having had to navigate all that came with being *special* and part of our little secret group. And it *was* possible I was overreacting to the latest enhancement to their *capabilities*, but I'd gone ahead anyway with asking Den to come over Sunday afternoon to work with the twins on self-defense.

The session with Den commenced with him saying to the girls the main thing with staying safe was *prevention*, so they needed to keep aware of their surroundings. He told them that most attackers are looking for an easy target and so they needed to be as difficult a target as possible. Next he'd said if someone approaches them from the front, the first thing to do is always step back. That it creates space between you and them, so they can't get close enough to cover their mouth and block them from calling out. He added that if they *attempt* to grab you, that they need to shout *Stop* or *Fire,* and to shout the same with each of the moves he was going to show them. The reason, he had explained, was to draw as much attention as you can, and these words work much better than simply calling out for *help*, and emphasized the key was to escape. He then pushed on with showing them some moves. First had been how to get loose if someone grabbed their arm, demonstrating to swing that arm away quickly and twirling your hand out from the opening of the person's hand. Then it was on to what to do if the stranger has both arms, demonstrating again with stretching out one arm, make a fist, then using the other hand to grab that fist, jerking both arms up hard and fast. After that, he instructed them on a few harder moves, showing what to do if someone grabs their shoulders from the front, starting with a groin kick and then do a double hammer strike down, which uses gravity more than muscle. And then last, he showed them what to do if they are grabbed from behind, teaching them the bearhug release move using their foot to stomp on the assailant's foot, slipping under their arms on the same side they stomped, then circling behind them and pushing them forward with all their force, before turning and running away. The move, he stated, was to get them off balance while creating more distance and time to escape.

My hope had been that they would have some *other* beneficial skills, and I might have less anxiety about their safety knowing they had learned the skills. Nevertheless, my worry had remained. I had even tried several attempts at meditating my stress away during their training, but I had failed each time to stay focused on myself while my daughters were learning to thwart an attacker. And instead of feeling they were safer after, I was now concerned over the possible circumstances that would force them into using these new skills. I had, however, gotten up the nerve to ask Den about his or the others having to involve humans in their lives, the top-secret part.

Den had conveyed that the only humans who knew about them had *needed* to know. Like with Leo, he had become exceptionally close with Max and Julian while working with them, and they'd built a trust through his business and of course later with Lane, who had been integrated into the secret world as a child much like the twins. Although, she and her fathers did not have any otherworldly abilities. I also questioned him about if they were going to integrate Jana into *the knowing*, and he had said it would be a matter of *trust* like with the others. He added that Jana had accepted the fake backstory, and understood the need for secrecy, but that only time would tell if she could handle the truth. I'd held back asking about what would happen if Kris and Jana wanted to have a future together because, similar to Den and Gavin, it would be the same issues with the slow aging and eventual heartbreak. The last thing I had said on the topic had been what Redmond had suggested to me, about how it would be good for Jana to have other humans there to soften the blow, should the time come.

My cellphone began ringing as I pulled into the driveway. "Hey, Derek," I said, hitting answer on the phone before rolling to a stop under the carport.

"Hey yourself, how's it going?"

"Just got home," I said, unlatching my seatbelt. "Need to change into my sparring clothes and head over to train with Den."

"How's the training going?"

"Really good. Haven't felt this fit in—well, ever." I grabbed up my small purse from the passenger seat. "Have you ever taken any martial art classes?"

"No, but I'd like to try Tai Chi since it's not just for self-defense."

"Ben teaches Tai chi," I said, remaining where I was in the A/C of the running car.

"Ya, I know. He explained to me that the slow intentional movements are a form of gentle exercise with moving meditation that benefits your mental and physical health."

"Sounds good to me. Maybe I should ask him to show me next time he's at South Haven, to help with stress, ya know."

"Nice balance with the other training too, I would imagine. I heard Darius and Lily went up to see Luc and Dunya for the long weekend.

"Yup," I agreed, draping my purse cross-bodied over my shoulder. "Lily mentioned to Redmond they were going. Asked if we wanted to go with them."

"How come you didn't go?"

"We promised the girls a family weekend, and Monday we spent the day at the beach, did a BBQ dinner. Then it was early to bed for all of us, but Derek... you can't just be calling to find out how we spent the weekend." I turned the car's A/C to low. "What's up?"

"Guess where I'm calling you from," he prompted, like a little kid.

I paused to imagine where he could be, but I had nothing. "Tell me."

"I'm in Ottawa—at North Haven. That's how I know about Ben teaching Tai Chi, we talked about it this morning. He gave me a tour of Ottawa, and we went by the new restaurant, too—it's not open for business yet, but I got to meet Kris and Jana. Everything seems copasetic with them so far in case you were wondering. Mason was at the restaurant too. Conversation with him was fascinating. He uses a voice app on his phone—and you know I love a clever app. Aaaand… I met *Jules*. She's taking me on a tour of the university campus tomorrow."

"Wow—lucky you!" I teased, but he was lucky. I hadn't even been up to see the restaurant yet. "Have you heard any news on Natalie— does Jules know if she's registered at any of the universities for the fall semester?"

"Funny you should ask—I inquired about the same thing, but no. Anyone who would have registered for Fall would have shown as having a *future start* status, she told me. She'll check again closer to December for the Spring semester. I think she's sweet on me—by the way. Told me how much she likes a man with brains."

"I bet she does," I said with a chuckle. "I haven't even gotten to meet her yet—lucky duck."

"Ha!"

"I'm assuming there's more as to why you're up in Ottawa, yes?" I checked the time on the car's dash.

"You're aware I've been working with Leo and Nic on the findings from the notebook, the experiments, right?"

"Yes, and?"

"Well, the most recent entries focus mainly on DNA."

"For like what? Familial DNA matches? You know that's how they found more info on Natalie's parents and the aunt, from one of those ancestry sites." I shut off the car. "Is that what you're getting at?"

"Uhm, kind of…," Derek said, pausing. I heard the sound of typing on a keyboard. "The notes mention genetic classifications and ancestral groupings within a population."

"Okay." I wasn't okay. I was lost. And it was starting to get hot in the car even with being in the shade of the carport.

"The notes refer to haplogroups typically defined by shared, inherited genetic markers or mutations. They can be traced through the analysis of mitochondrial DNA for maternal haplogroups and the Y chromosome for paternal haplogroups. A haplotype is a group of alleles in an organism that is inherited together from a single parent. Most organisms contain genetic material inherited from both parents."

"Oh my gawd—here we go," I said, opening the car door. "Clarity please, Derek."

"This kind of data helps researchers and genealogists understand the genetic relationships and ancestral origins of individuals and groups."

"Not that it makes things any clearer, but why do you think Thaddeus would be interested in this?" I sure wasn't.

"Leo thinks maybe his testing on halflings is not yielding any valuable results and now he may be *tracking* the migration of the Earthbound and their offspring."

"Frightening, but it makes sense." I shut the car door and leaned against it.

"He seems to be quite the supervillain."

"He's just a horrifying monster, if you ask me."

"That he is."

I let out a heavy sigh, then shuddered at the memory of the lab from my dreams.

"Lynn, you had brought up the question as to why he wasn't working on reproduction versus childhood lung diseases, considering his goal of creating a superior race."

"Ya." The alarm on the car *beeped* when I hit the lock button on my key fob. "Why pretend to help sick kids with lung diseases—and how does that further his cause?"

"Nic suspects it may have something to do with the similarities between the Earthbound and actual birds, how they and their wings function together."

"Mac and Olivia mentioned the Ottawa facility had an aviary, which was really weird."

"Right. The assumption is he is experimenting on the birds, too."

"Figures. The sick bastard."

"Do you know what happens to a bird if their wings are removed?"

"No." Sweat was beginning to bead on my forehead and upper lip. "Do birds need their wings in order to live? Maybe I don't want to know the answer."

"A bird's lungs are surprisingly unlike those of most other land vertebrates and are small compared with those of mammals. But because of the design and physiological complexity, they are among the most efficient on the planet. Their wings are connected to numerous inflatable air sacs that branch from the lungs into the muscles and even into the bones. And unlike mammals who breathe in and out, a bird's lungs inflate and deflate like bellows, causing a constant flow of oxygen in the lungs. They actually breathe in twice to complete one full respiration cycle, but I won't go into that."

"Great..," I started to say, but Derek went on.

"In comparison with you and I, who rely on a thick, muscular diaphragm to power our breath, the air sacs in birds are partly pumped by the action of hinged ribs and the furcula. The wings beat, the lungs compress and then expand, increasing air circulation during flight."

"Furcula?"

"It's the wishbone."

I wiped my sweaty face on the shoulder part of my sleeve. "So does that means they can or can't survive?"

"Well, birds don't *need* wings to eat, drink, or move around, only to fly. However, suffering a severed wing can be harmful to its physical and mental health. And Nic said that halflings are often born with physical complications, frequently lung issues being one of them, so it's possible it's associated with the whole latent wing thing."

"Did you find out anything else?"

"I'm trying to decipher more. There's a whole section on Epigenetics."

"Oh gosh—summarize, please." I stepped free of the car to allow the sea breeze coming from the beach swirling through the carport to pass over and cool me.

"It's basically the study of how our behaviors and environment can change the way our genes work. Your genes don't change, but how they function can. You follow?"

"Yup—gotcha."

"It's just a theory, but I think it all links back to the migration idea and how the different environments they encountered may have impacted the Earthbound."

Chapter 15 

The Celaeno Building, Saturday Night, October 1ˢᵗ, Ottawa

Lyndon arrived on the roof of the Celaeno facility to swiftly descend the stairs leading down to the building's top most floor. From there, he took the private elevator directly down to the lowest level that opened up across from the entrance to Thaddeus's personal lab next to the emergency exit stairwell that led up to the greenhouse. The only other way down here was through the greenhouse on the main level via these stairs.

When Lyndon had flown here with Zuriel almost a month ago, his fellow tracker had appeared in good spirits, as though focused on his return to South Florida. Lyndon, on the other hand, had been feeling a deep trepidation over his bringing Zuriel to see Thaddeus. He'd had to report something back to Thaddeus in preparation for their arrival and had texted his boss, stating that Zuriel had taken a chance on a lead. One he'd thought would bring him to where this woman had moved to. Lyndon had added that Zuriel had indeed found a woman who had relocated there. It was just the wrong woman, so unfortunately, the lead had not panned out.

Lyndon knew the truth. Zuriel had purposely followed the wrong woman north simply over pure fascination with the female. He understood the heightened interest. He had the same feelings for Lane. Although, he knew Lane—had known her for some time, and they had spent many hours together. She wasn't some woman who had simply caught his eye, nor had she been someone Lyndon had been watching from afar.

When Zuriel had stood before Thaddeus that day, he'd asked, *"What have you been doing all this time?"*

"I took the initial information Lyndon provided for me and," Zuriel had answered, scrambling further through the details of all he had discovered and the steps he had taken which had brought him to his most recent location.

Thaddeus had ignored Zuriel's explanation, stating, *"Lyndon informs me you were stalking some woman, the wrong woman."*

Lyndon had tried to help by explaining, *"Zuriel had only just discovered it was the wrong human when I had arrived to meet him."*

Thaddeus hadn't bought the excuse. *"This feels more like you have been wasting my time rather than following any worthy lead. Pursuing some worthless human female. He's hiding something,"* Thaddeus had mumbled to Lyndon then, before demanding, *"Leave him with me."*

When Lyndon had left the lab that day, the last words Thaddeus had uttered had been, *"Are you familiar with cellular regeneration?"*

And now as he swiped his security card over the panel next to the lab's door, the same unease he'd felt then was back, only this time its intensity had magnified tenfold. The security lock released, and Lyndon yanked open the door.

Thaddeus was nowhere in view, so Lyndon moved forward, his long strides taking him to the far side of the lab. He pushed aside one of the rolling privacy panels only to find more of the same—*nothing,* only a grouping of black cords that led along the floor into an open door on the right. A weak groan came then through the open door of the darkly lit room. Lyndon stepped over the cables, following them further to the doorway. He could already smell the rank stench of urine and body odor even before he crossed the door's threshold.

To the right of the entrance, two medical staff in white coats were positioned next to monitoring equipment and a portable patient X-ray. One of the medical staff was examining vials blood while the other made notes on a clipboard. The stench of something foul pulled his attention to the left.

In front of him hung a beaten angel, his friend… Zuriel. He was suspended several inches off the ground by straps around his shoulders and waist. Lyndon glanced up to see the straps were attached to chains hanging down from a hoist mechanism fixed to the ceiling. Zuriel's upper body was bare, his legs covered by hospital scrubs, the waist was stained with both dried and fresh blood. Next to him, in a tray on a small rolling table, were pieces of severed bone. Lyndon shut his eyes tight, then swiftly opened them again, stepping forward to stare into Zuriel's bruised and sweat-covered face. Bloodstains covered his cheeks. He was so gaunt, undoubtedly he'd been given little to no nourishment or fluids.

Thaddeus was holding Zuriel's head up by a fist of his hair. His eyes were closed, and his mouth hung slack as though he were unconscious. "When he wouldn't tell me what he found out—what he'd been hiding, I threatened him with taking his wings." Thaddeus yanked his head farther back. "I warned him—even asked him *do you want to lose your wings, lover-boy?* He finally told me." Thaddeus pointed to the wall behind Lyndon.

Above the doorway were two magnificent white wings, their tips edged in black feathers. Jabbed through the center of each wing were long metal rods that speared them to the wall. At the proximal end of each wing, the section that normally attached the owner's body, were the bloody remnants of fleshy bits that still clung to the bony protrusions of the wings' humerus.

Lyndon immediately stepped around Zuriel's hanging body to see open gashes and boreholes through which blood and what looked like pus seeped. The smell of both, along with the pungent scent of sweat, emanated from his skin. Lyndon wanted desperately to cover his nose and mouth to block the stench, but he remained stoic for his friend. Lyndon stared over at Thaddeus.

As though indifferent to Lyndon's rage, Thaddeus began removing the bloodstained coveralls he was wearing to reveal black trousers and a black linen short-sleeved shirt. "I know about Japan," he said, handing off the filthy jumpsuit to one of the medical staff.

"And… you took… his wings… anyway," Lyndon said through clenched teeth, turning back to the hanging angel.

"The fool infuriated me. I detest having my time wasted." Thaddeus adjusted the belt on his pants.

"He'll be waking up again soon…," one of the medical staff said, "…despite using a sedative heavy enough to take down an elephant."

"Will he heal?" Lyndon knew that severing the wings of his kind could kill them because it also cut off their heart and lung function, but Thaddeus must have found a way to remove them without further damage to the systems.

"Get out!" Thaddeus commanded, shooing the two medical underlings out of the room.

The two rushed out of the room without saying another word.

"He's a liability," Thaddeus said then. "Never has followed my orders—not from the beginning," he added cooly, smoothing out a tiny crease on the collar of his shirt.

Lyndon's jaw tightened at the blatant lie. Zuriel has always followed orders. He just hadn't followed them this time… because of this female. He didn't dare voice his thoughts out loud knowing how Thaddeus felt about all females.

"It was your error in judgment with sending him there instead of taking care of it yourself. Once again, this has been a complete and utter waste of my precious time." Thaddeus brushed invisible lint from his slacks. "I've already contacted my Japan facility. Sebastian is sending tracker Lazarus to follow up on the lead. And unless you see this *Westlake* woman here in Ottawa or know her exact and confirmed whereabouts, I don't want to hear from any of you failures." Placing his hands on his hips, he said, "Now, take this disaster-of-a-tracker away. Drop him off at the doorstep of that trivial human female. I never want to see his face ever again."

Lyndon watched through the open doorway as Thaddeus exited the small room and beelined it for the exit. He hadn't noticed earlier, but it appeared Thaddeus already had a packed bag waiting for him at the door, along with some fancy portable fish tank with Brutus already set to go.

"See that any perishables are removed from the fridge in my penthouse," he called back, stopping next to the lab's door. "I'm returning to Brazil at once and won't me back for some time." At those words, he grabbed up Brutus and his luggage and left.

When the lab door suctioned shut, Lyndon dashed from the room into the lab space to rip the bedding off one of the hospital beds. Draping it over his shoulder, he returned to the room, frantically searching for the controls to lower Zuriel down. He located them next to the light switch at the entrance to the small room. Gingerly, he lowered the wounded angel to within reach such that he could remove the strappings before wrapping the bedsheet around him. Then he carried Zuriel, cradled in his arms like a baby, out to one of the hospital style beds. He laid him face down, then began desperately rummaging through the cabinets and drawers in search of any medical supplies.

All he found were two large absorbent compress dressings and a basic first aid kit. In it were several adhesive bandages of assorted sizes, sterile gauze pads, adhesive cloth tape, antiseptic wipes along with hydrocortisone ointment packets, and one roll of gauze bandage. There were also two packets of aspirin in the first aid kit and four cold compresses, the kind you crack to make cold. Lyndon tossed all of it into a white garbage bin liner, not knowing what he might need later.

Other than the few measly items he'd found, the lab had been completely cleared out. Even Thaddeus's trophy bone cabinet had been emptied, his prized possessions relocated elsewhere. "It will have to do," he said to his unconscious friend. "Now, to get you up to the penthouse."

Even unconscious, Zuriel let out an agonizing *groan* as Lyndon carefully rested him down on Thaddeus's massive bed, this time on his side facing him. Lyndon dumped the medical supplies out on the bed next to Zuriel, then did his best to patch him up. Lyndon checked several times that Zuriel's heartbeat remained strong, and his breathing was a steady in and out, before leaving his side in pursuit of more provisions.

In the kitchen fridge he discovered one remaining glass bottle of the overpriced water Thaddeus insisted on having, its contents a mere inch of water left. Not that tap water wouldn't do for thirst, but there'd been no other food in the fridge nor the cupboards to appease hunger should Zuriel wake. He couldn't risk leaving to acquire food, so in desperation he checked the under-counter garbage bin.

Lyndon let out a sigh of relief considering it was the one and only time he was thankful Thaddeus was such a pretentious bastard. In the bin he found a generous, still wrapped refrigerated gift basket from some medical equipment sales rep.

He took the package back with him and set it on the floor next to the low bed. Unwrapping it he found that the gift offering contained boxes of assorted fancy crackers, several varieties of expensive still cool cheese both hard and soft, jars of expensive cocktail olives, individual packages of salted and unsalted almonds and cashews, and even a collection of high quality Swiss chocolate. "You will eat like a king when you wake," he said to his resting friend, then left his side once again to see what still remained in Thaddeus's barren domicile.

In the closet, the drawers and shelves were empty, though he did find a pair of jeans and a long-sleeved grey cotton pullover in the laundry basket. They appeared unused and only slightly rumpled as though Thaddeus had tried them on and then instead of returning them to the wardrobe had simply tossed them in the hamper. Unfortunately, there were no abandoned socks or shoes, so Zuriel would have to remain barefoot. *Whatever*. What he'd found would do perfectly to clothe Zuriel once he could get him out of here safely.

Lastly, Lyndon checked the bathroom, but all that had been left regarding pain meds was Vicodin, its expiration from several years ago, back when Thaddeus had tried it for recreational purposes. Lyndon too had used the stuff after he'd endured the sulfur burns on his face, but he hadn't liked how it made him feel. It did impact his ability to feel pain, although he'd had to take several at once to get any relief, and instead of concurrently bringing about feelings of contentment, relaxation, and overall wellbeing that the average person would feel, in his case it had induced the sensation of being detached from his surroundings, as well as nausea and vomiting, which were not a great combination. However, for Zuriel, it was all they had.

Returning to the bedroom area, Lyndon set the bottle of pain meds on the nightstand, then lowered himself to his knees next to the bed.

He leaned over to check Zuriel's breathing and heart rate again. Both were strong and steady. Using the loose end of the bed sheets Zuriel was wrapped in, Lyndon gently wiped away the lingering sweat and blood from the angel's now peaceful face. "I'm going to get you some help. Better help than I can give."

Chapter 16 

"Hey, *Aunt* Lynn," Lane greeted me when our video chat connected. "Did you guys do anything for Thanksgiving yet?"

"We were hoping our friends would be coming down to celebrate with us since flights from Ottawa to here are cheap at this time versus U.S. Thanksgiving in November," I said, noticing she too was sitting on her bed, like I was. "We had even gotten two boxes of wine and a few cases of beer in hopes of them visiting." Darius had been at us to get everyone to come down, and we'd hoped to have them here this past spring, but with us going to Iceland and finding Kris, it had been put on the back-burner. "We tried to coordinate for them to come down for Canadian Thanksgiving since we could make it a long weekend visit, but it was kiboshed when Alison's sister informed her she was coming from Calgary for it. Mac, we thought, might come down with Don and the boys, but her sister is hosting this year and since their parents are slowing down faster than any of them would like, Mac felt it best they stay local. I can't blame her. Olivia and her crew were all driving to Kingston for Thanksgiving to be with her sister and family. It is the year for sisters, apparently." I smirked, adding, "We even tried to coordinate for my brother James to come down to see me—*his* sister, but he'd surprised us on his last video chat by holding up a new black lab mixed puppy. Who he had adopted from the local shelter, and had jokingly named her Nightmare, *Night* for short, since she was a nightmare with all her chewing, saying he didn't want to leave her so soon." Everyone had busy lives, but we would figure out some way to get them here for a visit one way or another.

"I'd love to get a dog," Lane tossed out. "Would be nice to have one to hike through the Gatineau hills with."

"Oh, I really miss the patchwork of autumn leaves. We don't really get seasons," I said, admiring the rust-coloured sweater Lane was wearing, wishing we had more cold days to wear the ones I owned. "Is there a reason you haven't gotten a dog?" I hated to think of life without ours. "We've got two here that you can always come visit."

"I need to get myself down there—maybe once school is done. That's a big part of why I don't have any pets—wouldn't be fair to them with my current schedule. Someday though. And I'll reward myself in the meantime with a little vacation, down to South Haven, once school is done." She tucked a section of her wavy hair behind her ear.

"Sounds like a plan."

"So will you still be doing a Thanksgiving dinner?" She lifted her cellphone into view, briefly checking it for something.

"Ya, we're doing it tonight, sort of. It'll be just our four, plus Lily and Darius, of course. Lily usually spends major holidays with us, and she has adopted the Canadian Thanksgiving. Darius is always happy to be fed. But Redmond is doing pizza, not the traditional meal this year. That reminds me, I need to talk to your uncles about the plans for Thanksgiving with Redmond's family in New York City next month."

"Right, you get a second Thanksgiving with being in the U.S."

"A second chance to eat too much food too," I laughed out. "What about you—dinner with the dads?"

Lane tipped her head from side to side. "We're doing family dinner tonight too, along with Jules and Mason, and Kris and Jana, and anyone else who happens to be here. My dads always make too much food, just in case."

"Better more than not enough with that crew." I grinned.

"Truer words," Lane said, laughing then.

"Speaking of Kris and Jana, how are things with them?"

"Interesting," Lane said. "Kris took her shopping, got her all sorts of clothes and accessories and things she would need for a longer stay, since she hadn't really brought much with her. Jana told me she didn't like him spending so much money on her, but I reminded her that Uncle Kris was loaded and not to fuss over him paying for things."

"That can be tough for someone as independent as Jana."

"I can't wait to finish school and get a job—have more independence. I have a lot of freedom, but I still have to rely on my dads for money while I'm in school. And I hate it." Lane fiddled with the ear her hair was tucked behind.

"Count yourself lucky they've got you covered. Student loans suck to pay back."

"I know I'm fortunate to have parents who are able to support me. I don't take it for granted, but I still long for my independence."

"And you should want that—means you're not a freeloader. Jana probably feels like a freeloader, if you think about it."

"Ya, I can see that. I think she has been trying to give back by cooking. She and Julian have prepared some delicious meals together for all of us. And she spends her days with Kris at the restaurant working pretty hard, from what I hear."

"Does she seem happy? Does he?"

"Disgustingly so." Lane laughed again. "They spend most evenings together after they get home. And she and I have had some great talks too. You know how much I've longed for another female in the house."

"I do." I nodded. "So, do you think Jana will stay?"

"I'm guessing so—hoping so. However, I am finding it challenging to keep *secrets* from her. It's getting harder with Lyndon too." Lane pulled at her earlobe.

"I've wondered about that. How is your time with him going?"

"I'm not sure." Lane frowned. "Last evening I was helping at the group home for the residents' Thanksgiving, spending time with Taylor and the others who weren't out with family, and I had hoped to see Lyndon there for it, but he hadn't shown."

"Have you had much time with him lately?"

"Before that, yes, and we always have a terrific time together. I've even been down to the lower level where he has his apartment. You should see his chef's kitchen—it's spectacular."

"Wow, really?" A tracker who likes to cook. Interesting, I mused.

"Really!" she said with excitement, tucking loose strands of hair behind both ears this time. "And he loves to read. Has a whole wall of books. I wish you could see how he treats Taylor. They are so sweet together, especially when he reads to him."

"Those things I'm surprised to hear, considering his persona of being mainly dark and broody."

"And he's made it very clear that he does not like his boss, nor does he like working for him."

"Good!" I said, cringing at the thought of how horrid it would be to work for someone as evil as Thaddeus.

"He even shared a little about his previous work," Lane added, using air quotes for *previous*. "He said it was research on the biology of regeneration, but obviously I know the real details. Jules explained to me what he did before coming to Earth." Lane let out a sigh. "I feel like he wants to tell me things—private things, the secrets he keeps, the reality of his life, you know. And I feel the same way."

"I understand your desire to tell him your truth, but you can't, Lane."

"I know." Lane shook her head once. "Oh, and he's changed his appearance too since we've become friends."

"His appearance?"

"Nothing too drastic, just cleaned himself up. I've made a point to complement him, his clothes, his hair, you know, supporting the changes he's making. I think he wants to make a good impression on me." She played with her earlobe again.

"You'll have to take his photo—send it to me. I don't even know what the guy looks like, other than the fact he has a burn scar on his face."

"It's a bad burn—but just the one side." Lane lifted a hand to her own cheek. "He used to try to hide it using his long hair. But I can tell he feels more comfortable with me, and he keeps his hair back when I'm around now." Lane frowned again.

"What is it?"

"Lyndon was supposed to come to the grand opening at the restaurant too, but never showed then either."

"Do you know why he didn't make it to either event?"

"My guess is because of that fabulous boss of his."

"Gah!" I cringed a second time at the mention of Thaddeus. "Leo said he vanished again, so how's about we skip that topic?" I gave her an exaggerated, toothy grin. Leo's contact at the Ottawa facility had heard through rumblings of the other staff that Thaddeus had left again after only a month there. Though other than his arrival and departure, they had not seen him once during that time. And coincidence or not, last night had been the first sleep I had not had any bad dreams. For the past few weeks, I'd had various dreams about the angel combined with flashing images of the twins similar to the first, but with them huddled together in different locations, some places familiar, some not. Redmond and I were grateful the twins hadn't experienced the reoccurrences like I had and had only that first one over a month ago. Redmond, however, had *not* been grateful with my resorting to having one or two glasses of wine on the nights I'd been anxious over the thought of more nightmares. It had helped to keep me from dreaming, but in place of the nightmares, I'd woken in the morning with a hangover. "Tell me about the Grand Opening instead," I insisted, plastering another over the top smile on my face. It made Lane laugh, and her laughter released the growing pressure in my head. "I heard Rachel went. Mac and Alison said they dropped by to say hi to you all."

"Oh my gosh, Rachel and I had the best time! Wish you could have come up for it," she said, letting out another burst of laughter. "And yes, I got hugs from the ladies. Though it was a pretty young crowd, so they didn't stay long." She shrugged one shoulder. "Have you met Shayne?"

"Nope," I said, shaking my head. "But I do know he's Kris's new bar manager *and* another of the Earthbound."

"Right. He's also another good friend of my fathers. The bar staff think he's excellent. You still haven't met Mason or Jules either, have you?"

"Nope," I said again. "I'm already bitter I missed the grand opening, so don't rub it in about not having met the others yet, too." I made a frowny face, and she laughed.

"Oookaay, sorry," she said, holding in more laughs. "Let me see." She put a finger to her lips. "Of course my dads were there. Jules and Mason—he helped with the menu part. Ben, Nic, Leo, and Kris and Jana naturally. They had on the full staff, and the place was packed."

"Are the staff dressed in uniforms of some kind?" I asked, wondering how casual things were.

Lane went on to tell me about the details of the event, starting with the staff attire. "The waitstaff wears red t-shirts long or short-sleeved, with the logo in the upper left of the shirt and the tag line 'Get Snowed In' on the back, plus knee-length black cotton aprons with front pockets that tie with a long strap around the waist. All restaurant provided, of course. They were permitted to wear whatever pants they wanted as long as they were clean and presentable, and shorts during the summer of the same standard. The hosts/hostesses and bussers wear the same minus the apron. Management, Kris, Jana, and Shayne, wear either black or white, short or long-sleeved button-down shirts with the logo on the upper left like the other staff," Lane continued. "The kitchen crew all wear the traditional checkered black and white pants, with chefs wearing black double-breasted chef's coats. Dishwashers wearing the same *staff* shirt only in black."

"How does the place look now?" I questioned, my only memories being that of the previous bar from the 80s.

"The changes were done mainly to the second floor," Lane said, going on to describe the floor plan, the lay of the land as it were. The upper level had been renovated to have an upper balcony on the inside that looked over into the main restaurant area. The office too, was on the second floor at the back, next to a stockroom for non-kitchen provisions for staff, merchandise, bathroom, and cleaning supplies. "The upper restaurant space near the now open balcony has a lounge area and some small high-top tables with barstools. Behind those are several dining tables for seating of four or six, but they can be pushed together if groups are larger," she said, ending her description.

"Is there still a long bar you can sit at on the main floor?" I had a faint recollection of sitting at the far end of it and people watching.

"Yes—and fully restored," Lane said. "The bar has both a servers' station and patron bar seating at the center back with the kitchen behind the bar to the left, washrooms behind it to the right. Like the upper level, there are two similar lounge areas on the main floor, one near the entrance and another along the side wall furthest from the entry. Scattered throughout are the same tables for seating like the upper floor. The décor is ski lodge themed but with lighter wood accents and lighter fabrics than the traditional dark wood and heavier materials you might see at real ski resorts," Lane added. "Making it an all-season destination, so to speak. It is casual yet classy and still comfortable for the university crowd to come in and hang out."

"Seems like a place I'd want to hang out."

"I'll be hanging out there, that's for sure." She nodded several times. "On every surface, meaning dining tables, coffee tables in the lounge areas, the high-top and the bar, all have stacks of coasters with the logo name, and address on them for people to use or take home. There's also a plaque near the entrance and smaller table signs telling the story about the first Snow restaurant in NYC and how the owner's best friend owns and runs the place now."

"I like that idea of the place sharing a new backstory." I also like how detailed Lane was with her description. I could almost picture it. "What's the logo?"

"For the coasters, it's a stylized maple leaf on one side and the name Après SNOW on the other, with a snowflake for the letter O."

"Snow, snowflake—seems fitting." Though there was a little more meaning to the snowflake that only a select few knew. "I like the play on the name too, Après SNOW *after* snow, referring to after *skiing* and the ski lodge theme plus the new restaurant, which came *after* the original Snow restaurant. Very clever. Your Uncle Kris isn't just a pretty face." I smirked. "Now tell me about the food."

"I tell you, having a father who's a great cook and now Uncle Kris and Jana here feeding us—I have to say I'm no longer in haven—I'm in heaven. And same goes with the food at the restaurant."

"I'm so jealous. Although my hubby is a fantastic cook, so I lucked out there," I assured her.

"The event food was really cool. There was a special limited menu for purchase along with free food samples of other items, both standard and vegan options from the full menu, circulated by staff. They had a full bar setup plus special event beverages with a maple-flavored themed drinks."

"Mmmm, like what?" I always had Canadian maple syrup in my fridge.

"They had a locally brewed maple stout beer on tap, a maple shooter made with maple syrup and Canadian rye whiskey, aaand a *mapletini* made with maple flavored vodka. They did free desserts as well, made of mousse in hot chocolate, marshmallow, and maple flavors, all done up in plastic shot glasses for patrons to take home with them, if they wanted. There are replicas in glass of the plastic ones for purchase as part of the merch."

"How cool! What other stuff can you buy?"

"People can purchase tank tops, t-shirts long and short-sleeved, sweatshirts and hoodies from small to XXXL. They all come in either black, heather grey, or white with the same stylized snowflake in the name and maple leaf logo, with either a small logo and name on the upper left corner of the shirt or a large version in the center of the shirts. Everything is displayed in a large case at the front door near the hostess stand, and items can be bought from them or any waitstaff."

"I'm going to need to buy some shirts for sure." I already had a tall stack of sweatshirts and t-shirts but there was always room for more.

"I already bought a black long-sleeved one with the small logo. And I almost forgot, they had two local musicians come and play acoustic guitars and sing for the event. They were so well received that Kris has them coming regularly now Thursday through Saturday 6 - 8 and Sunday 11 - 4, only because they close at 5 on Sundays."

"Sounds like it was a great event, and the restaurant will be a great addition to the Ottawa landscape."

"I think so too. I'll send you some photos I took at the event. Hey, did you know there's no Thanksgiving or Halloween in Iceland?"

"No, but I can understand no Thanksgiving, since only a few countries celebrate. Bummer about Halloween, though."

"Ya. It was Jana who told me, but she said Christmas is highly anticipated, and preparation can start as early as September."

"Wow, that *is* early, but I do love the Christmas holiday season."

"Me too." Lane smiled much like a little girl, cheeks bunching, eyes twinkling at the mere mention of Christmas.

Personally, I felt the same way Lane did about the holiday. "Right now, I just need to get through these next two. Halloween first and then Thanksgiving."

Chapter 17 

Cleveland Hospital, Monday A.M. October 10th, South Florida

A giant of a man came through the now open emergency entrance doors, carrying an equally massive unconscious man. "I need some help here!" the giant called out to the staff. "Found the guy outside. Must have been trying to get in here. Kept saying the name Dr. Stone. Might be his doctor."

Monday wasn't a normal volunteer day for me, but I was doing an early-morning shift covering for a coworker. I'd been told that Mondays were the busiest day of the week and for most of my shift it had been, but it wasn't until I pushed the stray wheelchair I was returning into the ER that I experienced the full impact of it. A wave of senses crashed into me, my head dropping dizzily as I gripped the handles of the wheelchair to keep myself upright. The unexpected sensation, the one I'd come to associate with the Earthbound, engulfed me and almost brought me to my knees. I lifted my head to see… *Lyndon* standing at the far side near the ER entrance. Only reason I knew it was him was because I'd felt that familiar prickle of static electricity on my skin before at the group home, though this time it hadn't felt as razor-sharp. But the impact I was feeling wasn't from him alone. It was combined with the other Earthbound, an unfamiliar one Lyndon was now placing on a gurney. But there was a third, another Earthbound who heightened the sensation further, one I couldn't see, but was near enough I could feel them. I stared across at the Earthbound on the gurney, his back facing me. I glanced at the female doctor beside him as she lifted the back of his shirt and then wrote something on a clipboard. I continued to watch as they swiftly rolled the Angel into one of the examination rooms. When I turned back to where Lyndon had stood, he was no longer there, as was the sensation that had identified him to me. My brain was still buzzing as I rolled the wheelchair to its regular spot near the entrance. And as my racing heart slowed to a normal rhythm, it was then I realized the awareness of this mysterious third Earthbound had departed as well.

Senses clearing, I hustled it back the way I'd come, desperately trying to pick up on the trail for the injured Earthbound. His unique signature had felt more like a vibration against my skin versus the prickling Lyndon's invoked. I wasn't sure where they'd taken him now because he wasn't in any of the exam rooms. The vibration was faint, but I could still feel it as I walked my route through the hospital. At the first base station, I swiped my access card. The map showed no stray wheelchairs in this area and displayed only one in the Behavioral Health Center.

As I approached the center, the vibrations against my skin became more intense. I surveyed the area but saw no wheelchair. It must still be within the ward, I figured. Inside, where the injured Angel now was. Unfortunately, I didn't have access to this special area and normally staff left chairs on my side of the entrance hall for pickup.

The sliding security entry doors to the center suddenly swished open and out came a male doctor, a resident I'd seen before. He usually wore scrubs, but this time, his typically clean doctor's coat was dappled with fresh blood. He seemed surprised to see me and stopped short, as though to let me pass through the doors.

"Sorry, I'm just looking for the rogue wheelchair I need to pick up."

The door swooshed shut behind him. He turned back to the entrance and swiped his security badge to open the door again.

"Nurse," he called when it opened. "Can you help with the wheelchair?" He smiled then as the door shut once more, then he continued on his way.

The nurse he had called out to came through the sliding doors, pushing the abandoned wheelchair. "My apologies—I'm new and it's been a crazy morning," she said, then lowered her voice. "I'm not supposed to use the word *crazy*." She put her index finger to her lips and giggled.

This was my chance, I thought, aware I was conversing with a bit of a rule breaker, and asked, "Say, did they just bring in a new patient? One that was unconscious or may have been injured?"

"You bet they did," she said in a whisper. "That's what all the commotion was about. They said he was unconscious when they took him to the exam room, but then came too suddenly—ranting and raving. Something about how he was *'an angel, here to help those in need'*. They gave him a sedative, and he passed out cold. They called psych— us, I mean, letting us know they were bringing him up. The doctor checked his wounds and found they only needed to be cleaned up and re-bandaged."

"Re-bandaged?" I questioned.

"Someone had patched him up before coming here, it looked like, but it was clear he was off his rocker. Shame really for such a handsome fella. Now he's in a coma."

"What? A coma—how?" I asked, trying to keep my voice low.

"Uhm, he had a reaction to the sedative, apparently." She shrugged.

This nurse was no Florence Nightingale, that was for sure. "It is a shame," I agreed, taking the wheelchair by the handles. "Thanks... for bringing out the chair."

"No prob," she said, giving me a goofy smile before heading back into the ward.

I rolled my eyes and then began leisurely pushing the wheelchair up the hall towards where it belonged. At the end of the hall, I checked the base station again to see if there were any other misplaced ones I needed to retrieve. I was thankful to find, since my shift was also ending, that there were no more strays showing on the map.

After going to the staff lockers to retrieve my purse, I stepped into the nearest stairwell and checked to see I was alone. Then I called to the universe for my birthfather. "Gabriel," I said out loud into the bare stairwell, and then waited. *Nothing.* I waited a few more minutes, then called out his name a little louder, hopeful no one else could hear me.

A few more minutes passed and then Gabriel finally appeared before me. "You called?" he said with a smartass grin. He was casually dressed in worn jeans and a white long-sleeved linen shirt, the sleeves rolled up to his elbows.

I drew in a long breath, readying my words because what I had to say, had to tell him, was a doozy. "Let me begin by saying I'm fine—thanks for asking." Gabriel went to respond, but I cut him off. "You are not going to believe what just happened." Gabriel's eyes bulged, but he didn't attempt to say anything. "Lyndon…."

"What about Lyndon?" he interrupted.

I pursed my lips, then blew out a breath. "Lyndon was just here."

"What do you mean here?" he yelped in question. "Here-here?" he pointed to the floor.

"Yes, no, not here-here, in the ER."

He opened his mouth to say something, but I put up my hand to stop him. "For the love of… would you please let me get this out?"

"Sorry—go ahead." He wrang his hands like an old woman.

"Thank you," I gasped out, then went on to tell him about Lyndon and the injured Earthbound.

"So he's in there now?" Gabriel pointed to the wall of the stairwell, as though indicating the direction to the comatose Angel.

"You need to get in there—see who he is—see if you recognize him."

Gabriel disappeared, only to return several seconds later.

"Well?" I asked when he just stood there looking confused.

"He's one of Thaddeus's henchmen. Best kept in the ward sedated, if you ask me."

"Why would Lyndon do that?" I questioned, raising my hands in the air, shaking my head.

"You mean bring him to a hospital?"

"For Thaddeus?" I questioned again, but that didn't sit right with me. My phone vibrated in my purse, and I pulled it free to see that Redmond had sent me a text,

> *Are you on your way home? Darius called me asking if you were alright.*

I wrote back quickly, stating I was *on my way* and ended it with a green heart which signified I loved him, and I was okay. Then I texted Leo,

> *I need to speak to you in person. Can you come to South Haven?*

Leo wrote back immediately,

> *Yes, I can be there in a few hours. Is everything alright?*

I couldn't get into things right now, not here at the hospital, and I responded with,

> *I'm fine, we are fine, but something happened that we need to discuss. Redmond and I will meet you at South Haven.*

When I glanced up to look at Gabriel, he was frowning.

"Leo is going to meet us at South Haven," I said in explanation of my texting.

The frown on Gabriel's face deepened and then he said, "The real question we should be asking is, why *this* hospital?"

Gabriel rode home with me from the hospital. When I pulled into the carport at home and checked my cellphone, I found that Den had texted me, saying he and Marq were at South Haven waiting for Leo to arrive. Thankfully, he hadn't questioned what was going on, and in leu of an explanation, I asked Gabriel to go over and give them the details while I went into the house and explained it to Redmond.

Of course, Redmond lost his shit, but he calmed when I said Lyndon hadn't seen me. He then told me Darius had been calling, anxiously asking what had happened since obviously his guardian radar had gone off when I'd been hit with sensory overload at the hospital. While I changed out of my uniform and into jean shorts and a t-shirt, Redmond called Darius. He was still worried despite his radar alarms powering down, but Redmond had assured him I was fine and also suggested he meet up with us at South Haven.

When we arrived, we found Darius already in the workout area giving the beat-down on a punching bag. Den and Marq were at the computer workstation with Gabriel hovering over them.

"Gabriel brought us all up to speed," Den said, "and I spoke to Leo already—told him what happened. He should be here soon."

"Good," I said. I hadn't wanted to explain it again. Over Marq's shoulder, I watched as he brought up a spreadsheet on one of the computer screens, the one that listed the Earthbound.

Leo arrived moments later. "Redmond, Lynn," he said, coming to stand with us near the computer station. "Can you tell me what happened?"

I glanced at Den. "You said you told him."

"He did, but I want to hear it from you," Leo said. "Every detail."

So much for not having to explain it again. I let out a heavy sigh and then went over the details, every overwhelming feeling, the searching for the injured Earthbound, and what I'd heard from the nurse. "I wonder what they gave him that put him into a coma," I said.

"Maybe Benzodiazepine? It contains sulfur?" Leo said.

I just stared at him, as did Redmond.

"Ever since the incident with Kris, I've been keeping a list of medications that contain sulfur. And Benzos, as they are colloquially called, are depressants used for sedation or relieving anxiety, muscle spasms, even reducing seizures and sometime for hypnosis. You've heard of Valium and Xanax, those are brand names." Leo pulled in a long breath, appearing to hold it. "I can only imagine what might be going on inside his brain." Leo blew out the held breath through his mouth. "No visit from Purah, I take it?"

I raised my eyebrows and shot a quick glance at Den. "Sorry, no," I said, focusing back to Leo.

"I wish there was a way to summon her like you can with Gabriel." Leo stated.

I turned back to Den and gave him a few eyebrow raises. Den fought a grin but still raised his own eyebrows in recognition of the interest between Leo and Purah I'd pointed out to him months ago.

Leo's cellphone chimed then, and he pulled it from the back pocket of his khakis. "Update on the New York facility," he stated. "Addison has been spotted there with Marcus."

"Why would Addison be in NYC?" Marq asked, turning away from his review of the spreadsheet. "He functions out of the Norway facility."

"If he's in New York, who's with Kendrick in Norway?" Den inquired.

"No Idea," Leo said, leaning around me to look at the spreadsheet on the screen.

When my brain finally caught up to what was being discussed, I asked, "Who was in New York before Addison?"

"Zuriel," Marq said, tapping the name in his spreadsheet.

"Well, it's Zuriel who's in the psych ward," Gabriel announced then.

"What? You told me it was just one of Thaddeus's henchmen."

"Yes, but at the time I didn't think the *who* mattered."

Chapter 18 

The Group Home, Monday P.M. October 10th, Ottawa

"Lyndon, I was hoping to find you here," came Lane's voice from the entrance to the playroom. "We missed you Saturday for the Thanksgiving gathering." When she reached the table where he sat, she asked, "Where is Taylor?"

"It's his bath time," Lyndon said staring up at her. Her shiny black hair hung in subtle waves over her shoulders, and she wore a loosely tied charcoal coloured trench coat over an amethyst purple turtleneck and dark jeans. "Volunteers are done for the day. Why are you here?" he asked. Time with Lane had become one of his favorite parts of the day, but he hadn't been able to see her as of late. Because he'd been at the penthouse watching over Zuriel, this had been the first time in the past two weeks he'd seen Taylor as well.

"I came by to see if you were here," Lane said dejectedly.

Lyndon looked away to stare out the large window. "Shouldn't you be having Thanksgiving with your family?" he questioned gruffly.

"We had our family meal yesterday." Lane sat down in the chair next to him, pulling his attention back. "Did I do something wrong?" she asked.

"No, why would you ask that?" But he knew why. He was being an asshole. He was still upset over having to drop Zuriel at the hospital because he hadn't known where that woman, the doctor, lived, only that she'd moved to the area. The hospital had been the only place Lyndon had seen her, and he had brought Zuriel there in hopes of connecting the two. He'd given her name to the ER staff, suggesting she might be his doctor.

"You seem distressed. If it's not me—then what?" Lane questioned him. "Is everything okay?"

"Yes, I'm fine," he said, but he wasn't. He hated not knowing what had happened to Zuriel after leaving him at the hospital, but he couldn't stick around. There would have been too many questions, none of which he could answer. "Are you hungry?" he asked, changing the focus.

"I'm getting there, yes," Lane said with levity, standing and adjusting her purse to rest at her lower back. "Let's go get a bite to eat. I'll take you to my uncles' restaurant."

He stood then too, gazing down at her. "How about I make you dinner instead? I'd like to stick around here if that's okay with you." He forced a smile.

"Of course it's okay, and I would love that," she said, smiling sweetly back at him.

In his basement apartment, as Lane meandered over to his wall of books again, Lyndon pulled out the food items he'd purchased on the weekend in hopes of cooking something special for her. "What are you currently reading?" he asked, his mood lightening.

"Research papers," she said, the corner of her mouth lifting in a half smile. "I wish I had more time for casual reading. What about you?"

"Uhm, well, I just finished reading a new biography. *The Extraordinary Life of an Ordinary Man.*"

She gave him a puzzled look. "Who is the subject of the book?"

"Paul Newman—do you know who he is?" Lyndon drew a large cutting board from a low cupboard.

"Yes actually. I've watched a few of his movies with my fathers. The Sting, The Verdict, and Butch Cassidy and the Sundance Kid with

Robert Redford. Oh, and Cars when I was 8 years old—that one I saw in the theater."

"Cars? I'm not familiar with that one. Do you mean *Winning*? He had a role as a Grand Prix driver in that one."

"No, it was Cars. But I'm not surprised you don't know it. It's a kids' animated Pixar film with cars as characters. He does the voice of Doc Hudson a 1951 Hudson Hornet, who's the medical doctor and local judge for the car race in the movie."

He nodded slowly. There were lots of movies he hadn't seen, especially the animated ones. "The only kids' movie I've ever seen was Beauty and the Beast. Although I read the English translation of the original fairytale by Gabrielle-Suzanne Barbot de Villeneuve to Taylor. He loved it so much I got him a copy of the movie—we watched it together, but I found it quite different from the book. Taylor much prefers being read to than watching a movie I find." He couldn't ignore the parallel between him and Lane to the characters in the movie, and it wasn't the fact they both liked to read.

"The book is usually better than the movie adaptation," she said. "I loved being read to as a child."

"And now?"

She shrugged. "I listen to the occasional audiobook—but no one actually reads to me anymore." She laughed.

"I'd read to you, if you like."

"I would love…," she began, then switched to saying, "I love when you read to Taylor." She held his gaze. "And I love what you are wearing."

Lyndon's heart pounded harder in his chest as Lane stared at him. "That's kind of you," he said, brushing a hand down the front of his shirt. He hadn't put much thought into his clothes today, just black jeans and a grey pullover, but he was grateful just to have fresh garments on after spending two weeks with Zuriel in that penthouse. He'd barely taken any time to eat, let alone change his clothes.

"How did you like the biography?"

"I found it extremely fascinating," he said, pulling his gaze from her. "The memoir was actually edited by his daughter, culled from thousands of pages of transcripts he and his closest friends had compiled. It's a candid story about how he was often haunted by guilt and grief...." He paused to glance her way and found she was still watching him. "...and self-doubt, even though he was adored by the public. He had a traumatic childhood, but the most moving parts of the memoir, the parts I enjoyed the most, had to do with his love for his wife—their love for each other."

"That is fascinating," she said. "I might have to read that one myself."

"You are welcome to borrow my copy," he said, pointing to the bookshelves. "You can borrow any of my books."

"Thank you—I may take you up on that offer once I'm done with school." She halted her book perusing. "That's new," she said gleefully, pointing at the small table and chairs set up in the space between the end kitchen counter and the bookshelf. "How did I miss it?"

"It is new," Lyndon said, pleased at her enthusiasm. "I thought it would be more comfortable than sitting on the floor." He chuckled, enjoying their easy back-and-forth exchanges. He'd been quite pleased with his purchase of the two-person table and matching cushioned chairs. He'd even purchased placemats.

She stepped closer to the dining setup. "It's perfect." She ran a hand over the padded backrest of the closest chair. She removed her purse from hanging across her body to hook it on the back of the chair. "Although I would have been just as happy sitting on the floor if it meant sharing a meal with you." She smiled at him sweetly.

"Like an indoor picnic," he suggested. He would kneel bare-kneed on broken glass if it meant he could spend time with her.

"What are you making?" she asked, coming to rest her forearms on the end counter.

"Sushi," Lyndon said proudly. He'd been practicing the art in whatever spare time he found, also in the hopes of feeding her.

"Sushi? Really?" she rushed around the end counter into the kitchen space to stand near him where he assembled the ingredients. "I love sushi."

"That's why I'm making it," he said with an amused laugh, inspired by her joyful spirit. "I opted to create something traditional— a spicy tuna roll, something new...."

"Spicy tuna is my favorite," she cut in. "That one looks like it would be hard to make." She pointed at the square mosaic sushi roll.

He chuckled. "It just looks complex, but it is surprisingly simple to make. I can teach you."

"It's really beautiful—looks like art."

"Let's hope you like how it tastes. I made a Mexican roll because you said you also love Mexican food."

"You did? And I do."

"I still haven't figured out how to make a poutine roll."

"Is there such a thing as a poutine roll?"

"Not that I've found yet."

"I'm sure you will and have it mastered for next time."

He liked that she said *next time*. "I'll do my best."

A chime sound came from Lane's purse.

"Did you need to get that?" he asked, holding his breath, worried it might be something that would cause her to need to leave.

"I'm sure it can wait," she said, like whatever or whoever it was didn't matter. "What goes into a Mexican sushi roll?"

He let go of his breath. "Nothing too daring. Rice, avocado, diced tomatoes, chopped cilantro, sliced *jalapenos*...," he said, pausing to check that she liked the fiery pepper. When she nodded her approval, he went on, "Sliced cooked shrimp and soy sauce."

"Sounds delicious." She licked her lips. "Do you have a favorite roll?"

"Hmm, probably a dragon roll. It combines a variety of flavors and textures, including sweet, savory, and crunchy. Plus, I like how it resembles a dragon with the avocado arranged like scales on it." He grinned teasingly at her.

She gave him a playful smile, then scowled. "How come you didn't make one of those, then?" She leaned her hip against the counter.

He tilted his head to one side and frowned back at her. "Because these are especially for you."

"Well then, how can I help? I could set the table."

"That would be lovely. There are special plates and chopsticks there on the shelf," he said, finishing the last roll, pointing an elbow in the direction of the long shelf with the sushi dinner settings for two.

Lane moved around where he stood at the counter, then reached up and removed the sushi setups from the open shelf. Then she went back over to the table and divided up the dishes atop the placemats he arranged there earlier. The chime from her cellphone sounded from within her purse again. This time, Lane retrieved her phone from her purse. She glanced at it briefly before returning it, letting out an audible huff and a sigh.

"Everything alright?" he asked, placing the rolls side by side on a long narrow serving dish. He sensed his worry returning.

"Yes. It's just my fathers," she said, traversing back to where he prepped the meal. "I think they sometimes forget I'm an adult."

He didn't know what it was like to have parents, though Thaddeus often treated him like a child. "Are you sure?"

"I'm sure." She gave him several quick nods, then sat down in the chair facing his way.

"Okay," he said, still unsure. Finishing the food presentation, he placed wasabi and pickled ginger on either end of the serving dish, then he grabbed the bottle of soy sauce off the cutting table. "Because we can always do this another day if you need to leave," he assured her, hopeful she wouldn't actually leave.

"Absolutely not," she said, grabbing the set of chopsticks she had previously set on the plate. She made a fist around the utensils and shook them teasingly at him.

At her mischievous response, he scooped up the sushi display from the counter and headed over to the table.

When he set his creations down in the center of the small table, she said, "Especially not after you worked so hard on these magnificent rolls."

Her phone rang, but she ignored it.

Lyndon rested down in the chair across from her. "Shouldn't you get that?"

"It's probably one of my fathers," she said, seating the chopsticks properly in her fingers.

A different sounding chime jingled in her purse. "See, they left a message—I can check whatever it is they want later." She clicked her chopsticks as though eager to eat.

Lyndon poured soy sauce into the tiny bowls Lane had set atop each plate. "I'd love to be able to ignore my phone," he shared, setting the small bottle next to the serving plate.

"Is that why you were so troubled earlier? Did something happen with work?" Lane asked, reminding him how sour his mood had been before. Before she had changed it.

"I guess you could say that," he said, not looking at her, staring down at the colourful rolls.

"You can tell me, you know."

When he glanced up, Lane set her chopsticks down on the plate.

Could he, though? Could he actually tell her? Tell her the reality of what had been bothering him. Tell her what it was he truly did, Lyndon wondered. "Have you ever heard the name *Thaddeus Smyth*?"

"Yes, I think so… uhm… isn't he that… *entrepreneur* guy… the one doing research for… *sick kids*?" she questioned.

Her tone was unsteady, as though she didn't trust her own assumptions, and she shouldn't, Lyndon thought. "He doesn't care about the sick children. He's a horrible… *person*."

"I'm guessing this is your boss… you mentioned the name Thaddeus the last time I was here. But he can't be… all that bad… I mean… if he funds a place like this."

Again, her words seemed unsure. "You don't sound so certain."

Lane leaned in slightly over her plate, resting her elbows on the table, the fingers of her hands interlaced. "I asked you before, if you don't think he's a good person—then why do you work for him?" She rested her chin on her hands.

Lane had called him handsome, but Lyndon was uneasy with her staring so intently at his beast of a face. He shook his head.

"I know—it's *complicated*." Lane pulled her elbows from the table sitting back in her chair.

He wanted to tell her about all the things Thaddeus has done, how he was going to dispose of Taylor, explain why he was in his employ, but instead he said, "This group home was my idea."

"Your idea?" she questioned, as though confused over the bit of truth he'd chosen to share.

"Yes," he said, mirroring lane's earlier stance of leaning in with elbows on the table, fingers mingling together. "I told him it would make him look good, but that I would watch over things here. It fed his ego, and I got to watch over Taylor."

"Why were you a no-show for the Grand Opening of my uncles' restaurant?" she asked, her words suddenly edged with annoyance.

Lyndon dropped his hands and leaned back, blowing out a breath through his nose. He was grateful for the change of topic away from Thaddeus, but he had hoped not to address his absence from the event. He had planned to go to the grand opening, however, it was the day he'd had to take care of Zuriel. It was the same reason he hadn't been at the group home's Thanksgiving gathering. No one could help him, and as a last resort, he had taken Zuriel to the hospital. They couldn't stay at the penthouse, nor could he have kept him here. When he'd returned from Florida, he'd instructed the same two medical staffers who had been in the lab prior with Thaddeus, to clean up whatever mess he'd left in both the lab *and* in the penthouse. He had personally seen to taking down the wings and had wrapped them up and stowed them here in a secure place. He hadn't known what he should do with them, but he'd keep them safe for Zuriel. They were his, and he would be the one to decide their destiny. He drew his cellphone from his back pocket, glancing at it to check the time.

"Don't tell me you have another errand to run." The annoyance in Lane's voice had shifted, sounding more like disappointment.

"Nope," he said calmly, glancing across at her into her deep blue eyes. "It's almost Taylor's bedtime, and I promised him I would tell him a bedtime story. Would you like to join me after we eat?"

She gave him a gentle smile.

It was almost 9 p.m. when Lyndon finished with reciting the story of Wynken, Blynken, and Nod, the three children who sailed and fished among the stars, using a wooden shoe for a boat. He knew the poem by memory, having read it to Taylor several times, usually on particularly stormy nights.

"He's too old for the story now, but it always comforts him if he has trouble sleeping." Lyndon took a last glance at Taylor as he slept before closing the bedroom door. Then together, Lane and he walked back to the elevator, then rode it back down to his apartment.

"I've never heard this story before," Lane confessed as he opened the way back in. "It's cute."

"It's an old Dutch lullaby from 1889, so I'm not shocked you've never heard of it," he said, standing in the open doorway, watching as she crossed to the tiny dinner table.

Lane lifted her purse by its strap from the chair and then checked her watch. "I should get going," she said, though she remained where she was.

"Let me drive you home," he offered, in desire for further time in her company.

"I drove here," she said, producing a keychain from her purse. "Thank you for that delicious meal." She strode back over to him.

"You are very welcome—it was my pleasure." He stood in the hall, back from the opening to let her pass through, then followed as she walked the short stretch to the elevator door. He pressed the button to call the elevator. "Will you come for dinner again soon?" he asked, his heart thudding in his chest as he gazed down into her heavenly eyes.

"Definitely." Lane stared up at him, as if searching his face. "But promise me something…," she said, taking up his hand in hers, "… that you'll take me up on my offer to go to my uncles' restaurant sometime."

Lyndon's gaze dropped at her touch, and he stared dumbstruck at her delicate hand holding his. Then he lifted his gaze to look into her angelic face. He was lost in her mesmerizing eyes and lost for what to say. What a contrast they were, he the beast and she…. When he said nothing in response, she let go of his hand and he felt a squeeze in his chest at its absence. He watched as she turned her focus away from him and stepped into the now open elevator. As the elevator door began to close its last few inches, he said, "I promise," adding, *beauty*," in a whisper as the door finally shut.

"Where have you been?" her father Julian asked as she came through the door. Both of her fathers were standing in the kitchen.

"I was at the group home with Lyndon and Taylor."

"So late?" her father, Max, questioned next.

Lane hesitantly walked over to the kitchen. "He made us dinner. Then we read Taylor a bedtime story."

"Lane, we don't want you spending time with him anymore," Uncle Leo stated as he entered from the hallway into the kitchen area.

"Why? I thought you wanted me to watch over Taylor?" she questioned, removing her purse from over her shoulder.

"We did," her uncle said. "We just feel you may be getting too personally involved… with both of them."

Lane leaned her hand on the island. "So, you trust me to keep *watch* all this time, but now you're going to start treating me like a child?"

"It's just that…" Julian started to say.

"Just what?" Lane slammed her purse on the island.

Julian's face was grave. "It's not safe."

"I know all about the cruel things Thaddeus has done. Lyndon isn't like that!" she shouted, putting her hands on her hips.

"How can you be sure?" Max asked.

"Because we're friends. He's actually been opening up to me," she stated with conviction.

"Did he tell you he was in Florida?" Max inquired.

Lane dropped her hands. "Florida—no—when?" she directed at her Uncle Leo.

"Today." Leo's expression was weary.

"But I was just with him," she said, skeptical.

Uncle Leo took several steps coming to stand before her. "He was at a hospital there—the one Lynn volunteers at."

"How do you know that?" Lane asked, taking back her purse from the island and wrapping her arms around it.

"You are aware Lynn can feel us *and* the others, right?" Uncle Leo asked, placing a hand on her shoulder.

"Yes, but how does she know it was him?" Lane glanced at the anxious faces of her fathers, then back at her uncle's resolute one.

"She had that same feeling, the sensation she'd had the day she visited the group home," her uncle clarified.

"Maybe it was another Earthbound," she suggested, her words sounding as though she were pleading for it to be.

Uncle Leo raised his other hand to her shoulder and then said. "Lane, this time Lynn *saw* him."

Chapter 19 

The Women Are Persons Monument, October 18th, Ottawa, Canada

Gabriel stood next to the polished bronze figure of Nellie McClung brandishing a newspaper proclaiming to the world that Women are Persons, depicting the celebrating of their famous victory. The day's weather was a cool 12 degrees Celsius in Ottawa, so he'd switched out his usual summery clothing he wore when in Florida for a suitable fall outfit, consisting of dark denim jeans and the thick white Après SNOW sweatshirt he'd obtained over a plain white t-shirt.

"What an apropos location," Vretil stated, coming to stand next to the figure of Irene Parlby placed next to Nellie McClung. He wore an equally suitable outfit with jeans, a heavy grey thermal pullover under a charcoal and grey plaid flannel shirt.

"Oh, yes, the Famous Five," Uriel added, arriving second and next to the figure of Louise McKinney. He wore a similar outfit to Vretil, though his flannel shirt was red and grey plaid.

Raphael was last but only nodded at Uriel as he came to stand by his fellow Archangel. He glanced down at the figure of Henrietta Edward, who was seated next to McKinney. "Wasn't this on Parliament Hill?" he asked, observing the other figures in the circle.

"*The Women Are Persons* monument was created in 2000 and originally installed on Parliament Hill but was then moved here to the Plaza Bridge near the Senate of Canada," Gabriel informed them. "There are two other monuments in Canada, one in Winnipeg and one in Calgary." He smiled then at the fact that his fellow Archangels were dressed akin to triplets, Raphael having arrived wearing the same combination as the other two, his flannel shirt a combination of rust and brown.

"It's fitting that the likenesses of these women should find themselves next door to the Senate. The Persons Case was fought so women could be appointed to the Red Chamber, giving voice to underrepresented groups."

"I agree," Gabriel said. "It marks the day in 1929 when the historic decision to include women in the legal definition of *persons* was handed down by Canada's highest court of appeal." Gabriel scanned the area for their small gathering. "Where is Michael?"

"Traveling with Vicki," Raphael said, taking the seat next to the figure of Emily Murphy, whose figure in the monument gestured for passersby to come sit and think about how the world has changed. "Wasn't Ms. Murphy Canada's first female judge?" he asked then.

Gabriel turned to face Raphael where he sat now. "Yes, and that was even before women were fully defined as *persons* under Canadian and British law. Women had finally won the right to run in federal elections in 1921, but no woman had been appointed to the Senate."

"Why?" Raphael stood and walked over to Ms. McClung to view the newspaper she was holding with the 1929 announcement on the Persons case.

"Well, the 1867 Constitution Act allowed for the appointment of qualified persons to the Senate, and the general attitude was that it didn't include women." Gabriel shook his head. "This is what prompted the five to travel from Alberta to Ontario, to ask the Supreme Court in Ottawa for a legal interpretation of the term *qualified*."

Raphael glanced across at Irene Parlby, whose figure was gesturing to the newspaper in Ms. McClung's hands. "How did it go?"

"Badly," Gabriel said. "The Chief Justice said something along the lines that the word *persons* on its own included women, but the term *qualified persons*, excluded women since they belonged in the same category as criminals and children, and weren't fit to be appointed to the Senate."

"That makes no sense," Raphael said, wandering over to where Louise McKinney sat, hands folded and looking at McClung. "I like that the artist has captured this woman's sense of pleasure and pride in her face."

"It's victory," Gabriel expressed. Then he said, "Back then there was a higher power than the Supreme Court, the Judicial Committee of the Privy Council of England. So, in October 1929, they took their case across the Atlantic ocean to Lord Sankey. Ultimately, the Lord Chancellor delivered the decision they had long sought, acknowledging that politics had historically been a man's domain, describing the Canada's Constitution as *'a living tree capable of growth and expansion. The exclusion of women from all public offices is a relic of days more barbarous than ours. To those who ask why the word should include females, the obvious answer is why should it not'*."

"What happened after that?" Raphael asked.

"The following year, Cairine Wilson became Canada's first female senator," Vretil said, adding his own knowledge of the case. "This gave some women the right to be appointed to the Senate of Canada." He pointed at the Senate building.

"Though this decision did not include all women, but it did mark critical progress in the advancement of gender equality here in Canada," Gabriel advised them.

"I'd love a cup of tea," Raphael said, hovering over the figure of Henrietta Edward, who was holding up her cup of tea as if she was toasting the victory. "Who were excluded?" Raphael asked.

"Asian women were not granted suffrage until 1948 after WWII," Vretil advised. "Inuit women not until 1950, and it wasn't until 1960 that the vote in Federal elections was extended to all First Nations people, *and* without having to give up their treaty status."

"Painfully slow progress, yet still progress," Raphael expressed, traversing back over to sit again in the bronze chair next to the figure of Emily Murphy. "But Gabriel, I'm sure you didn't call us to this clandestine meeting to give us a history lesson."

"No, but today *is* the celebration of Persons Day," Gabriel announced. "These five women were champions in their own rights, and together they formed an unstoppable force that changed things for women in Canada and in all Commonwealth countries." He paused, glancing at each figure. "And I thought it a fitting location for a discussion about *our* infamous five."

Raphael dropped his head, then ran his hands through his short, cropped red hair. "Michael had the right idea with staying near his Charge."

"Your duty of watching over your Charges has long since passed," Gabriel said. "Why did Michael feel the need to be with Vicki on her travels, anyway?"

"For the same reason you watch over your Charge still," Vretil said.

"Your Charges are not your offspring—your daughter," Gabriel countered. "And I have granddaughters now as well."

Uriel came to stand next to Gabriel. "Will your duty end with them?" he asked.

"No, but...," Gabriel began to say, then halted to examine the question further.

"We all had daughters once, and granddaughters, and great-granddaughters and great-great-granddaughters," Vretil pointed out.

"Forgive me...," Gabriel said, interrupting him when he recognized the direction Vretil's words were headed. "...for my ignorance." Gabriel bowed his head.

"Your attachment to Lynn and her family is a raw circumstance for you," Vretil acknowledged. "But for us, with each generation, our own ancestry continues, and our attachment deepens."

"It doesn't simply end because the duty ended," Raphael stated. "Don't forget, we have watched over these Charges and their families for centuries. Unlike the rest of us, you are *new* to this emotional journey."

Gabriel raised his head to nod his admiration for their words. "I am terribly sorry. It was not my intention to draw you away from your... *families*."

"We are here now. So go ahead," Raphael requested.

"I have questions you may be able to answer," he said, "even more now that I understand the longevity of your devotion to your Charges."

"Has something happened to Lynn?" Uriel inquired, circling around to come stand near Gabriel.

"Nothing has *happened*, per se." Gabriel paused to arrange the information he wanted to deliver. "Are you familiar with an Earthbound named Lyndon?"

"Yes," Vretil said, moving to flank Uriel. "We know he is part of Thaddeus's alliance."

"And you know that Thaddeus has been trying to locate Lynn?"

"Yes," Vretil said again.

"It is Lyndon who was tasked with locating Lynn," Gabriel clarified. "And...."

"And?" Raphael interjected, standing again, crossing through the center of the monument to stand alongside his brethren.

"And... Lynn saw him... at the hospital she works at."

"Did he see her?"

"No, but...."

"But what?" Raphael interrupted again.

"He was with another of the Earthbound, a tracker named Zuriel. Lynn felt both of them before seeing them."

"Why...?" Raphael asked, though Gabriel held up a hand to halt any more from him.

"Lyndon was carrying Zuriel... into the emergency area—he was unconscious, injured in fact, we later found out," Gabriel specified. "I don't know what happened to him, but he's still in the hospital...In the Behavioral Health Center, in a coma."

Wordless glances were exchanged between the small host of Archangels.

As the three silently watched Gabriel, he continued. "Our first assumption was that Lyndon was there as part of his search for Lynn, but nothing has happened since the encounter. He has not been seen nor has Lynn felt him in the vicinity. Though I have no explanation as to why he chose to bring the injured Earthbound to that particular hospital."

"I'm guessing that's not all," Raphael asked, speaking up.

"She felt a third Earthbound."

"Who do you think it was?" Uriel asked, worry renting his expression.

"Thaddeus's people are accounted for... all but the tracker Ariadne. The Guards don't have a clue where she is."

"Have you seen this missing tracker before?" Uriel asked. "I mean, could you identify her if you saw her?"

"Definitely. She has long thick coils of white hair, the palest skin as though coated in fine powder. Her face shape, nose and mouth are identical to Amahle, though she wears no makeup. Similar to humans who have Albinism, her eyes also are of the palest colours, hers a light shade of violet, surrounded by long white eyelashes. She is quite striking, the most exquisite of the others from Pleiades. Gorgeous, some would say under ideal circumstance," Gabriel said.

"What do you mean by *ideal*?"

Gabriel grimaced. "Evidently, she is also the most lethal."

"You said you called us here because you had questions. Are you asking if we know why Lyndon was at the hospital, why he was carrying an injured Seraph, or is it why the other deadly one was possibly nearby?" Raphael glanced to Uriel, then to Vretil and then back to Gabriel. "Or is it as to why Lyndon had not sought Lynn out?"

"I suspected you wouldn't have answers to that—I was merely informing you of a most recent quandary. We have not spoken since December of last year." Gabriel paused. "My questions are of a separate nature, the first of which is regarding my granddaughters."

"Continue," Vretil insisted, as though sympathizing with his apprehension.

"Are any of you familiar with the term *magic mirrors*?"

"Does this have something to do with why my Charge—why Mackenzie, has been researching spells involving mirrors?" Uriel questioned, his expression discerning.

"Yes," Gabriel confessed, then he elaborated on what had happened with the twins and the mirror he'd built for them.

"It sounds similar to what is used in parapsychology and spiritualism," Vretil said. "I believe I saw mention of it in one of Alison's journals. A psychomanteum."

Gabriel, along with the others, stared dumfounded at their fellow Archangel.

"It's a small, enclosed room or area set up with a chair, dim lighting, and a mirror," he elaborated nonchalantly, as though the arrangement was common place. "The mirror is angled so as not to reflect anything but darkness, which is intended for communicating with souls of the dead."

Gabriel and the other two continued to gape at him.

"What?" Vretil panned their faces. "I'm not saying I believe in such things—I simply read about how research has been done on the topic."

"Similar to an acoustic mirror, used to reflect and focus sound waves?" Uriel said, echoing his friend's interest.

Ignoring Uriel and Vretil, Raphael said, "Speaking of obscure research, could it be twin telepathy?"

"Their prophetic gifts are expanding rapidly, but the twins couldn't explain what happened to them either, so I feel confident they were not the source of the incident." Gabriel huffed. "And I'm guessing none of you have encountered such happenings in your centuries of watching over your Charges?"

Gabriel got head shakes from each of them.

"Did you have any other questions for us, Gabriel?" Raphael asked impatiently.

"I do," Gabriel said. "Have any of you spoken with Archangel Diniel, of late?"

Chapter 20 

I'd felt someone, someone other than Lyndon and the injured Seraph he'd carried through the ER doors. Gabriel had identified the injured one as Zuriel, but I had sensed a third one outside the hospital. It had been faint, but the signature was nothing I'd sensed before. My assumption had been it was another of Thaddeus's people, but I couldn't be sure. When I was over at South Haven, after I'd had the not-so-fun, nerve-wracking, and unexpected run-in with Lyndon, I'd asked Den to show me the photos of all Thaddeus's people, managers and trackers. But upon reviewing the photos, Marq told me they didn't have photos of the trackers, just their descriptions. Although, Ariadne's appearance, I'd been told prior, was almost identical to Amahle, only she was albino, and though she had long hair like Amahle at the time they'd been trapped on earth, there was no guarantee she had kept it that way. Now, she, along with Thaddeus, were the only ones of his crew that Leo and the others hadn't been able to locate. Ariadne had been listed as a Tracker, but Marq had called her a *killer*. At the time I hadn't asked why but considering what I'd sensed and witnessed at the hospital, I needed to understand the *why*. Den explained to me that she'd killed one of Thaddeus's human henchmen when he'd tried to touch her one too many times. When I'd asked how she had done it,

Den said she used the tip of an arrow to slit his throat. Apparently, she was fond of bows and arrows. There was no way to know if who I'd sensed was Ariadne, but fortunately I'd not felt this third Seraph again, whoever it had been, and Darius too had felt no other threats.

In regard to Lyndon, I'd not seen or felt him at the hospital either since that day, but despite that, Gabriel had opted to stay close by at the hospital on my volunteer days. In addition, Den had made it a point to do aerial surveillance over our home at night and had taken Gavin up on his invite to come help out at the girl's school during the day, all while Marq monitored things using the security system he'd set up for us. Alison had made sure to write out all the details as she'd seen them unfold in her head upon my giving her the information. She always felt more comfortable knowing she had it all outlined in her notebooks. Mac, on the other hand, had doubled up on the protection spells around both hers and Alison's homes. She'd even amped up the ones at Olivia's house expressing to her she had wanted to refresh the existing ones verses telling Olivia the real reason she was amplifying the protection. We all knew Olivia was best kept in the dark regarding Lyndon, even if we couldn't confirm if he was a threat or not. Darius had then updated Luc and Derek about the current state of safety.

I'd been nervous at first, though as the weeks went by and nothing else happened, I'd felt fairly confident that if Lyndon was coming after me, he'd have done it by now. Because of that fact, I had requested everyone go back to their usual routines. They had agreed, but only once I'd promised them all that if I felt even the smallest tingle of an Earthbound, I'd alert them. For even more added safety, Redmond had gone as far as having Marq get me an updated cellphone with an app installed on it, which would allow for me to hit *one* button to alert them all.

I'd reached out to Mac and Alison as well, to let them know the scoop, making sure they understood the coast appeared to be clear and not to worry. Mac had conveyed she was still researching more on spells that involved mirrors, but so far, she hadn't found anything relatable. I'd left my conversation with the ladies on a happy note telling them I'd made a new doctor friend and how Grier had bought a place just up the beach from us. They were both pleased to hear it and knew how much I longed for a local girlfriend since moving to the small town we now lived in. When the pandemic hit shortly after we moved here, there had been no meeting anyone for quite a while. Getting back out in the world doing my volunteering was something I'd hoped would facilitate meeting new people. And as a result, I'd connected with Grier.

On an even happier note, Redmond and I had announced to Leo we would be going to New York City to gather with his parents and extended family for Thanksgiving. Leo wasn't a fan of *my* going, but when Kris had heard we were heading up to his old stomping grounds, he had graciously offered to reach out to Frank and coordinate with her on the possibility of hosting the event at SNOW. Luckily for us, Frank had been thrilled at the opportunity to host the shindig as a thank you for bringing Kris back. She had also promptly asked for me to send the number of family members and had stated she would attend to *everything*. Kris had also mentioned to Leo that as added security he would be there with us, so between him and Frank we would be in safe hands.

As for Lane learning about Lyndon being in Florida, well, she had been floored by what Leo had told her, but it hadn't been until I had gotten to speak with her myself that same night, that she'd fully understood everyone's apprehension about her spending time with him. I'd shared more about my life with her during our conversation too, about my growing up with the freaky spidey sense, about my interactions with the different types of angels, and even about the twins and their abilities, the ones we could confirm thus far. We had not spoken since then, but I considered she might be taking some time to absorb what she'd been told. Then this morning she had texted asking if we could talk again about *things*. That was a no-brainer, of course we could, and I texted back saying as much. And that I was free to chat after 10:00 a.m. if that worked for her.

My new cellphone rang at 10:05 a.m. and displayed the cute photo of Lane and her dads she'd sent me, indicating it was she who was calling.

"Heeey," I said, answering the call and putting it on speaker. I set my phone on the kitchen island while I made my breakfast.

"Hi Aunt Lynn. I'm driving and have you on hands-free, so you might hear some noise in the background. Thank you-thank you for making time to talk."

"I'll always make time for you, Lane. You could have reached out anytime," I stated, hoping to reassure her. "I hope you know that."

"I know… I just feel like…."

"Like what?" I asked, removing a basically empty bag of bread from the fridge drawer.

"Like a brat bugging her only aunt with drama," Lane huffed out

I removed the last pieces of bread from the bag and placed it in the toaster. Clearly I needed to get groceries. "You know, you're not the only female born into this," I reminded. "You are friends with Rachel. She's new to the whole angel thing too and I know she doesn't have to deal with it directly, but…."

"It does help to have a friend who knows what I know," she agreed. "I didn't have a lot of friends growing up. I was a loner and liked it, but it was hard not being able to have friends over. Now I'm starting to think maybe I should move out."

I pressed the lever down on the toaster. "I know you're not a child, but you still need protection."

"I'm not sure what I'm being protected from."

"Tell me why you believe in Lyndon so much? What exactly has convinced you to trust him?" I asked, rescuing a plate from the cupboard to put my soon-to-be toasted bread on.

"Haven't you ever had a gut feeling about someone? Ha—look who I'm asking," Lane laughed out, as if realizing what a silly question she'd asked. "Aunt Lynn, if you could only see him with Taylor, you'd understand."

I grabbed up the butter from the fridge and then honey from the cupboard. "When we visited with Taylor, Carlie told us he didn't like the male attendants, so I'm amazed to hear he likes Lyndon so much."

"He *adores* Lyndon. It is the sweetest thing when Lyndon caresses his little cheek and calls him *Angel*. Even more adorable is the way Taylor looks at Lyndon. He's essentially nonverbal, but when Lyndon calls him that, Taylor actually says the word Angel back to him. I can't explain it, but there's this *protective* nature to Lyndon—I feel it when I'm with him. I feel safe."

My toasted bread bounced as the spring in the toaster released them. "Lane… are you developing feelings for Lyndon?"

"I… I *feel* for him… for his situation. I get that it's complicated—he tells me that all the time."

"But…," I began, as I transferred my toast to the plate, "… it's more than that, isn't it?" I knew the answer, but still had to hear it from her.

"I really like him, Aunt Lynn," she confessed. "I just wish I knew what to do about it. My emotions are such a mess."

"I wish I knew what to tell you—to make this easier," I said, buttering my toast. "And I wish I could meet him. See him interact with you—see him in action with Taylor."

"That's not possible—I get it, but it sure would be helpful. It's a shame he knows what you look like."

I nodded, even though she couldn't see me. "That's an understatement." I chuckled. "Does he tell you about what he is doing, his job, or *who* his boss is?"

"He says he does research and runs errands for the guy. When we talked last, he asked if I'd heard the name *Thaddeus Smyth*—which I said I had. But I pretended I thought he was some entrepreneur who did research with sick kids. It's difficult to play dumb sometimes."

"I can see how it would be hard." I drew squiggles of honey back and forth over the toast.

"He didn't give me any details on the stupid asshole, other than he was a horrible person and that he doesn't care about the sick kids. And I already knew from my previous conversations with him that he hates the guy. That last time he mentioned him, I questioned him again why he would work for someone he clearly detests."

"What did he say?" I folded the first piece of toast in half and took a bite.

"He gave me nothing back on the subject, so I let it go. I didn't want to push."

"Do you think he trusts you enough to share *his* secrets with you?"

"He might. I wish I could tell him I know all about him and his kind—but I know that would be a huge mistake right now. I just hate the lying. Today will be the first time back at the group home since my helping with Thanksgiving."

"Right." After several group discussions over the last two weeks, with me included, we'd all agreed Lane could go back to volunteering, but she needed to be extremely careful.

"You're sure Lyndon didn't see you?"

"Yes, thank gawd. I'm not sure if anyone told you, Lane, but the other Earthbound with him was badly injured." I took another bite of my toast.

"Yes, Leo told me, said his name was Zuriel. He also said they didn't know what happened to him or why Lyndon brought him there. But Aunt Lynn...." She paused.

"What is it Lane?"

"I've heard that name before."

"What—when?" I questioned around a mouth full of toast.

"I'd asked Lyndon if there was anyone at his job that he *liked* working with and he'd said *Zuriel,* but also that he didn't really work with him much."

"Why didn't you say anything to Leo?"

"Honestly, I'm not sure why—just that if Lyndon liked the guy, and he'd been hurt, I'm not surprised he brought him to the hospital."

"You need to let Leo know—tell him you recalled this bit after we talked. That way, they won't keep you from the group home."

"Ground me, you mean?"

"Lane, all of this is way too much of a coincidence for my or for any of our liking," I stated. "You need to get Lyndon to tell you something—something that would convince the others we can trust him. If his loyalty is with Thaddeus, you can't *ever* have a real relationship with him of any kind."

"I know—I know."

"You keep saying *I know,* but the fact that Lyndon and the others don't know about The Guards is crucial. Knowing would put everyone in danger. So answering your earlier question, I guess that's what they are trying to protect you from, protect us all from." It was clear to me more than ever that Lane needed Lyndon to prove himself, to share something that would tell us we could trust him, that *she* could truly trust him.

"Okay, I just got to the group home—I'll call you later, let you know how it goes."

"Be careful," I said, just as a tiny text message icon displayed in the corner of my cellphone's screen.

"I will—and thank you, Aunt Lynn, for listening."

"Anytime."

Shoving the last of my toast in my mouth, I checked the message and saw it was from Grier. We'd been texting back and forth at least once a week since early September.

She'd written,

> *Happy beach morning. If you are not busy, would you fancy a coffee at my place?*

Most of our texts had been about topics such as the area, best places to eat, where to get deals on this or that, and about the beach house *must haves*, but we hadn't had any compatible time to get together yet. I'd already had my morning coffee, however I did fancy a little in-person get-to-know-you-time with my new friend, so I wrote back,

> *I'm already caffeinated, but my morning is open. See you in about 20 minutes?*

A few seconds later, she wrote back,

> *Great! The pumpkin muffins should be ready by the time you get here.*

Having a new friend just up the way was great, but having one who baked was even better. Plus, I could use a little walk to clear my brain and with the weather being slightly overcast, it would be cooler for the walk on the beach.

Normally I was barefoot for my walk on the beach because I wouldn't be walking on anything but sand, but I'd packed a pair of flip-flops in my little crossbody satchel before I left, just in case I needed footwear not knowing what to expect at the other end. I'd also packed the 'Welcome to the Beach' sign Redmond had made, and the twins had painted for her.

When I reached the sand dune at the entrance to the footpath down to the cottage, a flood of memories hit me from the time when Redmond and I had viewed and considered purchasing the tiny home. Walking down the sand footpath that merged into a wooden walkway, I recalled it had been rough bare wood when we'd walked it from the bottom of the stairs off the back deck out to the beach, but now the surface was smooth and painted a soft sky blue requiring no footwear at all. From off the walkway, I continued still barefoot around the left side of the house over a well-manicured lawn that led me around to the front steps. Like our beach house, this little cottage was also a stilted home built to withstand any potential storms or flooding. The underside of the home was similar as well, having a carport with an entrance to a smaller lower level, though there had been no inner stairwell to the upper level, it being just a room with extra space that held the utilities and the washer and dryer. Would make for good storage, I considered as I climbed the newly painted white staircase up to the main entrance door.

At the top, I found the front deck, along with the home's exterior had been freshened up with paint like the wooden walkway had with the same sky blue, its windows framed in the same renewed white paint as the stairs. I had loved the look of this quaint little home when I'd seen it years ago, but I loved it even more now with its renewed appearance.

Before I could knock, the front door swung wide to reveal a giddy, grinning Grier. "Hiiii! Happy Halloween! Come in-come in!" she squealed in greeting. The delicious aroma of fresh baked goods wafted out following her greeting. That day at the hospital when I first met Grier, she'd been in her professional suite, her hair in a tight bun at her nape, but today in contrast, she was in casual comfortable attire consisting of butter coloured terrycloth shorts and a matching short-sleeved yellow hoodie, her red hair up in a ponytail this time.

"Happy All Hallows' Eve," I greeted back, stepping through the door. "Wow, the place looks amazing," I added, scanning the open layout of the home. It still had the slanted beadboard ceiling, and the interior had been empty when we'd viewed it, but now it was adorned with wonderful coastal furnishings and beachy artwork on the walls.

"Thank you—I appreciate that. I've only ever lived in apartments, so it has been great fun fixing up this little place." Grier cupped her hands together at her chest. "Was it furnished when you saw it way back? It was a blank canvas when I viewed it," she said excitedly.

"Empty," I said, as I strode from the front door through to the living room. "Here," I said, drawing free the little housewarming gift from my satchel.

"Oh my gosh—that's fabulous—did you make that?" Grier gaped wide-eyes at me.

"Me no," I said with an amused laugh. "Ryley and Hayley and my husband made it for you."

"Lynn, it's truly wonderful." She clutched the small wooden sign to her chest.

"You sent me the paint colours you picked for the house, remember? Redmond matched them for the girls, and they painted the sign."

"I'll be sure to thank them when I finally meet them—but please tell them how much I adore it." She backed up, then turned to face the wall on the right of the entry. "Great spot for it, don't you think?" she said, holding the sign up to the wall over a cute shabby-chic entry table. "Welcome to the beach house," she said, reading the words on the sign.

"Excellent choice. Text me a photo once you have it up—and I'll show the girls."

"I will for sure," she said, resting the sign down on the table for now.

"Show me what you've done to the place." I removed my satchel and placed it on the table next to the sign.

"I haven't changed much. It was mostly just patchwork and paint, plus furniture. Come check out the kitchen first," she said with an enthusiastic arm wave in the direction.

I strode with her to the kitchen at the back of the house, which was more a nook with its L-shaped counter, containing a farm sink in the section next to the entry and a gas stove along the other section that extended to butt up to the fridge.

"I love that you painted the cupboards," I said, standing in the middle of the kitchen. Pale blue cabinets lined both the upper wall over the counter and lower. The opposite wall had double pantry doors painted in the same colour.

"I just couldn't have *every* room painted white," Grier said, nodding and admiring her kitchen.

"The blue is terrific," I said, glancing up. Like the living and dining room, the ceiling was a white beadboard, which paired well with the light neutral countertop and backsplash to create the illusion of an airy coastal kitchen, making the space feel much bigger. Even better, the far side of the kitchen exited out a sliding door to a back deck.

"Not much tricker treating in our area, I'm afraid," I said, spotting several bags of Halloween candy piled in a corner of the kitchen's counter.

"Aww, really?" Grier gave me a disappointed pout.

"Ya, not since before covid. Kids these days like to do group parties. It's not like when I was a kid, that's for sure." I shrugged. "We don't even buy candy anymore. Though Redmond always picks up a couple bags of the single wrapped Reese's cups for himself. And I make him keep them in the downstairs fridge, so I don't eat them." But I winked at her. "I steal one occasionally."

"That's a shame. More for me, I guess." She giggled. "I've always loved Halloween." She reached for a bag of mini chocolate bars, then tore it open. After plucking one from the bag, she leaned the opening my way. "Do you and Redmond dress up for Halloween?" Grier asked then.

I took a mini KitKat from the bag and began unwrapping it. "This year we are because we're taking the girls off island to a party at the roller rink. We're going for comfortable and easy, dressing up as hippies." I snapped the KitKat in two. "What about you?" I asked, then popped one half of the bar into my mouth.

"Well, I kind of cheat." Grier adjusted her ponytail, then snatched another tiny bar from the bag.

"What do you mean?" I popped the second half of the KitKat into my mouth and chewed.

"I usually wear a pair of hospital scrubs and hang a stethoscope around my neck." She smirked. "One year I put fake blood on the front of my top, but it kind of freaked the little kids out too much, so now I stick with the clean scrubs."

"Hey, scrubs are comfortable and easy—no shame there, sister."

"That's what I say," she said, scooping up and tossing our wrappers in the trash under the sink. "Let me show you the rest," Grier said, taking my hand and basically dragging me out of the kitchen back through the open dining/living room to the left and into a short hall. "Guest bedroom here," she said, coming to a stop and pointing to the entrance of the room.

I leaned into the small guest room to see it had a double bed with a white headboard and sea-foam green bedding. There were petite white wall sconces on either side over quaint nightstands that matched the style of the headboard. A large single-framed photo of a sand dune path hung on the wall opposite to the bed. "It's so cute," I said. The room didn't have much in it, but as a guest at a beach house, you didn't spend much time in your room other than sleeping and changing, so it was just right.

"Bathroom is here," she indicated, pointing left up the short hall.

I took a quick peek in the bathroom to see that everything was white, from the standup shower to the sleek toilet and sink. Even the walls were white shiplap, although the consistent white aided in making the tiny space look larger.

"That's the entrance to my bedroom there at the end. Come see how ideal it is," Grier said, moving forward and pushing open the bedroom door.

Like the guest room, this one had the same slanted ceiling that met up with the opposite slanted side over the living room and dining space. And she'd used a similar colour palette with soft hues of sea-foam green with hints of sea blues paired with sandy tones. This room had a king-sized bed with a padded headboard, flanked by similar yet larger nightstands, these having a drawer and a lower shelf, and big enough to have actual lamps on each. Suspended over the bed was a sweet crystal chandelier, the curving arms painted white complemented the charming feminine touches Grier had added. There was also a private bathroom with the same standup shower, sleek toilet, and dual sinks. A large picture window took up most of the far wall, displaying the view out to the beach. "Grier, this isn't ideal—it's perfect!" I turned to face her.

"Do you really think so? I just love it so much," she squealed.

"If it had been just Redmond and me, I would have snatched this little beauty up in a heartbeat."

"I feel so lucky my realtor found it for me." She cupped her hands to her chest again.

"I'm grateful they did too." It was nice knowing someone wonderful now owned it and I had that same great new friend close by.

"Let's sit in the living room. We can go out back to the deck once the shade finally covers it."

That was the issue with our deck, too. You had to wait for shade when it was too hot to sit out there. "Sure," I said, following her back into the living space. Like the guest room, the living room had a large picture window with a view over the front deck. I glimpsed out the front window, then glanced down at the pale wood floors. "I love the floors. Are they laminate?" I asked.

"Engineered hardwood," Grier corrected, before racing back to the kitchen. She returned with two pumpkin muffins on napkins. Handing me one, she said, "With the beach practically at my back door, the floors needed to be able to stand up to sandy feet." Grier rested down in one of two tan cushioned vintage bamboo chairs, then propped her feet up on the well-worn birchwood coffee table. "I put sisal rugs at the front and back doors to handle traffic."

"Smart." Instead of taking the other bamboo chair, I chose to sit in the deep slip-covered tan coloured sofa at the end closest to Grier. "We have similar fabric on our couches at home. Same colour too."

"Washable," she said, nodding, taking a big bite from her muffin.

"Swimsuit-friendly," we both said at the same time, ending our declarations with coupled laughter.

I took a bite of the warm pumpkin muffin and glanced back over the couch to the dining area, admiring the solid raw wood coloured table and chairs. Two of the four slat back farmhouse style chairs were painted in the same blue shade as the kitchen cupboards, the other two had been painted white. The dining area had a similar window to the living room one, with a view out the side of the house to what I could spy was a short wall of seagrape trees. I turned back to Grier. "I like how your window treatments are all sleek and modern and fit into the breezy coastal décor without sacrificing any of the practical benefits they provide." I smiled, nodding approvingly at her.

"They're sun controlled," Grier said, eyeing each of the windows.

"Sun controlled?" I took a second bite. "Thishis delishhus," I mumbled, mouth full.

"Solar shades," Grier clarified, giggling, and taking a bite of hers. Swallowing, she said, "They provide protection from UV rays. The strong summer sun can damage your skin—not to mention your furniture, but these shades filter the harsh unwanted part."

"Okay, we need these at our place," I said. "I'll have to tell Redmond about them."

"I'll hook you up—I got a guy," she laughed out. "Put it on your beach house must-have list."

"Done," I said, pointing at my noggin and chewing the last of the seasonal dessert. "That muffin was better than any Halloween candy."

"I only make them at this time of year. Like with the Halloween candy, I tend to overindulge." She patted her little tummy. "What are your daughters dressing as for Halloween?"

"Well, friends of ours made them wings for their birthday back in May, so the girls figured they could use them and go as...."

"Angels?" Grier guessed.

"Ha—no, *Egrets*," I said, the word *angels* still humming in my ears.

"Like the ones you see in packs out on the lawns here?" she questioned, pointing to the front window.

"Yes, exactly." I set my now empty napkin on the coffee table.

"Oh, how funny."

"They look hilarious. They're wearing black tights for the long legs, with white shorts and t-shirts over, and Redmond crafted them some long skinny yellow beaks. When they tried everything on, they walked around making stiff steps just like the birds." I chuckled, thinking about it.

"Please send me photos later," Grier asked.

"Okay, but yer gonna die when you see them," I said with another chuckle.

"Laughter therapy," she countered, giving me a one-handed thumbs-up.

"Grier," I began, anxious to ask this question, giving her a sly look.

"Lynn," she responded, mirroring my expression.

"How old are you?" I asked, holding back a laugh. I'd been curious about her age since we first met. Not that it mattered, my desire was for compatible friendships.

Grier giggled in place of a response, causing my laughter to break free. Then she said, "I turned 40 in February, a week after we met." She positioned her hands in a Madonna vogue style around her face. Then she sucked in her cheeks. "But I don't look a day over 39 and 3/4s," she added, sucking her cheeks in again before letting out another giggle.

"Ahhh, you look pretty damn good to me," I said, accepting the almost 15 year age difference, still grateful she was closer in age to me than I had thought. "That's why I was intrigued." I mirrored her vogue pose. Grier giggled again. "How's your practice?" I asked then, relaxing my face, cheeks tender from the sucking in.

"It's good," she said, reaching forward, tossing her used napkin on the coffee table next to mine. "But I do most of my work with my Miami patients via telehealth video." She shifted in her seat, crossing her legs at the ankles. "You're still volunteering at the hospital, I take it?"

"Yup," I said, rotating her way to lean my shoulder and body against the back of the sofa. I noticed Grier's hospital ID badge on the end table next to the sofa. "Why does your badge have a green *and* gold box around your photo? Mine only has the green box," I asked, picking up the badge from the small table.

"The gold box indicates to staff I'm part of the psychiatric team without identifying my role to patients." Grier loosened her ponytail, letting the red length of it down, then she swooped it back up into a loose bun on the top of her head.

Grier's actions with her hair reminded me of Mac and I felt a pang of missing my longtime friend, and I was reminded as well of her words on being at the clinic with Olivia, *'I'm just not so cool anymore with dealing with the heart wrenching stuff,'* she'd said. Hospital work was not for everyone. I glanced at Grier's ID badge again. "Like for when ER staff call psych down to evaluate a patient?"

"Exactly."

"How does the on-call thing work?" I shifted in my seat, tucking my feet under my butt.

Grier ran her hand around the back of her neck. "I'm on call nights only, from 9 p.m. until 6 a.m. Sunday through Thursday. I have my in-person appointments from 9 to 5, and the rest of the time is mine," she said, drawing her hand free from behind her neck. "Though I currently only have one in-person patient."

"Are they a new patient?" I already knew she wouldn't be able to elaborate on the details, but I had been wanting to ask her something else that had been renting space in my brain.

"Fairly new. I've been working with them for a few weeks now."

I pursed my lips, moving my mouth side to side as I mustered my courage, pondering whether I should ask my next question. I brought my hand to my necklace and ran it back and forth on the chain, then I asked, "Do your patients ever bring up their dreams in their sessions?"

"Oh yes, all the time. Why?" Grier did the hair loosening and swooping back up into a bun thing again.

"I'm not looking for a free psychiatry session, just some advice," I said. "But have you ever—or have any of your patients ever had dreams where you could swear it was real, but can't explain it?"

Grier stared down at the floor as if in a daze, as though plagued with recollections about what I just asked.

"Grier?" I queried, hoping I hadn't triggered a difficult memory.

"Dreaming," Grier said then, lifting her gaze back to me. "I have patients who talk about this." She nodded. "Oneironautics."

"Oneirona—what?"

"It's another name for lucid dreaming, the ability to journey within a dream in a conscious state. A person who can do this is called an oneironaut."

"Okay," I said, pleased Grier seemed knowledgeable on the subject.

"I've worked with both ends of the sleep spectrum, those who claim to never dream, and the dreamwalker whose dreams rival waking life."

A shiver ran down my spine. "What is a dreamwalker?"

"It's another term used for a lucid dreamer. I've been having fairly lucid dreams myself lately," she shared. "Are you familiar with lucid dreaming?"

"Maybe—not sure," I said, shrugging. I'd never heard the term before, but I was interested to know if this was what was happening to me, though mine felt more like my waking premonitions than just basic dreams.

"Lucid dreams are when you know you're dreaming while you're asleep. You're aware that the events flashing through your mind aren't really happening, but the dream feels real. Often, lucid dreamers are able to exert some or complete control over things like the dream's narrative or even the characters and environment."

Listening intently, I pulled up one of my knees to my chest, wrapping my arms around it.

"A dreamwalker can also be a person who often appears in or vividly haunts a person's dreams, usually in a positive way." Grier stared down at the floor again. "Or one who practices a type of out-of-body experience, astral projection, similar to the Indigenous traditions of gathering information from the dream world. It's practiced around the world," she added, tugging her attention away from the floor to look back at me. "And neuroscientists conduct research on the topic."

I stared at her and ran the charms on my necklace to the right.

"Lynn, are you having lucid dreams?" she asked then, staring back at me.

"Yes," I responded, running the charms back to the left.

Chapter 21 

Grier sent me home with ample food for thought concerning my dreams and she'd sent literal food home in the form of a plastic container full of pumpkin muffins in *thank you* to Redmond and the girls for her housewarming gift, along with a bag of KitKat minis just for me.

As I walked the stretch of beach from her quaint beach cottage to our beach side home, I pondered the information she'd shared about lucid dreaming. She had stated that neuroscientists didn't know exactly how and why lucid dreams happen, but they *have* found physical differences in the brains of people who do and don't have lucid dreams. Stating that the prefrontal cortex is bigger in brains of people who have lucid dreams and that they were often the type of person who tended to be self-reflective and go over thoughts in their heads. In one study where they tracked electrical activity in the brain while people slept, the researchers stated that lucid dreaming was a *between state* where the person was neither fully awake nor quite fully asleep. Grier also mentioned there were benefits to lucid dreams, which I'd been eager to hear, expressing how it may aid your waking life, with having less anxiety, better motor skills, improved problem solving and more creativity. When I'd asked her if there were any drawbacks to lucid dreaming she'd said, mainly poor sleep quality, though worst case there could be confusion, delirium, or even hallucinations but these were usually with people with existing mental health issues where the lines between what's real or not are often blurred. I had chosen not to share much about my dreams other than they often felt very real, especially regarding my tactile and smell senses.

Releasing my brain of the topic of dreams, I reflected back on Leo's comments from a few weeks ago about how he wished there was a way to summon Purah. Then I suddenly wondered if I was suffering from one of those drawbacks Grier had mentioned, delirium possibly, because I found it overly coincidental that right in this moment I was literally sensing Purah's presence as I approached the footpath to our backyard. But through the palms at the bottom of the path, I could see her tall form, so clearly I wasn't delirious.

When Purah eyed me stepping free of the overhanging palm leaves, she said, "Thaddeus was back in Ottawa, but he has departed again." She thumped her staff. She was in her usual gladiator attire, with the armor of white leather and metal pieces fashioned around her arms, legs and torsos, and the same helmet with its shiny silver metal and opalescent horn-like protrusions on all sides of it. Her hair was affixed in its customary thick white braid that contrasted with the rich dark colour of her skin.

"I know — Leo told me already."

"I see." Purah nodded, then smiled. "How is Leo?"

There it was again, that sparkle. She does have a shine on for him. Her iceberg coloured eyes did that backlit thing, glowing brighter at the mention of Leo's name.

"He's fine. But you can always ask him yourself." I gave her an amused smile.

"Oh, no, I couldn't." As dark as her skin was, I still could have sworn her face flushed.

"How do you know Thaddeus was there — left again?" I rested the muffin-filled container on one hip, my hand on the other.

"I was there, in his penthouse. All his clothing has been removed," she stated.

"So what?" I shrugged. "You already told us he was going to Brazil. Although Leo told me Thaddeus hadn't been to the facility there — he sent Nic to check. No one has seen him in months."

"I saw...."

"Saw what?" I interrupted, impatient over the vagueness of her declaration.

"Lyndon," she clarified. "He was in the Ottawa penthouse, tending to the wounds of an injured Earthbound—but when I returned, they were gone."

"You're talking about Zuriel," I said, switching to holding the container with both arms.

"Yes, how did you know?" She tilted her head to the side, the horns of the headpiece catching the sun's rays.

"I saw him… with Lyndon."

"Where?" Her body armor creaked as though she flexed all her muscles at the same time.

"Lyndon brought him here—to the hospital—the one I work at. He was unconscious."

"Why would Lyndon bring him all this way, I wonder?" She tightened her hand around the staff. "Could it be he knows now where you are?" Purah took a long stride in my direction, halting in front of me and stomping her staff. "Did he see you?"

"No. And he didn't stay. He was gone right after the doctor took over." I gazed up at her. She was magnificent to witness, and I wondered again if I was dreaming. Giving my head a shake, I said, "If he was looking for me, why would he leave?"

Purah glanced briefly over her shoulder. "When I was in the penthouse, I overheard Lyndon speaking. It startled me because for a moment I thought Lyndon could see me—was speaking to me, but he was speaking to the unconscious Earthbound."

"What did he say?" I hugged the muffin container.

"He had leaned in close to Zuriel's face and said that Thaddeus told him to make sure he—Zuriel, was gone, and that he never wanted to see his face again."

I shook my head. "But why bring him here? What could have motivated Lyndon to bring him to *this* hospital versus one closer to where they were?"

"Could it have been Zuriel who requested it?"

Instead of answering her question, I gave her a question of my own. "Who was it you said saw me in New York City speaking with the Watcher?" I asked. "Was it Lyndon?"

"No. It was Marcus. He runs the facility there."

"I see," I said. I didn't know the answer to Purah's question, and other than the name of the Earthbound she'd given me, the one who had seen me, Purah hadn't had anything else worth telling me that I didn't already know. "Could you use your gift of teleportation to search and locate Thaddeus, mainly so we all know *where* he was exactly?" I would worry about *what* he was up to later. "And I'll let Leo know you dropped by." Right now, what I needed to focus on was my family and our night of ghouls, goblins, and roller-skating.

She smiled, stomped her staff, then was gone in a blink of an eye.

When we arrived at the skating area, many of the twins' schoolmates and their families were already there. Most of the parents were in costume though there were still those few too-cool-for-school parents who had opted out of both the Halloween dress-up and the skating, choosing to sit back sipping their portable chiller mugs while hovering around the viewing areas in the food court.

Being the cool parents Redmond and I were, we'd dressed in our fun yet comfortable hippie getups. We were both wearing bell-bottom pants, but Redmond had chosen to wear a tie-dye shirt with his, where I'd opted for a bright pink top with a flower pattern on it with a matching head wrap. Redmond had added a suede vest with fringes along the bottom edge to his costume with a matching leather headband. And while Redmond had kept his hair the same as usual, I'd gone with braiding mine into two braids and tying off the ends with colourful macrame hair ties. Topping off my ensemble, I'd donned a pair of glasses with circular frames tinted in a light pink. I'd even painted a daisy on my cheek for added affect. The girls, of course, were in their matching bird costumes.

The place itself had been thoroughly decorated for the occasion, although on regular skate nights the décor was a mix of abstract shapes done in bright colours of the technicoloured rainbow on both the non-skating floors and the carpeted half-walls that surrounded most of the rink. The tables and seating available were an assortment of neon yellow, green, pink, blue, and purple. Even the skates themselves were done in bright colours. The skate floor was your typical smooth finished wood, the ceiling a standard white, but when the regular lights went out for certain songs, the space filled with the same techno colours in the lighting as was on all the surfaces. Next to the skate rental counter was a pro shop where you could get a wonky skate fixed or purchase skate paraphernalia should you desire it. Next to it was the food court, which had one counter for buying things like candy and fountain drinks, and the other counter was a variety of hot foods like hotdogs and French fries. Lucky for us, we'd eaten dinner before venturing out to the event. The far side had most of the seating, some for eating and some for watching the skaters. Closer to the pro shop was a long wall filled with arcade games and more seating opposite to watch the skaters.

While Redmond laced up his skates, the girls and I went to the pro shop to obtain ours. I still rented mine, as did the girls, since their feet were continuously growing, and it made no sense to buy right now. Redmond, on the other hand, had purchased his own skates soon after his first time roller-skating with the twins, mainly because he'd had to use the largest pair the place had and still they were not big enough for his gigantic feet.

Skates on and tied, I sent the girls off to the continuous circling of amateur and seasoned skaters. I still had the roller-skating moves, as did Redmond, but the twins skated much faster than either of us did.

For the first half hour, we relaxed on one of the bench seats off to the side within the roller rink's walls, watching all the skaters go round and round. The kids were dressed in a variety of costumes, from a simple pumpkin to the more elaborate witch, cowboy, fairy, pirate, the easily identifiable Spider-Man, and even an inflatable dinosaur. The other adults had on basic costumes like clowns, witches, or vampires, though the occasional creative adult had upped their game with witches from Hocus Pocus and a family of blue Na'vi people from Avatar. But the best was the Stranger Things group costume, done by the creative talents of a family of three. The daughter was dressed like Eleven in the hospital johnny gown, short hair skull-cap, and a bloody nose, the father was in a white lab coat dressed as the scientist and director of Hawkins National Laboratory, and the mother was in what could only be described as the quintessential 80s mom outfit. She had big hair, big framed glasses, a big shoulder padded white blazer, sleeves rolled up to the elbow, high-waisted jeans, and a shirt with geometric patterns in neon colours similar to the floor and walls of this establishment.

Since most of the parents here were in their 40s, we were considered old to have kids the twins' age made even more evident with several of the younger moms wearing racier versions of the traditional pirate, nurse or witch costumes. There was one over-the-top mom who had on an overly-sexy devil get-up with her husband, who clearly thought he was a stud, having dressed in a Mavrick Top Gun jumpsuit, made for a perfectly ridiculous pair, creating an even more entertaining view. But when the music for an oldies skate song *You Dropped A Bomb On Me* by The Gap Band started, I grabbed up Redmond's hand and led him out onto the main floor of the rink.

We skated side by side for the next half hour, through *Funkytown*, Kool & the Gang's *Celebration*, *Super Freak* by Rick James, and then into the song *You Really Got Me*, though instead of the original Kinks version, the DJ played the one from Van Halen. Our skate-in-a-circle slowed down after that, into a waltz with a song by the Bee Gees, *How Deep is Your Love*. Then when that slow song morphed into *Fireworks* by Katy Perry, the twins rolled up alongside to skate with us. I noticed then that one of my laces had broken, and I let go of Redmond's hand, pointing to my skate and indicating to him I need to get off. The girls picked up where I left off, each taking one of Redmond's hands to continue the round-and-round.

Rolling off, I went and sat down at one of the seats outside the rink's walls. I undid the skate with the busted lace and removed my foot to examine the lace more closely. The break was too far down the line to retie it up securely and I would need to get another pair if I was going to continue skating. As I removed my other skate and set it next to its mate, Hayley and Ryley rolled up next to me.

"Muuuum, we'rrrre huuungry," Hayley whined, attempting to skate backwards out in front of me.

"You ate before we left—how can you be hungry now?" I asked, tucking the laces into the top of the skates.

"Mum—exerting energy makes a person hungry," Ryley stated, lemon-skating back and forth in the space in front of me. "And we've been spending energy all night."

"Fine," I said, losing what energy I had left from just watching them. I spied Redmond near the sound booth chatting with the DJ. "I need to swap out my skates—roll on over there and ask your father to get you something to eat, okay?" I pointed over to where Redmond was.

"Okaaay," they both said, clearly ravenous, skating off without asking why I needed to change out my skates.

Starvation avoided, I grabbed up my skates and headed over in my socked feet to the skate rental counter.

My feet were small, and I rarely had any issues with getting the size I needed, but the teenage boy behind the counter said, "We don't have any available that would fit you. With all the kids here tonight for the Halloween party, we barely had enough to accommodate them."

"No worries." I said, sliding the skates up next to each other. I was relieved, actually. Because on the walk over, fully intending to get back out on the rink, I had come to a shocking and painful realization that I had a doozie of a blister forming.

When I turned to leave, he said, "I can re-string the laces, but it would take a minute."

"I think I'm done for the night but thank you." I smiled at the young guy, giving him the peace sign, then stepped over past the racks of skates to the wall of lockers. In contrast to roller-rinks in the past, these days they didn't keep your shoes when they swapped them for skates. Instead, you are given a key to a locker to keep your shoes in. There would be no more skating tonight for this flower-child. *"Groovy—not,"* I muttered, peeling off my socks to slide my feet into my flip-flops. Before closing the locker door, I tucked my socks into the small knapsack that held the rest of our shoes.

Pleased to be out of those blister makers, I searched the rink for Redmond and the girls. Instead of seeing him making another circle of the rink, I found Redmond still hanging near the DJ booth.

"Where are your skates?" he asked as I walked up.

"Where are the girls?" I asked, not answering his question.

Redmond's eyebrows bunched. "Thought they were with you."

"They said they were hungry, so I told them to skate over to you." I scanned the immediate area but couldn't see their white and black costumed bodies anywhere. "I'll check the bathrooms," I said, before turning and heading to ones near the pro shop.

"I'll check the food court," Redmond said, pushing off in that direction.

In the ladies' room, I checked the vacant stalls and called out the girls' names to the occupied ones, but my daughters weren't in there. What I did find were two tween girls putting on makeup in the bathroom mirror. One was dressed in a too-short cheerleader outfit, the other in a mini version of that risqué devil costume.

"I bet I know who your mom is," I said to the one dressed as the devil, followed by an amused laugh.

"What?" the 10-year-old girl going on 20 said, giving me a snotty look.

"Nothing—nice costume," I said with a snort, pushing up my pink tinted hippie glasses and yanking open the door. *"For a future succubus,"* I mumbled, taking my exit.

Redmond nearly slammed into me when I rounded the corner into the food court near the seating area for non-skaters. "Not in the food court," he said, panning the arcade area behind me.

"Not in the bathrooms either," I stated, doing my fiftieth scan of the skating floor.

"Outside, maybe," Redmond declared, pushing off again before I could even answer.

I dashed after Redmond, following him out through the main entrance to where I spotted the twins near the walkway from the parking lot. "What are you two doing out here?" I shouted, rushing over to where they were standing on the grass in their socks, skates lined up next to them.

"We were talking to…," Ryley began to say, but Hayley elbowed her in the side.

"Talking to who?" I searched the other side of the parking lot.

"Our friend," Ryley finished, yanking Hayley's costume beak down off her face.

"Give me that!" Hayley shrieked.

"Stop that!" Redmond said before I could. "What friend? I don't see anyone."

"An angel friend," Ryley said, dodging another elbow from her sister.

"Hayley, stop elbowing your sister!" I yelled. "Which angel?" I hadn't felt any angels, but then my senses had been bombarded with techno lights and disco music for the past hour.

Hayley glared daggers at Ryley. "Don't tell," she said in a too-loud whisper.

Ryley stepped forward, out of her sister's reach. "Archangel Diniel."

"Diniel?" I questioned, blinking in surprise. "How do you know her?" What the hell was she doing talking to my daughters, for that matter?

Ryley shot a rueful look over her shoulder at her sister. "She came to visit us at the house."

"What—when?" To say I wasn't pleased to hear about an angel visiting unannounced was more than an understatement, but I *was* thankful it had been someone I was knew and not someone I had the misfortune to be familiar with, considering who I'd ran into at the hospital only three weeks ago.

"When you and Da were on your date night," Ryley admitted.

"Why didn't you tell us?" Redmond asked, kneeling in front of them.

Ryley shrugged. "We thought it was okay since she's like Gup."

"This is all your fault," Hayley said then, pinching her sister's arm.

"Ouch!" Ryley screeched, batting Hayley away and causing her to stumble back. "Stop it!"

"It was supposed to be a secret," Hayley said, smacking her sister's arm. "You broke the promise to Diniel."

"We don't keep secrets," I said through clenched teeth, yanking the two apart.

"Yes we do!" Hayley screamed defiantly.

"Not from each other—we don't!" Redmond roared. "Now go in and return those skates." He pointed sternly to the entrance.

"But Da!" Ryley whined, stomping her foot. "They haven't announced the winners from the costume contest yet."

"Go!" Redmond roared again. "As of right now—you're both grounded."

"Grounded—why?" Hayley protested, kicking her skates over.

I blew out a frustrated breath and said, "For going outside without telling us. *And* for not telling us about Diniel." I held up both my hands. "And don't you dare say another word," I added, noting Hayley was ramping up for another protest.

Without uttering another word, the two promptly gathered up their neglected skates and then marched it back over to the front entrance.

"Can you please get the rest of the shoes from the locker? I need a minute to cool down." I handed Redmond the locker key.

"No worries, babe," he said, taking the key from my hand and rubbing my back. He gave my shoulder a little squeeze before following our two delinquents back into the Halloween party.

I released a heavy sigh, then pulled in enough breath to call out. "Gabriel!"

Chapter 22 

The Group Home, Monday P.M. October 31ˢᵗ, Ottawa

Lane placed her key fob on the security panel at the entrance to the group home and when the door lock clicked, she pulled open the door and entered. Inside she found the place had been decorated for Halloween with the typical cobwebs and happy spiders, along with strategically placed plastic pumpkins and bats, and it made her smile to see the staff had put in the effort. Despite the fun decorations, Lane was still anxious, and didn't bother to hang up her lightweight bomber jacket, unsure whether she would be staying or not since it wasn't one of her volunteering days. Instead, she headed to the playroom to find Taylor.

Along the short route, she passed staff members wearing their usual uniforms coupled with wild and wacky headbands consisting of waving antennae tipped with a variety of end caps like stars, googly eyes, and blinking lights, and again she smiled at their efforts. Stopping at the playroom's entrance, Lane spotted Taylor. Sitting next to him was Lyndon. He was wearing a long-sleeved pullover, in a colour she loved to see him in. A shade akin to the foliage of a blue spruce, and one of the many green hues that made up the spectacular colour of his eyes. Her heart pounded.

When Lyndon noticed her standing in the doorway, he waved, then stood, eagerly motioning for her to come over, pointing to the open chair next to Taylor.

Pulling in a quick breath, Lane crossed the room where they sat near the large windows. "Hello," she said eagerly to Lyndon, then noticed his cellphone resting on the table in front of him. She removed her coat and hung it over the back of the chair before sitting in the spot next to Taylor. "Hi Taylor," she said, signing the same greeting. "Sorry I haven't been in lately."

Taylor responded by lifting and showing her the masterpiece he'd created on the Etch A Sketch. It was a beautifully detailed image of a smiling pumpkin which was so well rendered that it appeared as though you could reach in and grab it.

"How wonderful," Lane said, just before he shook the image away.

Taylor turned back and began another sketch.

"Busy with school?" Lyndon asked.

"Uhm, yes," she answered nervously, thoughts of his being in Florida near her Aunt Lynn and the unknown reasons *why* weighing on her.

"I thought as much," Lyndon responded, though Lane kept her eyes on Taylor. "Still working with Julianna—Professor Forest?" he said then, causing her to look his way.

"Some—but I have another professor who needs to review my paper—the revisions I made." It was the truth. "How have you been?" she asked, detouring the conversation away from Jules. She hated lying to him, albeit she knew he was keeping things from her, too.

"I am well. And you, how have you been?" He smiled sweetly at her.

"Good—busy," she said, her shoulders tensing. She hated small talk almost as much as lying. She turned her focus back on Taylor. "How have you been, my little prince?"

"He has been a good boy," Lyndon answered on his behalf. He touched Taylor's cheek to get his attention, then signed the word 'good'.

"You've been using the ASL," Lane said, surprised yet pleased to see he'd been practicing signing with Taylor.

"I am trying, yes." He smiled again. "How are you finding your master's program?"

"Good," she said again, "It's challenging, but I love it." Lane relaxed her shoulders, enjoying his interest in her studies.

"Have you made any new friends at school?"

Her shoulders tensed again, and she blew out a breath.

"Sorry, did I say something wrong?" Lyndon turned in his chair to look directly at her.

"It's just…," she began, her shoulders slumping. "… you sound like my fathers." She stared down at her hands in her lap.

"My apologies. I'm not trying to pry." Lyndon's massive hand slid into view to rest atop hers.

She lifted her head and stared into his intense forest green eyes. "No-no, I'm sorry." She pulled one hand free to pat the top of his. "They have been asking me that same question every year since kindergarten." She gave him a quick grin. "But to answer your question, *yes*, a few. Why do you ask?" Lane straightened, reluctantly drawing her other hand free of his.

"You never talk about friends," Lyndon said, his face blanketing now with disappointment.

"Neither do you," she said, noting Lyndon's upset at her removing her hands from his.

"Are they in the same program—these new friends?" he asked, his expression impassive now.

"No." She shook her head.

Lyndon shot a brief glance at his cellphone. "How did you meet them?"

"On campus." She thought back to when he'd followed her that one time and how he had behaved. "Just a few girls, and Mason. He's Professor Forest's son," she added, realizing too late she shouldn't have shared that last bit. "She said she adopted him from an orphanage in Brazil because she couldn't have children of her own. He's the reason she is here—partly. She took the job when it was offered because she'd lost funding for her research, and Mason had wanted to do the program here anyway—so win-win," she rushed out, fixing the blunder. "I'm grateful for her help with *my* program," she added with an exhale.

Lyndon nodded, then turned his attention to Taylor.

Lane breathed in, then let go of another breath. "Lyndon," she said, drawing his attention back. "Remember when you asked if I had any aunts?"

"Yes," he said, his expression quizzical.

"Well, I've gotten to talk to one of them a lot lately—we video chat because she lives in Florida with her family," Lane stated, giving reason as to why their talks had not been in person.

"How are you finding the *chats*?" he asked, giving her his full attention, yet giving no indication that *Florida* meant anything to him.

"It's nice… wonderful actually, talking to her… having another woman to talk to about things… *relationships*. I can't talk to my fathers about that sort of stuff—not really."

"Relationships?" Lyndon's brow furrowed.

"Yes…," Lane said, drawing in a long breath. "I wanted to talk to her about… *you*."

"Me?" Lyndon's eyes glittered as if filled with emotion. "Lane," he said, before glancing around. "Let's go downstairs to talk about this." He stood from his chair.

Lane let the air out of her lungs slowly, as though doing so would summon her courage. "Sure, of course."

He turned to look at Taylor and touched his cheek again. "I'll be back in a bit, Angel." He stood, snatching up his phone off the table.

With only the "*swish-swish*" of her brown corduroy pants to accompany her, Lane followed as Lyndon led her to the elevator. She said nothing as they rode it down to the lower level. It wasn't until Lyndon opened the door into his private space that she spoke again. "I needed to talk to my aunt… about… my *feelings*… for you," she said, crossing to the far side of the apartment, noticing there were now two leather armchairs. Lyndon's well-worn one and a brand new one, the same tan colour, were arranged in front of the bookshelves. The door being shut sounded behind her as she regarded the seating arrangement.

"Feelings… regarding me?" she heard Lyndon question.

When she turned, Lyndon was there, right in front of her, staring down at her in disbelief. "Yes," she confessed, holding his gaze.

Lyndon said nothing, his expression that of bewilderment.

"The other day," Lane began, then swallowed. "I got in a big argument with my fathers and one of my uncles... they said they thought that my work here was supposed to just be volunteering, not *fraternizing*."

Lyndon stared at her, remaining silent and seemingly shocked at what she was sharing. Taking the leap, she said, "I told them I wasn't a child, and that I *wasn't* fraternizing... that we—you and I had a real friendship."

He continued to stare at her, his deep green eyes fixated on her every word.

"They asked if I was developing feelings for you and...." She paused. "... and when I didn't answer—they lost it." She blinked. "I told them if they met you—they would see what I see. What a good man you are."

"Lane, I...," Lyndon started to say, but she interrupted.

"I told my aunt I was starting to have more than *friendship* feelings for you," she added, taking another leap.

"But Lane...," he began again, cutting her off this time.

"But what?" she countered.

"... I'm not a good... man."

"Don't say that—yes, you are!" she shouted. "You've always been so kind and respectful to me. And I see how you are with Taylor."

Lyndon lifted his hands, palms upward. "Lane you don't...."

"I don't what?" Lane folded her arms over her chest.

"You don't know me."

"But I do," she insisted, tightening her folded arms. "You care about Taylor, this place, and you care about *me*—I know you do."

"You don't know the things I've done." Lyndon dropped his hands and lowered his gaze to the floor between them.

"What—for your boss?" Lane shifted her weight, rocking anxiously side to side.

"Yes."

"Just because you work for an asshole doesn't make you one by association." Lane released her arms, throwing them in the air.

Lyndon blew out a heavy breath, then pushed past her.

Arms still in the air, Lane turned to see he had rested himself down in the old armchair, the leather sighing as it accommodated his hefty weight. She put her hands on her hips.

Without lifting his gaze to her, he patted the seat of the new armchair, wordlessly indicating for her to come sit.

Surrendering, she further dropped her arms to her sides, and then she took the seat next to him. The feel of the new leather chair was soft and buttery, and she glanced at Lyndon to comment just as he reached over and effortlessly rotated Lane's chair to face him. Lane pulled at the neck of her suddenly too-warm sweater.

Lyndon leaned forward then, propping his elbows on his knees. Steepling his fingers, he asked, "Lane, do you… believe… in the *supernatural*?"

Lane felt her mouth gape, then quickly schooled her features. "Do you mean like ghosts and such?" *And angels*, she mused, keeping that thought to herself.

He nodded, folding his fingers into an overlapping fist.

"Okay, don't laugh but…," she began, knowing with confidence he wouldn't. "…. I'm a huge believer." She stared at him wide-eyed.

Emotionless, Lyndon rested his chin on his fisted hands and asked, "Have you ever experienced or witnessed something *otherworldly*?"

Lane's eyes felt dry from staring, and she purposely blinked. "Are you asking me this because it's Halloween?" she questioned, playing as though she didn't know the real reason.

"Halloween?" Lyndon straightened in his seat, shaking his head once. "No."

"Yes, I have," Lane confessed, playfully. "Have you?" She already knew the truth. The idea she should ask him to go with her to the Halloween party at Après SNOW suddenly popped into her head. She hadn't decided on a costume yet, but maybe this was something they could choose together.

"I have as well, yes," Lyndon replied, shifting her from her musing. "But… you probably wouldn't believe me if I told you."

"Try me." Lane cocked an eyebrow. "Bet I would."

"Lane, would you consider yourself a… *spiritual* person?" he asked then.

She knew where he was going with this but still asked, "What do you mean by *spiritual*? Like do I believe in God… or angels?" *Here it comes,* she thought.

Lyndon's cellphone rang on the kitchen counter where he'd left it, then vibrated its need for attention. Not answering Lane's question, Lyndon rose from the armchair, swiftly walking to the far side of the room to retrieve it. "Yes, I've been waiting for your call," she heard him say upon answering it.

"Not again," Lane grumbled under her breath.

Chapter 23 

Cleveland Hospital, Tuesday November 14th, South Florida

"Where are you?" Alison asked, through the tiny video screen on my cellphone.

"I'm at work—outside in the atrium. I just finished my shift." I shot a glance over my shoulder to see that I was still alone.

"Why didn't you wait until you got home to chat with us?" Mac asked.

"You said you were free when I texted, and we haven't had a chance to talk since before Halloween, so I took the opportunity." I slid further over on the bench to be fully under the shade of the covered employee break area.

"Did something happen on Halloween?" Alison asked, her pen and notebook at the ready.

"You could say that," I said, before leading them through the events of the roller-skating kerfuffle.

"What is this bitch up to?" Mac questioned.

"Mac!" Alison said in response to her outburst.

"Sorry—Archangel—I know, but what the hell is she doing?" Mac questioned again, bringing her huge black leather purse into view of her laptop's camera, rummaging through it like she was searching for a witchy weapon. "First Lyndon shows up for whatever-the-hell-reason, and now this angel is stirring shit up with your girls?"

"I know," I sighed out. It was a lot even for me, and I wasn't remotely okay with either visit. I sighed again. "I have no idea what she wants, but her request for secret keeping is a serious violation. I'll make sure Gabriel knows and he can put a stop to it. The girls understand what they did was wrong, but it's evident the influence Diniel has had on them."

Mac pulled her wand from her deep purse. "You mentioned you have a new doctor friend at work," she stated, using the wand to twist her hair up in a messy topknot.

"She's only on call so I don't get to see her at the hospital, unfortunately, but I did get to see her new place the morning of Halloween, though."

"That's right, she lives on the same stretch of beach as you," Alison recalled.

"Ya, it's just a 20-minute walk up the beach. Mac, you'd love the decor—I'll try to get some pictures to show you."

"Please do," Mac said. "Oh, to live on the beach," she added.

"Grier texted the day after Halloween asking how the skating had gone. I had to give her a vetted version of the details but gave her just enough information to convey I was scared to death when we couldn't find them. I explained we'd found them outside alone, but obviously I hadn't shared the reason they were out there, only that the girls were upset at us for making such a fuss."

"It's still the truth when you think about it. If someone—anyone, had lured them outside you'd have been just as scared and furious," Alison said.

I nodded. "'*Boundary pushing*' Grier had called it."

"We've all been there," Mac added. "Hey, have you talked to Lane since Halloween?"

"I did. She messaged me the day after Halloween, too. Told me she spoke with Lyndon on Halloween, and he was about to tell her something big, but then he got a phone call. She wanted to invite him to the Halloween party at Après SNOW, but she hadn't gotten a chance because he had to run. Didn't say where, but she said he apologized nonstop as he led her back up to the main floor and out to her car. He also promised her he'd go to the restaurant with her at some point, but she hasn't seen him since then."

"Did you tell her about *your* hectic Halloween?" Mac asked.

"Ya, and she told me a similar story about how she'd wondered off during a Canada Day celebration downtown when she was 10 years old and had basically aged her fathers an *equal 10 years* as they had put it, having a similar scare. She understood it wasn't quite as severe as with the girls, but the situation with seeing her fathers so terrified, had frightened her equally."

"How are the girls now?" Alison asked, jotting down the details.

"The girls were upset—but madder at us for making such a big deal out of it, but *frightened*, they had not been. I wished they had been more scared, but it was difficult to fully explain all the dangers out there, considering they aren't like the dangers regular kids have to watch out for."

"Still, those should have been enough to frighten them a bit," Mac said.

"You'd think. But like with surfing, they have always been fearless, but at this point, under these circumstances, it wasn't a good thing." I shook my head. "Lane told me you guys went to Après SNOW on Halloween."

"We did," Mac said. "Back in the 80s it was that bar Stoney Mondays, remember? It's changed so much since Kris and Leo renovated it."

"Changed for the better," Alison added. "Did Lane tell you about the staff costumes?"

"She said they did a zombie Scooby Doo themed mashup, but that was all she told me. She was too focused on Lyndon and their talk."

"It was excellent," Alison said, leading into the description of the t-shirts the staff had made to look like worn-out rags with bloodstains along with zombie makeup. "The managers did the Scooby Doo part. Shayne was dressed like Shaggy, Kris dressed as Fred, Jana dressed as Daphne, and Lane—she's not staff, but she went as Velma. She even wore the same big square dark-rimmed glasses the character wore."

"Don't forget Mason," Mac reminded.

Alison let out a giggle. "Right, Mason went as Scooby."

"Scooby?" I laughed out.

"He was the cutest," Mac said with a wink.

Alison put her hand to her neck. "He had the turquoise collar on, the one with the S tag on it, a tan shirt and khakis, as well as dog ears and a black painted nose."

"All the young ladies kept trying to pet him or hitch his collar to their leash, if you get my drift," Mac stated, giving me another wink.

"I hope Lane took lots of photos," I said. "If Mason's looks are even remotely like the other Earthbound, I'd say it was totally understandable he had the attention of the women."

"Based on his naturally tanned skin, dark hair and eyes, I'm guessing his father was from Brazil, yes?" Mac asked.

"That would be a good guess, with the majority of Brazilians identifying as white, brown, or black, but genetic studies show most have a mix of African, European, and Indigenous ancestry." Alison typed something on her keyboard. "Brazil's population also includes triracial descendants, sometimes referred to as *pardos*, who are mixed white-black people with some Amerindian ancestry, plus there are a significant number of black and Asian people," Alison, our resident ancestry guru, informed us. "Lynn, do you know who his father is?"

"Not sure—never asked. Guess I could, though."

"The party looked like it was going to be so much fun," Mac said, shifting her purse off her lap. "If I were 20 years younger, I would have stayed longer."

"But we're not, so we left early," Alison said, rolling her eyes. "Ken was still supervising a block party on our street when I got home, so I went and got another lawn chair and hung out with him until the last of the parents and young partygoers left."

"What about Don and the boys?" I directed at Mac.

"Well, they seemed pretty pleased with themselves when I got home. Carter and Declan are obviously too old for trick or treat, so the two of them and Don dressed up in scary costumes to give out candy at the front door. And from what Don told me, they put the neighborhood kids through the wringer scaring the piss out of them and asking them to do tricks for their treats."

I laughed hard at that image. "I hated when people did that to me when I was a kid, but I find it hilarious now. Like a rite of passage, kind of."

"Yup, me too—but don't tell Don I said so."

"And don't give my guys any ideas," Alison demanded. "Hey, have you heard anything from Gabriel—do you know if he met with the others yet?"

"That would be a *nope*. Been trying to reach him since Halloween, but I'll be giving him another shout once I'm done here at the hospital."

"Thought you said your shift was over?" Mac questioned.

"It is. But I wanted to see if I could get any more information on our coma patient before I go." I'd checked with the psych ward last week, but I still needed to circle back again to see if anyone had come to see their unconscious patient.

"Gotcha," Mac said.

"Okay, let us know," Alison said.

"Later, Lynn," Mac said.

"Later," I said back before they both logged off.

I paced back and forth outside the psych ward near the opening to the long hall that led to the main building, waiting and hoping my favorite overly chatty nurse, Alexis, would emerge. Her Tuesday and Wednesday shifts I'd found usually ended around the same time as mine. Funny fact, her first name actually means *helper*. The only reason I knew that was because one of the mothers I'd met while working in the NICU in Miami had given her newborn that name and shared the meaning of it. And well, this Alexis has definitely been a helper. Then, as if on cue, the doors to the Behavioral Health Center swooshed open and out came my helpful young nurse.

"Yo, Lynn—shift over?" Alexis asked, sauntering over to where I stood.

"Almost." I didn't want to give the impression I was waiting for her. "One more round before I go," I lied.

"Any update on the...," *Angel* I almost said, shifting then to, "superhero?"

"My superhero," she laughed out. "The guy who brought him in called the hospital and left a message asking how he was. Left his number for us to call him back."

"Did anyone call him?"

"I did," Alexis said.

"What did he say?"

"Just asked we call him if there was any change in his condition."

"Have there been any changes?"

She glanced over her shoulder at the sliding doors she'd exited from. "I was just supposed to tell the guy the patient was stable and then ask if he had any other info on him." She glanced up the hall behind me. "I felt bad for him. He seemed really concerned—not everyday someone puts themselves out there for a stranger, ya know."

"No kidding." I did know.

"So I told him what happened, about how he'd had a fit in the exam room and needed to be sedated, *and* that he was now in a coma." She glanced at the doors to the psych ward again. "I didn't mention which ward he was in, though. Not sure the patient would want strangers knowing he was in the loony bin, know what I mean?"

"That's understandable."

"If the patient comes to, I'll call and give the guy the update. I'd want to know if he makes it or not."

"And nobody else has called or come to claim him?"

"No, and he doesn't match any missing persons report either." Alexis reached into her purse's pocket and pulled out a pack of cigarettes. She flipped open the pack briefly, then slid it back into the pocket. "Finger prints aren't in any database, I was told. Therefore, I figure he's not a known criminal."

"Right."

"But I think he has money," she added.

"Why is that?"

"He came in wearing casual clothes, but when I searched the brand names on the labels, I found the pullover and jeans were high end and majorly expensive. But he had no ID, no watch, no jewelry of any kind. And we have no way to find out who he is, especially if no one claims him. I'd claim him." She gave me a devilish grin.

"Interesting," I said, but it wasn't, really. All the Earthbound I know seemed to have wealth.

"The guy who brought him in said he found him out front, and he was barefoot. But the weird thing was, his feet were smooth, no abrasions from walking on the hot pavement. Not sure how he got himself here. Cops said there were no abandoned cars in the parking lot, so someone must have dropped him off. Or maybe he is a superhero, like Superman, and he flew here."

"That sedative must have been his kryptonite," I teased, but I knew the truth. He was super something that was for sure. "How are you finding working here?" I asked then, wanting to keep her talking as long as I could.

"Entertaining," she said, looping her ID badge around the strap of her purse. "I'm trying to get assigned to the coma guy. He's pretty low maintenance at the moment. Just has the intravenous line to provide fluids and drugs. I'd need to tend to that, monitor him, check his wounds, check both his catheters, bathe him." She wiggled her eyebrows up and down. "Right now, the nurses take turns checking on him and sitting with him on their breaks. The head nurse actually sits and eats her lunch in the room. Even reads to him."

"Really?"

"Trust me, if you got to see him you'd know why. Drop dead gorgeous and seriously built. He doesn't need the oxygen mask now so you can see the full view of his face. Has a great ass, too. Though he was leaner when he arrived, dehydrated, and looked like he may not have eaten in a while. Looks almost perfect now since being hooked up for enteral nutrition. They use it for patients who can't take enough food orally."

"Wow." My *wow* was more about the reaction from the nurses, not about him getting fed through a tube. I was familiar with that part from my previous role in taking care of the babies in the NICU. Nutrients and fluids were delivered directly to the stomach through a feeding tube, or sometimes through a tiny plastic tube inserted into a vein. But I also understood the reactions to his appearance. All the Earthbound I'd met were gorgeous. Hell, all the angels I'd encountered had been spectacular in appearance. And I could totally see why Lane was enamored with Lyndon. Even from a distance, I had recognized how dangerously handsome he was, regardless of his scar.

"But like I said, he's pretty low maintenance, and he sure is a pleasure to look at," Alexis said.

My cellphone chimed, notifying me I had a new text. Checking, I saw it was from Kris, and he'd written,

> *Hey Lynn, got time for a chat?*

"Excuse me," I said to Alexis, pointing to my phone.

"Later," she said before spinning on her heals and heading up the hall to the elevators.

I texted Kris back with,

> *I always have time for you.*

Which he promptly responded with,

> *I'm still at the house, so let me get on my laptop to video chat. I'll ping you when you are ready.*

I had been waiting to hear from him mainly to double-check that the plans for Thanksgiving were all set, but I hadn't planned on a video chat. But when Kris's ping came, I made sure to be in the stairwell around the corner from the entrance to the psych ward, and ready with the video option again on my new cellphone. "Morning," I said to Kris in greeting when his face appeared on the small screen. From the looks of the background, he had himself set up at the kitchen island.

"Good morning to you. What's new at your end?" he asked, but he already knew all there was to know and that there was nothing *new*.

"Bupkis," I confirmed. "But I wanted to thank you again for offering to do this gathering for Redmond and me and his family."

"It's my pleasure. It's such a small group really, compared to the crowd the restaurant normally caters to. And we've rarely, if ever, been open on Thanksgiving, even for events, because we like to give the staff the time off to be with *their* families."

"That's kind of you."

He shrugged, giving me an innocent grin. "That was Frank's doing. Back then I couldn't have cared less. But I've learned that when you know better, you do better."

"I think you will be just fine," I assured him, just as a female figure passed behind him in the background.

"Who are you chatting with?" I heard a female voice ask.

"Hey, is that Jana?"

Kris turned away and said, "It's Lynn—come say *hi*."

Jana's lovely face came into view as she leaned in next to Kris. "Good morning," she said with an equally lovely smile stretching across her face.

"Hi Jana—good to see you again," I responded. "Lane told me all about the Grand Opening. Wish we could have come up for the big reveal. She also told me that you and Kris are quite the team. Lane sent me some photos, and I have to say the place looks amazing. I can't wait to come up and see it. I checked out the website, and the menu looks delicious too. Perfect addition to my hometown."

"I didn't know you were from Ottawa," Jana said with surprise.

"Yup, born and raised." I gave her a single head nod.

"I really love it here," Kris said then.

"I'm enjoying being here as well. The people are so nice," Jana added.

"I'm glad to hear that. Well, I won't keep you, Kris. I really just wanted to say thanks again—to you and Frank, for hosting the big gathering. And I guess the next time I see you will be in New York."

"You're going to New York, when?" Jana directed at Kris.

Uh-oh, silly me. I had assumed Jana was aware Kris was going, or at least knew about the family gathering. "My husband's parents live in New York City—we're heading there for a Thanksgiving family gathering—and Frank and Kris offered to host it at SNOW," I raced out before things could get problematic.

"Why didn't you tell me?" Jana asked, her focus still on Kris.

"I was—we were just confirming things and then I was going to ask you the favor of watching over everything at the restaurant while I'm away. It will only be a couple of days."

"Where will you be staying?" Jana asked Kris.

"I'll be staying in the condo above the restaurant. Lynn has done so much for us—my brothers, and Frank and I wanted to thank her by hosting this special gathering for her family."

"Kris—Jana, I have to get going. Kris, I'll see you in the big apple."

"Not a problem, Lynn," Kris countered. "See you then."

"Wonderful to see you again Jana," I added, giving her a quick smile.

She returned the smile. "Hope to see you again soon," she said.

"Later, you two," I said before shutting off the video chat. "*Yeesh*," I muttered. *"Let's hope Kris works out that little blunder."* I checked the time on my cellphone before sliding it into my back pocket. I needed to make another call, but this one didn't require my phone. "Gabriel," I said to the universe. I'd called out to him several times since the incident with the twins on Halloween, but he'd not shown his face.

"Hello—did you need me?" Gabriel asked, appearing in front of me, seated on a step halfway up the ascending stairs to the next floor.

I rolled my eyes. "You know I've been waiting on some kind of update from you—you told me you were going to meet with the other Archangels. So, do you have an update for me or not?" I put my hands on my hips in a manner like I was talking to the twins. "Oh, and I have a bone to pick with that Archangel Diniel."

"I do—I did, and I do, but tell me what happened with Diniel first," he said, standing up from his resting position to descend the stairs to the landing.

"You go first—I'm the one who's been waiting. Would have asked you about the mirror that day at South Haven, but I was a bit distracted after that Seraphim shit-show at the hospital." I leaned back against the rail of the stairs and folded my arms over my chest.

"Well, I didn't get much on the mirror, I'm afraid," Gabriel said straight out the gate. "I didn't get to talk with them until later, anyway. But Vretil said it sounded similar to some room setup used in parapsychology, used to talk to the dead. Although it's done in the dark, not normal daylight."

"Does he believed that's what's happening?" I loosened my arms, relaxing them down to my sides.

"He didn't say he believed it—just that he saw something about it in one of Alison's journals. Uriel mentioned an acoustic mirror, but those are used to reflect and focus sound waves. Oh, and Raphael asked about twin telepathy, and I told him the twins' abilities were expanding rapidly but that they were not the source of the incident. So like I said, not much."

"Not helpful." I sighed audibly.

Gabriel returned to his seat on the step. "Now before you tell me about your beef with Archangel Diniel, I just want to inform you that none of the Archangels I met with have spoken to or seen the angel in question."

Chapter 24 

The Warwick New York, Thursday November 24th, Manhattan, NY

Lane had texted me about her last interaction with Lyndon restating he made that promise about going with her to Après SNOW, but she had still not seen him since Halloween. She also told me she had finally updated Leo and Kris on what happened with Lyndon as well. We hadn't had much time for anything other than texting these past few weeks, but finally today we both had an early-morning opening for a quick phone call.

"Good morning," I said, when Lane picked up.

"How was the flight?" she asked. "Uncle Leo said he flew you first class for added security."

"It was quick," I said. "I don't care what the reason was. First class is the best," I joked. "Kris met us at the airport and brought us to the hotel."

"Where are you staying?"

"The Warwick New York Hotel. Kris booked us a junior suite there. It's got a King bed and pullout sofa for the twins, but they slept in the big bed with us last night. It's about a 10-minute walk from Redmond's parents' luxury high-rise condo in midtown and an easy cab ride to SNOW. He chose this hotel also because it's the best one to watch the Macy's Thanksgiving Day Parade."

"I bet the girls are excited about that. What route does the parade go?"

"I'm not terribly familiar with the city, but the hotel brochure says…." I flipped to the map. "… it starts at West 77th Street and Central Park West. Then goes down Central Park West to Columbus Circle, turns on Central Park South and then proceeds down 6th Avenue to 34th Street, making its final stop in front of Macy's Herald Square." That's the same location where I'd spoken with the Watcher I remembered. "Goes right in front so we can watch from our room. Doesn't start until 9 a.m.," I informed her. "We still have plenty of time to talk. Redmond and the girls are still asleep in our room." I grabbed the folded blanket from the far end of the couch that had been set out for the girls to use and set it next to me.

"You should have slept in—we could have talked another day."

"Nah, I'm an early riser. And it's rare I get a quiet morning to enjoy my coffee." I took a satisfying sip of my coffee.

"I can understand that," she agreed.

"By the way, I'm glad you finally updated Leo and Kris about Lyndon almost giving up the goods. It's best they know where you are at in that situation. Your safety is their priority—don't forget that."

"How can I not—I'm reminded daily."

"Laaane."

"I know," she huffed out.

"I'm guessing you've seen no sign of Lyndon?"

"Nope." She huffed again. "Still no update on the angel in the psych ward?"

"Nope," I said this time. "But I did speak to the chatty nurse again." I went on to tell her how the nurse said that in his state he was pretty low maintenance and that she was hoping to get assigned to him. And how the other nurses took turns checking on him and sitting with him on their breaks. "They all think he's gorgeous. I get it," I said, knowing angels, in general, were incredibly stunning. "And I can see why you are attracted to Lyndon."

"You do? I haven't been able to get a photo of him yet."

"Well, I hadn't had much time to assess him nor was I up close and personal, but he was enormous, and from what I remember, he had a gorgeous head of shoulder-length dark hair."

"He has incredible hair, and beautiful eyes—green like I've never seen," Lane remarked.

"With his size, it would be hard to go unnoticed, but he has managed to be stealthy, and those watching for him have not seen him at the Ottawa facility in quite some time. I haven't felt him either in my vicinity." I took another sip of my warm coffee.

"I guess that's a good thing?" Lane said, more as a question than a statement.

"Yes, I would say that." I nodded, even though she couldn't see me. "Hey, how are things with Jana and Kris? I didn't ask him last night, but when he and I video chatted the other day, Jana was only just hearing then about the family event and him going to New York. I got the feeling she was not thrilled."

"Really? I haven't heard anything about it. They seem blissful at work and home. Jana told me she loves working with Kris at the restaurant. Said it was fulfilling and fun and better than she could ever have imagined."

"Okay, good. I was a bit worried there was a breakdown in communication between them—with what Kris *could* talk about, anyway."

"She did tell me they were taking things slow on the romantic side, slower than she would have liked, but shared it was better than the alternative. Considering Kris is basically my uncle, I hadn't had much to say on the topic, but suggested maybe she make a move, show him *she* was ready for more."

I leaned my elbow on the arm of the couch. "It shouldn't be so complicated—but it is. I don't envy them."

"Me neither. With being so focused on my school life, I've never really had time for a romantic life."

"How old are you?"

"I turned 24 last March. I know it's old to not have had a boyfriend, but it has never been a priority."

"Hey, I'm all for waiting. Boys complicate things."

"I'll have time once I'm done my masters. Speaking of age, I found out Jana has her 33rd birthday coming up next month, and I made sure Kris knew, just in case he didn't already."

"Obviously, talk of birthdays is a tough subject to broach considering Kris wouldn't have a good answer for her should she ask when his was."

"When I talked to Kris, I told him I was surprised Jana hadn't even asked him how old he was yet. He said he wanted to plan a party for her at the restaurant. But because it *was* a difficult topic, he wanted to keep it a secret to avoid the birthday subject coming up."

"That's kind of messed up, don't you think?" I adjusted in my seat, bending my legs and tucking my feet to the side, then drew the blanket over my legs.

"I agree," Lane said. "I offered to help plan it but said that I also wanted to bring a guest. If I see Lyndon, I'm going to ask him to come to the birthday party. You guys should come up for the shindig."

"With Lyndon there?" I questioned, sipping my coffee.

"Right, shit."

"Promise that you'll give me all the details, since I can't be there."

"Of course. Birthday question aside, do you know what they are telling Jana about the search for her half-sister?"

"The truth actually, that they are watching for her, checking with the schools, police, hospitals etc.. Checking public records for anything new."

"I figured as much. When I asked Uncle Leo for an update, he told me it can be easier to find halflings when they reach adulthood and go off on their own because they have more records to aid in locating them."

"Ya, but Natalie doesn't have any records, not even a driver's license. And anything they have found has that old address associated with it." I made a mental note to ask Leo about other adult halflings when I got a chance to talk to him next.

"They had suggested to Jana that Natalie might not want to be found possibly because of the aunt or some other reason. But they assured Jana they wouldn't give up."

"Not much else they can do," I said, downing the last of my coffee.

"Seems so."

"Okay, my dear, I need to get a move on—but keep me updated on you-know-who."

"You got it. Later, Aunt Lynn. And you let me know how it goes there."

"Will do," I said before ending the call.

I refilled my coffee mug and then sent a quick text to Grier to say,

Happy Thanksgiving.

She had sent us well-wishes for our flight before we left, and shared that she would be volunteering with a few of her colleagues today at a Feeding South Florida event. I was grateful to hear she wouldn't be sitting alone for the holiday.

Grier responded back with,

Happy Thanksgiving to you, too! I'm just watching the sun come up. Can never get enough of the sunrises here.

I felt the same and wrote,

Enjoy! Have a great day!

I texted Lily next, letting her know all was good here, and to say *thank you* again. She and Darius were staying at our house to watch the dogs while we were away, but they were also going down to see Darius's mother for Thanksgiving in Miami.

This year Lily and Darius were bringing the Thanksgiving meal instead of helping cook it. They'd ordered all the fixings from the grocery store in advance and would be heating things up once they got to Darius's mother's place. She was getting up in years, and the doctors had told Darius her heart was getting weaker and would need someone to keep a better eye on her. It was soon after that, she began to struggle with things like cooking and daily chores. Darius had requested a companion aid person from the local agency, someone she could play cards with or do puzzles, and someone who she could cook her meals with, so she didn't feel helpless or waited on. Darius had arranged for an aid to come by three times a week to help her out, prep meals his mom could heat up or microwave, and do any heavy lifting like laundry and garbage out to the curb. When Darius had suggested it, his mom had refused to move up our way, despite Darius showing her the wonderful seniors' facility in town. She'd stated she had lived in this house since the day she'd married Darius's father. He passed away when Darius was 2 years old, and she was determined to stay until her own life came to an end. If her mind wasn't so sharp, Darius would have had her moved closer to him a long time ago, but even in her late 80s, she was still as smart as a whip. And she still doesn't like modern technology, though she does allow Darius to use his cellphone while at the house these days, but that's it. She adores Lily, and the two get on very well. Lily was raised by her grandmother in New York, but she passed away long before Redmond and she reconnected.

As I sipped my second cup of coffee, I turned the TV on with the volume low to find that the Today's Show Savannah Guthrie, Hoda Kotb, and Dylan Dreyer were apparently hosting the parade this year. Also scheduled were the cast of Pitch Perfect along with a variety of performers that Redmond would undoubtedly know like Bumper in Berlin, Betty Who, Big Time Rush, Fitz and the Tantrums, Paula Abdul, & Ziggy Marley, those last two I did know, but there were many more I didn't. When I flipped to the National Weather Service channel it showed the New York regional office was calling for morning temperatures hovering around 40 degrees for when the big parade was to get underway, with a light breeze from the northeast that would make it feel like 37 degrees. *"Good thing I packed warm clothes,"* I murmured to myself. I did love the feeling of wearing cozy clothes, and I missed the Fall season with living in Florida.

Just shy of 9 a.m., the twins were up and asking for breakfast. I was hungry too and asked Redmond to order room service so we could eat while we watch the parade pass by.

The 96th Annual Macy's parade's floats consisted of Tom Turkey, Green Giant's Harvest in the Valley, and several other food sponsored floats. There was New York Life's Toy House of Marvelous Milestones, Blue's Clues & You, Sesame Workshop's 1-2-3 Sesame Street being its 18th time, and Macy's People of First Light's first time showing. It ended with Macy's Singing Christmas Tree and of course Santa's Sleigh, which was always my favorite part of my hometown's Santa Claus parade which was usually done around this time of year.

At noon, when the parade came to an end, I got the girls into the shower to get them ready for the day. They had recently gotten their hair cut into bobs just above their shoulders because they saw that one of their surfing idols had cut off her hair. I had been fine with their request because it made getting them ready that much easier. I had packed each of them a holiday outfit consisting of slim high-neck long-sleeved sweater dresses with matching knit patterned leggings, Hayley's in a rose colour and Ryley's in a sage green, along with tan faux suede slip-on ankle boots.

"You two look terrific," I said when they both did a little spin in their cozy outfits. "You'll need to wear your coats today since you'll be walking around outside." I handed them their versatile mid-weight all-season jackets in darker matching shades to their dresses, both with the adjustable drawstring hoods buttoned *on* should they find the wind too cold. "And you look very handsome," I said when Redmond came out of the bedroom. He was dressed and ready in his black dress pants, a chocolate brown sweater that brought out the colour of his dark brown eyes, and a pair of brown leather lace-up boots.

"Why—thank you," he responded, reaching into the closet near the door. He pulled free the brown vintage leather jacket he'd brought with him, since it was a rare occasion he ever got to wear it back home in Florida. "We'll meet you at SNOW after we tour the Bethesda Fountain and the surrounding park area." It had been Gabriel's recommendation to see the fountain, and since the girls had loved the idea of seeing the bronze angel statue, Redmond's parents had suggested they meet up for lunch at The Tavern on the Green first, and then tour the park.

"Sounds like a plan," I said, tilting my head back for a kiss.

"Are you sure you can't come with us?" Ryley asked, playing with the toggle adjustment on the hood of her coat.

"I'm sorry I can't go with you. There are a few last-minute things I need to do for the get-together," I said, zipping up her coat.

"You're going to miss the *Angel of the Waters*," Hayley said, using the other name for the fountain.

"Get your father to take photos of the two of you in front of the fountain for me." I hated the idea of missing lunch with them and seeing the fountain, but I really wanted to have some time alone with Kris first, and to meet Frank and Ina before the onslaught of family began to arrive. "Have fun, be safe—love you," I said, holding the door open for them. Redmond and I had a long talk with the girls about our traveling, how they were not to go anywhere without one of us, and why it was we needed to be extra safe on this trip.

"Love you, too," came from the trio as they headed off down the hall to the elevators and on their quest for art and nourishment.

Alone in the hotel room, I took my time with getting ready and drying my hair, savoring the idea of wearing it down for once, since I readily wore my hair up in a bun or ponytail ninety percent of the time back home. When my hair was done, I donned a pair of charcoal grey wide-leg dress pants and my favorite periwinkle blue cashmere sweater, along with a similar pair of slip-on ankle boots to what the twins were wearing, mine in a matching shade to my pants. I'd not packed a jacket. Instead, I had chosen to bring a thickly lined wool wrap that, like the twins' coats, was a darker shade of my sweater, and perfect for car rides and brief moments in the cool weather. By 2:00 p.m. I was ready, and I called down to the desk to have them request a taxi to take me to SNOW on the upper West Side.

The taxi was waiting for me when I reached the main entrance to the hotel, but I paused, recalling that moment in time when I'd met and spoken briefly with the Watcher angel. I took a slow, steady look both ways up the street. Then, before I climbed into the taxi, I closed my eyes for a second to focus on if I could sense anyone otherworldly, but I felt nothing, no one. If there was anyone ethereal in the area, they weren't close enough for me to feel them.

On the drive over, I texted Kris,

Heading your way. See you soon.

He replied immediately with,

I'll be at the entrance watching for you.

As I exited the taxi, Kris already had the main doors to the restaurant wide open. He was spectacularly dressed in a crisp white tailored button-down dress shirt open at the neck and flat front navy dress pants. "We are almost ready," he said, ushering me inside before locking the doors behind us.

"Fancy-shmancy," I said, stepping into the main dining area to take it all in.

Tables were set up in a large U shape with enough chairs to accommodate our four, Redmond's mother's five siblings, which comprised her twin brother, two younger brothers who were a year apart, and the youngest, two sisters who were also twins, along with all their spouses, their children and their spouses, and their children. I'd given Frank the names of the potential attendees, which totaled an even 50 family members.

"Lynn!" Frank called out as she exited the kitchen. I recognized her by her photo from Marq's spreadsheet. She was dressed in a high-end deep purple, almost eggplant coloured pantsuit. Her midnight coloured hair was cut short with a long section of bang swept up and back to one side. She was as tall and almost as muscular as Kris, and she was magnificent to behold. "Wonderful to see you."

"Well, hello there!" I greeted her back. "Wonderful to finally meet you."

"We have 48 confirmed guests, but Kris made previsions for extra just in case," Frank stated, crossing to where Kris and I stood. She put out her hand for a handshake, but I took her hand and tugged her down for a hug. "All the extra food will go to feed those at the community center," she said through the embrace.

"You prepared the meal?" I asked Kris, letting the giant female loose from our hug, turning back to him.

"Of course!" Kris said, wrapping me in a gentle hug. "After all you have done for us, I wanted to make this event special for you and your family."

"Redmond is going to be so moved by all this," I gushed, wrapping my arms around him and hugging him back, smiling around his hunched shoulder over to an equally pleased Frank.

Kris released me and said, "You mentioned you wanted to talk before the guests arrived."

"Yes. I won't get much time alone once Redmond and the twins get here, let alone when the rest of the family arrives."

"I'll leave you to talk. Back in a bit," Frank said, striding off back to the kitchen, providing us privacy to talk.

"Come, have a seat." Kris extended a hand towards a lone table set off to the far side of the restaurant. "Tell me what's on your mind."

I took the chair with its back nearest the wall so I could look out at the beautiful Thanksgiving table display. "Thank you for all this," I said, admiring the elegant table settings and Thanksgiving themed floral center pieces.

"Thank you for letting us do this for you and your family," he said with a reassuring smile. "What did you want to talk about?"

"Jana," I said, giving no specifics. I unwrapped my wool throw from my shoulders and draped it over the back of the chair.

His smile turned winsome. "What about her?" he asked, fussing with the cuff of one of his sleeves.

"Well, first, how are things going?"

"Having her with me every day at the restaurant and in my home is heaven."

"Does she know that's how you feel?" I raised my eyebrows, knowing what Lane shared about the 'going slow' part Jana had concerns over.

"I tell her how much I appreciate her all the time. We spend almost every evening together talking and learning about each other. We have grown very close." Kris fiddled with the cuffs of his dress shirt. "But...."

"But?"

"I know she wants more I want more. But I'm not sure how to move forward considering the extenuating circumstances of my real existence," he said, staring down at his hands as he continued to adjust his cuffs.

"How long do you think you can go without telling her everything? You can't have a relationship based on half-truths." I tapped his hand when he didn't answer me. "How do you feel about her?"

"I'm in love with her," he breathed out in a gust of air, placing his hands on the sides of his head.

"Does Leo know how you feel about her?"

"Not that I've told him, but I'm sure he sees it," he said, resting his hands down on the table. "I can't imagine not having her in my life, Lynn."

"Lane said you both look blissfully happy, so I'm sure she sees it like you said." I put my hands over his. "It's time to talk to your brothers and figure out how you can move forward. I know that is a huge leap, but you can't keep Jana in limbo forever."

"I know, and I don't just want her to be my *girlfriend*, either." He glanced down at our hands.

"Not sure she knows that she is your girlfriend—officially, that is." I patted his hands, and he looked up. "A little birdie told me you're planning a party for her," I said, to shift the mood.

"A birdie named Lane, I assume." He slid his hands out from under mine, then leaned his elbows on the table.

"Who else?" I confirmed, grinning. "Considering you are planning a *birthday* party, I was wondering about the potential topic of DOB that might arise."

"That's a fiery topic," he said. "I keep meaning to speak with Leo on the subject. To see if he has a better answer for me to use than what I can come up with."

"With so many of you at North Haven, you'll need to come up with something that works for everyone, something plausible."

He nodded, shifting and leaning back to extend his long legs out under the table. "She has already questioned my being Lane's uncle, all of us being uncles, because of how young we look."

"Can you blame her?" I shrugged. "What did you say?"

"I just said that Lane's fathers labeled us as *uncles* to explain why we were all living together, should anyone question it. The title of uncle had started with Leo since he and Lane's fathers were so close. I explained that we already called each other *brother* because we had become family in our group home, and it seemed natural to use *uncle* with Lane as we joined the team. I also added that Lane calls us uncle, but she is more like a kid sister to all of us."

"And?"

"And she let it go." It was his turn to shrug.

"She's not going to let it go for long," I said. "Jana is going to want to know more, your birth *date* for one. Especially once she finds out you know about *her* birthday." I glanced briefly over at the table settings again. "She thinks I'm your executor, for heaven's sakes."

"Too many lies—I know. Be assured I'll be speaking with Leo when I get back on how to move forward, birthdates being on the top of the list." He shot a quick look over his shoulder at the door to the kitchen, then focused back on me. "Can I ask you something?"

I leaned forward, resting my forearms on the table. "Of course—ask me anything."

"It's about The Watcher you saw."

"Funny," I said, leaning back. "I was just thinking about him this morning, reflecting on the location of our hotel, how it had been right out front of the Macy's Herald Square where I met him."

"Ah, yes. That's right." Kris nodded slowly and gave me a tight smile.

"I've often wondered if I would ever see him again. We only spoke momentarily, but it was enough for me to be spotted by one of Thaddeus's people. And that's partly why I didn't go with Redmond and the girls. Better I'm not spotted on the street."

"Do you know much about them, these *Watchers*?"

"Some," I said. "Gabriel and the other Archangels told me and my friends about the different groups of angels soon after the gathering. We were told they reside in a realm known as Sanctuary and were advocates of The Fallen Watchers and were aided by Archangel Zadkiel."

"And you can sense them, right?" Kris ran the tips of his fingers over the back of his other hand.

"Yes, and they can sense and find each other. The twins can sense them too."

"What did this one say to you?"

"Not much. His interest had been more about the fact we could sense and see him while he'd been veiled. I don't recall sensing any other, but I was caught up with talking to him." I paused, my attention pulled to an exit door on the opposite side of the dining room. "Kris...."

"Lynn—what is it?"

"… I'm sensing." I shivered, but I wasn't cold.

"It's not Lyndon, is it?" Kris's attention followed mine as he stood from his chair.

"No, the other—the one I sensed but couldn't see." Leo and the others had assumed it had been another of Thaddeus's people, but I hadn't been so sure. In fact, I'd wondered if it had been the big-bad himself that was following, or should I say hiding. Purah had said Lyndon needed to get rid of Zuriel. Could Thaddeus have followed to see that it was done, I wondered. Lyndon wouldn't have known he was there.

"Can you tell where they are?" Kris asked, panning the large windows at the far side, then returned his attention back to me.

"Not sure… outside, I think—but they're moving." I threw my senses out, slowly probing the area, but I was struggling to pinpoint their key signature.

"At the hospital, could it have been one of The Watchers you sensed, that you're sensing now?" Kris questioned. His focus on me changed abruptly, and he stared over at the main entrance.

The doors opened wide, and through them came… the deep laughter of *Redmond*, followed by giggling twins skipping behind him in lead of their slow-moving grandparents.

"Let's continue this topic later," I said, getting up from my chair.

"Definitely," Kris said in relief, crossing with me to the middle of the room. "Redmond—good to see you again."

"Good to see you as well," Redmond said, going in for a manly embrace.

"I Iiiii Mum," Ryley squealed when she saw me. "Kriiiiss," she added, racing to meet up with us.

Kris scooped her up into an embrace. "Hello, little one," he said, enclosing her in his arms as he spun in a circle.

Redmond bent to kiss me, then I knelt to hug a yawning Hayley. "How was the park?" I asked her.

"The water angel is amazing," she whispered into my hug, then yawned again. "The park is big—we walked a lot."

I loosened my embrace on her just before Kris bent around me, seizing and scooping Hayley up into his other arm. "Hey, where is my hug?" he asked, spinning the two of them, making them both flop to one side and giggle.

Just then Frank and who I guessed by her slender, delicate stature and long pale blonde hair was Ina, came through the swinging kitchen door into the dining area. "What is all this nonsense?" Frank asked, hands on her hips, making a pouty face as if missing out.

"Ryley, Hayley, this is my very best friend, Frank," Kris said, coming to a stop in his spinning. "Frank, this is Ryley." He pretended he was going to drop her. "And this is Hayley." Hayley clung to Kris, ready for the pretend drop.

"Hiiii," the twins said, followed by more giggles over the possibility of being fake dropped again.

"Hello, ladies!" Frank said, reaching for Ina's hand. "I'd like you to meet my wife, Ina."

"It is delightful to meet you both," Ina said, greeting them with both hands out instead of a handshake. She was as tall as Frank and wore a similar pantsuit, though hers was lavender and in a much more flowy fabric. Her long hair was clipped up on one side with a silk flower in the same shade as her suit.

Kris bent at the knees to let the twins loose.

Free, they stepped forward, hands out in mirrored greetings.

"Wow—I want to be as awesome as you when I grow up," Ryley said, admiring Frank's muscular build.

"And I want to be awesome, like you," Hayley said to Ina, taking both her hands, giving a little curtsey as though Ina were royalty.

The twins switched places, extending greetings to the other.

"Do you have wings?" Ryley asked in a tiny whisper.

"We do," Ina whispered back, giving her a wink.

There was an advantage of safety with having Kris here, and knowing the twins would be well protected with Frank and Ina being here as well. But my senses were a mess having these new female Earthbound present together with Kris, their signatures mixing and splitting over and over as I attempted to get my bearings.

"Hi, Enzo, Nainseadh," I said, as my in-laws finally made it over to where we all stood. I gave each of them a soft hug.

"Frank, Ina, this is my husband Redmond," I said.

"Thank you for everything," Redmond said, shaking Frank's hand. "Ina, lovely to meet you." He gave them both a gracious smile.

"Ladies, this is Mr. and Mrs. Credente, Redmond's parents," I added. "Frank is our gracious host for tonight's festivities."

"Happy Thanksgiving," Frank said, stepping past me. Despite her size, she hugged each of them in a gentle embrace. "This is my wife, Ina." Frank stepped back graciously, making room for Ina to step up.

"A pleasure to meet you both," Ina said, embracing each of them as well.

"My goodness—Frank. This is a stunning restaurant. The tables are just so exquisite," Nainseadh cooed, clutching her purse to her chest.

"Beautifully done, Frank," Enzo said, reaching for a handshake. "And I thank you too for making this day so splendid for our family."

"It is our pleasure," Frank said, shaking his hand.

"And last but not least, this is our friend and co-host, Kris Snow."

Kris sidestepped over next to me. "Welcome," he said. "It is so marvelous to meet you both. I look forward to meeting the rest of your family."

Over the next half hour, the rest of the family members arrived, and Redmond left my side to greet them with his parents.

"Frank, you and Ina should sit down and eat with us."

"Oh, no, we couldn't," Frank declined, smiling at Ina.

"We never celebrate," Ina said, adding more refusal to my invitation. "And this is for your family."

"Kris and the others are family, so that makes the two of you family as well." I glanced back and forth between them. "You said it yourself, *there's plenty*."

"Plenty of what?" Redmond asked, finished with his greeting of relatives duties.

"Food," I said. "I asked Ina and Frank to join us."

"That's an excellent idea," Redmond agreed. "And I just heard that my cousin and his wife won't be coming because she's currently 8 months pregnant—so there will be extra seating."

"Yes-yes," Hayley said, jumping up and down.

"Please-please," Ryley added, clasping her hands to her chest.

"That is very kind," Ina said, smiling brilliantly at all of us. She turned her sweet smile to her wife. "We would love to join you."

Frank sniffled, wiping a rogue tear as though suddenly emotional. Then she said, "I'm just going to let the valets know the guest list is done." Frank turned and hurried off to the front entrance.

"She doesn't do mushy very well," Ina shared. "Let me go adjust the seating so that we can be nearer to you."

"I'll help you," Redmond offered. He gave my arm a gentle caress, then followed Ina over to the table with the vacant seats.

Hayley took up one of my hands, as did Ryley, the two grinning up at me.

I knelt down and then whispered, *"Did you feel anyone when you arrived?"*

"Yes," Hayley said, lifting the back of my hand to her cheek.

"I did, too. Did you?" Ryley asked me, mirroring her sister's action with my other hand to her cheek.

"Yes, I did," I answered, glancing back and forth at their adorable, grinning faces.

"The first one is gone," Hayley said in a quiet voice. *"But there's another one outside."*

I glanced over at the entrance. I could sense this other one now, the one outside, but with adjusting to Frank and Ina's new signatures and the shock of feeling the other from the hospital, I hadn't noticed the other unfamiliar sensation right away. "Can you go help your Da and Ina fix the seating?"

"Okay," they said in unison, releasing my hands and running over to help.

When Kris sidled up next to me again, I said, "I'm picking up on a new signature outside. But the twins felt them first."

"Another?" Kris's eyes bulged.

I nodded. "Are there any other Earthbound working here?"

"No, it's only ever been Frank and occasionally Ina, but… that may have changed. Let me go out and check with Frank."

Outside, Frank was rounding up the valets. "We'll be locking the doors for the event but keep your cellphones handy should anyone need to leave early and want their vehicle."

"Thanksgiving event?" questioned the voice of a familiar yet particularly vile Earthbound. Addison, who was one of Thaddeus's bunch, stood several paces away from the doors to the restaurant.

"It's a private party," Frank stated. "What are you even doing here—shouldn't you be slumming it in Norway?"

Addison smirked at her comment, then said, "Heard through the grapevine that you work here." He gave her a haughty grin. "Was just out for a stroll—thought I'd stop by." The bottom of his long grey trench coat flapped as the cool night wind swirled around them. He wore the coat tied tight at the waist, over dark pants and a dark shirt, and his blond hair was cut tight to his scalp, adding to his menacing appearance. He took a step closer, placing his hands behind his back as though to appear nonthreatening.

"Like I said, we are closed for the evening." Frank crossed her massive arms over her thick chest. "What do you want, Addison?"

"Me?" Addison pointed to himself. "Nothing in particular." He took another step towards her. "Say, where is that lovely mate of yours tonight?" He searched the space around her as if Ina were hiding behind her.

"She's inside—not that it's any of your business." Frank clenched her jaw.

The doors behind her opened unexpectedly, allowing for roars of laughter to escape the confines of the restaurant. When the Seraph took a step to the side, Frank mirrored his movement, blocking the view in through the doors.

"Sounds like everyone is having a splendid time," Addison said, endeavoring to see behind Frank again.

"Everything okay, Frank?" Kris asked, exiting and coming to stand at her flank.

"Everything is peachy-keen," Frank answered, eyes laser focused on the disgraceful Seraph.

"You must be Francesca's boss," Addison said then, taking another hesitant step forward. "Delightful place you have here."

"It's Frank's place. She's the boss," Kris stated firmly.

"I don't think I caught your name," Addison said, releasing his hands from behind his back, offering one in a handshake. "I'm Addison, an old friend of Ina and Francesca's."

"I didn't offer it." Unmoving, Kris scowled at the haughty Seraph. "Frank, the people are asking for you."

Without saying another word, Frank turned away from glaring at Addison to go back inside the restaurant.

Glowering still at Addison, Kris stepped sideways, taking Frank's place in front of the doors. He looked briefly over his shoulder as she went inside.

Addison returned to clutching his hands behind his back, then smiled meekly at him, nodding at his unspoken message which clearly hollered, *'You are not welcome here.'*.

Kris continued to watch as the lone Seraph turned and then leisurely strolled off in the other direction. *"What the hell?"* Kris murmured to himself, scanning up and down the street before he, too, returned inside.

Chapter 25

The Beach House, Friday December 16th, South Florida

Despite the unexpected and unwanted visit from Addison on Thanksgiving, the event had gone off without a hitch. Great food, tons of laughter, and good tidings were shared by all, including Frank and Ina, who had thoroughly enjoyed celebrating the holiday with us and Redmond's extended family.

Kris had taken it upon himself to inform Leo about Addison and about the other unidentified angel-related signature that appeared to be lingering near me. They had wondered if perhaps another Earthbound was working with Lyndon, another from the group cast out from Pleiades, stranded here on Earth by Thaddeus himself. Leo had stated that Anael and Thanael had lost track of several of them, adding that The Guards currently only knew the whereabouts of 75 percent of the originals. I had suggested that perhaps it wasn't me they were hovering near, and it was the other Earthbound Seraphim they chose to stay close to. There had been a unanimous response from all with the question of *why*, even from Redmond. I didn't know the answer. But I did have questions of my own.

Why had Lyndon brought Zuriel to a hospital, let alone the one I worked at? Did they know I worked there or lived in the area? If so, how? And why hadn't Lyndon or one of Thaddeus's other underlings not come after me? I still wondered if it was Thaddeus I had sensed. I didn't know Thaddeus's signature. He hadn't been in the Celaeno building when I'd been there. And why was this unknown individual concealing themselves from view? I hadn't shared this latest incident with my girlfriends up north, nor had Redmond shared it with Derek or Luc. The only ones who knew about it were Lily and Darius, for the plain reason they were local and needed to know if there was potential danger.

Yesterday when I'd gotten to speak with Lane, she'd said Leo had apprised her about Addison showing up, and how I'd sensed another, the same one from the hospital. I'd also learned from Lane that she and Lyndon had finally crossed paths at the group home. She had asked him for his cellphone number, and after he'd recited it, she sent him a quick *Hi it's Lane,* so he had her number in his contacts as well. At the time, Lyndon had been leaving when she arrived, and the exchange had been brief, with him overly apologetic again for having to go. But he did, however, agree to Lane's offer to accompany her to Jana's birthday party, which was tomorrow. Kris had informed Lane that Jana now knew about the party, and that he had dodged the inevitable question from her about *his* birthday, stating that this party was all about *her* and that they would talk about *his* at a later date. Apparently, Jana had succumbed to his pleas, Lane said, but Kris knew he and the others would have to come up with a solid explanation for her query soon.

On a lighter note, Hayley and Ryley hadn't had any angelic visitors since Halloween. In fact, they had behaved especially good since and had been rewarded for their good behaviour and for doing extra chores to make up for their mistake of keeping secrets. In addition, with Addison now confirmed as being at the New York facility with Marcus, and no action at the Norway facility since our caper, Zach had felt it was safe for him to travel, and he had made a rare visit to see us. While he was here, he and Den had taken the girls for an evening flight *after* they had practiced more of their self-defense moves again. As an added reward for making up for their poor actions, Redmond had told them they could rent a movie. They had chosen the movie *Disenchanted,* which was the sequel to one of their favorite movies, and they would be renting it tonight with Darius while we were out at the music event with Lily.

Right now they were rewatching the first movie *Enchanted* with their father in the living room in preparation for the sequel tonight, and the music and singing from the film was presently ringing throughout the house.

To avoid getting rooked into watching it again, I retreated to the kitchen to make them sweet and salty popcorn using melted caramel and sea salt. With the movie only just started, I checked the time on my cellphone to see it was 2 p.m. *and* saw that I had gotten a text from Grier. It read,

> *Got time for a visit?*

I did, and I wrote back,

> *I do.*

She responded with,

> *I'm out back on the beach. The temperature is perfect.*

It was a pleasant 68 degrees, and I replied,

> *It certainly is!*

"I'm heading over to see Grier—see you all in a little bit," I called out, waving at Redmond when he turned back, exiting out through the sliding door to the deck before he could protest.

I spotted Grier reclined in one of two lounge chairs out front, or outback as it were, near the entrance to the path to her beach cottage. "Hey, lady," I called to her.

She waved and pointed at the lounge chair next to her. "Have a seat," Grier said as I approached. She was dressed much like I was in black leggings and a long sweatshirt. Mine was grey while hers was a sunny yellow, and perfect for the cooler weather we sometimes got at this time of year.

"Why thank you—don't mind if I do," I said, easing myself down onto the padded lounge chair.

"What's the family up to today?" Grier asked.

"Redmond and the girls are watching a movie—rewatching, actually." I pointed at her. "OMG, that's who you remind me of."

"What—who?" she questioned, turning her head my way and lifting her sunglasses.

"The girls are watching Enchanted in preparation for renting the sequel Disenchanted tonight while we're out."

"I'm not familiar with the movies."

"I wouldn't think you would be," I laughed out. "It's a fairytale about a young typical Disney princess set to marry a handsome prince, but the evil stepmother sends the prince to New York City. The princess is then exiled from her animated world into the live-action world of New York City, where she is eventually rescued by a divorce lawyer, played by actor Patrick Dempsey. The film stars a slew of other famous actors, but it's the actress who plays the princess that you remind me of. Amy Adams."

"I've been told that before, actually—the Amy Adams part, not in reference to a fairytale princess. But I do like the *rescued by Patrick Dempsy* part." She grinned playfully, making me laugh.

"Hey, she starred with Henry Cavill in the Superman movies, too."

"He-llo!" she said, offering me a high-five.

I smacked her hand with mine and laughed again.

"Redmond said once I reminded him of a blonde Emily Blunt when we first met—note the *first met* part," I said using finger quotes.

"She has blonde hair now," Grier noted, dropping her sunglasses.

"True. But I don't see it. Most days with my greying hair mixing with the blonde, and wrinkles showing up on my face, I resemble more the disheveled character the actress played in The Quiet Place movie."

"Wait," Grier said, lifting her sunglasses again. "With that reference, I can totally see the resemblance now."

"Hey," I said, laughing and smacking her on the arm. "Tonight I'll try for the red carpet version of her."

"Where are you guys going tonight?" Grier rested her head back on the lounge chair, head still turned my way.

"To a music industry Christmas party." I grimaced.

"Is your husband a musician?" she asked, turning on her side to fully face my way.

"Yes, and no. He owns a recording studio off island, but he also plays in studio with some of the bands and sometimes for fun at gatherings." He hasn't played for us in a while, I mused.

"Do you attend a lot of these events?"

"Never. Redmond sometimes, Lily always. Only reason we are going is because Lily had asked that we attend with her because it was so close and not in Miami."

"Lily?"

"She's Redmond's second in command, but she basically runs the studio now. She and her boyfriend Darius are close friends of ours. They actually met through us." I turned on my side, facing Grier.

"Oh, so the four of you are going together—how nice." Grier tugged an elastic hair tie from around her wrist and fashioned a loose braid of her long red hair. It was a tad windy, and I was thankful I'd pulled mine back in a ponytail.

"Well, no, not exactly. We're attending the party with her, and she offered to drive so that Redmond and I could have a couple drinks and *'let loose'* as she put it, but Darius isn't going. He offered to watch the girls for us as he was *'No way going to put on a stupid suit and would rather die than attend some fancy music bash'*. He never goes." I shook my head and rolled my eyes. "Lily is good with it because she prefers to flit around meeting and shmoozing with the music artists and industry bigwigs and said she *'didn't need to drag a giant wet blanket around with her'* as she did so. I'm not a fan of dressing up either, so I can't blame him."

"Have you ever wondered why it is you don't like dressing up or dresses?"

"Wondered—no. But I chalk it up to having three older brothers and lots of guy cousins in my life growing up. Keeping up with them didn't lend itself to wearing skirts and dresses. Now I just feel more comfortable in pants." I bent my arm up to rest my head on it. "Yer not trying to shrink me, are you?"

"Absolutely not, just my natural curiosity about human nature and what makes people comfortable or uncomfortable."

"I'm big on comfort."

"Me too—most people are," she said, mirroring my position. "People often think of comfort or being comfortable as the feeling of physical or psychological ease, often described as a lack of hardship. Comfort is a particular concern in health care, like providing comfort to the sick and injured, which can facilitate recovery. A level of psychological comfort can be reached by recreating experiences that are associated with pleasant memories, like engaging in familiar activities, keeping familiar objects around, and consumption of comfort foods. Or in your case, clothing comfort." Grier tucked a loose strand of hair that had come loose from her braid behind her ear. "Comfort is related to various perceptions… physiological, social, and psychological needs and after food, *clothing* is one of the significant objects that serves for comfort requirements. It provides aesthetic, tactile, thermal, moisture, and pressure comfort. And things like colour..," she said, pointing to her sweatshirt. "… fabric, and style of clothing and other clothing related variants. This type of comfort is necessary for psychological and social comfort. And it is why the colour yellow brings me joy."

"Wow, I never looked at it that way, but I can totally relate to a lot of those clothing comfort needs."

"Most people don't realize how much clothing plays a part of our overall, well, *comfort*." She giggled.

"I knew you were a smarty-pants."

"You're funny. I really just like what I do." Grier flicked the tail of her braid as though deflecting the complement, then she asked, "Do you normally stay local for Christmas?"

"It depends. This year is just the four of us. Oh, and my cousin Gabriel usually drops in. Last year Redmond's parents were down since we missed a few during the pandemic, but they usually like to travel over Christmas and this year they're going to Italy to visit family friends of his father's."

"Ooohhh, I'd love to go to Italy someday."

"Me too—pasta is my favorite food group." I was suddenly hungry.

"Cheese is mine." Grier put the fingertips of one hand to her lips and did a chef's kiss with them. "How about your side of the family? Are they local?"

"Actually, I'm not originally from the U.S.—I'm from Canada. But most of my family has been gone for some time now. I still have a brother who lives up in Canada—so it's just the two of us left now. We video chat on Christmas eve—it's become a tradition from when the girls were born."

"Video chats are great when friends and family are far away," she said sympathetically.

"What about you—are you originally from Florida?"

"No." She shook her head. "I grew up in Southport. It's a small town in North Carolina."

"Why does that sound familiar?" I said, pushing my sunglasses up on my head.

"Have you ever seen the movie *Safe Haven*? It was originally a book written by Nicholas Sparks." Grier tucked her hands into the sleeves as though for warmth, then rested her head back on her bent arm.

"Yes, I loved that one." My hands felt a tad cold too, and I copied her sleeve idea.

"Well, that was filmed in my hometown. Along with *The Secret Life of Bees*, that was a novel first too, and *I know What You Did Last Summer*, which, believe it or not, was loosely based on a book as well. There were a bunch of other movies filmed there, too."

"Did you live there when any of them were being filmed?"

"Safe Haven and the *bee* one, no, but the *I know what you did last summer* movie was filmed back in 1997, when I was 18 and right before I went off to university. Didn't really get to see much filming, but I find it fun to see places that are familiar in films."

"Ya, I love when that happens, too. Redmond always laughs at me when I point out when something is filmed in Canada."

"Why does he laugh?" Grier rubbed the end of her nose with her sleeve.

"Because it happens a lot. Plenty of films depicted as being in the U.S. are often filmed in Canada for some reason. Might be less expensive, I don't know." I shrugged. "If I recognize a certain setting, I look it up on my cellphone right then to see where it's filmed, and more often than not, it's Canada. Redmond expects it now." I chuckled.

"Oh, that is hilarious. Canada is another place I'd like to visit."

"It's beautiful in winter if you enjoy things like skiing and ice skating, but it's even more spectacular if you travel during the other seasons, especially fall." I felt a little homesick all of a sudden.

"I get the feeling that you miss the changing seasons."

"I do. And summers in Florida are brutal."

"I have to agree."

"Will you be going back home to see your family for the holiday?" Feeling the chill of the wind, I bent my legs up, tucking them in under the bottom of my huge sweatshirt.

"No. I haven't been back in almost 4 years, not since my father passed away from a sudden heart attack."

"Oh gosh, Grier—I'm so sorry. What about your mom?"

"She passed away when I was twelve, suicide."

"Grier, I…." I understood how horrible it was being in the *I lost my parents* club.

"It was a long time ago," she said with a shrug. "She'd been struggling with mental instability and depression for several years. The doctors back home couldn't seem to help her. One of the small town challenges." She shrugged again. "It's the reason I went into psychology."

"Do you have any siblings?"

She shook her head. "It was just me and my dad." She released an audible sigh.

"And I take it you two were close?"

"Thick as thieves." She gave me a sad smile. "My dad raised me basically. I don't really have any other close family *or* friends, for that matter. Spent most of my time devoted to my studies, building my practice, and then connecting with several prestigious hospitals."

"All that focus must have paid off, and you said you love what you do." It wasn't a question, more my observation of her time well spent.

"It has—and I do love it, yes. I started doing virtual sessions when covid hit and still do so now. I relish working from home, even more now with living here."

"It's wonderful you can help people all from the comfort of your home."

"There's that *comfort* word again." Her smile was joyful this time.

"Say, why don't you come over, do Christmas with us?"

"Oh no, I couldn't intrude."

"No intrusion, you can finally meet Redmond and the twins."

"To be honest, I've gotten used to doing Christmas alone, and I enjoy the quiet time. But I so appreciate the lovely offer."

"No worries, I understand—but if you change your mind."

She nodded "Thank you."

"Will you be working over the holidays?" I asked, sitting up, releasing my legs from under my sweatshirt. I adjusted the backrest of the lounge to be more upright, then leaned back against it. My bare feet were cold now, and I spread my legs with the lower half over the sides so I could dip my feet into the warm sand.

"Some," Grier replied. "And I'm on call for the hospital if they need me. The holidays can be difficult for a lot of people."

I turned my head to look at her. "You mentioned you did in-person sessions, too."

"Yes, but I just have the one patient currently." She paused, glancing down at her watch, then she glanced back to the path.

"What is it?"

"Nothing. I have a session with him today, is all."

"Are the sessions going well?" I asked reluctantly, knowing the session details were confidential.

"I'm not sure, to be honest." Grier tucked her hands back into her sleeves.

"How long have you been working with this patient?"

"Several weeks, actually a few months almost, now that I think about it." She squeezed her sleeve cuffs together.

"I know you can't tell me anything, but are you feeling uncomfortable having them *here* for sessions?" I pointed to her beach cottage.

"No," she said, pausing. "I'm not sure—but I get so flustered when he's here." She put her covered hands to her cheeks as though shocked she'd spoken the words. "I know I should refer him out—but he insists on being treated by me."

I drew a breath in through my nose and said, "What is it that's impeding your ability to treat him?"

"It's just—I can't believe I'm saying this, and oh my god I feel so unprofessional telling you—but the man I'm treating is soooooooo gorgeous," she rushed out before putting her cuffs over her mouth. "I've been dreaming about him too," she muffled through the fabric of her sleeves. Then she covered her eyes.

I tightened my lips, drawing them in my mouth, unsure what to say, but my thoughts screamed, wowsers! Then I reached out and gently pulled her hands from her face, so they rested in her lap.

"Sorry," she said, rubbing her sleeves together at the cuffs.

"Grier don't worry—everyone needs someone to talk to, you know that. Even if it's just a friend." I reached out and wrapped my hands around her covered ones. "What you are dealing with mustn't be uncommon in your profession."

She nodded slowly.

"Dreams can be challenging on the psyche too—you told me that." I squeezed her hands. "Look, I know you're doing a solo Christmas, but what are you doing for New Year's?"

She shook her head and gave me a weak smile. "No plans."

"We're not doing anything fancy, but we have some local friends coming over. Our neighbors a few houses over, do fireworks on the beach that we can see from our back deck. Do you think you'd be up for celebrating with us?"

Her small smile widened then. "New Years sounds great, actually. New home, new job, and it would be nice to bring in the new year with *new* friends."

"Excellent," I said, letting go of her hands. "Okay, I'll text you the details," I added, drawing my cellphone from my leggings pocket and checking the time. "Crap, it's 4 p.m. already. I better skedaddle. I still need to feed the troops and then beautify myself. Need all the time I can get for that." I pushed up from the lounge chair. "And regarding your patient conflict—maybe talk with a close colleague about how to deal with the… *discomfort*."

"I've been considering that." She gave me a reassuring smile. "Have a good time tonight," she said, artfully changing the subject.

"Thank you." I gave her the peace sign. "Later," I said, before rushing off.

"Send me a photo of you all dolled up," Grier called after me.

"I hate getting dressed up!" I called back to her. "I should make you come over and help me." I pointed a stern finger at her like I might follow through with dragging her with me.

Chapter 26 

An hour after I got home, Darius and Lily arrived at my front door. Darius was dressed in his usual gym clothes of shorts and a tank top, even though the weather had gotten cooler. In fashionable difference, Lily was rocking a sparkly two-piece outfit with a long-sleeved top cut off at her midriff, and a floor-length skirt with a thigh-high slit. She also wore 5-inch black stilettos that brought her to a height of 5 foot 5, and she moved in the shoes like she'd been born to wear them.

"I'll help you get ready—do your hair," she graciously offered, noting my wet hair, patting the small tote bag she had with her.

"Redmond is taking a shower in our bathroom, so I'm going to get ready in the girls' bathroom," I said to Lily.

"Where are the twins?" Darius asked, before heading to the couch to find a comfortable seat.

"Changing into their jammies for your movie night," I said, excited for them. I wished I was staying home watching movies and eating junk versus playing grownup at a fancy party. This was the start of their two-week holiday break from school that didn't have them back until after the new year. "Movie snacks are on the kitchen counter."

"Perfect—thanks," Darius said, glancing back over the back of the couch to the kitchen.

In the girls' bathroom, Hayley and Ryley sat on the side of their tub while Summer and Snow rested on the floor at their feet, all watching as Lily began my transformation by blowing out my hair into long smooth waves down my back. She did my makeup for me next, lining my eyes in black liner, lids in dark plum eyeshadows, and a hint of blush, leaving my lips nude except for a shine of lip-gloss. She had brought an extra pair of fake lashes and had put them on me too, stating it would help emphasize my eyes with my glittery outfit. The outfit Lily had found for me was a one-piece all black wide-leg jumpsuit, with an elegant deep V-neck and long sleeves in a similar sequin fabric to hers. Thankfully, my wedge sandals only had a 2 ½ inch heel and were the perfect height for the inseam length of the jumpsuit. I'd gone minimal with my jewelry, diamond studs for my ears, a large black diamond costume jewelry ring for my right hand and my usual wedding rings for my left. I already had a tiny black clutch purse that was just big enough to hold my cellphone, ID, and the lip-gloss I was wearing.

"Done," Lily said, walking in a circle around me. "Another stunning success."

I turned to look at myself in the girls' full-length mirror, then pulled Lily in view of the mirror. "You look like a Rockstar," I said. In contrast to me, Lily had styled her hair in a rockabilly updo, and had on long shoulder-duster earrings, and silver bangles as cuffs stacked 4 inches deep on each wrist. She had a similar small purse, but hers wrapped around her hips with a thin black chain like a low belt. She'd also donned black eyeliner and fake lashes, though her eye shadow was a fan of sparkling navy blue to match the swipe of blue in her upswept blonde hair.

"And you look like a masterpiece," Redmond said as he entered the bathroom from the hall.

"I know," I said to him with a smirk, running a hand down the length of my smooth hair. If it weren't for my training with Den, I would never have been brave enough to wear something so… *snug*, but I was feeling very confident in my body these days, and went with bravery over fear, and was ever thankful it wasn't a dress. "And you look effortlessly handsome." He had taken all of a half an hour to get ready and stood tall and dashing in a Givenchy inspired all black suit, with matching black shirt, and tie. Redmond looked amazing, and he sure could fill out a suit. He had leaned out having lost any extra weight he'd gained around his midsection. Even though he had gotten a bit soft since the birth of the twins, his training this year and mine these past few months had gotten us both back into shape and then some.

"Okay, people, let's go!" Lily said, urging all of us out into the hall. "It's a 40-minute drive to the venue and we have just under an hour to get there."

"It's only six o'clock," I said, checking the time on my cellphone. "I thought this thing didn't get cranked up until eight."

"It doesn't, but I like to be at these events before the music industry's whose-who start arriving so I can properly greet them as they enter the main mingling area." Lily hustled us down the hall to the front foyer.

"Hiii Darius," Hayley said as she jumped up on the couch next to him.

"I got the snacks," Ryley said, running from the kitchen, carrying the bags of chips I'd set out earlier on the counter. She climbed up on the other side of the couch next to Darius.

"Girls—you promised to let Darius know if you get any visitors tonight. Don't forget."

"We will," they both said in agreement. "Den's here," they added, just as I felt his presence.

"I know," I said, followed by a heavy knocking at the front door that yanked my attention from the twins. I strode over and opened the door. "What are you doing here?" I questioned, staring up at Den as he took up all the space in the entry way. He was wearing dark sunglasses comparable to what the Agent characters wore from the Matrix movie. I noticed then he was dressed in a similarly elegant suit to the one Redmond wore, though his collar was unbuttoned, and he wore no tie.

"I'm here to escort all of you to the party," he said nonchalantly, as though we were all in on his plan. "Leo thought it best I stick close while you attend an event with such a large crowd of unknown individuals."

"I know quite a few," Lily said, coming to stand near the entrance. "And there will be plenty of security there, I'm sure."

"Leo didn't mention anything to us," Redmond interjected. "Not that I mind the extra safety and security." He turned my way and gave me a pleased smile.

I focused back on Den. "So then what—yer going to act as my bodyguard for the night?"

"Something like that." Den pointed a hand to the driveway. "Your ride awaits."

Redmond, Lily, and I leaned out through the front door to see a stylish stretch black Lincoln town car in the driveway. And the only reason I recognized the fancy model was because I'd seen several similar when I'd lived in Miami.

"Sounds good to me," Darius called from his place on the couch. "Less worry for me."

"Alright then—let's get a move on it," Lily said, standing half out and half in the doorway. "Lynn, you got your purse?"

"Yup," I said, snatching it up from the small table near the front door. "Wait," I said, taking my cellphone from my purse. "Den, take some photos of us before we go."

"This is one of America's most iconic resorts," Den said as we drove the last stretch along the lushly landscaped 1,040-foot, palm-lined drive to the Florentine Fountain at the entrance to The Breakers Palm Beach. "Featuring an eight-story palace, twin Belvedere Towers, and graceful arches throughout, situated on 140 acres of oceanfront property, and recognized as a AAA Five Diamond property listed on the National Register of Historic Places," he remarked, adding more on the history of the venue.

"Quite the place," I said, recalling the photos and what I'd read online about the Italian renaissance-style hotel.

We pulled up to the event entrance and Lily said, "Perfect, I've got 15 minutes to spare." And while we got out and Den handed off his keys to the valet, Lily rushed off up the steps to the main entrance in search of her perfect greeting spot.

Redmond was delighted to let Lily do all the greeting, though I knew he would be expected to do some of the meet'n greet. I was content with simply people watching from the sidelines.

"This private road is modeled after the Boboli Gardens in Florence," Den said, pointing back the way we came and then at the fountain.

I nodded, attempting to settle my nerves while taking it all in. And as Redmond and I took our time, leisurely entering through the main door into the breathtaking lobby, Den continued with his history lesson.

"This lobby was influenced by the Great Hall of the Palazzo Carrega in Genoa, circa 1560," he said, sliding his sunglasses into the breast pocket of his suit jacket.

I tilted my head back to admire the vaulted, frescoed ceiling with its intricate hand-painted details, then dropped my gaze to look at Redmond.

"Nice place," Redmond said, raising his eyebrows.

I looked to the left, then to the right of what had to be over 50 meters of impressive lobby space. Two towering evergreen trees and a sculptured menorah illuminated the hotel lobby. The magical ambiance of the holidays was evident in the lush foliage, modern trimmings, and elegant embellishments, along with twinkle lights, ornaments, and ribbons and bows. The furniture was an elegant collection of upholstered sofas, lounge chairs and tables, reflecting a modern design scheme, with vibrant hues echoing the carpet's shades of blue and green. "The carpet is the true centerpiece," I said, glancing up at Den.

"The custom-designed carpet was inspired by the paintings of French Symbolist Odilon Redon," Den said, buttoning up his suit jacket. "It's hand-tufted floral motif was woven in one piece... by 35 weavers on a loom, using the finest New Zealand yarn in over 70 unique colors. It measures 161-feet by 25-feet wide and weighs 1,500 lbs.," he elaborated. "But the magic is in the details and this venue is teeming with them." He shot a quick look over his shoulder. "They spend 11 months planning and then 6 days decking the halls of the magnificent entryways, the loggias and courtyards. Including thousands of soft lights that wrap the royal palms and date trees we saw when we drove up the hotel's main drive."

The whole aesthetic was elegant and sumptuous, and I grinned at Redmond. However, as expected, the main entrance was also edged by random media people and photographers.

"Events like these often come with an extra level of stress with working with celebs," Den shared, bending closer so I could hear him better.

He wasn't kidding, I mused. It was a music industry event, and the music was booming, adding to my already fraying nerves over being at such a lavish party. Den, working as a professional bodyguard, must have attended similar events, having guarded some seriously high-profile clients.

"The job of an event organizer can end up being a precarious balancing act with trying to keep things orderly, flowing and on time." Den pointed to a well-groomed middle-aged man in a dark suit, bordered by two frantic younger women baring the same matching tailored dark outfits. "If they are good at their jobs, you won't even notice them."

Together Redmond and I, followed by Den, passed through from the main lobby into what Den called the Mediterranean Courtyard. The outdoor space was framed by classic balustrades, accented with tropical flora reflecting the resort's romantic style.

"That way takes you to the South Loggias used for conference registration and hospitality services," Den said, pointing to the right. Then he pointed straight ahead. "Through there is the Mediterranean Ballroom where they have this event's sit-down dining services for the industry elite. And left is the North Loggias, which leads into the social club, where everyone can mingle," he explained, further giving us the lay of the land he'd obviously researched for this protective detail.

"For the dregs like us," I said, turning to my left, exploring for anyone I might recognize. Through the 15-foot tall arched windows that overlooked the courtyard from the ballroom I could see the elaborate fresco-painted ceilings that were lit up by the large Venetian-style chandeliers, but I couldn't make out the faces of the people in the room. I turned right, observing the outdoor space. Before I took another step, Den gently took my arm and eased me back behind him as a long-haired rocker wearing a loud pink and black suit approached Redmond.

"Hey, Red-man," the wild-looking character said to Redmond, grabbing and shaking his hand quickly as he passed by.

Stepping back out from behind Den, I said, "Who was that?"

Redmond turned to look at me. "Hell if I know," he laughed out. "We'll have to ask Lily."

Celebrities, VIPs, industry professionals and other influential guests of the high-profile invite-only gathering mingled with each other throughout the courtyard and further in through the open doors of the North Loggias. We continued our journey passing through the space and into the chic HMF social club, named after the resorts founder Henry Morrison Flagler. It too was decorated for the season, but it also gave a modern nod to the classic speakeasy era and high-class American glamour. Two bars stretched both sides of the lounge, which was filled with sounds of laughter, more music, and clinking glasses, with everyone dressed to the nines.

"At the far side is The Circle Ballroom," Den said, steering our attention. "But you'll see it's currently set up with a dance floor and a raised platform behind it for the bands," Den added, completing his dialog on the event areas.

The ballroom had a soaring domed ceiling with an ornate crystal chandelier hanging from a stylized gold-leaf sunburst, surrounded by eight oval fresco-painted murals depicting Renaissance landscapes. The room itself was as Den had said, contained the dance floor and band stage at the far side, but the rest was arranged perfectly for a cocktail party with tall tables to stand at and rest your drinks on, but no chairs. Behind the stage, out the similar 15-foot windows as shown in the courtyard, were spectacular softly lit ocean views.

For the next hour we walked the room, lightly mingling with and checking out the whose-who of the event.

"Would you like to dance?" Redmond asked, offering his hand when Meghan Trainor's *Made You Look* came over the speakers. It was one of the twins' favorite songs right now.

I smiled playfully at him, then I took his hand. "I'm in!" I shouted as the music grew louder.

We continued our dancing after the first song into OneRepublic's *I Ain't Worried*, on through Imagine Dragons' *Sharks* and the erotic song *Unholy* by Sam Smith, ending on a slowdown with Adele's *Easy On Me*.

When the slow song ended, Redmond guided us to where Den stood patiently waiting. Then he leaned down, his mouth next to my ear. "How are your feet?" he asked, sympathetic to my plight of wearing high heels. Then he turned his cheek, offering me his ear.

"So far, so good," I assured him, despite my feet starting to ache. "Do you see Lily anywhere?" He was taller than most of the guests, and that made it easy for him to scan the room.

He shook his head, then said, "Yes, there she is!"

As though a powerful presence was coming through, the crowd parted like waves in an ocean. When the last few people stepped back, Lily emerged from the sea of guests. "Heeeey," she shouted when she spotted us.

"Hey," I yelled back, through the boom-boom of the music as she began to cross the short distance.

Just then, the same long-haired rocker in the pink and black suit who had addressed Redmond earlier caught Lily by the elbow. "Shade," I heard him say to her through the music eruption. They embraced briefly and then Lily pointed to us.

"Red-man," the guy said again when he saw Redmond.

"Redmond, Lynn, this is Sam Black from *Pink'n Black*, the band," Lily said in introduction. "He's the lead singer in the band playing tonight."

Redmond grinned at me before greeting the rock'n roller. "Sam — looking forward to hearing you live," Redmond said, patting the guy's arm.

"Sam's band is looking for a new place to record their next album," Lily added, full of enthusiasm.

This Sam Black put his hand up on Redmond's shoulder and then said, "Come meet our producer."

"It'll only take a few minutes," Lily said, directing her words at me.

I smiled, knowing this was a big deal.

"Sure," Redmond agreed, nodding at the eager twosome. "I'll be back soon," he said then, the statement directed at me. He squeezed my hand, then kissed my forehead before rushing off with Lily and Sam.

"*Great*," I sighed out in a low voice. We'd managed almost two hours of freedom before Lily had swooped in and accosted my husband, stealing him away to converse with some famous music producer and the lead singer of this latest band he was promoting. I waved to Redmond as he was pulled away by an enthusiastic Lily, the three of them swiftly swallowed up in the crowd of music elite. My titan of a bodyguard remained with me.

"Here," Den said, tapping my arm and handing me what I knew to be a high-tech covert earpiece. "You'll be able to hear me better over the music and crowd." He stepped back behind me, then slightly to my left.

"Gotcha," I said, after placing the earbud into my ear. "This is perfect, actually. Now you can tell me about Addison being in New York."

"We figured with Zuriel out of commission, Addison must have been asked to cover the New York facility with Marcus. As you know, Zach said the Norway lab has been quiet."

"Yes, but do you think Addison was only there because Frank owns the place?"

"She did say both Marcus and then Thaddeus made appearances there, so maybe that was all it was, curiosity."

"Let's hope so. It was too close for comfort in my books."

"Mine too."

"I'm sure it's been discussed amongst your brothers, but what is your take on this undercover Angel? Do you think it's an Earthbound?"

"Don't you?"

"We all assumed it was because of Zuriel and Lyndon, but Kris asked me if I thought it could be one of The Watchers."

"Why would they be following you, now especially?"

I shrugged. "To be honest, I worry that it's Thaddeus," I shared.

"Everything points to him being in Brazil."

"Does it though? No one knows where he is. You only think he's there. I asked Purah to search for him and I haven't heard a peep from her."

"Well, don't you think if Thaddeus was aware of your whereabouts, wouldn't he have already snatched you up?"

"I'm not looking to test my theory. So maybe he's keeping an eye on the other Earthbound, seeing if Lyndon follows through with his tasks, seeing if Addison does as he's told."

"He's too egocentric. And it's not like him to micromanage his people. He'd rather break them after if they fail at their task."

"Okay." I turned to him and gave him a weak smile, then turned back to the crowd of people mingling. "I heard Kris dodged the dreaded birthday question," I stated, changing subjects.

"I guess you haven't heard the latest on that."

"What did I miss?"

"Jana confronted Kris again about his birthday."

"When? What did he say?"

"Today. Lucky for him, we'd come up with an explanation on the topic."

"You did?" I turned back to him, my eyes bulging. "What's the story?"

"That the only records they had were from the foster system and none of us knew our real birthdays."

"And she bought that?" I fiddled with my earpiece.

"He told her it was why we had all been brought to that particular group home. The story we agreed upon was that we had been brought there at different times as toddlers or babies, foster records only stating we'd been abandoned in some way or form, no records to say who we were, only a number to identify our existence, and an estimate of our ages. The only date on the records had been the one stating when we'd been found by the police. And Kris told her that our foster parents chose our first names for us but let us choose our own surnames when we were old enough. And that until then we'd been known as the Haven boys."

"It's reaching, I have to say, but plausible," I said, turning to him and nodding.

"If Kris and Jana are ever going to have a real relationship, he's going to need to tell the truth—the real truth."

"And that is why we never get too involved."

My brain went to my questions about Den and his relationship with Gavin, but I kept those queries to myself. Instead, I asked, "Speaking of getting involved, what are your thoughts on Lane bringing Lyndon to the birthday party tomorrow?"

"I… I want to believe what Lane says about him… so we'll see. Kris and Leo need to see him in person with Lane, confirm what his agenda is with her."

"His agenda?"

"Well, all I know is he hates Thaddeus like the rest of us—so there might be hope for him yet."

I glanced back at him again, but he only gave me a tight smile. "I guess we'll see," I added as a topic ender. My stomach grumbled as a waiter with a small tray of canapés swept by, leaving in his wake an aroma of something decadent and cheese laden. We'd eaten dinner with the girls when I'd gotten back from my visit with Grier, but I was feeling a bit peckish now, watching as the waitstaff with trays filled with a variety of finger foods shuttled by. When one of the waiters slowed stopping next to me, I snatched up one of the accompanying napkins and two of the hors d'oeuvres from the tray. I bit into one and gagged instantly discovering the puffed pastry contained pureed mushrooms. When I was sure no one other than Den was looking, I spit the contents from my mouth into the napkin, then flashed him a sickly expression.

"What?" he questioned in my ear.

"Mushrooms—gah," I grumbled. Den just shook his head. And of course, this event was too extravagant to have trash bins close by, so I had to find another way to dispose of the evidence. Luckily for me, a waiter with glasses of sparkling champagne passed by and offered me one. "Where is the ladies' room?" I asked, taking the offered fluted glass from the tray. He pointed back towards the side entrance to the lobby, then smiled. "Thank you," I said before he walked off. Then I took a quick sip to wash away the horrible taste of fungus. "I need to go to the ladies' room," I told Den, even though I knew he'd heard my exchange with the waiter. I took another big gulp of champagne before setting the glass on a nearby table, then I turned, heading back through the social club in the direction of the lobby. Den turned instantly and followed along close behind me. Through the doors, I spotted the sign indicating the location of the bathrooms and I hurried towards them.

In the ladies' room, I tossed the napkin in the closest trash bin as I noticed two women fixing their makeup in the mirrors closest to the door. I didn't need to use the facilities, but I did need to wash my hands. Besides, I'm sure Den wouldn't have appreciated the background sounds anyway had I needed to. I passed behind the women over to the sink at the far end.

Finished washing, I took one of the thin cloth towels from the shelf above the sink and was unexpectedly hit with a ripple of dizziness.

"Are you okay?" one of the women asked, as though noticing my distress.

"I'm good," I lied, gripping the edge of the sink's vanity counter. "Just food sensitivities. I'll be fine." I let my head drop forward and pulled in a cleansing breath. *Oh my gaaawd*, my brain screamed, and I drew in another slow breath of air.

"I never eat at these events," the other woman said.

"You okay, Lynn?" came Den's voice in my ear.

I turned my head, watching as the two women exited the bathroom, and then said, "They're here."

"Whose here?"

"I'm sensing… it's the same feeling I had at the hospital."

"Lyndon?"

"No, the other from the hospital—same one I felt in New York."

"How could they know you would be here?" Den questioned.

"How could they know I would be in New York?" I countered. With the sensation still buzzing over my skin, I promptly exited the bathroom to address Den in person. "Maybe someone was hanging around the studio," I tossed out as I came up next to him. "We'll have to check with Lily."

"Are you still… *feeling* them?" he asked, concern blanketing his face.

I nodded, then we both began scanning the lengthy stretch of the lobby.

"Let's go out to the courtyard," Den suggested, motioning for me to move forward.

Outside, we once again scanned the vicinity, but the sensation had lessened some. "Ballroom," I said, chin nodding in the direction of the entrance to the Mediterranean Ballroom.

In the ballroom, the sensation was even weaker, and I shook my head when Den looked down at me. "Loggia?" I said with a shrug before heading back through to the courtyard and left into the South Loggia Registration area. The tingling was scarcely present on my skin as I glanced left up the narrow hall to see nothing but an exit door. Then I looked right past plush seating areas that dotted the space between us and the doors that led to the other end of the main lobby. "I can barely feel them," I said, turning back to the doors we'd come through.

"What about checking out the social club again?" Den suggested, as though running out of ideas.

"Whatever," I said, frustrated. "We need to find Redmond and Lily, anyway." My feet were now killing me, too. "They'll still be in the social club, I'm guessing." My phone vibrated in my purse, and I pulled it free, thinking that maybe Redmond was looking for us. It wasn't him, it was a text from Grier. I grinned despite my current situation and aching feet. I'd sent her the photos Den had taken of us before we'd left, and based on her response, I knew for certain she and I were going to be *great* friends.

Her message read,

> *Okay, with your fit body in those photos, I'm going with Ms. Blunt's character Rita, from Edge of Tomorrow, but strictly going off that fabulous jumpsuit, I'd say you've achieved Queen Freya status from the movie The Huntsman.*

Chapter 27 

Yesterday, when Jana had asked Kris again about his birthday, he finally explained the story behind his avoidance on the issue. It was a wild one and a heartbreaking one. No records. No idea who their parents were, and nothing stating when each of them was born. They only had estimates on their actual ages too, having been put in the foster system so young, with their current ages somewhere between 35 and 40 at best guess, with Leo being the oldest and Hayden being the youngest, and Kris in his late 30s. It had been hard to believe, but the details behind where he came from weren't something any of them ever chose to share. She figured it must have been embarrassing growing up having to explain why they had no family history, and no accurate date of birth, but it didn't seem to bother Kris. He said he understood her need to know, but he just didn't like having to explain it. His foster parents sounded like wonderful people, especially taking on so many young boys and making their world feel normal under such unusual circumstances. She'd told Kris that they could pick a day just for him to celebrate his existence and the fact that he was born. She also said she couldn't imagine a world without him in it. He'd responded by saying he felt the same. It had been Lane who had asked about her birthday and when Jana had told her it was this month, Lane had suggested a party at the restaurant. She also said Kris had loved the idea since he'd missed out on all her other birthdays and that he hated the idea of missing out on any more. Jana guessed that meant he wanted her to stick around for a while.

She'd never asked Kris outright if he had been dating someone before he'd lost his memory, though she had learned that none on the *team* were married or had ever been. In fact, there had been no mention of women in their lives other than Jules, and it was clear she wasn't anyone's girlfriend. Jana had wondered if their reservations about getting involved with someone had to do with their mission, considering it was a covert operation and how complicated it had been for them to disclose it with her. It's not something one would easily share, like how many siblings you have. Jana understood it was a big deal that she'd been included in this part of their lives, and she was grateful they were searching for her half-sister.

Last night Leo had given her the update on Natalie, stating Jules had checked the university registration database again where she and Ben worked, searching the updates for the January students, and had found Natalie's now visible profile on the list showing her in Future Start status. And ironically enough, she was registered to be in one of Ben's classes. Unfortunately, though, she had that old address of hers attached to her file. That meant that they were going to have to wait until she started class to actually find her. But they were one step closer.

Jana had spoken to Geir numerous times over the past several months, although all she told him was that things were good with Kris, going slowly but still going well. She hadn't shared with Geir the intricacies of what Kris and his brothers did when they weren't at their day jobs, or even about how she had a half-sister, mainly because she wasn't sure what she was allowed to tell him, but it was hard keeping things from him. As long as she shared she was happy, he would be happy and wouldn't pry.

Jana *was* happy, and she'd told him so when he'd called her first thing this morning to wish her a happy birthday. It had been 7 a.m. Ottawa time, and still dark out when she'd answered the call in bed, Geir stated he hadn't wanted to wake her any earlier. The sun had risen by the time she'd hung up their call, and it was then she noticed a tiny rose bush had been placed on the small desk in her room. She had admired the one Lane had in *her* room and had mentioned it to Kris, so she had a pretty good idea of who it was from.

When she'd finally gotten out of bed, she saw the small pot had a note card tied to it with a pink ribbon that matched the tiny rosebuds. The card read, *Happy Birthday, Jana*. Signed with just *Kris* and a hand-drawn heart next to it. He had already told her last night how grateful he was to be celebrating her birthday with her, and how much he loved spending time with her these past months, but she still didn't feel confident he wanted more. She was seriously attracted to him, had been from the beginning, if she was being honest with herself. She thought there had been *heat* between them before, and he'd kissed her with such passion when she'd first come to his home, but she worried now that things wouldn't ever progress. When she'd talked to Lane about their *slow-moving* relationship, Lane had suggested *she* should make a move, show him she was ready for more. But she'd not gotten up the nerve to do so yet.

Kris had mentioned last night he'd be going to the restaurant early this morning to do some work and get things ready for later, adding she was to take the day off since it was her birthday. Jana hadn't said *no* and had enjoyed falling back to sleep after Geir's call. At 10 a.m. she'd gotten up and showered, readying herself for the day ahead.

After blow-drying her hair, Jana returned to the bedroom and noticed that she had gotten a text from Kris.

He'd written,

> *Good morning, Birthday Girl!*
> *Can't wait to see you at the restaurant later.*
> *Working on your surprise ;)*

Which made her smile, although it also meant he wouldn't be home in between, but he had written he had a surprise for her and that made her smile twice.

A soft knock sounded then on her bedroom door.

"Come in," she called, setting her cellphone back on the nightstand.

The door opened to reveal a grinning Lane. "Happy Birthday!" she said in a singsong voice. "How is your day looking so far?"

"So far it's been perfect," Jana said. "Morning call from my friend Geir in Iceland, a happy birthday text from Kris...." She paused to point at the tiny rose bush Kris had left for her on the desk.

"Oooh it's so cute," Lane said, crossing the room to admire the gift. "The pink is even prettier than the yellow one I have."

"And I get to see your gorgeous face to start my day," Jana added, pulling Lane in for a hug.

"Did you eat yet?" Lane asked, as Jana released her from their embrace.

"No, but I'm starving."

"My dad—Julian, just made a batch of confetti pancakes in honor of your birthday, so I'd get a move on and get some before the ogres in the house eat them all."

Jana laughed and then said, "Truer words."

"Come on then," Lane said, tugging on her sleeve.

When the two of them entered from the hall into the kitchen space, no one was eating at the counter island and only Julian was there.

"Don't tell me the pancakes are all gone," Lane whined.

Jana just laughed because it was typical for food to go fast around here.

"Have no fear," Julian said, opening the oven to reveal a hidden stack of pancakes.

"Fantastic," Lane said then, making Jana laugh again.

Julian set the two of them up, each with a small stack of warm, colourfully dotted pancakes and a plate of bacon he had also skillfully hid in the oven. "By the way, Max and I will be taking you over to the party," Julian told Jana.

"Okay, great," Jana said to him.

Julian pulled a book-shaped wrapped gift from under the counter and set it next to Jana. "Happy Birthday," he said then.

"Julian—you didn't have to get me anything," she gushed, hugging the package against her chest.

"It's the second book of that series I started you on," he said with a wink.

Jana grinned. The first book had been seriously steamy, so she could only guess where book two would take her.

"I'll be bringing your gift to the restaurant later," Lane said. "And I'm bringing a date." Lane gave her father a side-eye look.

Jana glanced at Julian to see he was doing a fatherly eyebrow raise in response, but she said nothing. She recognized that look. It was the same expression she remembered her own father giving her on occasion. Jana turned her attention back to Lane. "Is this the one you work with at the group home?"

"Yup," she said, side-eyeing her father again. "Speaking of which, I have to head there now, so I'll see you all later."

"See you then," Jana said. She didn't dare look at Julian. She already knew he was watching Lane leave. Instead, she stared down at the gift-wrapped book. When she heard the front door close upon Lane's departure, she tore open the wrapping and said, "Thank you so much for this—I thoroughly enjoyed the first one." She clutched it to her chest again and looked up at Julian. He was still glaring at the front door.

"Good morning, and Happy Birthday," came Leo's deep voice from behind her. "

"Good morning to you and thanks," Jana said, turning his way. He carried with him a hardcover book as he strolled from the interior door of his suite.

"Hey, Julian, thanks again for a fun breakfast," he said to the brooding father. "We don't get many festive, colourful breakfasts these days, not since Lane was younger."

"Will you be at the party later?" Jana set the book from Julian on the island.

"Yes, but I have something to attend to beforehand, so I'll be a bit late." He turned his attention back to Julian. "You and Max are bringing Jana to the party, yes?"

"Correct," Julian said. "I too have some things to attend to as well before the day is out." He turned to face Jana. "I'll come by your room around 5ish and we'll head out. You're going to love this one." He tapped the book and winked at her again, then turned and headed in the direction of the laundry room.

Grinning, Jana focused back on Leo, and asked, "What do you have there?"

"Well," Leo said, shooting a quick glance at her birthday present. "I see you have already received a book as a gift." He rubbed his hand over the cover of the one he held. "Have you ever read *The Great Gatsby*?"

"No, I haven't, not yet," she said, admiring the blue cover of the book.

"I don't read much fiction, but this is one of my favorites." Leo caressed the cover again. "And I know you like reading, so I wanted to give you this copy as a gift for your birthday." Leo handed her the book.

"That is so kind—and I love to read," she said, opening the cover. "Oh my, this is a first edition." She stared up at Leo, stunned. "This must be worth a fortune—I couldn't," she stuttered out, still staring at him.

"Yes—yes you can," Leo said, covering her hand with his and closing the book.

"I don't know what to say," she said, slowly drawing the book to her chest like she'd done with the one Julian had given her.

"I've read it a hundred times—I just hope you enjoy it."

"I haven't met a book I didn't like," Jana said, stealing a look at the cover again.

"Let me know what you think," Leo said before heading back the way he came. "Oh, hey." He paused at the door, glancing back at her. "Did Kris ever tell you when Natalie's birthday was?"

Jana shook her head. She knew how old she was, but she hadn't thought to ask when she was born.

"Soon—January 1st," Leo said, before opening the way back into his suite.

A New Year's baby, Jana considered, watching as the door to Leo's private quarters closed.

Jana spent the rest of the day in bliss reading the first of her two birthday book gifts. And by the time Julian knocked on her door at 5 p.m. she was ready and in her new dark blue jeans and the cranberry red sweater Kris had bought for her. She had never celebrated her birthday with a party like this. It had usually been just her and her father, but she was truly excited now for the night's festivities.

"Kris told us the upper section is reserved for just the party," Max said, opening the way into the restaurant. "But the rest will be open to patrons."

"That way, the staff can come up to the party area and still not miss out on their shift."

"Smart," Jana said. "Saturday nights are the best—wouldn't be fair to them if Kris closed the whole place, and they missed out on tips."

As they reached the bottom of the staircase to the upper level, Mason came rushing out of the kitchen. His hands were flying with ASL, clearly stressed over something.

"What's wrong—slow down," Jana said, doing her best to understand what he was trying to say. She had been practicing learning ASL with Mason since she'd started working at the restaurant and was usually pretty good at deciphering his quick fingers.

"Come Max," Julian said. "Let's go see what is so urgent in the kitchen."

Mason quickly signed, "Happy Birthday", then rushed after Max and Julian.

Letting the others deal with the kitchen issue, Jana proceeded up the stairs. Once at the top, she saw the space had been elegantly decorated in tasteful party decorations with a bar set up for private service. Next to it she noticed a small table with what looked like a stack of more book-shaped gifts. She grinned with the anticipation.

"I guess people know you love to read," came Lane's voice behind her.

Jana laughed amusedly, glancing back over her shoulder, then whirled swiftly to face Lane, astonished by the man who stood next to her.

"Jana, this is Lyndon," Lane said. "Lyndon, this is our birthday girl, Jana."

"I wish you the happiest of birthdays," Lyndon said in a deep voice, bowing regally in response to the introduction.

"Thank you—I'm thrilled to meet you finally," Jana said, shaking herself from gawking at him. "Lane has told me some wonderful things about your work with her at the group home." Jana had gotten used to being around huge men, but she hadn't expected Lane's date would be another colossally huge one.

"She is a welcome addition to the wonderful staff there," Lyndon said, smiling graciously.

"That is lovely to hear—I know she enjoys her time there," Jana said. *He was a handsome one. I'll give Lane that*, Jana thought. Shame about the scar, but with those stunning green eyes and lush dark hair, it was effortless to overlook. "Mason," Jana said then, noticing him standing silently at the top of the stairs. "Did everything get worked out?" She'd almost forgotten there had been an emergency in the kitchen.

Mason nodded.

"Come," Lane said then, waving Mason over. "Mason, this is my friend Lyndon."

Mason held out his hand for a handshake, but Lyndon just looked at him intensely.

Jana looked to Lane. *I think I smell a hint of testosterone*, Jana considered.

"Mason and I both go to Ottawa U, and he has been helping my Uncle Kris with the menu here."

Mason signed, "Hello." Then used the voice app on his wristwatch phone. "Hello," the voice simulator said for him.

"You can hear… but you use ASL," Lyndon said, sounding impressed.

"Do you know it?" Mason signed before using the voice app again.

"Some," Lyndon said with a humble smile. "I'm learning."

"I've been teaching one of our residents at the group home and Lyndon has been practicing with him," Lane shared, smiling at Lyndon proudly.

"Jana," came Kris's voice from the stairs, pulling everyone's attention his way.

Kris took several long strides, coming to stand in front of Jana, ignoring the others. "Happy Birthday, beautiful lady," he said, taking both her hands in his and kissing the backs of them.

"Uncle Kris," Lane said, drawing Kris's focus away from her. "This in Lyndon."

Still holding Jana's hand, Kris stared at the enormous man.

"Good to meet you, Lyndon," Kris said, giving what looked like a forced smile.

"I am grateful to make your acquaintance," Lyndon said, but there was no bow from him for Kris.

"Where is Uncle Leo?" Lane asked, checking in the direction of the stairs.

Jana observed as Kris yanked his gaze from Lane's date. "He will be along soon," Kris said to Lane. Then he turned to Mason. "I need your help with the surprise." Kris leaned in and gave Jana a soft, lingering kiss on her cheek. "I'll be back shortly." He stared into her eyes, and she was momentarily lost in his. He glanced Lane's way. "Please get Jana something to drink, would you?" he asked, letting go of Jana's hands. Then he was off, rushing back down the stairs to the main level.

Mason gave a smile and a wave to each of them before chasing Kris down the stairs to the kitchen.

Jana turned to face Lane and Lyndon just as a *"cough"* sounded from behind them. This time, Julian and Max now stood at the top of the stairs. *Yup, it was definitely an excess of testosterone she was detecting,* Jana mused.

Lane blew out a loud sigh. "Lyndon, I'd like you to meet my fathers, Julian and Max." Lane extended a hand to each of her parents respectfully, making room for them to come stand next to her between her and Jana.

Max smiled tightly, extending a hand in greeting.

Lyndon stared down at it for a heartbeat, then swiftly clasped the man's hand for a firm shake. "It is an honor to meet Lane's parents," Lyndon said, before proactively extending a hand to Julian.

"We've heard wonderful things about you, Lyndon. It is lovely of you to accompany Lane to the party," Julian said, taking Lyndon's hand.

Lyndon shook Julian's hand, in what appear to be in a much softer manner. "I'm not much for parties, gatherings of any kind for that matter, but I could not refuse Lane's invitation. And now that I am here, I am grateful for the opportunity to meet you both."

"We don't normally do big parties either, but this was my idea," Lane said, as though hoping to ease the parental tension. "And I felt we were all due."

"Here-here," Max said in agreement. "Would anyone care for a drink?"

"Thought you'd never ask," Jana joked, feeling the tension lessoning.

"Did you do anything special for your last birthday?" Lane asked, pulling Jana's focus from watching Max and Julian navigate their way to the bar area.

"In Iceland, peak season for travelers is during the summer, but as you also know, Christmas is an exciting time too, preparation starting as early as September, and because my bakery was always busy around my birthday, I rarely had time to celebrate with anyone other than my father."

"Excuse me, did you say you're from Iceland?" Lyndon asked, cutting in with his inquiry.

"Yes, I arrived from Iceland in August," Jana said. "Have you visited?"

"No... I... no... but I hear it is... *fascinating*," Lyndon hedged out, as though he had something else he wanted to say.

"It is—and I recommend everyone should visit at least once in their lives," Jana said fondly.

Lyndon smiled meekly at Jana, but he had no response.

"What do you think of the new restaurant?" Jana asked him then.

Lane directed an arm for Lyndon to take in the full view, then she said, "I think you and my uncles did a wicked job with this place."

"The décor is splendid," Lyndon acknowledged, moving closer to the overlook to the main level to further observe the patrons. "It's an extremely... lively place."

"Thank you Lane—Lyndon. I hope our customers feel the same way," Jana replied. She noticed then Lyndon was gripping the railing so tight his knuckles were turning white. Jana turned with the intention of saying something to Lane, but she had already moved to the far side of the overlook and was speaking with her fathers.

Lyndon spun around then, an expression of disbelief painted across his face.

"Is everything alright?" Jana asked, wondering if perchance he had a problem with heights.

"Yes—please excuse me," he said, rushing past her to the stairs to the main level.

When Lyndon hit the bottom step, he couldn't believe what he was seeing, *who* he was seeing. It was *Shayne*, one of the Seraphim from their home star in Pleiades, cast down by his tyrant of a boss. "What are you doing here?" Lyndon said in demand, reaching out and gripping the arm of the Seraph as he approached the service bar.

Shayne reeled, his fists clenched and up for a fight at the abruptness of the contact. "You!" Shayne barked, yanking his arm free of Lyndon when he saw who had accosted him.

"What. Are. You. Doing here?" Lyndon questioned again.

"If you must know, I work here," Shayne said with a scowl. "And I'm good friends with the owners."

"You're friends… with Lane's uncles?" Lyndon asked, confusion rushing through his brain. Lane was in unusually close contact with several of the Earthbound from Pleiades. First Julianna, her university professor, and now this one working for her uncles, Lyndon examined.

"Lane? How do you know, Lane?" Shayne asked, his brow furrowing. "And what are *you* doing here?"

"I am here at Lane's request—for the birthday party. For Jana, the mate of her Uncle Kris, I believe."

Shayne circled around through the entry into the bartender's space, retrieving a bin filled with tiny glasses. He set the bin on the bar, then asked, "What are your intentions with Lane?"

"Why is she any of your concern?" Lyndon asked, checking over his shoulder that no one could overhear them.

"Because I am also friends with her parents," Shayne revealed, grabbing up another bin of used drink glasses from behind the bar.

"She and I are friends… close friends," Lyndon confessed, unsure why he was wasting his time telling him this. It was true. They were friends, though Lyndon longed for more. He wished to hold her hand in his, to caress her delicate cheek, to press a gentle kiss to her blush-coloured lips.

Shayne slammed the bin on the bar top. "Good—keep it that way," he bit out, wrenching Lyndon from his thoughts. *"Does she know what you are?"* he asked in a low voice then.

"No," Lyndon said, shame tightening his chest as though he'd been caught speaking his desires aloud.

"Do you plan to tell her?" Shayne questioned, his voice still quiet.

Instead of answering, Lyndon narrowed his eyes and countered with, "Does her family know what you are?"

Shayne pointed a scrutinizing finger at Lyndon. *"If you do anything to hurt her, I will…,"* Shayne said through clenched teeth.

"I would never hurt Lane," Lyndon declared, straightening his posture in a protective stance like he was her guardian. "I would sooner die than cause her any harm."

"Everything okay, here?" came an unexpected query behind Lyndon.

"Lane—Hi, yes," Shayne answered. "Was just chatting with your friend here, Lyndon was it?"

"Yes—very good talking with you," Lyndon responded before turning to face Lane.

"Hey, Shayne." Lane gave him a little wave. "I was wondering where you got off to," Lane said to Lyndon, lacing her arm around his, then guiding him towards the staircase to the upper level.

Lyndon's body warmed in response to the intimate contact. "Your fathers are very delightful," he said, flustered. "And your uncle seems very nice as well." Lyndon shot a look towards the bar to see Shayne the bartender, observing them as they ascended the stairs.

"They are protective—overly protective, if you ask me," Lane said when they reached the upper level.

"Lane, Lyndon!" Jana's joyous voice called when she spotted them. Gathered around her were several of the restaurant staff, based on their outfits, Lane's fathers, and another enormous man.

"That's my Uncle Leo," Lane said, as though noticing he was staring.

"Haaappyyy biiiirthdaaaaaaay tooooo youuu," came a baritone singing voice behind them. Lane's Uncle Kris strode forward from the staircase, serenading the birthday girl while carrying a large cake.

"Happy birthday to youuu," Lane sang, adding her voice to the celebratory song, her spirited voice making Lyndon smile. Lane took him by the elbow then, steering him this time nearer to the group.

On closer inspection, Lyndon saw that the cake was covered in tiny blush-coloured rosebuds. Up from the center spiraled three candles aglow with yellow flames. *Why three candles*, he wondered.

"Jana is 33 today," Lane said, unexpectedly answering his brain's question.

"Lane," Lyndon began, causing her to look up at him. "I… feel protective of you, too." He had taken notice of how massive Lane's Uncle Kris was, and now he surveyed this other one, both of them bigger than him even. Granted, her uncles appeared more youthful than he had anticipated.

"I like that you said that." Lane drew her hand down his arm, ending with a soft squeeze of his forearm.

"When is your birthday?" he asked, then instantly regretted it, knowing he'd inadvertently opened a tricky dialog.

"March," she said. "When is yours?"

Lyndon drew in a breath. "Taylor's birthday is the only one I celebrate," he said in leu of an answer to her inquiry.

Lane smiled sweetly at him. "I'm glad you are here with me." She brushed her fingers against the back of his hand, then said, "I was going to ask you to go with me to the Halloween party they had here, but you got called away again. And you never told me what happened." Lane tilted her head inquisitively.

Lyndon pressed his lips together, then he said, "A friend of mine… remember when you asked if there was anyone at work I liked?"

"Yes." Lane nodded.

"Well… Zuriel was injured, and he's in the hospital," Lyndon clarified. "You were with me… in my apartment when they called with an update. That is why I had to leave you that day."

"Is he okay?" Lane's brows pinched together.

"Unfortunately, no," he said, dropping his gaze to look down at the floor. Lyndon's heart swelled, the stress of the situation lessening a tad with sharing this with her, though he wondered how far he could take his disclosure. Looking at her again, he said, "He had a serious reaction to some medication they gave him and… now he's in a coma."

"My gosh!" Worry filled Lane's lovely face. She reached for his hand, but then pulled back as if she'd lost her resolve. "What now—what can they do for him?"

Lyndon shook his head. "It's a waiting game now."

Without hesitation this time, as though now resolute, Lane wrapped her hand around his. "Then we wait."

Chapter 28 

Leo had been given the details on the events from the music industry Christmas party from Den, and he and the others had discussed at length about who they thought might be hovering around. None of them could come up with a plausible individual other than it being one of Thaddeus's crew. Addison, it seemed, had relocated to New York City, temporarily or permanently, they didn't know, but his showing up at the Thanksgiving gathering had struck added concern, especially with the other lingering and hiding out of view. Leo had played with the idea of it being Thaddeus himself, but there were no indicators he was even in North America, let alone specifically South Florida. Besides, he wasn't known for his subtlety or lack of control, and he would have pounced on his prey without hesitation had he been the one hiding in the shadows. Kris had suggested the possibility of it being one of The Watchers, but the others had felt it was a bit of a reach, though nothing, no one, was off the quandary table.

Further to that discussion, they had deliberated over the troubling question of whether they could trust Lyndon or not. Kris and Leo, along with Lane's fathers, had watched and scrutinized every interaction he and Lane had while at Jana's birthday party, but it hadn't been until Shayne had shared his encounter with Lyndon from that night, that they had truly grasped the depth of friendship Lyndon had with their young female family member. When Shayne had asked Lyndon about his intentions with Lane, his response had come off like an alpha male guarding his mate, but the jury was still out on whether he was someone they could trust. As far as their concerns regarding Jana, since she hadn't known about their scrutiny of Lyndon, to her it appeared as if the party was a wonderful success, and she had also accepted the narrative Kris had told her about their birthdays and foster home situation. As much as they wanted to tell Jana the truth, Kris specifically, they knew it was much too soon to bring her into their otherworldly reality. Plus, in addition to dialog with the partial truth, they'd had to keep the facts of their urgency with trying to find Natalie from Jana as well.

So far, luck had been on their side with Natalie showing as registered for classes at the university Ben and Jules taught at, but the need to locate her was of the utmost importance. Natalie had already surpassed the crucial age of 20 but was swiftly edging towards her 21st birthday in January, mere days away. The knowledge Natalie could sprout wings at any time weighed heavily on each and every one of them, and tensions were high. Without knowing her location precisely, they couldn't aid her should the need surface, nor could they shelter her from the enemy should they learn of her existence. Keeping Mason's genealogy a secret, short of separating him from his mother, had been the only ploy they'd had in protecting him *and* Jules, but they'd been fully aware of her pregnancy and the birth of her son. Natalie, being out in the world basically solo, was the least ideal situation.

Even after all this time, they still didn't understand why the 20th year was so crucial. Leo had speculated on the theory it was a latent hormonal trigger due to the slow aging and longevity that came from their Seraph parent. Those who made it to adulthood were usually healthier, more athletic, and noticeably more striking in appearance. They had no idea what Natalie's health was like at this point, whether it was good or bad, but if she went through this transition without assistance from those with experience in such matters, it would be more than her health and body that would be harmed, the damage it could do to her psyche would be unrepairable. Even if she were somehow able to come to grips with the fact she had physical wings, the function and knowledge of how to use them would not be instinctive. She'd need to be taught, and this was the best-case scenario.

Leo's cellphone vibrated next to him where he sat behind the bar. "Things are copacetic here," he said, answering a call from Kris. "How goes the hunt?" Leo got off his bar seat and strolled towards the main doors. He had offered to manage things at the restaurant this morning, while Kris and Jana were off shopping for last-minute supplies for their Christmas gathering at North Haven.

"I would hope so," Kris said into Leo's ear. "Place doesn't open for another two hours, but that's not why I'm calling."

"What's up? Is there a shortage of candy canes or eggnog?" Leo joked. This year for Christmas, Lane had insisted they get a real tree, a tall one to boot, to set up in the main living space. Lane and Jana had done all the decorating of the restaurant and the house, plus the decorations on the tree, but Jana had insisted they needed a tree *topper*, and it was the reason she and Kris were out hunting for one this morning.

"Nope. Julian took care of those supplies already," Kris said. "We just need your vote on the tree topper. You're the last to vote, by the way."

"What are the choices?" Leo asked. Christmas had become a fun thing when Lane was born, only to peter off as she had gotten older, but with Jana, another lover of the season in the house, Lane had revived her enthusiasm once again. He and the others all had as well.

"Uhmm…," Kris said, as though hesitant to answer. "It's between two of Jana's favorites."

"Okay—tell me," Leo demanded in jest, reaching for the latch above the door handle to unlock the way in for staff who would be arriving soon.

"You get to pick between a star or an… angel," Kris tossed out finally.

Chuckling, Leo said, "I vote for *angel*." When Lane was younger, they had always used whatever topper she'd hand made that year, and when she was in her teens, they'd reused whatever decorations had survived those earlier times.

"*It's unanimous,*" Kris said with a hearty laugh. "We'll be back in an hour," he added before ending the call.

Leo crossed the way back to the bar and slid his cellphone into the back pocket of his jeans only to have it vibrate again. Retrieving and answering it, he said, "Hey Shayne." Leo hit the speaker, then set his cellphone back on the bar.

"Think I've found your girl," Shayne said.

"What—how?" Leo questioned. "Where?"

"I was just at The Laff visiting the owners, and a young woman came in, one who looks suspiciously like the halfling you've been looking for—matches the photo you sent out, though you couldn't miss her if you saw her."

"Is she still there?"

"No. She was just picking up her final paycheck."

"You let her go?"

"Here me out—she said something to the owner about starting school at the university in January. Asked about future shift options that might work with her school schedule. But the owner said they were already filled."

"Shayne!?" Leo yelled, anxious for him to get to the point. "You should have followed her."

"Hold up," Shayne said, "Sounded like she was in need of a job, school being full time and all. So, I introduced myself, told her I was the bar manager at Après SNOW, and suggest she go over there—that you might be looking for more staff come the new year. She seemed thrilled at the idea—said she'd drop over before heading home."

The bell over the door jingled, causing Leo anxiously to glance up, but it wasn't one of the staff who had entered. He sucked in a breath through his nose, then calmly said, "That's excellent, thanks. She just came through the restaurant door." Leo blew out the heavy breath and hung up. Then he circled back around to the front of the bar to greet his anticipated yet unexpected visitor. "Season's Greetings," he said to the young woman with the uncanny beauty. "We're not quite open yet. How may I help you?"

"Hi, yes—sorry," she said. "I'm Natalie Harwood. I met your bar manager earlier, and he suggested I come by. He mentioned you might be hiring."

Leo kept his expression stoic, though he was filled with relief at seeing her standing before him. "What is your availability?" he asked, even though he knew they didn't have any openings.

"I'm attending Ottawa U full time in the new year, so I'm available to work nights and weekends."

Leo turned and reached behind the bar. "We have most of our staff set up for the new year, but we can put you on the call list." He smiled, however, he still held back his excitement over catching such a serendipitous break in their search for her. "Here," he said, handing Natalie his business card for the restaurant. "Go here to fill out the application form with your phone number and *current* address." He pointed to the website on the card. "I'm Leo, by the way—I'm one of the owners here." He held out his hand.

"Pleased to meet you, Leo—that would be great!" Natalie said, taking the card and then shaking his hand. "Thank you—I promise I'll get on it as soon as I get home." With a hopeful smile, Natalie zipped up her winter coat and was off back out into the crisp, cold weather of the morning.

Leo watched as their latest subject of interest exited out the main door, turned right, and passed in front of the large windows, and proceeded up the snow-cleared sidewalk.

The kitchen door swung open then as Mason entered into the restaurant space. "Who was that?" he signed, just as Natalie disappeared out of view.

"Believe it or not—that was our mystery girl, Natalie," Leo said, leaning an elbow on the bar. "I guess we don't have to wait for her to start class next year, after all."

Chapter 29 

The Beach House, New Year's Eve, South Florida

Since the resulting unrest of the music industry Christmas party, there had been loads of dialog, catchup, updating and deliberating with those in *the knowing*.

The Guards had been given quite the boon with Shayne crossing paths with Natalie and her showing up at the restaurant looking for a job. Leo had explained the whole thing to Redmond and me, how she'd filled out the online application that same day. It was a huge relief to have her accurate contact information now, but things were still tense with her being at the end of her 20th year. As much as they wanted to go to her home, they were aware that ambushing her was not the right approach. Instead, they'd set up surveillance near her home. Ben and Jules, along with Mason and Lane were all on the lookout for when she started school in the new year.

They'd notified Anael that her daughter had been located and she'd been grateful to hear the news, but she had no intention of coming to Ottawa to meet her. She had not and still did not have any desire to be a parent. Apparently, her only goal had been to understand the human experience of pregnancy and childbirth, but her interests ended there. When she'd given up her daughter for adoption, she'd made financial provisions for her and the adoptive parents. She had not known about the death of the parents, nor had she known about her going to live with the aunt. Luckily, the aunt had no knowledge of the future provisions that had been set up for Natalie once she reached adulthood. This task had been transferred to Leo to facilitate the next stage for her daughter's financial inheritance. Anael, along with the rest of us, was thankful Natalie would not be falling into the clutches of Thaddeus and his menace alliance.

With regard to the music industry Christmas party turmoil itself, Den and I had updated Redmond and Lily of the happenings that night while they had been shmoozing, but I'd left it up to Den to inform Leo and the rest of The Guards. We'd asked Lily if she remembered seeing anyone unfamiliar hanging around the music studio and she'd said some woman had come by asking about services, but there hadn't been any men other than the music clients they were working with. However, she did mention the studio had the same promo poster in the front window as in the one displayed in the front lobby of the event's venue, and it displayed all the details for the party. Meaning that anyone who had passed by the studio would have knowledge of the event, but they still wouldn't have the knowledge I would be attending.

The unidentified angel had been at the hospital, the Thanksgiving gathering in New York City, and then the music Christmas party, but they had not approached me at any of these events, nor had they done anything to harm me since, so I had still wondered if it really was me they were interested in. In each of these incidences, another Seraph had been present. First with Lyndon at the hospital, Thanksgiving there had been two Seraphim, Ina and Frank, plus Addison, but my theory had been quickly quashed when Den pointed out that the only Seraph at the party had been the one hiding, he didn't count. It was true, and I chose to leave the mystery solving up to him and the others while I turned my attention on to the holidays.

As per my brother James and my girlfriends up north, Christmas in Ottawa had been a bit of a cluster storm. My hometown had received 12 cm of snow in November, but by mid-December it had all but melted as warmer temperatures lingered over the area. At that point, they'd seen less than a centimeter. A *white Christmas* is defined as having at least 2 cm of snow on the ground on Christmas Day. Leading up to Christmas, Tuesday and Wednesday's weather had been rainy, with temperatures around four degrees warmer than normal. Temperatures around the freezing mark had been forecast for the end of the week and into the weekend, with the weather man stating there's very little snow in the immediate forecast, and the city would likely be seeing more fog than flurries. James had reminded me that back 50 years ago, we'd have an 85 percent chance of a white Christmas, therefore it was expected. In the last 10 to 15 years, it's been more like 70 percent, and in the last 7 years, 4 have been white and 3 have been green. Subsequently, the residents of Ottawa had been astonished when told by the weather forecasters that *Santa Claus better bundle and buckle up*, and that a powerful winter storm was about to sweep across eastern Ontario burying the region in snow mixed at times with rain, ice pellets, and freezing rain.

By the time Christmas eve was on them, Ottawa had already received more than 13 cm of snow, and several millimeters of rain, with more snow expected through the day. Blizzard-like conditions including blowing snow, whiteout conditions, and at times zero visibility among many of its municipalities caused treacherous conditions, with a state of emergency being declared because roads became impassable for emergency services, appealing to residents to stay home if possible and avoid all travel. Major highways near Ottawa were closed from late morning December 24 until early morning on December 25, with widespread power outages exacerbating the conditions.

The weather here in South Florida hadn't been remotely as bad as Ottawa, but we woke up to temperatures in the low 30s, with an afternoon high in the low 50s on Christmas eve. Friday, the day before, the girls had been exhausted from surfing with their dad and Gavin all morning. Den and I had watched from the beach. I can surf, not like them, of course, but I still preferred watching from the sidelines. The girls were fearless, which added to my own fear when watching them. It was soon after on Christmas Eve morning when the weather shifted severely for us also, but we still ventured out to the downtown off island farmers market. I'd embraced the colder temperatures, because it made it feel like Christmas and gave us the opportunity to wear our cold weather clothing, in particular the holiday sweaters the twins had picked out for themselves. We didn't often go to the market, but the vendors were always friendly and offered a diverse selection of delicious foods and locally handcrafted items.

In the evening we had enjoyed our usual Christmas eve French onion soup with my brother via video chat. The gifts James had sent to us had arrived earlier in the week. He and I always preferred handmade gifts, and he had sent us his own handcrafted wooden Christmas ornaments. The adorable little framed ornaments each had a loop of brown twine attached to the back so they could be hung on the tree. Inside, the frames held wallet-sized watercolor paintings he'd done. He'd painted one for each of the girls of their likeness, one with Redmond and me, one with Summer and Snow, and one with him, Radar, and Night, aka *Nightmare.* We had chosen to open our gifts from the girls on Christmas Eve so that James could show us what the girls had sent him. Marq and Den had helped the girls with their gifts, all in the theme of *family.* Den had made sure James's gift had gotten to him on the 23rd, so he would have it to open with us Christmas Eve.

The girls had fashioned a gift similar to the butterfly painting they had done for Redmond and me, using their handprints to create the butterflies with instruction from Marq showing them how to do the fine paint work, nonetheless they did the majority of it all themselves. For our gifts, Ryley had made a wooden frame and within it she'd placed a poem she'd written for us about Christmas and family. We couldn't have been prouder of her writing skills, a talent we had seen blooming this school year, and we'd encouraged her to read it aloud for all of us,

Christmas with family, a time so dear
Gathered around the tree, filled with cheer
Laughter and joy, filling the air
Memories made that we'll always share

The smell of cookies baking in the oven
The sound of carolers spreading their love
The warmth of hugs and smiles so bright

Filling our hearts with pure delight

Children's faces lit up with glee
As they open their presents for all to see
The love and kindness that we all show
Makes this Christmas with family the best we know

From the youngest to the oldest, we all come together
In this moment, nothing else matters
We share stories and recall the past
Creating bonds that forever last

The love that surrounds us is so pure
A love that will always endure
Christmas with family, a time of bliss
A time when we cherish the ones we miss

So let's raise a glass to family and friends
For the love and joy that never ends
May this Christmas be filled with love and light
And may we cherish each moment, day and night

So here's to Christmas with family, so true
May it bring happiness and blessings to you
Let's celebrate together, hand in hand
For in each other, we'll forever stand.

Hayley's eye for composition had been her new emerging talent, and she had made a similar frame donning the word *family* on it, but she had filled hers with a collage of photos. Den had given her some of the photos, having asked Lane to take a few at North Haven, so there were a variety in the collection with Lane and her fathers, Julian and Max, along with different groupings of Den, Marq, Zach, Leo, Kris, Ben, Nic, Jana, Jules and Mason. Redmond had helped provide her with photos as well. One from the Ottawa trip for our anniversary with my friends and their spouses, one with Nana and Poppy, Ina and Frank and the four of us from Thanksgiving, one with James and his doggies, one of Darius and Lily, Luc and Dunya together from their visit on Labour Day weekend, and one with Derek and my girlfriends from when he'd visited Ottawa. Both gifts from the twins couldn't have been more beautiful and heartfelt, and more accurate on the theme of family.

On Christmas morning, Gabriel had made an appearance with the offer of making us all breakfast, a breakfast frittata, in fact. He'd made a mess of my kitchen with the eggs, heavy cream, diced bacon, onion, tomato and spinach and the sharp cheddar cheese, stating he had watched an online cooking class on how to make it, and believe it or not, it had actually been quite yummy. Then, after the delicious breakfast, the girls had opened the rest of their gifts. However, Den had asked that we all meet at South Haven, sharing they had a special treat for all of us.

When we had arrived, Den had their massive TV set up with a live video feed from North Haven giving us the treat of sharing this time with those up north. In the center of the main living area, they'd placed a real Christmas tree decorated in a variety of ornaments, including hand-painted shells with everyone's names on them. The top of the tree had a ceramic handmade starfish which had been created by Marq. Under the tree were gifts for each of us, including Lily and Darius, who had also been told to meet there after their Christmas visit with Darius's mother. Ryley and Hayley had been thrilled by their surprise and how it had added to the idea of family. Our gift to them had been the jukebox Redmond had procured. He'd loaded the box with the 100 absolute best songs in history, with the catch that they had to come here to South Haven to hear them and visit.

There had also been a long dining table set up, and we'd gathered around for a lovely traditional meal of turkey dinner with all the fixings, stuffing, mashed potatoes, vegetables, gravy, and cranberry sauce. For dessert we'd had the quintessential Canadian dessert of butter tarts, the rich and gooey mini pies typically baked in a muffin tin, having a flaky crust filled with the delectable goodness of butter, sugar, syrup, eggs, and sometimes raisins or nuts—perfect for holidays or any day for that matter.

In addition to the jukebox gift, Ryley had written another poem for them, and as we'd assembled around the tree again, she had read it aloud to us,

Gather 'round the tree so tall
With loved ones, we stand in awe
The magic of Christmas fills the air
As we come together, a family that cares

The laughter echoes through the night
As we share stories and hold each other tight
Memories made, traditions upheld
In this moment, our hearts are swelled

The warmth of love surrounds us all
As we celebrate, both big and small
Grateful for the bond we share
Christmas with family, beyond compare

So let us cherish this special day
For in each other, we find our way
Through joy and laughter, love shines bright
Christmas with family, a beautiful sight.

There had been no grumbling from anyone, unless you counted the tiny bit of bellyaching that had come from Hayley. She'd wanted to see her shell on the tree and Den had ally-ooped her up to view it, but what she had really wanted was to move her ornament next to Den's. It had been then Den told her he wouldn't be here for New Year's Eve, but Leo would be in his place. When she'd complained about swapping, Den had said, *"Did you know that in French, you don't say, I miss you. Instead you say, tu me manques, which means you are missing from me."* And those simple words had eased her woes. However, the best part of the get-together was the fact there had been no talk of Thaddeus, Lyndon, prowling arcane angels or the coma patient angel, and had solely been a lovely time with family.

On Boxing day, I'd gotten a chance to speak with Lane privately about her time with Lyndon over Christmas. He'd asked her to spend Christmas Eve with him and Taylor, stating that Taylor is the only one he spends the day of Christmas with. Lane had gone to the group home unsure what to expect, but it had turned out to be a lovely evening spent listing to Christmas music and watching the snow fall outside through the large windows in the playroom. There had been no other residents there, and they had been able to talk freely. At Taylor's bedtime, Lyndon had read him one of his favorite Christmas stories, *The Gift of the Magi* by O. Henry, which told the sentimental story of a young husband and wife coping with the challenge of buying gifts for each other while having little money to do so. The wife cuts off and sells her knee-length hair to buy a chain for her husband's heirloom pocket watch, and the husband sells his treasured watch to buy his wife a decorative comb for her hair, capturing the moral lesson about gift-giving. And regarding gift-giving, she'd been pleasantly surprised when Lyndon had presented *her* with one. It was a framed, handmade custom star map that had been created by both him and Taylor. Taylor's contribution had been a water colour night sky background and the constellation he'd drawn using his toy stylist tool. Lyndon's efforts had been transferring the image Taylor had created, the *Asterism*, Lyndon had called it, onto the water colour background set in the handmade white frame he had made. Below the image in beautiful calligraphy, he'd written the words *Omnia Vincit Amor*, meaning Love Conquers All. Lane had recognized the constellation Pleiades right away, but she'd said nothing when Lyndon had gone on to explain its significance, being it was among the nearest star cluster to Earth, but we all knew it's true importance.

Lane had been grateful for the invite and hadn't pushed the idea of spending Christmas day together, mainly because her family would not have been okay had she invited him to their home. The birthday party at the restaurant was one thing, but having Lyndon in their home clearly came with a completely different set of issues. Despite what the others were feeling about him, Lane felt the party had gone quite well and they'd grown closer because of it. I'd ended our call saying I believed she genuinely trusted Lyndon, but that I also felt deep concern over the complications her affections for him could bring.

Come late afternoon, what I had begun to feel, unfortunately, was that a cold was trying to get ahold of me, and I had been down for the count ever since. Yesterday, Leo had brought me a sweet, earthy concoction he had made with elderberries to remedy it, and now today, to my amazement, I was feeling fit as a fiddle. As for it being the coldest

Christmas here in recent history, Saturday through Monday's temps around the 30s and highs hardly breaking the 50s, Wednesday the weather had shifted back into the 70s, then upper 70s on Thursday and Friday, and today it was in the low 80s.

Last year at this time I'd been just learning about The Guards and the rest of the Earthbound, about Anael's daughter for whom they'd been searching for and the part about Kris having gone missing, which had prompted flashes from my horrid dream about the angel suspended from the ceiling with his back cut open. I'd seen Thaddeus's private lab firsthand, and there'd been no patients, no sick children, and certainly no massive angel hanging from the ceiling. The real mind-warp, though, had been the reality that these Earthbound Angels, my now expanded family, literally had wings. Back then, I hadn't wanted to burden my friends with these details, but I knew I couldn't have kept it from them. And today, setting up for another video chat in the living room, I had similar reservations about updating them on the latest happenings.

When Mac and Alison, Luc and Dunya, Olivia and then Derek swiftly appeared on screen, I nervously greeted them all with, "Happy almost new year's!"

A fluster of similar greetings, coupled with joyous smiles, were returned by all.

"Where's Redmond?" Luc asked.

"He took the girls to the grocery store for me—wanted me to have more rest. I had a cold all last week, so I hadn't been able to do my usual food shopping." *Who was I to refuse the kind gesture,* I considered, grinning back at my friends on the screen. "Everyone survive the crazy Christmas weather?" I asked. All but Derek had experienced some form of disruptive seasonal weather. In his neck of the woods, in North Carolina, temperatures had been generally in line with the statewide average, although Derek had told us the areas along the coast had been slightly warmer and opposite to what the rest of us had experienced.

"Other than having to shovel snow too many times, all is good at our place," Alison said, adjusting a sofa cushion behind her back.

"Same here," Mac expressed.

"Warm and cozy here," Dunya shared, looping her arm around Luc's.

"Status quo for me," Derek added, biting off and chewing the end of a candy cane.

"Has anyone heard from Vicki?" I asked.

"Last I heard, she and Eric were flying to Prague for the holidays," Olivia stated, fiddling with one of her earrings that resembled tiny snowmen.

"Why Prague?" I questioned.

"She said something about wanting to see the world famous Christmas markets," Olivia added with a casual shrug.

We spent the next hour sharing and updating each other on how our Christmas holidays had been unfolding, ending with me detailing our wonderful time spent at South Haven, plus the description of what James and the twins had made for us.

"You'll have to send photos of all the handmade gifts," Mac said. "They sound so sweet."

"I sent Den the photo of us from my trip to Ottawa," Derek said. "That was a great visit with you all—and I got some quality time with Nic and Leo to go over my findings from the journals."

"All the photos Den gathered for Hayley were so perfect," I gushed.

"Lynn," Derek said then, "remember when you questioned why Thaddeus wasn't testing reproduction instead of diseases?"

"Okay—that's it for me folks," Olivia promptly said. "I'm not interested in hearing anything to do with that monster." She logged out before any of us could say a word, but that was fine. The things I had to tell them would have freaked her out, anyway.

"Yes," I said, ignoring Olivia's abrupt retreat. "Not that I want him doing reproduction testing on halflings, but considering his interests were in populating the planet with new Seraphim, it made more sense to me."

"Well, the last few pages of his journal focused on that topic."

"What do you mean?" I asked, watching Derek clack away on his computer.

"In the last entry, there was a list of what I assumed were patient names. However, when I'd given the list to Nic, he ran the names through several medical databases."

"Long shot, I'm sure, but did he find any of the names?" Alison asked, her pen and notebook now at the ready.

"All of them," Derek said.

"What? Was it some kind of patient study?" I asked.

"Nope. They were names of doctors, endocrinologists."

"What?" I said again, shaking my head.

"Reproductive endocrinologists, to be more precise," Derek elaborated.

"Seriously?" Mac asked, clearly as astonished as I was.

"Yes, in fact it was a list of top physicians in the fields of gynecology, obstetrics, fertility and reproductive studies, from around the world." Derek took another bite of his candy cane.

"Holy shit!" I said then, recognizing my hypothesis was correct.

With the hook end of the candy cane hanging from his mouth, Derek said, "The first names on the list are located in Brazil. When Nic did more research, he found they were part of something called *The Perffeto Group*, who are leaders in assisted human reproduction." Derek maneuvered the end of the candy cane into his mouth and bit down. "They specialize in advanced treatment and diagnostic procedures in the field of in-vitro fertilization. Denmark is widely recognized as a leading destination for IVF treatment, but there were no doctors on the list from that country."

"Must be why he went to Brazil," Luc tossed out, rubbing a hand over his jaw.

"Possibly, but get this," Derek said, chewing the last of his holiday treat. "What I found even more interesting is one of the top fertility clinics is located on the upper-east side in New York City. There's even a top rated place in Los Angeles that has the highest IVF Success Rates."

"So why wouldn't he just go to either of those?" I asked.

"My question exactly," Derek said, smacking the palm of his hand on the top of his desk.

"Maybe it has something to do with regulations or government influence," Alison suggested. It was a smart assumption since she did have personal experience with IVF and all the BS that went with it.

"That never stopped him before," I noted with a heavy sigh. "Speaking of never stopping, I have a few things to tell you," I stated, before going on to tell them about sensing the same hiding angel from the hospital at both the Thanksgiving gathering and the music Christmas party. They had the same questions as the others about who it might be, but I didn't share my guesses. I only inferred that maybe it wasn't one of Thaddeus's crew, since they hadn't made any kind of move on me. "On a happier note," I said, shifting dialog, "we're having a small New Year's Eve get-together with fireworks on the beach." I wasn't sure about them, but I needed to clear my head of the topics on disturbing covert angels and the potential of horrific medical testing. "My friend Grier is coming over, too," I highlighted for good measure.

There had been an immediate alteration in the mood, so it was obvious I wasn't the only one who had needed the change in topic. We spent the next half hour discussing all our New Year's Eve plans.

Before the end of the call, Dunya offered the salutation, "Salaam." Which is an Arabic word used as a respectful gesture meaning *peace*.

Each of us responded in kind with various well-wishes for the new year, then signed off with promises to circle back as soon as everyone could find a compatible time.

Chapter 30

I'd texted Grier on Christmas day with a photo of us still in our pajamas surrounded by a mess of torn decorative Christmas paper from unwrapped gifts, with the message, *Wish you were here* and a Santa Claus emoji. She'd written back with one word, *Yikes* and two emojis, one with a scared face and one laughing. What was funnier was I had been feeling like both those emoji faces with having to clean up and at how ridiculous we looked. Then she'd written saying that next year she'd come over in her pajamas and help me tidy up, to which I had responded with, *It's a date.* But at least Grier would be spending new year's with us this year and she was to arrive here anytime.

At 6p.m. there was a knock at the door and when I opened it Grier greeted me with, "Happy New Year!" Food container in hand, she smiled cheerfully back at me. Grier had on black skinny jeans with a black long-sleeved knit shirt covered in tiny shiny black sequins, and flat black sandals to match.

"Happy New Year to you too—get in here. I love your outfit," I said, taking the container from her and setting it on the side table so that I could give her a hug.

"Oh thanks," she said, giggling in my embrace as though happy to be here, and I squeezed her tight, just as thrilled to have her here.

"Your hair looks gorgeous. You should wear it down more often," I said, releasing her. I'd pulled mine back in a French braid knowing

I'd probably be too hot, and the twins had asked I do pigtails for them since their hair was still short from the bob cuts.

"Thanks," she said again, giggling, brushing one side of it back over her shoulder.

"What did you bring?" I asked, curious, snatching up the container from the front table.

"Well, you said you were doing all night nibbles and charcutier, so I made cranberry brie bites—the recipe makes 24, but I doubled it."

I popped the lid to see a beautiful flaky puffed pastries topped with a creamy red and white mixture. "They look perfectly delicious," I said, pressing the top back on the container.

"They need to be warmed up," Grier said before looking past me into the living room. "Lynn, your home is fantastic."

"Thank you—we love it here." I motioned Grier forward through the living room and dining area, where some of the food had already been set out. "I'll set your hors d'oeuvres with the others that need heating up," I said, setting her container down next to a stack of serving platters on the kitchen island.

"My goodness, that's a lot of food," Grier said, the look of shock blanketing her face. "Thought you said it was a small gathering." She walked around the dining table, surveying the food offerings. "Great top, by the way," she said, pointing at my silver and gold sequin sleeveless shirt.

"Thanks—I'd planned to wear it with these jeans on Christmas, but it was just too damn cold. Now the weather is perfect for it. And yes, it's a lot of food, but you have to see who we're feeding to understand the volume," I laughed out.

"Muuum?" Hayley shouted from down the hall.

"I'm in the kitchen!" I called back. "Come meet my friend!"

Summer and Snow softly lumbered up the hall from the girls' bedrooms into the kitchen.

"These are my furry girls," I said. "Summer." I patted her side. "And Snow." I ran my hand over the soft fur of her head.

"Beautiful," Grier said, as the two leaned into her legs as she patted them.

Even though Redmond had told them on numerous occasions not to, both Ryley and then Hayley sock-slid down the hall into the kitchen area. Summer and Snow padded off to the open space near the living room couches and rested their big furry bodies down on the floor.

"Hiii," Ryley said, arriving in front of her sister, hand already out for a shake. "I'm Ryley."

"Hello, Ryley. I'm Grier—nice to meet you," she said, shaking Ryley's hand. "And you must be Hayley," she said then, turning her focus to Hayley.

"You know my name?" Hayley asked.

"Of course," Grier said. "I've heard all about the two of you from your mother."

Hayley took up both of Grier's hands in her tiny ones and smiled up at her, then said, "I love your shirt."

"Why thank you," Grier said, bending at the knees to be at eye-level with the girls. "I thought it was perfect for the festive night."

Hayley let go of one of Grier's hands to run her little fingers along Grier's arm over the sequin sleeve.

"Fun, right?" Grier said, releasing Hayley's other hand, mirroring her by running a hand over her opposite arm.

Hayley smiled again and nodded. Then she turned to look at me. "I like your top too, Mum," Hayley said, reaching her hand up to flutter the shiny sequins on my blouse.

"Well, thank you—and you girls look festive too," I said, noting Redmond must have helped them pick out their outfits. They had on matching jeans and similar tops, both of which were long sleeved concert t-shirts Lily had gotten them from the Five Finger Death Punch concert event she'd attended. The shirts were cool, it was just the scary red X's for eyes and fang-toothed skull of their mascot *Knucklehead* on them that gave the images such a harsh impression.

"I wanted to thank you both also for the lovely beach house warming gift—it's perfect," Grier said, straightening.

"You're welcome," Hayle said. "Mum showed us the photo of where you hung it." She beamed up at Grier.

"Can we eat any of this?" Ryley asked, ignoring them, hovering over a tray of her favorite pigs in a blanket.

"Yes, just don't eat all of them," I said, glancing at Grier and giving her a wink. "There are napkins and paper plates in the center of the table—use them, please."

Hayley joined her sister and together they began transferring their favorite nibbles from the platters to their paper plates. "Can we sit out on the deck?" Hayley asked, a stacked plate in one hand, napkin in the other.

"Sure," I said. "There's soda in the cooler out there if you get thirsty."

"Baaabe! Do you know where my black belt is?" bellowed Redmond as he rushed from our bedroom into the living room, carrying his *brown* leather belt. "Oh, sorry—Hi!" he said sheepishly when he realized I wasn't alone. He was wearing the same shirt as the girls, only Redmond's was short-sleeved.

"Grier, this is my husband Redmond," I said in introduction. "Your black belt should still be hanging with your suit from the Christmas party."

"Nice to finally meet you, Grier," Redmond said with a wave. "Excuse me, I'll be right back."

"Nice to meet you toooo," Grier called as he dashed off then in the hunt of his other belt.

"Boys," I said, shaking my head. "What can I get you to drink? I've got red wine." I tapped one of the bottles next to the arrangement of wine glasses. "White wine is in the fridge, and we have an assortment of beers and sodas, unless you'd prefer just water." I pulled open the fridge. "And Redmond set up coolers on the deck with more beers and sodas," I said, sliding yet another food tray from the lower shelf, this one a pumpernickel bread bowl filled with spinach artichoke dip. I snatched up the accompanying large plastic bag of torn pumpernickel bread and then shut the door. "I'm having red wine."

"I'll have whatever you're having," she said before taking the platter and plastic bag from my hand. "Let me do that while you pour the wine."

"Gladly," I said, thankful for the aid. I took one of the already open wine bottles and two glasses from their spot on the island, then happily poured some of the contents into the wine glasses. "Here," I said, handing Grier one of them.

"To new friends," Grier cheered, clinking her glass with mine.

"Cheers—I'll drink to that," I said before taking a sip of the luscious liquid.

"Mmm that's a good one," Grier said, savoring her sip and nodding at the deliciousness of the wine.

A forceful *knocking* sounded at the front door.

"I got it," Redmond shouted, returning from the bedroom and heading to the front foyer. "Hey, Leo—Zach—brothers, come on in," I heard him say when he opened the door. The sound of back slapping followed his words.

"More guests—come," I said, urging Grier in the direction of the front door. I'd felt their unique signatures before they'd even knocked.

"Leo, Zach, Happy New Year," I said as we rounded from the dining area into the living room in view of the front foyer. Everyone, it seemed, had opted to wear jeans this evening, including the two massive Seraphs who were wearing almost identical shirts. Leo had donned a white long-sleeved pullover, and Zach was in a sage green one.

"Hi Lynn, Happy New Year to you too!" Zach said, his grin wide.

"Happy New Year all," Leo added.

"Guys, this is my friend Grier—she owns a beach cottage down the way." I turned to her, but she had stopped short, her mouth agape. "Grier?"

"Haah-haa-hiii," Grier stuttered out as though her brain had short-circuited.

Ah yes, I mused. I'd gotten so used to the appearance of the Earthbound now I had forgotten what they must look like for the average person. Both Leo and Zach were fiercely handsome and charismatic, and it was no wonder Grier was stunned into silence.

Stepping in, Redmond said, "Leo and Zach are good friends of ours from Ottawa. They are vacationing here, staying just up the road at one of the properties they own."

"It is always wonderful to meet a friend of Lynn and Redmond's," Leo greeted, stepping forward to shake her hand.

When Grier just stared down at his hand, Leo shot a look my way.

"Grier's one of the doctors at the hospital where I volunteer," I said, filling in the awkward silence.

Grier smiled and giggled in response when Leo took up one of her hands in his. "Pleased to meet you… Leo," she finally said, staring up into his face.

"It is my pleasure to meet *you*," Leo said before taking over the introductions. "This is my brother, Zach." Leo extended an arm to Zach.

"Zach—lovely to meet you," Grier said, finding her composure.

"Milady," Zach said, graciously, taking Grier's hand and bowing.

Relinquishing Zach's hand, Grier brushed a side of her long hair over her shoulder.

"Guys," Redmond said then, "what can I get you to drink?"

"I'll take a beer," Leo said.

"Me too," Zach added, following Leo and Redmond over to the kitchen.

Then, as though abruptly woken, Grier said, "Lynn, mind if I check out the back deck—I'm a bit *warm*." She waved the hand that Leo and Zach had held in front of her face, turning away to look out to the deck. "It looks magical with all the twinkle lights strung along the roofline."

"Absolutely," I said, needing to have a private chat with my Seraph friends, anyway. "Don't let the girls talk your ear off, though."

"I think I might like that," she said with a laugh, tipping her chin in the direction where Leo and Zach stood, giving me a few eyebrow raises before sliding open the door.

Overhearing, Leo said, "I find they have interesting perspectives." He gave a playful grin as he popped the cap off his beer.

"I wouldn't doubt it," Grier said with a nod and a sweet smile before sliding the door shut behind her.

"Lynn," Zach said, when the door shut. "I already told Leo and the others, but you should know too."

"Know what?" I asked, anxious, even though the sliding doors and the windows of the house were all storm glass blocking any conversation from being heard.

"The birds are gone from the Ottawa facility," Leo answered for him.

"So?" I shrugged.

"And Marcus is gone too," Leo added, glancing at Zach.

"Tell me!" I demanded, running the charms of my necklace back and forth again.

Zach swallowed, then said, "The Norway facility is being shut down and Kendrick has relocated to the facility in New York City."

"Are you sure?"

"I spoke to some of the staff as they were being ushered out of the building. One of them said they were told funding for the place had been reallocated to a new initiative."

"Derek told me about the Reproductive endocrinologists," I said then.

Leo nodded slowly. "Yes, an interesting change in direction for Thaddeus, I must say."

"It's unnerving if you ask me." I shot a glance towards the patio door. "It has to have something to do with these other changes." I played with the charms on my necklace.

"Are you and the girls still having those nightmares?" Leo asked.

"Nothing since before Halloween." I no longer felt the need to get back into that lab, *but*. "I think I need to get in to see that comatose Seraph though," I said, raising the charms to my lips, desperate to get into the psych ward now.

"Let me work with Zach on a way to get you in," Leo suggested.

"I got your back, Mata Hari," Zach said. "And it seems like I'll be relocating."

"Mata Hari?" questioned Grier as she came in through the patio door from the deck.

"That's a long story," I said, flustered, realizing I hadn't heard the door open. "Zach works as a firefighter," I redirected at the possibility Grier may have heard more.

"I've been working in Norway, but I'm not needed there now. So, possibly relocating back to Ottawa."

"Or *here*," Leo cut in.

"Muuum," Hayley bellowed from the now open patio door.

"Yeeeeeesss?" I bellowed back.

"We're still huuungry," Ryley said, pushing past her sister through the open door.

"Come say hi to Zach and Leo first, then you can fill your plates up again."

"Zaaach," Ryley squealed, rushing over to embrace the blond giant. "Hiii Leo," she said, just as Zach tossed her into the air his way.

"*Hi, Leo. Hi, Zach,*" Hayley said to them in an almost inaudible voice, a pout filling her face.

"What kind of hello is that?" Zach asked, quickly snaking an arm around her middle to lift her. "Leo," he said with a chin lift like he'd conveyed more. Then simultaneously they tossed the twin they were holding into the air in the other's direction. The girls shrieked in delight as they were thrown, then caught by the other. "Again," Zach said, tossing Ryley this time in the air, retrieving Hayley as she was flung his way. Once more, the twins squealed with joy.

"Alright, aaalright," I said to Zach and Leo. "Cut that out, you two, before they throw up." I glanced at Summer and Snow who still lounged on the floor in the living room. They'd barely raised their heads at the commotion.

"Muuum," Hayley protested, her pout returning as Zach set her down.

"Sorry, Mom," Zach mocked, making his own pouty face.

I narrowed my eyes at him, then laughed. Changing focus, I said, "Didn't you girls say you were hungry?"

"Yes!" the twins said in unison.

"Okay then, fill your plates before Darius gets here."

The girls did as they were instructed, then returned to the deck.

On cue, there was a loud rapping on the front door and even though I couldn't sense him, I knew it was Darius. Without asking, Redmond set off to the front door and the rest of us followed.

Redmond opened the front door and was swiftly lifted into the air bearhug style by an eager Darius. "Hi, Darius," Redmond grunted.

"Dude! Happy New Year," Darius said in response.

"Lily, get over here," I said when I saw her little hand waving from behind the crushing hug.

Large cooler bag in hand, Lily scooted around Darius as he set Redmond back on his feet. "Hi-hi-hi," she said to Redmond, then Leo and Zach, respectively, rushing past them over to me for her own hug.

"Oh-my-god-I-love-your-hair," Grier rushed out, spotting the blue swipe in her rockabilly updo when Lily freed me. "Your outfit from the music event was on fire!" She giggled. "Hi—I'm Grier."

"Lily—Grier, Grier—Lily," I said, promptly acquainting the two.

"Great to meet you," Lily said. "And thanks on the outfit. I find dressing up a gas—Lynn hates it." Both she and Darius were in jeans and almost matching red t-shirts with images on them resembling *ugly* Christmas sweaters.

"Oh, she's told me," Grier said in agreement, nodding, the two of them laughing together.

"Hey—ganging up on me already?" I gave a fake sob, then said, "Whatcha got there?" I pointed at the cooler bag Lily had dropped before hugging me.

"Beef tenderloin gorgonzola bites," she said smugly, knowing they were one of Redmond's favorites. She glanced back over her shoulder to see if he'd heard, but Redmond was busily chatting with the guys.

"Do they need to be heated up?" I asked.

"Nope—this thing keeps them hot," Lily said, grabbing the bag and heading to the kitchen. Taking one of the serving trays, she piled the meat skewers on it, then set the offering with the rest of the food trays on the table.

"I don't mean to be rude—and I know I'm short, but Lynn, are all the men in your life giants," she asked then, glancing over at the four strapping men.

"Mostly," I said, jokingly, though I wasn't joking. Most were quite literally giants.

"Good things come in small packages," Lily said, establishing she was on team petite and not team goliath.

"Yeaaaah!" Grier cheered, getting on board with the short-girl power.

"Everything looks delicious," Leo said, returning with the guys to survey the dining table spread.

"Dig in," I said, addressing everyone. "Redmond made jalapeno poppers, bacon wrapped dates, and baked chicken wings. There's a charcuterie board with a variety of meats, cheeses and crackers. Next to the pumpernickel bread bowl with spinach artichoke dip, there are a variety of other dips, aaand pigs in a blanket that I just noticed the girls have all but devoured." I turned on the oven. "Plus there's bruschetta I still need to put in the oven and Grier brought cranberry brie bites that need to be warmed, so eat up," I added, opening the fridge to retrieve the last items.

Leo along with Darius, Zach and Redmond dove in and began filling the larger version of the paper plates the girls had used with the array of options before them.

"Get in there ladies, before these monsters eat everything," I recommended. I'd seen the members of The Guards eat on numerous occasions, and Darius of course. I opened the oven and slid Grier's bites and my bruschetta in, knowing the food would be going fast.

Lily, Grier and I filled our own plates and then took up residence in the living room to eat while the others chowed down at the dining table in close proximity to the food platters.

"Babe," Redmond called from across the room. "The neighbors just texted they're down at the beach—they have a fire pit set up."

"Do they need any help?" I asked.

"Texted that they might," he said, confirming my assumption.

"I'll help," Zach said, getting up from his spot at the table.

"Sounds like a good idea, Zach—thank you." I raised a knowing eyebrow at Lily. "Can you bring the girls with you?" I asked Redmond. "Lily, Grier and I will meet you there."

After tossing all the used paper plates in the trash, Redmond led the twins and the remainder of our guests to the beach, while we three ladies got better acquainted. Conversation was filled with talk of the holidays, the small beach town we all now lived in, and our diverse career paths.

"Do you know anything about *psychology* as it relates to fertility?" I asked, remnants of my earlier conversation with Derek and the others still lingering.

"I've read several studies on the topic," Grier said. "Why do you ask?"

"The topic came up in a video chat I had with some friends. One of them used IVF, and I was curious about how psychology might come into play." I glanced at Lily. Redmond had already updated her and Darius with the details of the call.

"Well, infertility counseling should be considered before, during, and after the treatment," Grier began. "It's a complex relationship between infertility and its psychological impact on couples undergoing the treatment. To begin with, the drugs don't only have physical side effects, they can have psychological effects as well."

"Like?"

"Mood changes, sleep disturbances, anxiety, depression. Then there's the real issue of being diagnosed as *infertile* which can be an emotional experience for couples, causing various psychological problems like anxiety and depression as well, along with eating disorders and lowered self-confidence, and other issues like social isolation, decreased communication between partners and difficulties in marriage altogether."

"I know my girlfriend, Alison, worried constantly during her treatments—it was debilitating."

"This is where the role of psychotherapy comes in," Grier stated with a sympathetic smile. "It's been well known that interventions like counselling and psychotherapy for infertile couples have the power to decrease psychological problems and considerably enhance the conception rates."

"I never asked her if she sought help or not," I said. "But their last try was a success. They have a son."

"I love hearing the success stories," Lily said, giving a small smile.

"Me too," Grier said. "The relationship between stress and infertility can be a vicious cycle. Does that give you more insight into the topic?"

"Yes—stress has a bigger impact than I originally thought," I confirmed, considering the type of stressors Thaddeus could possibly put on his test subjects. I ran the charms back and forth on my necklace.

"Is that your talisman?" Grier asked, pulling me from my thoughts.

"What?"

Grier reached over and tapped the hand I was gripping my charms with.

"Redmond gave this to me on our first Christmas together," I said, clasping the grouping between my fingers and leaning towards Grier. "The tiny butterfly is in honor of my mom." I splayed them out to explain the meaning of each charm. "The XO kiss and hug symbol signifies good friendship, the fancy number 4 is the symbol for tin—in tradition for our 10th anniversary." It was also the atomic symbol for the number 50, which Redmond had gotten as a tattoo on his 50th birthday. "What did you mean by talisman?" I asked, resting back in my seat.

"You've heard of four-leaf clovers and rabbits' feet, right?" Grier asked, adjusting in her seat, tucking a foot under her butt.

"Yup," I said, nodding.

"I have a lucky guitar pic—I keep it in my purse," Lily said, nodding too.

"Those are considered talismans," Grier affirmed. "And like other things, such as quartz or precious stones, they are all thought to bring luck, health, and happiness. Or in the case of the Hand of Hamsa and crucifixes, even the yin-yang symbols provide strength and comfort, often worn as an amulet or charm."

"Maybe it *is* my talisman," I considered, lifting the group of charms so I could look at them.

"That sliding thing she does with it—is an anxious *tell* of hers," Lily informed my friend the psychologist.

Grier raised her eyebrows but said nothing.

"You two cool if I head down to the beach?" Lily asked then, pushing up from the couch. "Need to make sure Darius is staying out of trouble." She chuckled.

"No worries—the twins can be a bad influence," I said, giving her a knowing grin. "Take another plate of whatever is left down to Darius, would ya? Saves me having to package it all up."

"Sure—and I'll take whatever's left with us when we leave," Lily said with another chuckle, taking a plate and filling it up with the leftovers. "Don't be long," she added, waving.

"We'll be along soon," I assured her as she went out the patio door with what I was sure would be Darius's fifth plate.

"You've got some wonderful friends, Lynn. Some huge friends, too." She giggled, then raised her eyebrows. "Leo and Zach kind of remind me of that patient I told you about."

I moved to sit beside her in Lily's now empty spot. "How is that going?"

"Okay." She shrugged one shoulder.

I turned to face her. "Just okay?"

"We're still meeting once a week—been doing that since October."

"And?" I mirrored her, tucking up one of my feet.

"And I don't think I'm making any progress with him. But like I mentioned before, part of the problem is that he's just so *hot*—makes it difficult to have sessions with him." Grier shrugged both her shoulders and shook her head as though defeated. "Are you still having nightmares?"

"Nope—not since October, but I still have some pretty realistic dreams.

"What are your thoughts on what I told you about lucid dreaming?"

"Honestly, this may come off weird, but I actually get premonitions and such in dreams and when I'm awake."

"I must admit, you do have an intuitive way about you," Grier said, nodding her acceptance. "Do you believe in dream telepathy or telepathic lucid dreaming?"

"In the idea of one person being able to consciously travel or interact within the dream of another person?" I stated, recalling the details she'd shared the last time we'd talked about it. "I'm not sure, but I've experienced some wild stuff, both sleeping and awake. But I'm guessing you do. Am I right?"

"I didn't always believe." She paused. "But... after some of the unusual things I have experienced of late, I'm beginning to." She paused again, glancing back over the couch to the wall of windows that looked out to the back deck. "Have you ever seen the movie *The Cell*?" she asked then, turning forward again.

"I have actually, the one with Jennifer Lopez. It's an excellent movie—albeit the bad guy was disturbingly sick in the head and the imagery gave me the serious creeps." I gave her my repulsed face.

"Seriously sick in the head," she agreed. "What was depicted in the movie is what's called a computer-mediated psychotherapeutic action, or like in the movie *Inception*—did you see that one?"

I nodded. "Another excellent movie."

"They did something similar, but through the direct intervention of another sleeping person. In these movies, they also explore the ramifications of whether a sleeping person *should* enter the sleeping brain of another, as opposed to allowing another person to enter *your* brain. The reason being, it can be an unpleasant shock conditional upon the mental state of the *host* or the preparedness of the *guest*."

"I can totally understand that—saw it in the movies," I said as several terrifying images cycled through *my* brain.

"We talked last time about how to have a lucid dream. Do you remember?"

"The part about priming your mind and raising your chances of dreaming lucidly?"

"Correct," Grier said, sitting up, tucking her other foot under her as though her enthusiasm on the subject was rising. "Some researchers have tried things like *reality testing*, where you pause at different times during your day to determine if you're dreaming, testing something normally impossible in a waking state or harder in a sleeping state—like reading a page in a book."

"What about dream diaries?" I asked, remembering vaguely that I'd read about them.

"Some studies showed people had more success with a log, because they were more focused on them." Grier tipped her head from side to side like she was on the fence. "Other research found it didn't help but may be useful combined with other methods. Methods such as wake-back-to-bed or mnemonic induction of lucid dreams—also known as MILD, where the person is instructed to wake up after 5 hours of sleep, stay awake briefly, and then go back to bed to try to enter a REM sleep. With MILD you do the same 5 hours sleep, but when you wake you say to yourself several times that when you dream — you will remember that you're dreaming. These methods are good because they use your prospective memory."

"The act of remembering to do something in the future," I said, recalling from our discussion on how to trigger a lucid dream. The patio door suddenly opened then, and we both glanced over.

"Mum," Ryley called from the open door, smiling. "They're getting ready to do the fireworks." She bounced up and down on her toes.

"Okay, let everyone know that we're on our way," I said, planting my feet on the floor to get up.

"It's almost midnight," Grier said, showing me the digital time on her watch.

"We better get a move on," I said, standing and reaching for her hand to pull her up.

At the top of the path to the beach, I found Lily standing a few feet back from the firepit. Darius had Ryley up on his shoulders now, and Hayley was up on Redmond's. Leo was over with our neighbors, as was Zach, our resident fireman and expert in pyrotechnics, supervising the *safe* deployment of the fireworks. And as our small group began the countdown for the last 10 seconds of the current year, I encircled an arm around my old friend Lily, then wrapped my other arm around my *new* friend Grier. Then, together through shouts of Happy New Year, we all watched as the rockets shot off and ushered in a new year.

Chapter 31 

Lyndon attending the birthday party with Lane had been a huge leap for him, though he was grateful he had gone. It had been nice to meet her parents and her uncles while participating in such a joyous occasion as a birthday. Lane's family members were kind and welcoming *and* protective, Lane had said as much, but he couldn't blame them. He too was protective of her, but part of that came from his struggle with the connections Lane seemed to have with not one but two of his fellow Seraphim from Pleiades. It wasn't that they were a threat to her, it was quite the opposite. Shayne was a close friend of the family, and he too seemed protective of Lane, and Julianna was aiding Lane in her studies, so she claimed. The battle in his head was more about the established proximity she already had with several of his kind. But right now, his biggest concern was Zuriel.

He'd been told on the last call from the nurse that there had still been no change, but he'd come back to the hospital to see for himself. What he hadn't expected to hear when he requested to see his friend at the admissions desk, was that the patient was under a Baker Act in the psych ward. She had said behavior health center, but he knew what that meant. She'd also told him that visitors were not permitted in the center without a doctor's permission. And he couldn't enter the hospital itself without registering and providing ID, which he was not willing to do. He told the woman he'd return another time, considering he wouldn't be permitted to see his friend, anyway.

It didn't mean he had given up on seeing Zuriel, though. He'd searched the hospital map for the location of the ward and had noted there was a helipad on the roof for air ambulances with an entrance to two sets of elevators and two stairwells, one of which let out adjacent to the main doors of the behavioral health center itself. He'd found it interesting there were no security locks on the roof entrance but arriving at the correct floor he'd swiftly realized there would be no way to get into the ward itself. To add to the difficulty, there appeared to be some kind of Mental Health Awareness function going on based on the display boards in the area out front of the ward, and there were a ton of people attending.

From his vantage point just around the corner near the event, Lyndon scanned the faces of the people coming and going, the grouping a mix of medical personnel and regular citizens. The chances of him getting into the ward on his own were slim to none, it appeared, and he contemplated the idea of calling the nurse who had provided him the updates. He had gotten the impression from her calls that she had provided him with more information than she should have already, and his hope was maybe she would break the rules again. He could call, letting her know he was here and wanted to speak to her in person, then hopefully persuade her to escort him in to see his friend.

He was just about to step forward from his discreet location to make the call when he shockingly spotted an unexpected face. His *target*, the woman he had come to know as Lynn Westlake, stood next to one of the exhibition tables. He watched as she turned and then strode towards the other hallway, stopping just before the security doors. *Had Zuriel's hunch been right about coming up here*, Lyndon speculated. Could it be it wasn't just about the other woman, the doctor he had been watching?

Lyndon remained where he was near the stairs observing as the woman pulled out her cellphone, using his enhanced hearing he zeroed in on her call.

"He's here again," she said into her cellphone. *"Lane, trust me, I know it's him."*

"Lane, what the hell—that can't be," he murmured to himself, sharpening further his hearing to catch the caller's voice.

"Can you see him?" came the all too familiar voice of his beloved, confirming it truly was *his* Lane.

"No, but I'm not interested in searching him out either," the Westlake woman said.

See who Lyndon wondered, and why was his target speaking to Lane about this person? Who was this woman to Lane?

"Did you find out anything more about the coma patient?" he heard Lane ask then.

Lyndon had told Lane about Zuriel, about his condition, but how could she know he was here in this hospital? How could this woman know, for that matter?

Continuing to listen in, he heard her say, *"When I spoke to the same nurse as before, she said it looked like he had been beaten. Cops told her they think it may have been a possible kidnapping. But the nurse said she doubted it, being how big he is she couldn't imagine someone able to overpower him. She overheard the doctors discussing the case, and they'd considered it may have been consensual BDSM gone wrong, no safe word or something she'd alluded to."*

Thaddeus had been the one who had beaten him, Lyndon wanted to scream.

"What kind of wounds?" Lane questioned.

"Said he had huge gashes on his back and boreholes like his back had been drilled into. The interesting thing—the nurse called it a funny thing, whomever he had been with prior had patched him up with care, probably saved his life," she answered.

Lyndon knew he had, but he'd not been able to do more for his friend.

"You mentioned Zuriel was the only one he liked at his job, so maybe he patched him up. Still doesn't answer why he brought him here to this hospital, though.

"Whoa—what?" Lyndon questioned under his breath. Had Lane been talking to this Westlake woman about *him*? Could Lane have knowledge of the Pleiadeans who had been cast down, Lyndon speculated. She was close with two of them. If so, did that mean she already knew what *he* was? Had that been the reason behind all the questions she asked him? Had she been testing him to see if he would tell her his secrets?

"Did the nurse say anything more?" Lane inquired.

"Only that there has been no change," the woman answered, taking a glance behind her.

Who was it this woman was watching for, Lyndon speculated.

"Is he still there?"

"Yes, I can still feel him."

"She can feel me," he all but blurted out, covering his mouth with his fist. He pulled back from the corner and flattened himself against the wall as if it would help hide him. It wasn't just the Archangels and The Watchers as they had assumed. She could feel him too, and more than likely the others stranded here on Earth. *"How the hell do you know Lane?"* he whispered into his fist, spying around the wall again. Then he recalled how Lane had told him about speaking to an aunt who lived in Florida. Could this woman and the aunt be one and the same? The same woman Thaddeus has had him searching for all this time? How could it be? How could any of this be possible? What else had Zuriel discovered, and why hadn't he told him? Calming his breathing, he tuned in to listen again.

"He must be here checking on him. I'll call you back," he heard her say then, ending the call with Lane.

Lyndon watched Lane's aunt — Ms. Westlake — his *target* for a few more moments as she mingled with the staff, then he retreated to the roof to make his escape. He landed several miles away in a secluded nature preserve with the intention of calling Thaddeus. He was still in Brazil as far as he knew and he'd be furious with him for calling, but he needed to know if Zuriel told him anything more than the lead in Japan.

"Didn't I say not to call me?" Thaddeus's irritated voice spewed from Lyndon's phone. He'd been smart to put it on speaker, it abating the risk of that vicious voice damaging his eardrum.

"I want to know if Zuriel told you anything else?" Lyndon practically demanded.

"Other than his fraternizing with that human female, no. I already told you I tortured info out of him about Japan, so why are you pestering me with this?"

"Did you tell Sebastian—did Lazarus track down the lead?"

"Who do you think you are to be questioning me—you dimwit?" Thaddeus roared.

"What did they find?" Lyndon asked, disregarding Thaddeus's rage.

"Fuck all!" Thaddeus roared again.

"Nothing?" Lyndon ran his palm across the back of his neck.

Thaddeus growled out a breath. "If you must know—they found that Lockridge person—the husband, but that Westlake woman wasn't with him, nor was there any evidence the bitch was ever in Japan," Thaddeus huffed out. "Dead end—and don't contact me again unless you have a lead."

When Lyndon said nothing, Thaddeus said, "Or is that it—do you have a lead?"

Lyndon remained silent. If this woman truly was Lane's aunt, could he turn her over to the likes of Thaddeus? Lane had expressed how wonderful it was having this aunt, this woman in her life.

"Well?" Thaddeus prodded.

Lyndon squeezed the cellphone. If anything were to happen to this woman, it would crush Lane, and he couldn't let that happen. He would never hurt Lane.

"Lyndon!" Thaddeus shouted through the cellphone.

"No... no lead," he said, squeezing his eyes shut and ending the call.

Chapter 32 

Natalie walked through the door into the front hallway, followed by Teeny, the two of them kicking off their winter boots onto the mat. Before proceeding into the living room, Natalie hung her bomber jacket and Teeny's long wool coat on the hooks in the front hall.

"Good to be home," Natalie said, dropping her bookbag on the floor near the L-shaped sofa, then she plopped herself down at the far end that ran along the bay window, tucking her legs up under the oversized sweatshirt she'd borrowed from one of her roommates. Since starting school, her attire had mostly been leggings, sweatpants and sweatshirts and her insulated coat with having to cross the university's courtyard back and forth for some of her classes in the dead of winter.

"I've barely talked to you, let alone seen you this past month," Teeny said, resting herself down in the corner of the couch.

"Oh, I know—that's why I texted you to meet me here," Natalie said, noting Teeny had on her bar staff shirt for The Laff. She had spent Christmas with Teeny and her family doing things Italian style with baked pasta, braised beef, Brussel sprouts with almonds and for dessert, panna cotta and panettone sweet bread, which had been a welcomed change from her usual diet of pizza, chicken wings and

French fries and boxed macaroni and cheese. But the last time Natalie had seen Teeny had been New Year's Eve to celebrate the combo of the new year and her birthday. They'd stayed here just the two of them while her roommates had gone out to party, but the guys had brought her and Teeny out late morning the following day, on her actual birthday, for what they had dubbed a *hangover breakfast*. "Only reason I'm even home is there was no in-person lecture for my last class today. But of course we were given an online assignment in place of it."

"Did you have any idea your classes would monopolize so much of your time?" Teeny asked, leaning back and extending out her legs on the stretch of sofa opposite Natalie.

"I knew there would be a lot," Natalie said, "I have virtual sessions and in-person sessions—some recorded some not, online—prerecorded, and mandatory in-person and virtual sessions I have to attend in real time, but it's not just classes," she added before going on to explain her weekly curricular of activities. "My school year is divided into 13 blocks, each 4 weeks in length, and primary care sports medicine makes up 6 of those blocks alone. I have lectures in Physiotherapy, Athletic therapy, Orthotics and Bracing, Massage therapy, Exercise physiology, Kinesiology, Sport psychology and Concussion care, Osteopathy and sport-specific assessments. I even have an Eating Disorders Clinic as part of my program."

"Isn't that why you chose this sports and exercise medicine program, because of the diversity of exposure to multiple specialties?"

"It is," she said, exasperated.

"And don't forget Nutrition class with that hunky Mason," Teeny reminded, reaching for the sofa pillow near her feet.

"How could I forget?" she said. Besides the fact that Mason was brutally handsome, he had been a welcome addition with providing help in her nutrition class. She had met Mason and her other new friend, Lane, while she'd been in the Learning Crossroads center checking out the job board. Natalie had originally thought Mason was deaf since he'd used ASL and had spoken to her that first time via a voice app on his wristwatch. Lane had been the one who had informed her he was only mute. Still, thrown off by his looks, she'd stupidly asked if he read lips but then recalled he could actually hear. He'd whistled and given her a thumbs up, then graciously explained how most people figure he's deaf because of his signing, but the preconception came in handy for *eavesdropping*, he had joked then. She later found out he'd been born without vocal cords but since you didn't need them to whistle, he often used it for communication of a sort along with ASL and his voice app.

"Any luck finding a job?" Teeny asked, hugging the sofa pillow.

"I thought I'd have time for a part-time job, but as it turns out, I don't," Natalie said. On the first day of school, when she had met Mason and Lane, she'd shared that she was looking for a job, and how she'd recently applied at Après SNOW, expressing how she thought it was a great new bar and an excellent location. Coincidently, Lane had said her uncles owned the place and that she'd check to see what the status of their staff was. "I also have to do a minimum of 50 hours of documented supervised sports event coverage for my CASEM diploma." It was the prerequisite needed to take the Canadian Academy of Sport Medicine exam she'd been informed during orientation on day one. "Hopefully, I can get something come spring when school winds down. I'll be running out of cash by then."

"Sounds to me you need to bring your stress level down some," Teeny said. "Didn't you say the university had a wellness lounge? Maybe you could spend some time there with Maaaason," she teased.

"I have been using the uoWellness app," she said, ignoring her friend's taunts. The app she'd learned from Lane was a one-stop solution for health and wellness designed by students, for students, and tailored to university life, making the wellness journey simpler and engaging. Lane was a seasoned student similar in age to Natalie's roommates, and she had been the one who showed her the app and had provided her with a few tricks with getting around campus that even her roommates didn't know. Natalie had also learned Lane knew ASL as well, that she had taken an elective course online with the University to learn it and that Mason helps her practice. When Natalie had said she'd love to learn, Lane had given Natalie her cellphone number, saying to text her, and she'd send her the details on the course. Lane had also been the one who had brought her to the Wellness Lounge, stating it was a place you could study and get away from the chaos and commotion of full-time university and her sometimes noisy roommates. It's a judgment free space open to all students with free wellness-focused activities with more than just study rooms. There was a light therapy room, balance room, and a plant room, and they even had workshops and therapy dog sessions. *It could be fun to go to the lounge with Mason*, she thought to herself, but chose not to elaborate on it with her friend. "Are you working tonight?" she asked Teeny instead.

"Yes, only because I switched my regular day shift with another bartender for tonight."

"Friday night is always good money," Natalie recalled.

"I know, but I hate dealing with the Friday and Saturday night party crowd." Teeny squeezed the sofa pillow. "Not working Saturday nights means I can attend your Feast of Saint Valentine's Day party."

"Palentine's Day," Natalie corrected, tucking her hands in the sleeves of her sweatshirt for warmth.

"Right, the anti-valentines, *Palentine's* Day party," Teeny amended. "Did you know that Saint Valentine was the patron saint of lovers, people with epilepsy, and beekeepers?"

Natalie raised her eyebrows. "I did *not*."

"I read that Saint V was a Roman priest and physician who was beheaded during the persecution of Christians by the emperor Claudius II Gothicus, his body was buried on February 14th which has been observed as the Feast of Saint Valentine—Saint Valentine's Day, since at least the eighth century."

"Killed for his beliefs," Natalie acknowledged.

"The day is meant to honor his death and burial, but some historians believe the date is in reflect of the Catholic Church's attempt to replace the Pagan celebration of *Lupercalia*—it's a fertility festival," Teeny added with a chuckle.

"Wow—aren't you the smarty-smarterson," Natalie said.

"I'm not just a pretty face in a tiny package, you know." Teeny did an air kiss, then winked. "What are you guys naming the party this year?"

"Cupid's Conspiracy," Natalie said. "You're too smart for your own good."

"Are you inviting Mason?" Teeny asked then, giving her a couple of eyebrow raises.

"Yup, Lane and Mason," Natalie confirmed. She'd texted Lane first because she was fun to hang out with and would aid the nervousness she felt around Mason. Back when she'd met them both, Mason too had given his number, offering to help her practice ASL if she chose to take the course. She hadn't had time for additional studies, but Mason had turned out to be a good study partner. She was still interested in ASL, but she had been more interested in Mason, and her curiosity about him had morphed into a serious crush. She wasn't sure if he was interested in her though, since witnessing the attention he always got from the other female students.

"Great—can't wait to meet Lane, and that Mason sure is a treat to look at." Teeny winked at her again, this time with more exaggeration.

The sound of the front door opening abruptly interrupted Natalie and Teeny's luxurious yet recently scarce friend time. The two of them turning their attention from each other to the loud voices of her roommates Kelly and Kerry.

"There's an envelope for you," Kerry said when he came into view, still wearing his university hockey jacket. He tossed the letter pile on the dining room table. "Hi Teeny."

"Hi, handsome," Teeny said, blowing Kerry a kiss. Teeny knew he was gay, but she still thought he was the better looking of the two.

Kerry and Kelly were twins, and it was their mother who owned the rental property they lived in. Their mother was a successful, busy real estate lawyer who had wanted a child but didn't have time to date, so she'd opted to use fertility assistance instead of waiting to find a man. She had gotten her wish for a successful pregnancy but had been surprised to find out she'd been carrying twins. During the gender ultrasound, the doctor informed her the twins were girls—hence the names, but when the twins were born, to her surprise again, they'd turned out to be boys. And she'd chosen to keep the names since she'd been using them for most of her pregnancy.

"Where's Brady?" Teeny asked. We all knew she liked Brady and that he had a crush on her, but he was too shy to act on it.

"Studying at school," Kerry said with a knowing grin. Teeny was intelligent and quick-witted, but Brady was scholastically smart, and his hyper focus on school was why his dating skills and sometimes social skills were often lacking. Kerry and Kelly were both on hockey scholarships, though Kerry hadn't needed the added assistance since his grades warranted an academic scholarship as well.

"Hey Teeny-weeny," Kelly said mockingly, greeting Natalie's friend. He hadn't taken his jacket off either.

"Don't call her that," Natalie said, getting up from the sofa.

"I can take him," Teeny said, standing and putting up her fists.

"You sure it's for me?" she asked Kerry, crossing the living room over to the table.

"Says *Ms. Natalie Harwood* right on the front of the envelope," Kerry stated, tapping a finger on it. "Nice sweatshirt," he said, recognizing it was his.

Natalie grinned at him, then grabbed the envelope to read the front before tearing it open.

"What does it say?" Teeny asked, coming up beside her.

"Says I'm supposed to contact the *North Haven Estate Lawyers*."

Teeny leaned in as though trying to read the letter. "What is it about?"

Natalie glanced up at her. "It's regarding my birthmother."

"You gonna call them?" Kelly asked, coming to stand next to her and Teeny, making a show of how much taller he was than Teeny

"Back up, stalker," Teeny said, elbowing him in the ribs.

"I uhm… I don't…," Natalie mumbled.

"Didn't you say you wished you knew more about your birth parents?" Kerry asked.

"Yes, but what if it's bad news?" Natalie questioned. "Think I've had enough bad news for one little lifetime."

"What if it's good news?" Teeny interjected.

Natalie reread the letter a second time.

"We're going to head out," Kerry said then, poking Teeny in the shoulder. "Meeting up with Brady."

"Nat, you want to come out with us?" Kelly asked as though hopeful.

"I have to watch my money," she answered, glancing up from the letter.

"How about you, Teeny?" Kelly inquired, twirling a length of her hair around his finger.

"Don't hold your breath," Teeny said, swatting his hand away. The two actually liked each other as friends, but they also enjoyed this back-and-forth sarcastic banter.

"Call them," Kerry said, pointing at the letter in Natalie's hand. "Them come meet us," he added, grabbing Kelly by the arm, hauling his brother with him to the front door.

"You too, Teeny-weeny," Kelly jokingly commanded before his brother shut the door.

Teeny shook her head at Kelly's demand, then she asked, "You gonna call?"

"Says I have to call this lawyer guy, Mr. Zachery Glacier," Natalie said. The name showed above the signature at the bottom of the letter.

"Do it," Teeny said, checking the time on her phone. "Text me later with the details—need to bolt or I'm going to be late."

"I will." Natalie set down the letter to give her friend a hug.

Letting go of Natalie, Teeny said, "Promise?" She pointed a stern finger at Natalie as she backed towards the front door.

"I promise," Natalie said, yielding, watching as Teeny donned her long wool coat and slipped into her winter boots to head back out into the cold.

Natalie waited several heartbeats after her friend left, before dialing the number provided for this Mr. Glacier person.

After an exchange of introductions over the phone, Natalie said, "The letter says you have information about my birthmother."

"Yes," Mr. Glacier said. "Are you available to go over things?" When Natalie didn't answer right away, he asked, "Would you be comfortable with me stopping by now? I'd like to finish this up today, if you don't mind."

"Sure," Natalie agreed. She couldn't see why not.

A quick 30 minutes later, Mr. Glacier was at her door and Natalie guided him in to sit at the dining table. He was dressed casually for a lawyer in a waist-length, winter coat over jeans and a pullover, and based on his appearance was more *Mr. Tall, Blond and Gorgeous*—she would tell Teeny later. For now, she did her best not to stare directly at him as he sat down and retrieved a folder from the briefcase he'd brought with him.

"Ms. Harwood," Mr. Gorgeous Glacier began.

"Call me Natalie," she interrupted, giving him a friendly smile.

"Natalie," he began again. "You have been left some money from an associate of your birthmother."

"What—Who?" she asked, gazing at him as he smiled warmly back at her.

"The person is not named," he said, looking down at the paperwork in front of him. "The funds were provided anonymously." Glancing back up, he said, "We originally contacted your aunt who raised you, having been informed about the death of your adoptive parents." He paused, his expression sympathetic. "My condolences."

"Thank you," Natalie said, setting her cellphone on the table next to her. "As for my aunt, I wouldn't exactly say she raised me. Good thing she didn't know about this additional inheritance. She gambled away the money my parents left me." Natalie blew out a breath. "I didn't even know there had been any money until I found the letter from the other lawyer."

"My associates met her. She was…," Mr. Glacier started to say.

"She was an awful person," Natalie finished for him. "Bitter over having to take care of her sister's kid." Natalie glanced at the papers, feeling a sting in her heart over missing her parents. "Found out my aunt was given money too, but she lost it all gambling as well. It's the reason we lived in such a shithole." She glanced at the lawyer. "Sorry."

He shook his head. "No need for sorry," he said, dismissing her swearing.

She nodded once. "I contacted the bank—took what was left of my money, and left the *bitch*—my aunt, the minute I turned 18," Natalie said, attempting to mind her manners this time. "With being in school full time, I don't really have time for a job, so any funds would be welcome." She slumped in her seat knowing she sounded pathetic, but facts were facts.

"I don't think you're going to have to worry about work. The money you've been left is substantial."

Natalie straightened in her chair. "How substantial?"

"Enough to grant you monthly increments of $2500 over the next 4 years," he said.

Natalie felt her mouth gape.

"There's only one stipulation."

Of course there was, she thought, slumping again.

"The monthly payments will continue as long as you remain in school and up until you graduate. The funds had been held in trust until such time you chose to attend a higher educational institute on a full-time basis."

Natalie wondered how they could have known she was going to university.

"An account is now open and activated in your name, but here is your first check. The payments will go into this account automatically starting February and continue on the first of each month."

Natalie stared down at the check as he slid it her way. Who cared how they knew about her attending school. All that mattered now was that she wasn't going to starve, and she could continue to pay her rent and then some.

"Here are the account details," Mr. Glacier said, standing then and handing her the remaining papers.

Natalie stood, extending her hand. "Thank you sooo much—you don't know what a lifesaver this is."

"My pleasure," he said, shaking her hand. "I can see myself out."

Natalie felt as though she were in a dream as she watched the handsome lawyer who had saved the day leave out her front door. Shaking herself, she snatched up her phone from the dining table, then dialed Kerry.

"Tell me you're calling to say you're coming out," Kerry said through the phone in leu of a hello.

"Nope," Natalie said, smiling into the phone. "I'm calling to say that this year's anti-Valentine's Day party is going to be on *me*."

Chapter 33 

Since his encounter with the Westlake woman, Lane's aunt, at the hospital in Florida a month ago, Lyndon hadn't spoken with Lane, but he had been following her to school. Lane hadn't exactly lied to him, but she hadn't been forthcoming with how much she actually knew about him and his kind. He'd needed to take a step back from in-person contact with her, and instead he'd been watching her interactions with Julianna, and her school chum Mason who Lyndon had met at the birthday party, but it had been her frequent exchanges with some other young female student that had interested him the most. There was something about this girl's appearance he found intriguing, and it wasn't because she was strikingly attractive, it was that something about *her* pulled at him, pulled at reaches of his foggy memory banks.

Lyndon stood in his usual hiding place inside the Learning Crossroads building, watching as Lane and Julianna conversed over coffees they'd purchased from the Tim Horton's coffee shop on the premises. When Julianna answered a call on her cellphone, he noted Lane retrieving *her* phone from her purse. Then his cellphone vibrated in his jacket. Withdrawing it from the inner pocket, he saw ironic as it was, he had received a text from Lane.

She'd written,

> *Happy Valentine's Day!*
> *I know you've been crazy busy, but we haven't seen each other in weeks, and considering it's Valentine's Day, I thought I'd take a leap and ask if you wanted to get together tonight.*

They had exchanged a few texts back and forth following Christmas but after this situation with his target being connected to Lane, he wasn't sure he could trust his own judgement. His texts, since last seeing Lane on Christmas Eve, had been mainly excuses for his evasiveness and not being around, alluding to it being his boss's doing. He hadn't seen anything during his surveillance of Lane that convinced him that anything sketchy was going on with her, but he still had a long list of questions he didn't know how to get answers to. But he missed her. The emptiness in his heart at her absence had been unbearable. Taking his own leap, he wrote back,

> *I would love that.*

Lane wrote back right away, saying,

> *I have a friends' gathering to drop by first, then I'll be right over.*

Lyndon slid his cellphone back into his jacket pocket and returned to observing Lane.

"This is what you've been up to," came an unexpected, familiar, yet annoying voice. "Watching Julianna and some human woman," Addison said, catching Lyndon off guard.

"What the hell are you doing here—you're supposed to be in New York," Lyndon shot out.

"Thaddeus asked me to check up on you," Addison said. "Did you already tell him Julianna was here in Ottawa?"

"Not yet. I've been watching her to see what she's been up to." He glanced over her way. "He'd have me do it, anyway. And if I find she *is* up to something, I can tell him such."

"Is there something going on between you two?" Addison asked, sneering.

"Julianna and me?" Lyndon questioned, taken aback.

"Wait—no, it's the *human* female—isn't it?" he said then.

Lyndon glared at him.

"Good for you—the whole *Beauty and the Beast* thing—I get it—nice," he added when Lyndon said nothing. "How did you two meet?"

"At the group home—Julianna is her professor," Lyndon bit out.

"So you're stalking them both, then?" Addison said, rocking on his heels.

"You need to leave," Lyndon said, ignoring the foolish question.

Addison didn't leave, instead he clasped his hands behind his back. "Shall I tell Thaddeus what I found out—what you have been up to?"

"I'll take care of telling him about Julianna," Lyndon said, turning to face the Seraph. "But if you feel the need to tell him anything—tell him you found *nothing* out of the ordinary—that I spend my free time at the group home." Lyndon poked Addison in the chest. "Got it?"

"She's cute—I may have to check out this group home myself," Addison said, as though baiting Lyndon, releasing his hands from behind his back.

Lyndon grabbed Addison by the lapels of his overpriced designer coat and threw him up against the wall, pinning him there. "Don't you ever," Lyndon threatened.

"Ever what?" Addison asked innocently.

Lyndon pressed him into the wall. "If you so much as try to talk to her, I'll rip your tongue from your body. If you touch her, I will…." He paused. "…Just stay away from her," he added, letting go of Addison

"You'll what?" Addison asked, goading him further.

Lyndon grabbed hold of Addison again, this time around his throat, and leaned into his face. "I. Will. Kill. You," Lyndon said, drawing out each word, pushing his intentions home. He gave Addison a forceful shove against the wall, then let go.

Addison stumbled, then turned, swiftly walking in the opposite direction, away from Lyndon.

Lyndon focused the other way to see the professor was still in view, though Lane had left. He thought it best he told Thaddeus about Julianna before Addison did, and he pulled his cellphone from the pocket of his coat once again.

"Why… are… you… bothering me!!" Thaddeus screamed into Lyndon's ear. He would have put the asshole on speaker, but he was in a public place. Not that the bastard's aggression couldn't still be heard.

"Thought you should know Julianna is in town—but I've been watching her, and she appears to pose no threat."

"Why the hell is she there?"

"I… overheard she's working at a university here now—because the research job she'd been on lost funding," he scrambled out, having not anticipated it would require further explanation.

"What research?"

"The research she was doing in the rainforest—regenerative therapies on the vegetation there," Lyndon clarified.

"Sounds more like your expertise—or used to be. I'm setting up a new laboratory in a new location, but I'm intrigued about this past work of hers," Thaddeus said, as though more interested in Julianna's research than the fact she was in town. Lyndon knew there was none of Thaddeus's crew at the Brazil facility, but he wasn't interested in hearing about his latest endeavor. Then, as though Thaddeus's interest was abruptly lost, he said, "I'm over it. I have better things to occupy my time." Then he hung up.

Lyndon was relieved Thaddeus was now preoccupied with his new venture and it meant Addison, Thaddeus's new lapdog, could go back to his duties at the New York facility. At this point, Lyndon couldn't care less about what Thaddeus was up to, as long as he left him out of it. Still, he needed to confirm why Julianna was here, not for Thaddeus, but for himself. Leaving his spot in the shadows, he strode forward across the courtyard. "Julianna," he said, approaching where she stood.

Julianna looked up from her phone, startled. "Lyndon." She scanned the surrounding area. "What do you want?"

"I just want to know what you're doing here," he said, hoping her answer proved Lane hadn't been lying to him.

"I work here—teach here," she said, glancing around again.

That's what Lane had told him. "What happened to your work in Brazil?"

"The funding ran out. Luckily, a colleague of mine mentioned the professor's job here—put in a good word, and they offered the position to me," she rushed out, the details more confirmation Lane had not lied. "I suppose you've told Thaddeus I'm here?"

"He knows," Lyndon said, nodding. "But I told him there was nothing to worry about."

"Look, I have no interest in Thaddeus—and the last thing I need is him sniffing in my business," Julianna said, adjusting her purse on her shoulder, and sliding her hands into her coat pockets.

"Lane mentioned you have a son—that you adopted him from an orphanage."

"Lane?" she questioned, her brow furrowing.

"I believe she's a student of yours in the master's program, yes?"

"How do you know Lane?" Julianna asked, taking her turn at a query.

"We're friends," Lyndon said, pacifying her confusion. "Does Lane know what you are?"

"Now why would I need to tell one of my students about my… *origins*?" Julianna asked, removing a hand from her coat pocket to place it on her hip. "You say you're friends—do you plan on telling her what you are?" She gave him a smug grin.

Lyndon glanced away, then turned to leave without answering. After several strides toward the parking lot, he shot a glance over his shoulder to see Julianna heading in the opposite direction towards the Center for Advanced Research in Environmental Genomics, where she taught several of her classes. When Julianna paused to use her cellphone, Lyndon turned and continued on his way, done with spying for the day.

"Ben, are you still here at the school?" Julianna asked, stepping up next to the closest building to avoid the winter wind.

"Yes. Why—what's up?" Ben asked.

"Lyndon just confronted me—asked why I was here," she said, leaning back against the brick facade of the old building. "He asked about my son—said Lane told him."

"Lane told him?" he said, shocked. "What did you say?"

"Nothing. But he did ask if I planned on telling Lane what I am."

"Do you think Lane told him about Natalie?"

"Anael's daughter—no? If he knows, he didn't share it with me. I think I convinced him I'm strictly here for the teaching job and that's it." Julianna pushed away from the building. "I'm heading to class now—but meet me in the Wellness Lounge after."

"Okay, I'll meet you," he said.

"See you then," Julianna said, ending the call and rushing off.

Addison stepped forward then from the shadows near the building Julianna had rested against. *"Anael has a daughter?"* he murmured to himself. *"Won't Thaddeus be pleased to hear this news?"*

Chapter 34 

A month had passed and still Zuriel's condition hadn't changed, but I'd not felt Lyndon again since that day at the hospital. It was obvious he wasn't there for me, considering the location in which I had detected his unique signature resonating. I'd not sensed him at all during my shift and it hadn't been until I'd been standing at the event table near the Behavioral Health Center that his distinct resonance shuddered across my skin. Zuriel had to be the reason Lyndon had been there, but once again, it didn't explain why he had brought him to my hospital in the first place.

As I walked from Hayley's bedroom through the bathroom into Ryley's room, picking up damp towels and tossed clothing, I heard my cellphone chime loudly from the kitchen. On my way up the hall, I threw the rumpled clothes and towels into a basket in the laundry room as I passed by. Retrieving my cellphone from off the kitchen island, I checked and saw Lane had sent me a text message.

She'd written,

Got time for a video chat?

Other than finishing the laundry, I was wide open for time, plus Lane and I needed to have a talk, and I wrote back,

I always have time for you!

Instead of using my laptop for the video call, I plopped myself down on the couch with just my cellphone and waited for Lane to dial me through the video app.

"Hi, Aunt Lynn," she greeted as our faces unblurred on the screen.

I waved at her on my tiny phone screen. "Hiiii, Lane."

"I'm sorry, I've been wanting to talk to you—but I've been head-down with my research for school." Lane, it appeared, was on her laptop in her room.

"I heard from Olivia that you and Rachel went to Après SNOW for New Year's," I said, letting her know my spies had eyes.

"We did—it was a blast," Lane said as she slid her arms into a sky blue coloured zip-up hoody. "I was going to ask Lyndon to come, but Rachel was bringing several of her nurse friends she works with at the hospital and wanted it to be a *singles* thing. Nic came too—he never goes out. But I think he was keeping an eye on me." She raised her eyebrows knowingly and made a tight smile.

"I hear you befriended Natalie," I said, not quite ready to jump into the Lyndon topic.

"You'd really like her—she's funny and smart, and Mason and I have hung out together with her several times at the university. She's having a party tonight at the home she rents with her roommates—she invited Mason and me."

"A Valentine's party?" I asked, curious about the idea.

"It's for everyone, singles and couples. The purpose is an anti-romance event focused on friendship. Her roommates apparently do it every year."

"Cool, I like the concept." I paused, then said, "We need to talk about what happened at the hospital."

"I know," Lane agreed, glancing down, her hands coming into view as she began picking at the corner of a fingernail. "I haven't seen him since Christmas," she said then, still fiddling with her nail.

"Have you talked to him?" I asked, bringing one of my knees up and resting my foot on the couch.

"No," she said, returning to look at the video screen. "We have been texting, but not much since you and I talked the day he was at the hospital. He's been vague in his texts and aloof in his communication with me, and I don't understand why." Lane picked at her fingernail again.

"Do you think he's been in Brazil with Thaddeus?" I asked, wondering myself.

"I highly doubt it—he hates the guy, *and* he told me he never travels with him. Besides, he would never leave Taylor for any great length of time." Lane ran her hand through her hair, twisting it and holding the length of it next to her shoulder. "I texted him this morning, and he agreed to see me tonight." She fiddled with her ear. "Told him I had a friend's party to go to first."

"What are you planning to do?" I rested my cellphone against my knee, leaning my elbow on the armrest of the couch.

"I'm going to the group home after making an appearance at the party—I told Mason I'd go. I really just want to get Lyndon and me back on track," she said, letting her hair loose, it spinning free to spread over the back of her shoulders. "I thought we made such great progress after Jana's party and with Christmas, but he's been so busy with…."

"Traveling to Florida," I cut in.

"Yes, that too." Lane reached out an arm, bringing her cellphone into view as she checked. "He hasn't shared much in his text, but I get the impression he is not happy." She looked up from her phone and frowned.

"I haven't sensed him since that day, by the way. And I don't think the others consider him a danger."

"You think so?" Lane rested her cellphone to the side.

"Well, they haven't implemented any added security, not that I think we need it. They know if I feel even the tiniest tingle, I can alert them with the app on my phone Marq installed for me," I assured her. "Leo has been at South Haven on and off since Den left for his regular facility watch in Amsterdam. And Zach relocated here." I shrugged, rubbing the back of my neck, then rested my elbow on the armrest again. "No sign of Thaddeus still, though. The consensus is he's in Brazil, potentially sourcing fertility specialists." I shivered at the notion, then pushed the thoughts away. "Do you think you'll ask Lyndon about what's been going on—why he's been MIA?"

"Probably." Lane nodded slowly.

"Do you think he will share more?" I asked, leaning the side of my face against the palm of my hand.

"I'm counting on it. Plus, I want to ask him about the question he posed to me about believing in the supernatural. See if that opens him up more." Mirroring me, she leaned her elbow on her desk, resting her cheek against her palm.

"That's a good idea, since he's the one who brought it up in the first place." I relaxed my forearm down on the armrest. "Speaking of supernatural, how is Jana handling the fact that Natalie has been found?"

"Jana hasn't met her yet, but she knows they've located Natalie. They've made provisions through Anael for her financial security, Zach told me when he was up here. They need to establish a plan for divulging the details about Jana being her half-sister, too. Kris has something planned for Jana tonight for Valentine's, he told me." Lane smiled then, clearly a romantic at heart.

"I can't imagine how difficult it must be to navigate a relationship like that." I shook my head.

"Tell me about it," Lane said, rolling her eyes, fully aware of the difficulties. "What are *your* plans for Valentines?"

"Date night at home while Zach babysits the girls." I gave Lane a wide grin.

"With raising kids, I bet you could use a night alone," she said, pointing a finger at the screen.

"Tell me about it," I said, rolling my eyes this time, conveying her same sentiment. Lane let out a burst of laughter, and I laughed along with her. "Tell me something good—non-angel related."

"I'm almost done with my thesis for my master's degree," she said, her voice heightening with joy.

"Oh, you must be so excited."

"I am—and anxious too. But I met with Jules this morning to set up a time to practice."

"Practice?" I gave her a *what* face.

"She's going to help me prepare for when I have to present at the end of the month," she explained, followed by a nervous grin.

"Then it's nothing but rainbows and job hunting after that," I joked.

Lane laughed again. "Jules found me an intern placement with one of her contacts. But unfortunately the main work isn't local, so it means I'd be travelling some." She gave me another nervous smile.

"It will be good for you to get out of dodge now and again—out from under those overprotective males you live with."

"Right—hadn't thought of that," she said. "But I wholeheartedly agree."

I figured she hadn't focused on that part. "Okay, my dear—I need to make another call before the afternoon gets away from me. Let me know how things go with Mr. Lyndon *and* be careful. That's your protective aunt talking." I stuck my tongue out at her.

"I will—and I will." She stuck out her tongue at me then. "I got to get a move on it, too. Later Aunt Lynn."

"Later, Lane," I said, waving goodbye as she ended the call.

In the laundry room, I put the stuff from the basket into the washer and pressed the start button. Then I returned to my spot on the couch and hit dial on my cellphone for a regular call with Mac, then hit speaker. "Happy VD," I said when she answered, knowing she wasn't a fan of Valentine's day. "What do you have planned for this night devoted to love?"

"Game night," she tossed back, unaffected.

"With Don and the boys?"

"Just Don," she said casually. "Carter has a date, and Declan is doing a pizza party at a friend's place." I heard barking in the background. "Can you call me back on video? I want to show you my handsome boy."

"Sure," I said before hanging up. I hit the icon on my phone for video chat.

"Look at this gorgeous face," Mac gushed, bringing the face of her gigantic bull mastiff Fergus into view of the screen.

"Nice bandana," I said, admiring the big boy's red and white heart patterned doggy neck wrap.

"Had to get my special boy something—he is the love of my life, you know," Mac said all serious like, then she kissed Fergus on the head and let him free. With his massive face no longer blocking the view, I now saw that Mac was in her office.

"Of course," I said, grinning. "What are Olivia and Alison up to—do ya know?"

"No idea—didn't ask. Probably gross romantic stuff." She made an *ick* face.

"Lyndon was at the hospital again," I blurted, then chewed the corner of my lip.

Mac stared at me for a heartbeat, then dropped her head into her hands. "And here I was thinking all was well."

"It's not *unwell*. I don't think he was there for me, Mac. I didn't feel him at all during my shift—wasn't until I was near the psych ward that I felt him. Zuriel is the reason he was there." At least I hoped that was the excuse.

"Doesn't explain why he brought him to your hospital," Mac said, eerily echoing my earlier thoughts.

"Did you want me to tell the others?" Mac asked, as though the thought of conveying the latest news was exhausting.

"Just Alison. Redmond updated Luc and Derek. And we told Lily and Darius," I shared, eager to lesson her burden.

"And I take it you're not going to tell Olivia?" she asked, stating the obvious.

"Would you?"

"Nope." Mac shook her head, then reached for something on her desk. Then she waved what I saw now was her grimoire in view of the screen. "I've been afraid to ask, but have you had any more mirror incidents?"

"Not a one," I said, expressing my relief.

"So I can drop the research on mirror spells, yes?" she asked, setting the grimoire on the desk in front of her.

"For now. If it happens again, I'll let you know." No one could find the answer to this weird mirror business, not even Gabriel.

"Greeeat," Mac drew out. "What little I found, hedged a tad too close to the dark side of magic, for my liking."

"Sorry, Mac," I said, feeling remorseful. "On a fun note, Redmond and I are doing a Valentine's date night here at home, too," I sing-songed, pushing for levity.

"With the twins?" Mac tilted her head to one side in question.

"Just Redmond and me. The girls are doing a movie night over at South Haven with Zach.

"Lucky them," she said, smiling playfully, making me laugh

"We need this time alone, though, you know."

She blew out a heavy breath. "Time alone will get easier once the girls reach the same age as my boys. It's also the age when they stop wanting to hang out with you too," she added, as though bummed at the fact.

"They are already growing up too fast—I wish they had slow aging like Zach and the others. I wish I had it too," I admitted.

"Don't we all," Mac agreed with a chuckle.

I laughed and gave her a nod.

"Keep me posted and I'll update Alison on the latest. But be safe, Lynn," Mac said, serious again.

"I will. And say happy Valentines to Don for me."

"Will do. Send Redmond and the girls my love."

I gave her the peace sign. "Chat at ya later."

Mac blew me a kiss, then signed off.

I checked the time on my phone, then went to the laundry room again to toss the now washed items into the dryer. One of the things on my list today was to go talk to Zach about what he and Leo had come up with for my getting into the psych ward, but I hadn't wanted to share that part with Mac. She was already stressed out about this Lyndon stuff.

When I walked into the training space at South Haven through the garage access, I found Zach doing pullups in the squat rack.

"Looking to get in a quick training session?" he asked when he saw me.

"As much as I enjoy your *company*," I said, "I'm grateful to skip my training today. I don't need any scrapes and bruises for my date night."

Zach just laughed and then continued with what I was sure was his five-hundredth pullup.

"I spoke with Lane this morning—told me about she and Mason hanging with Natalie. They're going to a party at Natalie's house apparently," I shared, though I'm sure he was well aware.

"Leo has been keeping an eye on her at the university since her transition could start any day—it's exceptionally late for a halfling," Zach confirmed before letting go of the bar and dropping to the ground. "

"Are there any other adult halflings?" I'd been wanting to ask Leo, but Zach would answer the question for me.

"We only know of one other—besides Mason," Zach said, taking a long stride over to sit on the bench next to the mats. "But there could be more—hard to say," he added, sadness creeping into his normally cheerful face. He snatched one of the small towels stacked at the end of the bench.

"Who is this other one?"

"Shea O'Sluaghain. Her mother's name was Shrina—she died in childbirth and her parents raised her." Zach wiped his face with the towel. "Shea should be close to 30 years old now," he said, dabbing his face.

"Interesting names," I said, taking a seat next to him.

"Interesting spelling too. It's pronounced *Sloan*, but spelled with an O apostrophe," he said, spelling out the remaining letters. "Her grandfather was Irish, and her grandmother was Arab." He draped the towel over his shoulder.

"Interesting combination of cultures," I acknowledged. "What about the father?" I shifted a leg over to straddle the bench to face Zach.

"That is unknown at the moment," he said. "But I saw photos of her mother—she was lovely. She looks like an Egyptian Sophia Loren."

"What about Shea—what does she look like?" I asked, smiling.

"Like Cleopatra—she even wears the thick black eyeliner," Zach said, tapping a finger next to one of his eyes. "But… she's missing her legs from below the knee," he said then, stealing my smile.

"How did you find her?"

"Den found her. He was doing one of his bodyguard gigs for some diplomat and their kids at a concert in Madrid, and Shea was with them."

"Lucky find," I said, recognizing how fortunate they had been, especially Shea.

Zach nodded. "Timing," he said then.

Timing was key—boy, did I know it. "What happened to Mason's dad?" I asked, curious for more.

"Ya, well, that's another harsh story," Zach said. "Jules and he had been secretly seeing each other—they worked together, so it was a big no-no, but they had only been dating for a few weeks when he'd been out in the field—the field being the rainforest in Brazil, when an old Kapok tree that was being cut down came down and crushed him."

"Holy shit," I said, bringing my hand to my mouth.

"Worse—Jules didn't even know she was pregnant at the time."

I fisted my hand against my mouth and said, "Poor Jules."

"Nic was stationed in Brazil then, he helped her through it all."

"Thankfully, Mason is healthy too," I added, needing more lightness.

"Yup—Nic helped him through his transition as well."

"Good guy—that Nic. You're all wonderful—Redmond and I are grateful to have you all in our lives—I hope you know that."

"We're grateful for you all too," Zach said, smiling again.

"How long do you think Den will be away?"

"With Thaddeus on the loose, Den, Marq and even Ben have been watching their locations more closely." Zach pushed up from the bench. "I have your disguise ready, by the way—for getting into the psych ward."

"Really—already?" I asked, getting up off the bench.

"Come, I'll show you," Zach said, striding over to the computer stations set up on the far side. "I found a past employee from like 15 years ago, whose status shows as still having security access to the area." Zach handed me a photo of a woman with shoulder-length curly grey hair. "She was already going grey in her last ID photo, so I just enhanced and aged it some." He handed me the new security ID badge. "Marq instructed me on how to make it using her image, but with the updated hair and added glasses, and with the same purple wine stain birthmark on her right cheek." He tapped a pile of clothing. "Got you hospital clothing, too."

"Well done!" I said, picking up the scrubs and physicians' coat. "Oh, damn."

"What?" Zack asked, taking the coat from me.

"It's not the clothes," I said, holding up the ID badge. "It needs to have a gold border around the image too, not just the green. Only the staff from that ward have both." I handed it back to him.

"Easy fix—leave it with me. I'll have it ready for when you come back with the girls."

"No worries," I said, patting him on the back. Wasn't like I'd be venturing to the hospital tonight. "I'll be back around 5p.m., cool?"

"Perfect!," Zach said. "Tell the girls I'm making buffalo chicken nachos for dinner and popcorn for later. I also got them an exclusive early release copy of the Spider-Man: Across the Spider-Verse movie that doesn't come out in theaters until March."

"That was sweet of you."

"Den got it for them actually, he has a connection with one of the voice actors. But don't tell the girls the part about the movie—I want it to be a surprise."

"Okay, I'll just tell them you have a surprise," I said, before taking my leave.

When I got home, Redmond already had the girls packed for their time over at South Haven, so all I had to do was get them bathed and into their jammies for drop off back with Zach. As though as like clockwork, Hayley and Ryley were bathed, changed, and ready to go with little effort.

"Bye Da," Ryley said, giving her dad a kiss and hug. Hayley did the same but added a, "See you tomorrow" before the two of them headed downstairs to the carport.

"Have a good time and say hi to Zach for me," Redmond called down the stairs to them.

Then when we got to South Haven, in complement to the earlier efficiency at home, Zach had my disguise and the new badge ready for me when I arrived with the twins.

"Girls—be good for Zach—you hear me?" I called as they ran off and jumped up on the massive sectional couch in the main living space. Zach had tv-trays set up on one side for them to eat while watching the movie. The other side, which I only just realized was a pullout couch, was made up with loads of pillows and blankets for them to sleep on.

"Here," Zach said, pulling my attention back, handing me the small black canvas bag with my undercover garb in it. "There's adhesive for the facial prosthetic in there too, along with a hair stocking to keep your hair back for the wig," he added.

"Thank you for doing this," I said, patting the bag. "And for that." I pointed to the fantabulous sleep-over arrangement.

"Anytime," he said with a playful laugh. "And you know I mean it."

"Who knew giants could be the best babysitters?" I joked. "Have fun," I called to the girls.

"Byyyye, Mum," they yelled back in unison, already wanting me gone.

"You have a fun night, too," Zach said then, laughing, turning me around and easing me towards the door to the garage.

I pulled into the carport, then reached for the canvas bag with my disguise, then thought better of it and tossed it in the backseat. I hadn't told Redmond about the plan to get into the psych ward yet. And I certainly didn't want to tell him now and put a damper on our night, either.

As I came through the door into the kitchen from the lower level, I could smell the aroma that told me Redmond was making one of my favorite dishes, salmon pasta bake. "You are the best," I said, wrapping my arms around his waist as he stood at the island working his magic.

He lifted an arm up over me and kissed the top of my head. "I never get to make it now, since the girls refuse to eat fish anymore," he said, returning to his prep work.

"Not since they realized they could talk to them," I said, removing my arms from around him. "Gonna take a quick shower—back in a flash."

When I returned, clean and in my tank top and matching pink pajama bottoms, Redmond had two bottles of my favorite wine from Nappa California set out on the dining room table. He, too, was in pajama bottoms, but he wore a navy t-shirt that matched his pajamas. "Shall we eat?" he asked, bringing the meal he'd made to the table.

Over dinner we chatted without interruption and on topics we didn't bring up around the twins. They being one of the topics, but life had been fairly smooth with them, even with the unexpected visitors at the Thanksgiving gathering. Ryley and Hayley knew not to keep any visitors a secret now, but fortunately we hadn't had any since. There had also been no scary mirror or nightmare occurrences either, thankfully.

"Lane told me Kris was planning something romantic for Jana tonight," I said, sipping my wine.

"Must be tricky wanting to move forward but having to keep so much a secret," Redmond said. "It took you time before you could tell me about your… *weirdness*."

"Weirdness?" I pretended to jab his hand with my fork, then I stole a tiny piece of salmon from his plate. "My secret was easier to tell than what Kris is hiding from Jana," I said, grateful my life didn't carry the same weightiness.

"Love conquers all," Redmond said then, pouring more wine into my now empty glass.

"*Omnia Vincit Amor*," I mumbled, recalling the words on the gift Lyndon had given Lane.

"What was that?" Redmond asked, taking both our dinner plates from the table and walking them over to the kitchen sink.

"Nothing—just that I love you," I said, appreciative of everything he did for me and brought to my life.

"Feel like sitting on the deck by the firepit?" he asked before going up the hall to the laundry room.

"Is that a trick question?" I called, pulling a quilt from the blanket box next to the couch.

Redmond returned with two warm-out-of-the-dryer sweatshirts. "Great minds think alike," he said, pointing to the blanket in my arms. "It's cold out—we might need both." He grabbed up the wine bottle from the table and went to the patio door.

"I got the glasses," I said, snagging both from the table and following him out onto the deck.

Cuddled together on the patio couch, we sipped our wine in silence, stargazing and listening to the sound of the waves hitting the shore. "Bottle is empty," Redmond said, getting up and heading inside to get the other one.

"I think it's getting too cold—I'm coming in," I said, but he was already out of earshot despite the door being left open. Ready to go back in, I shut off the firepit and then dragged the blanket with me.

"You done?" Redmond asked, setting the bottle on the kitchen island.

"Too cold," I said, folding up the blanket and setting it on the bench at the kitchen table.

"With Den away, I'm guessing you didn't train today?" He came around the island to where I stood next to the table and put his hands on my shoulders.

"No, and I probably wouldn't have either, had he been here. I didn't need any new cuts or bruises." I grinned up at him.

"Or the sore muscles?" He rubbed my shoulders.

"When aren't they sore?" I said with a chuckle.

He pulled me closer. "How about I give you one of my famous massages?"

"Is that another trick question?" I asked. "You haven't given me a massage in a *very* long time. Not since before we moved here."

"I know," he said, leaning down to kiss me. Then he reached over to the kitchen island to retrieve a tiny gift bag. "Happy Valentine's Day."

I took the bag and peeked inside. In it was a lemon grass scented candle in a glass jar, and a bottle of massage oil, the kind that heats up. I looked up at Redmond to say thank you, but he was already walking away towards the bedroom. He glanced back briefly while slowly pulling his t-shirt over his head, then disappeared into our bedroom. Saving my *thank you* for later, I set the gift bag down on the table, then ripped off my sweatshirt and draped it over the back of one of the dining room chairs. Then I grabbed up the bag again and the second bottle of wine, before racing after my masseuse.

Chapter 35 

In Iceland, they don't celebrate February 14th, Valentine's Day. In fact, they have two special days, Kondaur, known as Wife's Day, in January, and Bóndadagur, known as Husband's Day, celebrated near the end of February, neither of which Jana had ever participated in. So, when Kris told her that he was planning something special for Valentine's day she had been thrilled. The birthday party he and Lane had planned for her had been fantastic and it had made her feel even more welcomed into Kris's family. Christmas too had been wonderful with so much warmth and comfort. Kris's brothers had even set up a live video feed on Christmas day to include everyone who could not be in Ottawa with them. It had been lovely to see Lynn and her family as well, for everyone to be part of that joy filled time of year. Even New Year's Eve had been great with working at the restaurant for the event and being a part of the wild and crazy evening full of fun and laughter. She and Kris had kissed at midnight, and it seems that second kiss may have sparked the elevated intimacy they'd had since.

Their regular evening spent together had shifted from just talking and handholding to the next level with cuddling that led to more kissing and several intense make-out sessions on Kris's couch in the lower level of his private suite. Despite the passion and obvious arousal she knew they both were experiencing, each time they partook in one of these sessions, Kris eventually pulled back, restraining himself from going further, even with Jana's coaxing. Despite the different levels of intimacy they shared, each evening ended the same way. Kris would escort her to her room then kiss her goodnight at her door as though he were dropping her off at her family home like her impatient father waited inside. She was grateful their relationship had moved to the next level, but she found she wanted more. There was still so much she didn't know about Kris, and what she did know had to be kept a secret, most of the details unclear. Even the information on his earlier years at the group home had been terribly vague. Kris kept reminding her that what mattered was now, not the past, and she did her best to keep her curiosity from affecting their time together. Perhaps tonight there would be more, or at least clearer confirmation of what she meant to Kris. Either way, she planned to tell him how she felt about him. And she had something special for him, too.

Since food preparation was a challenging secret to keep in this house, Julian had leaked Kris's surprise about him making her a special dinner, so she in turn, told Julian to share with Kris that she was making the dessert.

While Max watched from his spot at the kitchen island—he had done the grocery shopping, Jana and Kris, along with Julian, who knew where everything was in the kitchen, worked together to prepare a delicious Valentine's Day meal for the four of them. The rest of the house was on their own, Julian had informed them. And of course, even though their food was being prepared together, they would be enjoying their meals as couples in the privacy of their own spaces.

"Do you always celebrate Valentine's Day?" Jana asked Max and Julian.

"We try to do something special, sometimes extravagant—sometimes just something simple," Julian answered, retrieving a mixing bowl from a lower cupboard for Jana.

"But each day we honor the love we have for each other," Max added. "Not just on this day."

Jana smiled at Max, then at Julian, loving the sentiment.

"Do you have any travel plans this year?" Kris inquired, rolling up his sleeves in preparation for constructing *his* version of a classic British beef Wellington. "By the way, I'm doing individual mini beef Wellingtons so we can each carve and savor our own pastry-wrapped beef roast."

"Clever," Max said, clapping his hands in enthusiasm.

"Future travel—nothing until June," Julian said, mixing the traditional duxelles of minced mushrooms sauteed and deglazed with Madeira for Kris's creation.

"What's happening in June?" Jana asked.

"Julian wants to go to New York City for the 53rd annual pride march," Max shared.

"What's so special about this one?" she asked.

"Nothing," Julian said. "We just haven't been to New York for one in over 20 years."

"We should all go," Kris suggested, adding the protective barrier layer of country ham over the tenderloins. "Frank and Ina would love it if we all went."

"I only met them that one time—I would really enjoy getting to spend more time with them," Jana said, retrieving the ingredients she needed from the fridge for her dessert. Then she paused, a memory of something tickling her brain.

Julian leaned over her way, nudging her from her thoughts, inspecting the items on the counter where she'd set up to start her dessert. "I thought you were making Fudge Truffle Cheesecake?" he questioned.

"Oh, I was—but when I found out Kris was making individual beef Wellingtons, I decided to make individual desserts too. So I'm making Chocolate Lava Cakes." She took a quick glimpse Kris's way.

"My favorite!" Kris tossed out, as he added the outer cloak of puff pastry to his masterpiece.

"A little birdy told me that," Jana said, winking at Julian. "And I'm making chocolate-covered strawberries, but they take 2 hours to set so those can be a treat for later in the evening." She winked at Julian again, then laughed. She giggled, in fact, because she was having a fabulous time with them chatting and cooking together. The *together* being the best part.

Kris smiled warmly at her then said, "Alright, my part is done—30 minutes in the oven, then we let them rest for 10 minutes before serving."

"I've never had this dish," Jana said, placing the four greased and floured ramekins aside. Then once again she scrapped down the inner-sides of the double boiler containing the melting butter and chocolate. "My cakes will take about 10-13 minutes and need to cool for 5, so I won't put them in until yours is halfway done."

"That will be perfect," Kris stated. "I can check the internal temperature then. The goal for the beef is rare to almost medium-rare and when the thermometer registers at 115 degrees Fahrenheit."

"I'm preparing classic mashed potatoes and a zesty arugula salad to go with it," Julian added, pulling the salad ingredients from the fridge. "Potatoes are already cooking." He pointed to the large pot bubbling on the stove.

"Did I mention I bought fresh bread and picked up an elegant Bordeaux wine to go with the meal?" Max declared, sharing his contribution to the lovely dinner being made.

"Yes you did, Dear," Julian confirmed, ruffling his husband's hair and kissing him on the cheek. "The Chateau Fonplegade will be a satisfying addition to the meal."

Max grasped Julian by the arm, then gently drew him closer for a more passionate kiss. "You are what satisfies me," Max declared to Julian.

Overhearing Max's words, Jana glanced over at Kris. When she saw he was already watching her, an unexpected flush warmed her body. Kris gave her a wicked smile, as though he knew how she was feeling. Flustered, Jana quickly looked away and turned on the electric mixer to beat the sugar and eggs she'd added to the large mixing bowl Julian had gotten out for her. Then she combined the melted chocolate and the other ingredients before pouring the batter into the prepared ramekins. Images of intimate touching and passionate kissing from her time alone with Kris rushed across her mind as she did her best to maintain her composure.

"Let me help you with that, *Hun*," Julian said, startling her yet saving her from her imaginings. "We'll put the ramekins on a baking tray, so they are ready to go in."

When everything was done and had rested the appropriate amount of time, Julian and Max prepared portable trays with the special dinner for each of them, such that they could transport their individual meals to their private dining spaces.

Before Jana and Kris left the kitchen with their trays, Max said, "I set up TV tables in your living room, Kris—for you to set your trays on." Then he placed one of the bottles of wine he'd procured under Kris's arm for him to take with us. "There's more if you need it," Max said as he placed wine glasses on our trays.

"I almost forgot," Kris said, adjusting his arm grip on the bottle while still holding the tray.

"Thank you, Max," Jana said, appreciate of his kindness.

"Have a wonderful evening, you two," Max said as he followed Julian, the love of his life out of the kitchen.

Jana rested back in her seat on the couch, contented and full from the dinner, the dessert, and the wine.

"I'm going to get another bottle of the Bordeaux," Kris said. "I'll be right back."

"Grab some of the chocolate-covered strawberries too," Jana said as he went out the door into the main living space. She didn't need more wine. She was already feeling the effects from the first bottle.

Feeling *bold* as well, she got up from the couch and proceeded up the stairs to Kris's bedroom. She'd only ever been in his room that one time when she'd first arrived, although she'd thought about being in bed with Kris many times.

Through the doorway into Kris's bedroom she saw that nothing had changed, and it was neat and tidy like it had been the first time. But then noticed as she panned the room that there were a few more pillows on his bed, and there was another framed photo on the mostly empty bookshelves.

Jana crossed the room and picked up the new photo. It was one of her and Kris in an embrace from the night of her birthday party. She smiled, happy to see the addition, and ran a hand around the edge of the frame. Jana set the photo back on the shelf, then focused her attention on the one of Frank and Kris from the gay pride event in New York. *"What?"* she murmured, seizing the frame from the shelf. The banner displayed the words 30th Annual Pride March on it, sending Jana's wine fogged brain into a spin. *"Hadn't Julian said they were going to attend the 53rd annual pride march?"* she questioned, mumbling to herself. *"How can this be from 23 years ago?"* Jana stared at the photo. Frank looked almost the same, though her hair had been shaved close to her scalp and died purple, but other than a slightly longer hairstyle, Kris looked exactly the same.

"Jana," she heard Kris call from the lower level, followed by his footfalls up the stairs.

"Here you are," he said, smiling at her, open wine bottle in one hand, chocolate strawberries on a plate in the other.

Still holding the pride photo, she said, "I'm going to ask you a strange question."

"Okay, I'll try to answer it," Kris said with a shrug.

"When you were in Iceland, I bought you some toiletries, deodorant, shampoo… and shaving products."

"I remember," he said, setting the wine bottle and plate on the nightstand next to the bed.

"Now I know you used the deodorant and shampoo because I could smell them on you. But…." Jana paused her words taking a step closer to get a better look at him. "You never showed stubble on your face, but I don't recall you ever using the razors and shave cream." She took another step closer, examining his face. Then she glanced down at his exposed forearms. "And you don't have any hair on your arms or legs," she said, recalling how bare his legs had been when he had worn shorts.

"I…," Kris began. "I never used the razor, correct." He stared back at her for a halted moment. "It seems I have extremely slow hair growth, and well, I don't have hair anywhere other than my head and face—I can grow a beard and mustache but it's very slow—not sure why—it's just always been that way," he added fumbling out his words. "It's a genetic variance, Nic told me, like with my sensitivity to sulfur, it's an anomaly."

"Kris—are you up there?" came Nic's frantic voice from the lower level, then he appeared in the doorway to the bedroom.

"Jana," he said, noticing her. "Sorry to interrupt—but Mason is on his way here with Natalie." Nic stared at Kris with an intensity she'd never witnessed on him in the time she'd been staying here.

"Why is Mason bringing her here?" Kris questioned, his eyebrows pinching.

"She was supposed to be hosting a party at her home—but when Mason arrived to help with the decorations, she told him she hadn't been feeling well—then shortly after she said her upper back was paining her."

"How far away are they?" Kris asked.

"Should be here any minute," Nic confirmed.

"Maybe you should call Jules to come over here," Kris suggested, then he glanced over at Jana. "Looks like you'll get to meet your sister sooner than we thought."

A loud whistle echoed then up through the stairwell and into the open door of the bedroom. "That's Mason," Nic said, quickly turning and descending the stairs back down.

"Stay here," Kris said, rushing off after Nic.

Jana remained where she was, her mind still fuzzy from the wine and reeling over the confusion over the photo and what Kris had just shared about more of his abnormalities. "I got her," Jana heard Nic yell, followed by the pounding of footsteps so loud Jana could hear them through the walls that divided Kris's room from that of Zach's next door.

"What's happening?" Jana asked when Kris reentered the bedroom.

"We think Natalie is having some kind of allergic reaction," Kris said, his words not making any sense to her. "She's stable for now."

"Why aren't you taking her to the hospital?" Jana questioned, uncertainty flooding her.

"Remember we told you about Natalie having those unique genes?"

"Yes, but?" Jana shook her head.

"Well, apparently Natalie used some antibiotic cream her friend Tina gave her for an acne breakout—the cream contained sulfur."

"She has the same allergy you have? Wait, are you one of these people too—who carries the rare gene?"

"Yes, I guess you could say that." Kris turned his attention to the doorway as Mason entered the room. "Where's Lane?" Kris asked him.

Mason shrugged, then signed something too complicated for Jana to understand.

"Thought she was going to the party with you?" Kris questioned.

Mason glanced at her, then to Kris, signing what Jana interpreted as, "See you later," but then realized it meant Lane would see *him* later. Then Mason was gone again out the bedroom door, the sound of pounding footsteps ensuing shortly after as he returned to Zach's room.

Jana ran her hands over her temples and through her hair, struggling to keep her wits. When Kris just stood there staring at her, she dropped her hands, letting her arms hang at her sides. Then she took several slow strides to stand in front of him. Staring up into his face, she asked, "How old are you?"

"It's not polite to ask a person their age," he said in a lighthearted feminine lilt.

"Julian said the pride march in June would be the 53rd—but that photo…." Jana peered over her shoulder at the bookshelf and pointed. Turning back, she said, "The banner said 30th annual pride march—that would mean the photo was taken in 2000." Jana noted the moment the realization hit Kris, his expression changing from teasing to one of remorse.

"Jana," Kris implored, placing his hands at her elbows.

"Explain to me how you *and* Frank look as though you haven't aged a day in almost 23 years," Jana demanded, staring up at him.

"I can explain," Kris said, rubbing the sides of her arms.

Jana shrugged his hands away and stepped back. "I assumed you were close in age to me—but even if you were 40, that would put you in your teens when this was taken—and you are definitely not a teenager in this photo—nor is Frank." She walked over and stood next to the photo on the shelf. "Tell me it's a tribute to that year—something you and Frank did for fun at the restaurant in New York." Jana's heart pounded in her chest as she waited for his answer.

Kris took a tentative step towards her. "Remember when you told me about Superman—the books—the movies—the TV shows etc. and I didn't recall any of it?"

Jana frowned. "Yes—what does that have to do with this photo?"

He took another cautious step in her direction. "I know who Superman is now—it all came back with my memories. How he was from Krypton—his archenemy was Lex Luthor—and how kryptonite was poisonous and could even kill Kryptonians," Kris rambled out.

"What are you talking about?" she questioned, clearer headed, no longer feeling the effects of the wine.

"Kind of like what sulfur does to me," he said, as though it made any more sense.

"And?" she asked, frustration consuming her now.

Kris took another step forward. "And… even Superman had a day job."

"Is this some kind of joke?" Jana threw her hands in the air. "Whatever, Kris, I'm starting to think your allergic reaction stole more than just your memories—it may have robbed you of your sanity, too." She glanced at the photo of her and Kris, then tapped the frame of the pride photo. "Still, it doesn't explain this photo."

Pain-filled cries penetrated through the barrier between bedrooms, jerking Jana's and Kris's attention over to the far wall.

Without hesitation, Jana pushed past Kris to the doorway, then took the stairs two at a time. Kris followed close behind as she went through the already open door into Zach's suite and up the stairs to the bedroom. Through the doorway, Jana spotted Nic next to a woman on the bed, *Natalie*. She was shirtless, her back facing them. Jules was on the other side of the bed, holding Natalie's arms. "What are you doing?" Jana demanded.

"They are trying to help her," Kris said, coming to stand behind Jana, gently wrapping his arms around her.

Jana gave into the comfort and leaned back into Kris as he embraced her. "What's happening to her?"

"She's transforming," Nic said, moving down the bed to brace Natalie's legs.

Jana drew in a quick breath. "What in heaven's name…?" Jana said on the exhale, stunned speechless, watching as the skin on her sister's back reddened then altered to purple. Deafening screams tore from Natalie's lungs then as the skin of her back morphed to black and then ripped open as white bony protrusions burst free from the wounds.

Chapter 36 

Lane stared down at the text on her cellphone from Lyndon, the one he'd sent saying he would *love* to see her. She had told Mason she was going to meet him at Natalie's party, but she was too eager to see Lyndon, especially after all this time apart.

When she pulled her car into the parking lot of the group home, she sent a text to Lyndon.

I'm here. Meet you at the elevator?

She'd mentioned the elevator in hopes they could go down to his apartment. Taylor would already be in bed by now, though her intentions were to talk with Lyndon alone. Moments later, a message came back from Lyndon.

He'd written,

I will send up the elevator to you.

Which indicated he was already down in his apartment, and even better Lane thought, with not having to suggest they go down.

Lane grabbed for the present she'd gotten Lyndon from the passenger seat, then exited her car. Using her security fob, she went into the group home. The elevator was already waiting for her when she reached the end of the hall.

Riding the lift down to the lower level, she took off her winter jacket, then drew in a cleansing breath to settle her nerves. As she exited the elevator, she half expected to see Lyndon waiting for her in the doorway to his apartment. But when she came up to the door, she found that it wasn't just closed; it was locked. Without hesitating, she knocked twice and then waited. The sound of the lock disengaging was followed by the doorknob twisting, but the door only opened enough that Lane could see that lights were on in the apartment. It wasn't like Lyndon to not greet her at the door, so she pushed it open further before taking a step inside.

From the doorway, Lane could see Lyndon was sitting in his armchair, his legs extended, feet resting on the ottoman. He was wearing dark blue jeans similar in shade to the ones she had on and a t-shirt in her favorite colour on him, forest green, that played off the colour of his eyes. "Hi," she said, stepping into the apartment, feeling a tad timid.

"Hi," Lyndon said in return. "Come have a seat." He patted the armchair next to him, the one she had come to accept as *hers*.

Lane hung her jacket on a free hook near the door, then took off her boots before striding across the short distance to the small lounge area set up next to the bookshelf. Without sitting, she handed him the gift she'd brought. "Happy Valentine's day." She smiled at him, but he did not smile back.

"You brought me a gift?" he questioned, frowning and reaching for the red paper-wrapped package, the colour matching the deep red sweater she wore.

Lane stood there watching as he unwrapped her gift, his scowl transforming into one of astonishment. His face brightened, and he smiled, staring down at the framed photo Lane had taken of him and Taylor. "Thought it would be nice to have a photo of the two of you here in your… home," Lane said, still feeling nervous.

Lyndon placed his feet on the floor and slid forward in his seat. "I've never done Valentine's day," he said, gazing up at her. "Sorry, I didn't get you anything."

Normally she was the one gazing up at him. "It doesn't matter — I'm more interested in just time with you, anyway."

"Sit," he said, patting the chair next to him again.

Lane dropped her purse next to her chair, then sat silently observing Lyndon as he stared lovingly at the framed photo. Then he turned in his seat towards the bookshelf. As though to make room, Lyndon shoved a loose stack of books upright and against the side of the shelf, then he set the frame in the new open space. He stared at it for a moment, then turned back to look at her. "Thank you. It's a thoughtful gift."

Lane just smiled, unsure of what to say. Something felt different with him, but she couldn't put her finger on it. "How have you been?" she asked, hating they weren't talking like they usually did. She thought she might give him a hug this time when she saw him, but he hadn't even greeted her at the door.

"Busy," Lyndon said, staring at her.

"Is everything alright? You seem… *distant*," she said, but it was more than that.

"I have a lot on my mind." He glanced over at the photo on the shelf.

"Anything I can help with?" Lane questioned when he lingered on the photo. When he didn't answer, she reached out and touched his hand, the one resting on the arm of the chair.

His focus instantly returned to her, staring down at his hand where she was touching him.

Lane squeezed his hand and immediately, as though instinctively, he placed his other hand atop hers. When he raised his beautiful green eyes to look into hers, she shifted from her seat onto the ottoman in front of him. "I missed you," she said in a shy voice, shifting and leaning forward so their knees touched.

He opened his mouth as if to say something, then paused to look down at their joined hands.

"Lyndon?"

He glanced up as though bewildered.

"Remember when you asked me if I had ever witnessed something *otherworldly?*"

Lyndon stared back down at their hands. "That was nothing," he said, like he was brushing it off. "I feel silly for even bringing it up."

Lane was trying to give him an opening to share more with her. She knew everything, but she needed for him to *want* to tell her. She feared if she told him the truth, that she'd known about him all along, he might kick her out and that would be the end of things. Lane didn't want to take that risk. She knew—she had known for some time that she'd already fallen hard for him, and she wasn't willing to lose him. "If I tell you a secret—would you share one of yours with me?" It was a long shot, but she was running out of options to get him to talk.

He tilted his head, his expression this time unreadable. "What secrets could you possibly have, Lane?" he asked, his tone cynical.

Lane drew in a long breath and then said, "I want to kiss you." She shifted her gaze to his full lips, but he didn't smile like she hoped he would. Then she glanced back to his eyes to find them shut tight. Embarrassment flooding her, Lane realized then she'd been too forward and had mistaken his feelings for her. She went to pull her hand free, but instead of letting her go, Lyndon held her hand tighter and opened his eyes.

Tears pooled at the corners of them as he gazed longingly into hers. "Lane," he said then, her name spoken as though he were in pain.

Her breath caught in her throat, but she wouldn't falter this time, and she quickly leaned forward, pressing her lips against Lyndon's. As his warm mouth welcomed hers, she pressed deeper into the kiss.

Lane heard her cellphone chime in her purse and Lyndon broke their connection, resting his forehead gently against hers. "You should get that," he said in a low voice.

"It can wait," Lane countered, pressing her mouth against his once more. Her phone chimed again, then a third time, but she didn't stop. She had been wanting to kiss him like this for so long.

"What if it's your parents?" Lyndon said, taking a breath.

"It's probably just Mason," she said, stealing another kiss. "I told him I'd meet him at the party—but I changed my mind. He'll be fine— he has a crush on the girl hosting the party."

Lyndon stared at her mouth, then licked his lips. "I've thought about kissing you as well." He leaned back to look at her fully. "Let me make you dinner," he said then. "It will be my Valentine's day gift to you." He kissed her quick then stood. "Have you eaten already?" he asked excitedly, sidestepping out from behind the ottoman and walking to the kitchen.

"No, I haven't, and I am hungry," Lane said, though she was hungry for more than just food now. But she was pleased at the change in his disposition.

Lyndon opened several cupboards and then checked the fridge. "How about pasta?" he asked, glancing over, holding the fridge door open.

"Pasta is my favorite." Lane smiled at him. She really did love pasta.

This time, he smiled back at her. "Great—I already have everything I need to prepare it." Lyndon pulled out cherry tomatoes, butter, and parmesan cheese from the fridge. Then he retrieved a box of farfel pasta and a large bottle of extra-virgin olive oil from the cupboard above the stove. He set all the ingredients on the large cutting board, then pulled free a pot for the pasta and a large skillet for what Lane figured was for whatever sauce he was going to make.

Lyndon's cellphone vibrated once on the kitchen counter then chimed notification of a text or email, Lane assumed. It always vibrated and rang when it was a call, but still she stood and let out a sigh, believing her time with him would be cut short now.

But then, when Lyndon checked his phone, instead of responding back, he did something unexpected.

"Did you just shut off your phone?" Lane asked as he set his phone down on the counter.

"Yes, I don't want to be bothered this evening," he said, taking a lemon from the decorative bowl on the counter near his phone.

"Can you do that?" she asked, walking past the small dining table next to the short end of the L-shaped kitchen counter.

"I just did," Lyndon said, before tearing a few leaves of fresh basil from the tiny potted plant next to the sink. Then he proceeded to fill the pot with water and then placed it on a stove burner to heat up.

"Will you let me help?" Lane asked, leaning her elbows on the counter.

"If you like," Lyndon said, then handed her a garlic bulb and a state-of-the-art garlic press. "You can press the garlic."

"How many?" she asked, enjoying their interactions.

"All of them," he said. "I hope you like garlic."

"I love it actually," Lane said. "And it's best if both parties like it if there's going to be more kissing." She laughed when he stared wide-eyed at her.

"Makes sense," he said with a playful smile.

Lane joked and flirted with him as he prepared their meal. "Your butt looks cute in those jeans," she said boldly, grabbing placemats, napkins and cutlery to take over to the dining table.

"Stooop," Lyndon said teasingly, as though trying to stay focused on heating the olive oil in the skillet. He tossed in some red pepper flakes into the oil, allowing them to bloom.

They continued to banter back and forth as Lyndon added the garlic Lane had pressed, along with the cherry tomatoes he'd cut into halves into the mix, topping it off with the fresh basil, butter and parmesan. Before draining the pasta, he scooped about 1/2 cup of the pasta water from the pot then poured it into the skillet to thicken the sauce. "The pasta is al dente," Lyndon said, adding the drained pasta into the skillet. "It will cook for 2-3 minutes—then it will be ready." Ending his skillful cooking, Lyndon squeezed fresh lemon juice over the pasta and then stirred, coating everything with sauce.

Lane opened the fridge and pulled out the pitcher of water. Then she filled two tall glasses and brought them to the table.

"Ready?" Lyndon asked as he plated the pasta.

"Absolutely," Lane said, taking her seat at the table.

As Lyndon set the dinner plate in front of her, he leaned down and kissed her gently on the lips, lingering a moment before pulling away.

"Delicious," Lane said, staring at him as he set down his plate and sat.

"You haven't even tasted it yet," he said, chuckling and unfolding his napkin.

"Oh, but I have," Lane said, giving him a flirtatious wink.

"Eeeat!" Lyndon said, shaking his head.

"You like it," Lane countered, raising an eyebrow.

"I do—now eat your food," he admitted.

Lane did as she was told, and she was grateful she did. The food was absolutely amazing, and she didn't say another word until her very last bite. "Lyndon, you are a fabulous cook." Lane licked the last bit of sauce off her fork.

"I do like to cook." He shrugged. "But I enjoy it most when cooking for you," he confessed.

"I'm serious—you could be a professional chef," Lane praised. "Have you ever thought about doing it—cooking professionally?"

"Me, naaw," he said, shaking his head, standing and removing their plates from the table. Lyndon set the dinnerware into the sink, ran some water over the dishes, then quickly returned to the table. "Come, let's get more comfortable," he said, offering her his hand.

Lane took his hand and allowed him to lead her back to the lounging area. When Lyndon sat in his worn leather chair, she plopped down in her newer one and gave her full tummy a rub. "Is it the money?" she asked, taking a chance at getting to the heart of why he remained working for Thaddeus.

"What?"

"The reason you stay working for that guy?"

"No," he said, extending his long legs and resting his feet on the ottoman. "I have plenty of money."

Lane extended her legs too, tapping her sock foot with his. "If you have money, why do you stay here—in the basement apartment?"

"I stay because I'm afraid of what will happen to Taylor and to this place if I leave."

"So you stay for the group home *and* Taylor?" Lane had shared part of what she knew the first time they had talked about him, but she knew the full story as to how Taylor had come to be there. He had been given back to Children's Services when Thaddeus had determined he was defective, having been diagnosed with autism. He had been born with an enlarged ribcage and vocal cord damage, along with missing the lower part of his legs, but now he needed specialized care. She also knew about the unusual birthmarks he had on his shoulder blades.

"Yes," Lyndon said, placing his forearm on the armrest and leaning her way. "This is his home… and it's my home now, too.

"Then why don't you take him out of here—make a new home somewhere else—just the two of you?" Lane questioned. She honestly didn't understand why he would stay.

"Again, it's complicated." Lyndon reached for her hand.

"Tell me," she said, taking hold of his outstretched hand.

"I have other duties that often take me away and I can't always watch over him." Lyndon rubbed the back of her hand with his thumb. "He is in good hands here—the staff, they adore him, and he loves them. I can't directly provide the care he needs like the trained professionals here can. And I'm certainly no doctor, but he has special physical requirements and conditions that will change as he grows and gets older, as well." He gave her a woeful smile.

"Then maybe get your own private home, and just volunteer here instead, like me," Lane said, shifting in her seat to lean his way.

Lyndon squeezed her hand. "Taylor needs me… and I need to be more than just a volunteer for him."

Lane frowned, then huffed. "You act as though you have to atone for something. Is protecting Taylor your penance?" Lane brought her other hand over to hold his in both of hers.

"No—I just don't trust him," he said, glancing at their hands.

Lane narrowed her eyes. "Who, Thaddeus?" she said angrily.

"Yes—he's a wretched… *person*," Lyndon spat out, continuing to gaze at their hands.

"Stop working for him—it's like an albatross hanging over you robbing you of your peace," Lane said, her anger for his boss rising.

Lyndon looked at her this time. "I can't… not yet." He shook his head once.

"So what—you think if you stop working for him—he'll do something to Taylor?" she said, rushing out her conviction.

"Yes," he said forcefully.

"For what reason?" She frowned and shook her head.

"To punish me," he said, softer this time, returning to look at Lane's hands.

"Because why?" Lane demanded, giving his hand a gentle tug.

Lyndon glanced up at her once again, unease spreading across his handsome, scarred face. Then he said, "Because… he's my *son*."

Chapter 37 

Home Office of Dr. Grier Stone, February 14th, South Florida

He was never late. So why had Grier checked the clock on the wall half a dozen times in the past five minutes? She knew he would be on time because she had been treating him twice a week for over 5 months, and he was her last appointment of the day. He'd requested a later appointment time than usual, asking if they could do their session today at 7 p.m. versus their earlier time on Fridays.

When Grier had moved north from the fast-paced city of Miami up to the small beach town just south of Vero Beach, the tiny beach cottage had been the perfect purchase for two reasons; one she wanted an actual house versus the high-rise style apartment she had normally lived in, and two, it had a converted lower level space that she was pleasantly surprised made for an excellent home office, it having a separate entrance for patients in the carport under the stilted home. The interior renovation had been beautifully done. Just past the entry into the now-office, on the right was a tiny half-bath, on the left was a small kitchenette/coffee bar and an under-counter fridge with bottled water, and a variety of teas and coffee set up for her patients. The large open office space had simple décor and a look of what you would expect for this sort of practice. There were two high-back armchairs in a neutral shade of beige, facing a lengthy sofa in a similar fabric, separated by a sleek, modern looking coffee table. Behind the sofa was an equally modern style desk and chair. Behind the desk space against the wall was a large bookcase filled with a variety of books in regard to her area of study and research, along with a few seaside knickknacks she had picked up at a local home décor store. The laundry machines that had been in this space prior had been replaced with a stacking washer and dryer set and moved to the main house in a spot between her ensuite bathroom and walk-in closet. No personal items were in the room, other than several framed degrees that hung on the wall to the left of the bookcase. Nothing to imply this was anything other than the professional space it was meant to be and not an extension of her personal home.

Anxious, Grier moved from her desk and headed for the door even before she heard the knock. Opening the door, she paused, taken aback by the sight of him. Grier had always been considered petite, so his height of what had to be over 6′ 4″ only dwarfed her further. He was a fit, muscular man in what she had assumed was in his mid-30s, well-groomed with short dark hair parted to one side, a more professional looking cut compared to his usual casual attire of dark jeans and white t-shirt, though she appreciated the contrast. She took in a deep breath, then swallowed. "Good afternoon, Zuriel. Please come in," she directed, using her best professional voice.

"Dr. Stone, please call me Z," he said, offering her his usual magnificent smile that traveled from his sensual lips up to his equally magnificent pearl-grey eyes. A gentle ocean breeze passed through the open door, carrying the scent of him with it. He always smelled of freshly laundered clothes and vanilla, mixed with a faint masculine earthy scent.

Get ahold of yourself, Grier—professional, she reminded herself. She smiled in response to his request as he entered through the doorway and continued on to his regular spot on the sofa. Grier followed behind, using the moment to gather herself.

Sitting down now across from him in one of the professional wingback chairs, she reached for the tools she used during her sessions from off the coffee table that separated them. Her methods may seem a little old-school to some of her patients, using a pencil and notepad, but she found it removed the disconnect that was often created when clacking away on a laptop while a patient poured out their fears and feelings to her.

"I watched over another last night," Zuriel started, jumping right into things, even before she could get her notepad open.

"Now, Zuriel," she interjected, stopping the same dialog he had used in many of their sessions prior.

"Z," he reminded her with a salacious grin, the corners of his gorgeous eyes crinkling.

She forced herself to look down, but the sound of his voice alone captured her, leaving her searching for her words. With her eyes focused on the new blank page of her notepad, she retraced the date she had just written. Taking in a deep breath, she centered her thoughts. "Zuriel," she began again, ignoring once more the variation of his name he had requested. "We've talked about dreams. These are just that, dreams—they are not real. We've worked on this for several months now, yet you're still not willing to accept these facts." Still, she kept her eyes down, knowing his expression would be stern. She had seen it many times, his eyebrows knitting together, not from her comments, but from her use of his name.

"What fact?" he asked, as if goading her.

She glanced up, letting her focus go to the bookshelf at the far wall. "That dreams are not real, and that you are not an angel sent to… watch over." She had numerous journals on dream studies and dream interpretation, and she had even written an article on it for the APA. But she knew what was coming next, knew he understood, and she also knew that he liked this game. She wasn't sure why she let him play it, but she did. She shifted in her seat then, crossing her legs and pressing her spine against the back of the chair, returning her focus to the notepad on her lap.

"Fallen… angel," he stated, saying the word fallen as if it were painful for him to speak. That voice of his, smooth and masculine, sounded as if next to her ear. A whisper of warm breath brushed her skin, causing her to glance up.

His expression was smug, as if pleased with himself, almost as though he had read her thoughts, and a smirk had replaced his smile this time, she noticed.

Professional Grier, she recited in her head. "Yes, I know — you keep telling me this. That you believe you're a fallen angel and that it's your job to watch over those in need." Feigning calm, she reached a hand up to touch her earlobe, the one she swore she had just felt his breath caress.

His pleased expression faded, replaced then by firm words. "I don't believe I'm a fallen angel — I am a fallen angel." He leaned forward, placing the palms of his hands flat upon the coffee table as if to push further his statement and conviction.

A small sigh escaped her as she recognized his desperate need for her to believe him. She took in a breath. "Why do you think you're a fallen angel?" she questioned, breathing out, trying to keep her breathing steady yet still playing her usual move in this game. She took in another deep breath, preparing herself for more.

"Why do you think I'm not?" he shot back, before she could go on, countering her move.

Diverting her eyes, she refocused again on the mostly blank page of her notepad. It was her move. "Do you have proof that you're an angel?" She glanced up then, letting her breath out slowly.

"Do you have proof that I'm not?" he answered, leaning back, settling against the couch again. He steepled his fingers in his lap as if he had announced *checkmate*.

She looked down, pretending to be making notes, flipping pages as if reviewing past entries, all the while trying to devise something professional or at least something clever to say back, but she had zilch.

When she said nothing, he went on with detailing everything in the same way he had in their other sessions, this time explaining who and how he had helped those in need since his last appointment with her. She kept her eyes on the pad as he continued, nodding occasionally and jotting down notes on each experience he shared. The banter went on between them for the next 40 minutes. Then Zuriel paused his recalling, and then said, "I was in your dreams last night." His voice was low and throaty, an almost growl. His hand unexpectedly touched hers and she glanced up.

She hadn't realized he had moved, but he was now sitting in the chair next to her, no longer on the couch across as he had been moments ago. She hadn't been startled by this shift in the space between them. In fact, she was surprisingly calm, even with the sensation of his warm strong fingers stroking over the back of her hand. She was surprised by his touch, but what surprised her more was how his contact eased her. She blushed then, feeling her cheeks blazing with heat as she attempted to gather her wits. "Don't be ridiculous...," she said, stopping short, caught in his gaze as he stared at her, into her, transfixing her.

He spoke again. "I was there… you know I was." The sound of his voice soothed her. His tone was firm, yet his words caressed like that of a lover's touch, and she was suddenly blanketed in what felt like a full body blush of heat. When his hand heated against hers, she pulled it away, scrambling for what little composure she had left.

With her eyes back on her notepad, she said, "I rarely dream. If you were in my dreams—I would know it." She blew out a breath. "Besides—I am not in need," she lied. The words stung her tongue as she looked up again. Her palms were sweaty, and her cheeks burned again. Very professional, Grier, she chided herself.

"Oh, but you are," he contested. A sensual smile joined his smug conviction.

"Cling-Cling," went the old-fashioned wall clock she used to keep her sessions on schedule.

Saved, yet still unable to form an intelligent response, Grier stood and began moving swiftly towards the office door. She stopped and placed her hand on the doorknob, but before she could turn the knob, Zuriel's warm hand covered hers. His breath trailed across the back of her neck, and she shivered, letting out the tiniest gasp.

"Wear your hair down tonight," he whispered against her ear. Then he removed his hand from atop hers, allowing her to continue with opening the door.

Nervously, she reached her other hand up to pat the braid she always had twisted up into a tight bun. She never wore it loose, at least not in front of patients. Giving no response to his comment, Grier turned the knob and yanked open the door, desperate for more than just the cool ocean air. "I'll see you next Tuesday, Zuriel," she said in as professional a voice as she could muster. "And please, think about what we discussed."

Without another word, he passed through the open door, striding through the carport, but then stopped halfway. He turned, glancing back at her with that knowing stare he often gave her.

She gave him back her best poker-face, despite the growing weakness in her composure and in her knees. "See you next week," she added, before closing the door. She leaned against it and blew out the breath she had been holding. He couldn't know about her dreams, could he, she wondered. He was playing with her, she was sure of it. But why?

He had come to her seeking help, hadn't he? She had taken him on as a patient, hoping to relieve him of these delusions, but they were no further along on that mission, even after so many sessions. She had explained to him he was human, emphasizing it by stating, "*Why would an angel be visiting a psychiatrist?*" All he had said to her in response was, "*Yes, why indeed?*" And she had been dreaming about him — lustful dreams, which had made each new appointment with him increasingly difficult. Cursing aloud, she touched the back of her neck and then her ear, recalling the caress of his breath, the memory causing her to shiver again.

Before bed, Grier changed out of her clothes and into her pale blue terry bathrobe. Then she went through the nightly ritual of washing her face, brushing her teeth, and flossing, and then securing back her waist-length hair. Pulling her long coppery tresses over her shoulder, she crisscrossed the divided sections, capturing them into a lengthy braid. She left the ensuite bath into her bedroom in pursuit of changing into something comfy for bed.

Like always with her routine, she opened the top drawer of her dresser to grab one of her many Dr. Seuss themed nightshirts, but then she hesitated, glancing down to the bottom drawer. Changing her usual habit, she pushed the top drawer back in without selecting something to wear, then bent down to pull out the bottom drawer.

A soft breath escaped her as she brushed her palm across a lavender silk negligee that was folded neatly within the drawer. This one she had purchased more than a year ago, foolishly hopeful of potential romance in her future. Sadly, it had yet to be worn. Her last intimate relationship had been over three years ago, and since then she had moved homes, changed cities even, and had buried herself in work, focusing on research and patient treatment, leaving little time to even meet someone new. On a whim, instead of donning her usual nightly garb, she pulled the delicate piece of clothing from its confines. She removed her bathrobe, draping it temporarily over the chair next to the dresser, then slid the nightgown over herself.

The silken fabric cooled like cream over her warm skin. Standing in front of the floor-length mirror next to the dresser, she admired how the fabric smoothed over her curves. The colour was perfect for her; the shade complementing her complexion and hair. Yawning then, she took one last look at herself in the mirror before grabbing up her bathrobe and hanging it on the back of the bathroom door.

Before climbing into bed, she hesitated again. This time to loosen her hair from its plait, running her fingers through the long wavy tresses to release it. She then slipped between the sheets and giggled, noting each rebellion to her usual routine. After a quick plumping of the pillows behind her head, she reached for a book from her nightstand. Grier considered reading the latest novel from her favorite paranormal romance author as her guilty pleasure. She gave another yawn, adjusted the tiny lamp at her bedside, and then opened the book.

Something jarred the bed, and she startled, sitting up abruptly. She must have dozed off, she considered. But then swiftly realized that the bulb in the bedside lamp must have burned out, because with having the window blinds lowered she was in complete darkness with no moonlight to bathe the room.

"You wore your hair down," spoke a dreamy—yet familiar voice through the darkness.

She should have been frightened, but she wasn't. The timbre of the voice calmed her. She had heard it in her dreams before, and in her office. "Zuriel," she breathed out.

"Z, please," he whispered from the dark.

Her skin grew warmer at the sound of his voice, and she threw back the duvet bedcover in response, leaving only the top sheet covering her body. She could see nothing through the darkness, though she knew she had heard him, and she knew his scent. That glorious masculine scent, clean and sensual, and delicious. She could almost taste it.

There was movement then on the bed as her remaining covers began sliding gently away and off her body.

"Dr. Stone."

"Call me Grier, please," she purred sleepily.

A buzzing noise sounded near her head. "What is that?" she said, annoyed, her eyes still shut.

Then she opened her eyes and sat up, dropping her book to the floor. Stunned, she gazed around her dimly lit bedroom to see her bedside lamp was still on. Shifting her attention, she cut a glance in the direction of the noise. Her cell phone vibrated next to her on the nightstand. Grabbing it, she recognized it was the hospital calling, but then the vibrating stopped. She'd missed the call. Staring at the screen, she watched as the tiny icon for a voice message appeared in the upper left-hand corner. Then she hit the voicemail button and listened to the message.

In the message, the nurse explained they'd had a situation with a patient refusing to take their meds, that he wouldn't take them without the doctor present. She hit save on the message just in case, then checked the time on the phone. It was 3 a.m. and clearly several hours before her usual wake-up time. Sadly, she realized she had been dreaming again. She'd had vivid dreams in the past, but never had they been like these, nor had they been so sensual as with her midnight visitor, and never so real.

Shaking it off, she scrambled to get dressed in her typical work clothes of dark slacks and one of her many light-coloured tailored blouses. Then she pulled back her hair into a tidy bun. Passing through the living room, she snatched up her purse and keys from the sofa table, and then was off and out the door.

Twenty minutes later, she was parked and walking through the main doors of the hospital's psychiatric wing. As she rushed through the entrance, she gave a hurried wave of the faculty badge to the night guard she had hung around her neck, and he buzzed her in. On the short drive over, she had called to tell them she was on the way, so he had been expecting her. She had been on call for this location for months now, but this was the first time they had called her to come in for anything.

As Grier rounded the corner near the nurses' station, she almost ran straight into a young nurse in light green scrubs holding a computer tablet. Next to her stood a young male orderly of substantial stature. Both stood just in the doorway of the first patient room. Peering past them, she saw a frail young man in his early 20s, wearing white pajamas, sitting on the end of a bed.

He grinned up at her. "Now I can take my medication," he agreed, reaching out for the pill cup the nurse had been holding in her hand. After gulping down the pills with the water that had accompanied them, he grinned up at Grier again. With a yawn, he crawled into his bed, pulling up the plain white covers to his chin much like a child would. With the heavy sedative in his system now, the patient rapidly drifted off to sleep.

"He has never refused his meds before, Dr. Stone," the nurse stated, glancing up from Grier's security badge. "We've been trying to get him to take them since before lights-out at 10:00 p.m. The other patients, due to the ruckus he readily makes, wouldn't get proper sleep if he didn't. We were running out of options, so that's why we paged you—sorry."

"No worries. It's my first call. If he acts up again, consider an earlier time for meds, perhaps a half dose at dinner, topping him up at lights-out," Grier stated, trying to reassure the nurse.

Alarms suddenly began sounding from down the hall.

"Nurse!" an orderly called, exiting from a patient room down at the end of the hall. "The monitors on the angel are going off."

"What?" Grier questioned, following the young nurse as she took off in the direction of the room where the alarms were signaling, the word angel humming in her ear.

"We have a patient who arrived back in October ranting something about being a fallen angel," the nurse said before rushing into the room.

Fallen angel? Grier wondered as she entered the room. From where she stood, she could see the room had two beds. The closest one was empty and the other she could only see the foot of the bed. The rest was hidden behind a floor-to-ceiling curtain the young nurse had disappeared behind, splitting the room in half. Near the foot of the mostly hidden bed were multiple monitors. One of them had an alarm going off. The nurse reappeared from behind the curtain then. "That's so strange," she said. "All of his other readings are normal—it has to be the machine. I'll change it out with a spare and then put in a call for the technician."

"What happened to him?" Grier asked, tentatively approaching the curtain, the word angel still resonating in her head.

The young nurse went over to the monitoring machines next to the empty bed. Before rolling the replacement over, she drew in a long breath and made a face like she was hesitant to share the details. "Well… we had to sedate him that night." The nurse paused, fiddling with the machines that were in view. "He was out of control—ranting, kept saying 'he was here for those in need'," she said, glancing up, stopping mid-sentence. "Dr. Stone, are you okay?"

Grier closed her gaping mouth, then opened it again to speak. "Who is he?" she asked, taking another tentative step closer.

"He had no identification on him, but he had mumbled a name before he'd been sedated." Adding to the details, the nurse said, "He had an allergic reaction to the drugs the doctor told us—been in a coma ever since. The administration did not want him moved, just in case he woke up and began ranting or acting out again. We have him in the right ward, they figure." The nurse nodded as though she agreed with the hospital's handling of things. "We hoped someone would come and claim him, but no such luck yet."

Grier's breath caught in her throat as she took her last step finally to round the curtain. *That face.* Staring down at the man's magnificent face, she watched as his eyes moved gently back and forth under heavily lashed lids. Keeping her eyes fixed on the patient, Grier took another step closer. As she reached the head of the bed, the rapid beeping associated with the faulty heart monitor slowed to a normal rhythm. "Who's his doctor?" Grier asked, swallowing hard.

The nurse pushed the replacement monitor aside and grabbed up the chart from the end of the bed. Flipping through to the back page, the nurse answered, "Says here... you are?"

Grier glanced over to find the nurse gawking back at her. Snatching the chart, she scanned the page only to find that her name was most definitely showing in the physician's name box. Under the patient box, she read aloud the name. "Zuriel." Lowering the chart, she turned to gaze back to the handsome man in the bed. She lingered on his stunning yet familiar face.

At that same moment, his lids fluttered open, revealing magnificent pearl-grey eyes that sparkled up at her.

"Hello, Z," she said with a gentle smile.

Chapter 38 

The Beach House, in the wee hours, February 15th, South Florida

The strong odor of harsh cleaning product and bleach permeate my senses as the fog clouding my vision dissipated. I'm in the lab again and I am standing before the clinical-style desk, but there are no notebooks lined up along the back of it and the office paraphernalia is no longer there. The pin board that once displayed the beautiful butterflies is practically empty, bar the single white butterfly. This one wasn't part of the grouping before. This one resembles the butterfly I'd seen in Norway. To the left, the glass cabinets that contained plant samples and rows of bottles are now empty. Past the desk, in the middle of the room, are the same two folding privacy partitions that extend out from the side wall and meet in the middle blocking the back section. I push through the rolling barriers, but the surgery stations with all the fancy equipment that had been here previously have been reduced to a surgical platform on one side and the metal autopsy table on the other. Over to the right, the door to the small room is open, though no black cords lead along the floor to it.

I'm standing in the doorway but there is no medical staff or equipment in the room like before, and thankfully there is no massive angel hanging from straps attached to a mechanism on the ceiling. The reek of sweat and rancid stench of pus-filled open wounds no longer permeated the air as it had before. And though there was no evidence of it in view, what had remained, now mingling with the stink of bleach and cleaning solutions, was the distinctive metallic scent of blood.

I step deeper into the room and turn around. There, above the door on the wall, is a board similar to the butterfly display board. But instead of butterflies pinned to it, there is a massive set of white, black-tipped feathered wings. Similar to the butterflies, they were affixed to the board with huge silver nails. But unlike the butterflies who still have their wings attached to their torsos, these wings are missing the owner's body and cut flush with traces of flesh and dried blood still visible on the white feathers nearest to where the wings would have attached to their host. When I turn back around, I am no longer in the small room in the lab, instead I am standing in a hospital room, a patient bed before me. In it rests Zuriel, unconscious and attached to several steadily bleeping monitors. Leaning over his peaceful face, I can see his eyes are active under heavily lashed lids. Suddenly his eyelids open and I am staring down at the most beautiful grey eyes. His lips move then, silently mouthing the words, help me, and I… sat up in bed.

"You're awake," I whispered into the night as my dream faded. Checking the clock on my nightstand I saw the time read 4 a.m. and Redmond was sound asleep in the bed next to me. The soft snores coming from him only occurred when he drank too much and it was the only evidence that we had finished off the wine, because I wasn't feeling hungover for whatever reason.

Sliding out of bed, I stumbled, tripping over what I could see by the light of the moon were my rumpled tank top and pajama bottoms next to the bed. Grabbing them up, I left the bedroom and shut the door behind me.

In the kitchen, I quickly pulled on my tank and pajama pants and then donned the discarded sweatshirt I'd left on the dining chair. Before grabbing my purse and keys, I slipped into my running shoes and then headed down the staircase to the lower level.

"What are you doing Westlake," I mumbled to myself as I got into my car. Who was I kidding, my intention was to get into that psych ward right now using the disguise Zach created for me. I glanced into the backseat, checking to see the black canvas bag was where I'd left it. Then I slowly backed out the carport and down the driveway.

At the hospital, I pulled into the visitors' parking area, taking a spot furthest from the lamppost so I could swap my sweatshirt and pajama pants for the disguise. Already in the scrubs, grey curly wig and dated eyeglasses, I stood next to my car with the driver's side door open as I shrugged into the white doctor's coat. Then I draped the security ID badge on the lanyard around my neck. Closing things up, I locked the car and slid my keys into the deep pocket of the coat. To avoid having to walk past security, I went around to the side of the atrium to the staff entrance instead of going through the main doors.

Keeping my head down, I ran my security badge over the access pad. When the light on the pad switched from yellow to green, I yanked the door open. Safely through the door and walking to the entrance for the stairs, I had this overwhelming feeling I was forgetting something. I paused inside the stairwell, focusing my senses on Zuriel's distinct signature. The resonance was weak, but I followed it up to the stairs to what I knew would be the stairway entry just around the corner from the entrance to the psych ward. At the top of the stairs on the second floor, Zuriel's signature was much stronger, and I didn't hesitate to yank open the door to the floor.

Two steps in from the stairwell opening, my head pounded like I was suddenly hit with the hangover I thought I'd dodged but it was even worse. The back of my neck began to tingle, followed by a wave of nausea so overwhelming I found myself gambling whether I could make the quick dash across to the unisex bathroom right in front of me before throwing up first. I swayed, then froze as the sensation of static electricity prickled down both my arms. Then the metallic sound of the entry latch for the door to the stairwell clicked behind me. Struggling not to vomit, I turned slowly around, only to come face to chest with an enormous figure who filled up the full opening of the doorframe. Then I gingerly tilted my head back to stare up at him.

Stunning eyes glowered down at me, scrutinizing, moving from the top of my head down to my ID badge, and then back up to my face. His eyes narrowed and his brows furrowed into a menacing scowl, as if endeavoring to see beyond my façade.

"You," he said in a deep questioning voice, further examining me. His eyes widened, and then his mouth gaped. "It's you," he said this time as though it made his first declaration clearer.

I went to step back, but his hand moved so fast it blurred as it wrapped around my forearm. I stared up at the towering figure helpless, as all the self-defense moves I'd mastered rapidly deserted my memory banks. It was then, as his massive fingers tightened around my tiny forearm, I *remembered* what it was I had *forgotten*. The purple wine stain facial prosthetic was still in its special container inside the canvas bag in the front seat of my car, I realized.

His eyebrows rose then with an expression of understanding that spread across his face as he roared his recognition, "WESTLAKE!"

* * *

BONUS CONTENT
CHAPTER 37 THE EXTENDED VERSION
LEARN MORE HERE > www.nlwestaway.com/free-read

The Guard Trilogy Extended Series

Book 6 – Haven Found
Much more to come…

Learn more about author N. L. Westaway
at www.NLWestaway.com